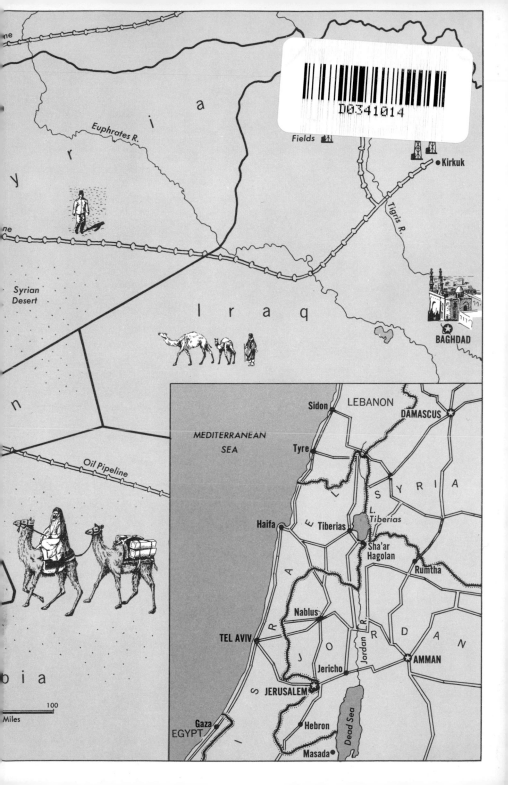

Euphrates R.

Fields

Kirkuk

Tigris R.

Syrian
Desert

I r a q

BAGHDAD

Sidon   LEBANON
                    DAMASCUS

MEDITERRANEAN
SEA   Tyre

L   S Y R I A

Haifa   E   Tiberias   L.
                          Tiberias

                          Sha'ar
                          Hagolan

                                    Rumtha

Oil Pipeline

                    Nablus

                R
TEL AVIV   A   J   O   R   D   A   N

            S   Jericho   Jordan R.   AMMAN

            I
            JERUSALEM

b i a   Gaza
            EGYPT
100   Hebron   Dead Sea

Miles   Masada

THE TOWER OF BABEL

By the same author

THE TOWER
OF BABEL

A NOVEL BY

Morris L. West

William Morrow & Company, Inc.

NEW YORK 1968

Published simultaneously in Canada by George J. McLeod Limited, Toronto.

Printed and bound in the United States of America by The Haddon Craftsmen, Inc., Scranton, Pennsylvania

Designed by Paula Wiener

Library of Congress Catalog Card Number 68-14801

ACKNOWLEDGMENT

Many generous friends in several countries gave me their time, knowledge and counsel while I was writing this book.

Some cannot be named. Some have suffered greatly. All must remain anonymous.

I offer them my public thanks and my private prayer for peace upon all their houses.

M. L. W.

And they said, Go to, let us build us . . . a tower, whose top may reach unto heaven. . . . And the Lord came down to see . . . the tower which the children of men builded. And the Lord said, Behold, the people is one and they have all one language; . . . Go to, let us go down, and there confound their language, that they may not understand one another's speech. . . . Therefore is the name of it called Babel; because the Lord did there confound the language of all the earth.

(Genesis, xi, 4–9)

THE TOWER OF BABEL

ONE

SHA'AR HAGOLAN . . . OCTOBER, 1966

The watcher on the hilltop settled himself against the gnarled bole of an olive tree, tested his radio, opened his map case on his knees, focused his field glasses and began a slow meticulous survey from the southern tip of the Lake of Tiberias to the spur of Sha'ar Hagolan, where the Yarmuk River turned southwestward to join the Jordan. It was eleven o'clock in the morning. The sky was clear, the air crisp and dry after the first small rains of autumn.

He studied the eastern ridges first, swinging from north to south down the contour line that marked the border between Syria and the demilitarized zone of Israel. The hills rose brown and empty from the border to the jagged saddle. There were no herdsmen. No sheep, no goats. There was no sign of life from the village piled like a heap of white blocks against the flank of the mountain. He held a long time on the ruins below the village, because sometimes the Syrians posted a crew there ready to traverse the valley with machine-gun fire. Today the ruins were empty too. The trenches next—that long crisscross of scars on the southern spur which the Australians had dug in the war of 1918. They were inside Israeli territory; but sometimes the raiders used them as a sally point for nighttime forays against the kibbutz. A small herd of fallow deer were cropping peacefully between the upper and the lower lines of trenches. He watched the deer for a long time, because they were shy creatures, easily startled by a sound or a movement. Then he turned his attention to the vineyards at the southern end of the valley. They were brown now and withering in the late autumn sun. They offered no cover for man or beast.

Northward from the vineyards were the two long carpets of plowed land separated by a thin finger of turf. The brown turf could not be plowed, because, by some folly of the mapmakers and the draftsmen of the Armistice, it had never been designated as arable land; so to dig it or even to cross it was to expose oneself to fire from the invisible gunners on the Syrian side of the frontier. Yigael was working the first plot now; he was driving the new tractor and dragging a harrow that raised a high gray dust cloud in the still air. Yigael was his brother and at midday he would take over the watch, while another man drove the tractor. Northward again were the banana plantations that stretched lush and green almost to the shores of the lake. At night they too were a danger area, because they provided good cover, but in the daytime the hills behind them were too bare and exposed, even for the boldest guerrillas. . . . So, it looked like another quiet day in the valley of Sha'ar Hagolan. He took a long swallow from his water bottle, then switched on his transmitter and made a negative report to the army post just outside the demilitarized zone.

The tractor made one traverse of the field, then another and another, so that the valley reverberated to the hypnotic beat of its motor, and the dust cloud shimmered like a ground mist in the sun. The last traverse brought the tractor close to the finger of turf. On the turn it canted sideways into a ditch and, for a moment, it seemed as though it were about to capsize. But Yigael was a good tractor man. He gunned the motor, wrenched the wheel hard in the opposite direction

and righted the vehicle by driving it straight across the turf.
The watchman gasped and sprang to his feet, waiting for the
gunfire. None came. Yigael drove the tractor fast across the
narrow promontory towards the second plowland. There
was still no gunfire. In five seconds he would be safe.

Then the mine exploded; the petrol tank blew up and
Yigael was tossed into the air like a rag doll with his hair
and clothes on fire. . . .

TEL AVIV

In his large bleak office on the fourth floor of the Operations Building, Brigadier-General Jakov Baratz, Director of
Military Intelligence, sat at his desk studying a report of the
incident at Sha'ar Hagolan. He called a set of coordinates to
his aide, who marked them on the map with a small red cross
surrounded by a circle and then added a notation to the list
in his hand.

"That's the fourth incident in the Revaya-Sha'ar Hagolan
sector, sir. Sabotage of a pipeline, sabotage of a pumping
station, sabotage of three dwelling houses and a water pump,
and now this."

The brigadier added a rider of his own. "Four incidents
in nine months. Nuisance stuff, designed to provoke us into
military action in a demilitarized zone."

"What do we do about it, sir?"

"We? Nothing." There was a sour irony in his tone. "Kap-
lan in Tiberias has already reported by telephone and in
writing to the Mixed Armistice Commission of the United
Nations. Tomorrow the memorandum will be acknowledged
and the Mixed Armistice Commission will constitute a formal
inquiry. A month, six weeks from now the Commission will
render a formal finding: to wit, that a mine of unidentified
pattern was set by person or persons unknown on a strip of
land called the Green Finger in the Sha'ar Hagolan area.

They will also note that an Israeli tractor encroached upon the above-named strip and was blown up in consequence. Conclusion: that person or persons unknown were responsible for an illegal act in planting a mine in a demilitarized zone and that an Israeli, regrettably dead, committed an illegal act of encroachment. Action indicated: nil."

"But we bear the brunt of the blame as usual."

"As usual," said Baratz dryly. "But in strict legality—and the Armistice Commission is a very legal body—we are the only people who can be identified. We have a dead man on our doorstep." He paused and then added a sober afterthought. "But the tally is getting high. We've had forty-seven sabotage attempts from August last year to October this year. We also have a new government in Jerusalem. Very soon somebody's going to start shouting for action. I can't say I blame them. . . . But not now, not yet."

"When, sir?"

Baratz felt a pang of pity for him. He was very young, very eager, but still a novice in the cold trade of military intelligence and political maneuver.

"When? We don't decide that, Captain. The Prime Minister decides in Jerusalem with the Cabinet and the Chiefs of Staff. We offer information, estimates, an opinion of probable consequences. . . . And we hope to God we're right in half of them. But if you ask me what may force us into reprisals, I will say anything that happens here, for instance. . . ." His bony finger stabbed at the map, pointing to the thick wedge of land between the southern border of Lebanon and the eastern frontier of Syria. It was closely dotted with crosses and circles that ran from Metulla southward down the Jordan cleft. ". . . Or here, on the Sharon plain; or in the Shefelah; or on the Dead Sea, between Ein Gedi and Arad. . . . It's the pattern we have to think of, always the pattern."

"A man was killed this morning, sir; a peaceful farmer. Isn't he part of the pattern too?"

"We lost six million dead in the holocausts, Captain. Israel is built on their ashes. Remember that." Then, more gently he asked, "Have we heard anything from Fathalla?"

"Nothing yet. He hasn't sent a radio signal for ten days. We can't raise him either."

"I know," said Baratz moodily. "I'm worried about him. Call me as soon as you have contact. That's all."

The young man saluted and went out, closing the door behind him. Baratz stood staring at the map, where the red ink was spattered like blood spots and the cryptic military symbols told the story of a daily battle for survival.

The map was as familiar to him as his own skin and he reacted instantly to every itch and prickle on its surface. Sometimes in his troubled dreams, it *was* a skin; a living human skin, stretched tight and pegged down over a narrow ground between Egypt and Jordan and Syria and Lebanon and the sea which was its lifeblood. Suddenly the skin would erupt into swellings and pustules and out of these would come legions and legions of soldier ants, marching in serried ranks until they blotted out the skin and ate through it to the bare ground. When the ants left, the ground would be covered with bones, over which the voice of the ancient prophet chanted a threnody.

"The Power of the Lord laid hold of me and by the Spirit of the Lord I was carried away and set down in the midst of the plain which was covered with bones. Round the whole extent of them he took me, where they lay thick on the plain, all of them parched quite dry. Son of man, he said, can life return to these bones. . . ."

Then, in the dream, there would be a silence while he waited for the promise of resurrection that should follow the threnody. But the promise never came and he would wake, sweating and terrified, knowing that if the ants took over the land there would be no resurrection any more and that the House of Israel would be blotted out for ever.

Sharp and strident the telephone rang. He crossed swiftly to the desk and answered curtly, "Baratz here."

"Jakov, this is Franz Lieberman, I've just seen Hannah."

A cold hand crisped around his heart. He felt himself trembling. He grasped at a pencil to control the tremors.

"How is she? What do you think, Franz?"

"I think you should leave her with us for a while, Jakov."

"How long?"

"A month. Maybe two or three. She is on a long journey this time. We shall try to follow her and turn her back when she is ready to come."

"Is there nothing you can do?"

"Oh, yes. There are treatments, of course. But no guarantees. You know that."

"I know it. Be gentle with her, Franz."

"Like she was my own," said Franz Lieberman.

"When can I see her?"

"I'll call you. Trust me, Jakov."

"I do. Who else is there?"

He put down the phone and sat a long time staring at the palms of his hands as if, like a cheiromancer, he could read in them his wife's future and his own and the future of all those for whom he stood, a secret watchman in a twilight world. But cheiromancy was a magical art and he did not believe in magic any more than he believed in the God of the Fathers, who could sit removed in his heaven while six million of his chosen ones perished in a monstrous hecatomb. And this was the irony of his situation, that in him, an appointed trustee of the continuity of Israel, the continuity was already broken. The hands which lay before him on the table were not anointed to a priesthood. No prophecies were written in their leathery palms. They called down no benediction from a silent sky. They were artisan's hands, apt to the working of wood and metal. They were soldier's hands, that could strip a gun and assemble it again from stock to muzzle swifter than most. They were lover's hands, which had once wakened Hannah to triumphant ecstasy, but which now were powerless to draw her back from her haunted regression into the past. Closed in the naked room with his map and his secrets, he was engulfed for a moment in a black wave of despair. Then slowly the disciplines of a lifetime took hold of him: the wave receded and he began to think clearly again.

Fathalla was his first concern: Selim Fathalla, whose Arabic name signified Gift of God, who ran an import-export business in Damascus and was friendly with men in high places in Syria and who lived in daily risk of his life, because his real name was Adom Ronen and he was a Jewish agent. Every week, by one means or another, he filed a background report. The means varied considerably. Every day, at different times and on different wave lengths, Fathalla made radio contact with Tel Aviv. Sometimes an Israeli pilot brought in a coded letter from Cyprus. Sometimes a consular driver, who crossed every day at the Mandelbaum Gate, delivered a gift from Jordan to a girl friend in Jerusalem. Occasionally the message came from Rome or Athens, because Fathalla was an inventive man with a sense of humor and a great care for the security of his network. But for ten days now, there had been no word and Baratz was troubled. . . .

DAMASCUS

He could not remember how long he had been ill. Time had become a capricious dimension, in which he was held for a while and from which he slipped back into a restless eternity of fevers and nameless fears and tangled dreams. Time was the slanting of sunlight through the carved fretwork of the shutters, the shape of the tamarisk outside the open window and the white minaret of the mosque beyond it. Time was a white moon in a purple sky. Time was a woman's face and the touch of her hands and the smell of rosewater. But the symbols were elusive and when he tried to cling to them, they drifted out of focus and dissolved into confusion. Until now . . . until this moment in which he lay, timid but restful, and felt the world solidify around him.

He was aware of his body first. It was cool and dry. There was no sensation of pain, but only of a pleasant weakness and detachment. The coverlets were crisp under his fingers. The pillow was soft against his stubbled cheek. When he opened his eyes, the first thing he saw was the great lamp of beaten copper that hung from the white vault of the ceiling. Every cleft and figuration on it was familiar from a hundred nights of contemplation. So there was no possibility of illusion. If the lamp was there, he was there.

Directly opposite his bed was the window alcove, hung with silk drapes and furnished with a divan and a taboret inlaid with mother-of-pearl. The shutters were closed over the windows, so that the carved traceries of shisham wood made a dark pattern against the blue sky outside. To the left of the alcove, in the center of a white wall, was the huge panel of blue faience which he had brought from Ishfahan. . . . Everything was there—familiar and reassuring; the Bokhara rugs, the glowing tiles, the small group of miniatures painted on ivory, the scimitar in its golden scabbard which he had bought from Ali the swordmaker. Then, faint but clear, he heard the cry of the sweetmeat seller and, after it, the long wailing summons of the muezzin, distorted by the amplifiers on the unseen minaret. Suddenly he was blissfully and childishly happy, because Selim Fathalla was alive, in his own bed, in his own house, in Damascus.

It was strange how lovingly he clung to this identity, how much he enjoyed it, how laboriously he strove to reinforce it. It was not a disguise: it was an authentic self, organically complete, without which he would have felt lost and lonely, like a brother bereft of his twin. The other self—named

Adom Ronen—was complete too. Even their twinship was total, because there was between them a fraternal conflict whenever the interests of the one threatened the comfort or security of the other. Their dialogue was a mirror-talk, colored always by the fear that one day the mirror-man might disappear, or the man before the mirror might walk away leaving his image locked for ever in the glass. And each had the same problem: that with every passing month it was harder to know which was the image and which was the man.

In this shabby tortuous city only Selim Fathalla was real: Selim Fathalla the conspirator from Baghdad who, when the Baathist party was suppressed in Iraq, turned up in Damascus to ask for asylum from his Syrian comrades. He carried letters from party chiefs who were known to be in hiding and from old friends in the American University of Beirut. He brought money too—a large credit with the Phoenician Bank. He brought a nimble knowledge of the import and export business which he had learned in Rashid Street in Old Baghdad. Because of the letters and the money he was received, if not with warmth, at least without too much suspicion. Because he was amiable and openhanded, he made friends quickly. Because he was a bold trader and a hard-line Baathist as well, he was soon serviceable to the Government which, having expropriated industry and socialized agriculture and destroyed its merchant class, was faced with the problem of selling its national product in a free market.

Selim Fathalla made no vulgar display of his success. He understood that a guest must observe the decencies if he is not to excite the jealousy of his hosts. So, he bought himself a house in the old quarter of Damascus near the bazaars, behind whose blank walls he lived a life of discreet luxury and entertained friends from the Party and the Army and diplomats from Moscow and Prague and Sofia. These latter found him an informative acquaintance and a sound guide to the backstairs politics of the Arab world. He was a good

Moslem too—if not noticeably devout; but he was seen often enough at the mosque and had friends enough in the Ulema to testify to his orthodoxy.

He fell in love with his secretary and made her his mistress. But he would not marry her because she was half French and a Christian as well; and such a marriage would have given offense to those who now approved his good taste in women. He was eager for trade and drove hard bargains— as what Iraqi did not?—but he was not greedy enough to make enemies and not foolish enough to cheat the Government; so that, in the end, even the redoubtable Safreddin, who was Director of Public Security for Syria and Head of the Extraordinary Military Tribunal, came to trust him.

But Adom Ronen, the mirror-twin, was in far different case. He was neither comfortable nor content—and at times he found it hard to respect himself.

He was a prisoner in this whitewashed room. In fact he was confined to a far smaller space: a tiny chamber hardly larger than a wardrobe which was hidden behind the faience panel. Here he wrote his reports and photographed documents and stored the incriminating equipment of his trade. From here, a mocking voyeur, he watched the wild couplings of Selim Fathalla while he remembered his own wife and child in Jerusalem. Here, every day, he relived the intimate tragedy which is called "The Divided House"; because Adom Ronen, the agent, was divided and subdivided against himself.

He was a ghetto Jew from Baghdad who had organized the exodus of his people and yet had never achieved his own —because he was never quite sure how much he wanted it. He was the Zionist who found the House of Israel a dull place to live in and yet committed himself to jeopardy to preserve it. He was an adventurer cursed with a missionary urge; a cynic burdened with guilts that itched him like a private leprosy.

It was he who had created Selim Fathalla and endowed him

with that placid amorality by which he endured. It was he who plotted and schemed in secret, while Fathalla fondled his Syrian mistress or sealed bargains with Safreddin in the name of Allah. And yet he loved Fathalla and Fathalla loved him. They depended, each on the other, for sanity and for simple survival. When Adom Ronen found the burden of himself intolerable, Fathalla cajoled him into satiric amusement. If Fathalla could sleep quietly, it was because Adom Ronen kept watch over the lobes of his brain and a ward over his heedless tongue. But Selim Fathalla had caught malaria in Aleppo and had lain eight days in delirium; so that neither knew what he had said or who might have heard it. . . .

He threw back the covers and eased himself into a sitting position on the edge of the bed. He felt light-headed but stronger than he had expected. He stood up, supporting himself against the wall. Then, when he was sure of his balance, he walked gingerly to the window, threw open the shutters and perched himself on the divan, looking out into the garden.

The tamarisk plumes drooped in the still noonday air. The potted geraniums made a flare of color against the gray walls. The single rose bush beneath his window was already half in bloom. From the mouth of the crusader lion, a thin runnel of water trickled musically into the stone basin. Hassan, the gardener, knelt in the middle of the small patch of grass, as if on a prayer carpet, weeding it carefully and snipping it with handshears. The murmur of the streets and the babble of the adjoining markets were hushed to a soft monotone. This privacy at least was still inviolate.

As he breathed the faint dusty fragrance of the rose blooms, he thought of Emilie Ayub and wished that she were with him to bathe and massage him and coax the passion back into his depleted body. But she would not come until he summoned her, because this was the role that he had de-

termined for her: the discreet and serviceable mistress who
kept herself private for her man and preserved his dignity
among his Moslem peers. It was a role that seemed to satisfy
her, although it was less than satisfactory to him. Yet he dared
not trust her with a larger one, because it was better to endure
a solitude of the spirit than to risk his neck by sharing the
secret of the twins.

The knock at the door startled him. He took a long moment
to recover himself before he called: "Come in."

The heavy door creaked open and old Farida ushered Dr.
Bitar into the bedroom. Bitar was a tall, flexible man who
always reminded him of a bamboo, bowing to the wind. His
face was long, lean and smooth as a woman's; his hands were
soft, expressive and always beautifully manicured. His voice
was incongruous: a deep resonant bass, which should have
belonged to an opera singer instead of to a physician. There
was a theatrical quality too in his entrance. He waved the old
woman out of the room with an ample gesture and then stood
in the middle of the bedroom, legs astraddle, surveying his
patient.

"So! We are better today. We have no fever. We think we
are fully recovered."

Fathalla grinned at him from his silken perch and answered
lightly enough, "I feel very weak—and I stink like a beggar
in the bazaar."

"Take a bath, my friend. Eat lightly, drink lots of fluid.
In two days you will be a new man." With the same dramatic
calculation he moved into the alcove and sat down facing
Fathalla. He took hold of his wrist, felt his pulse and nodded
sagely. "Good! A little fast, but good. You know, of course,
that you are infected for always. If you are to avoid more
attacks, you will take Paludrine tablets all the time. I gave
the prescription to your girl. She will bring them home
tonight."

"When can I go back to work?"

Bitar shrugged. "A couple of days—unless there is liver damage, but I don't think there is." Then he added a terse thought. "You talk in your sleep, my friend. That's dangerous."

Fathalla looked up startled. "What did I say?"

"Names—like Jakov Baratz and Safreddin and others which we both know but would rather not hear. You talked about the killing of kings and a man in Cyprus who sends messages. Other things too . . ."

"Did anyone else hear me?"

"Your woman, Emilie Ayub. She was with you night and day during the fever."

"How much did she understand?"

"I don't know. I didn't ask. She didn't comment. It's clear that she loves you; that may be enough."

"Did I talk about—other women?"

"Not to me. To her? I hope not."

"I'm scared," said Selim Fathalla.

"Good!" said Dr. Bitar. "If it makes you careful—good!"

"Have you heard any more news?"

"Not directly; but we have had six editorials attacking King Hussein and naming him a tool of foreign imperialists. In view of what we already know, the timing is significant. Also Safreddin called me twice to inquire about your health. I told him I would report to him as soon as you were well enough to have visitors."

"Should I call him?"

Bitar chewed on the question for a moment, then spread his soft hands in a gesture of indifference. "As you wish. It's a courtesy that might buy you a little information."

"Let's do it now."

He walked a little unsteadily to the telephone and dialed the private number of the Director of Public Security. A few moments later the flat familiar voice answered.

"This is Safreddin."

"Colonel, this is Selim Fathalla."

"My dear man!" Safreddin was instantly cordial. "You've had a bad time. Bitar told me. How do you feel?"

"A little weak. But the fever's gone. . . . You really will have to do something about malaria control in this country."

It was a poor joke but apparently it pleased Safreddin. He laughed and answered amiably, "I'm studying the new program now. I'm adding a footnote that we cannot afford to lose good friends like you."

"Dr. Bitar has confined me to the house for a couple of days. I wondered if you would care to pass by and have a cup of coffee with me."

"Of course, yes. Shall we say ten o'clock tomorrow morning?"

"I'll expect you, Colonel."

There was a long pause and the crackling on the line was muffled as if a hand had been placed over the mouthpiece of the telephone; then the hand was removed and Safreddin spoke again.

"There's something I'd like you to think about, my friend. You may be able to help us."

"Any time," said Selim Fathalla easily. "What can I do for you?"

"When do you send your next consignment to Amman?"

"I'll have to check the list, but I think on Wednesday the twenty-fifth. Why?"

"We'd like you to carry something for us."

"What sort of something?"

"Guns," said Safreddin blandly. "Guns and grenades and plastic explosives."

"Oh! . . ." Fathalla's surprise was genuine but he acted it with special emphasis. "We can carry white elephants if you like, Colonel—just so you arrange our clearance at the Jordan border."

"In this case . . ." Safreddin let the phrase hang for a

moment as if he did not want to commit himself to a conclusion. "In this case, my friend, we may want to dispense
with a customs clearance."

"Oh!" said Selim Fathalla again. "Then we should plan the
job together. Let me think about it, Colonel. I'll try to have
some suggestions for you in the morning."

"You're a good friend," said Safreddin gently. "I want
you to know that we have much confidence in you."

"I'm delighted to hear it, Colonel."

When he put down the receiver, Fathalla found that his
hands were trembling and a small clammy sweat had broken
out on his forehead. When he told Bitar what Safreddin
had asked, the physician whistled softly and tunelessly. Then
he fell silent. Fathalla said:

"It smells. It smells like a dungheap."

"I know," said Dr. Bitar. "There are a hundred ways of
running guns into Jordan without a customs check. Safreddin
knows them all. He's used them all at one time or another.
Why does he need you? And why is he so public about it?"

ALEXANDRIA

On the western sweep of the Grand Corniche of Alexandria, near the Palace of Ras-el-Tin, there was a villa set
in a garden of palm trees, lawns and flower beds. Even now
it had an air of faded opulence although the glory had
departed from it when its Greek owner lost his faith in the
Nasser regime and decided to cut his losses, abandon his
diminished Egyptian capital and live on his investments in
Europe. The garden, too, had a run-down air; the white
metal furniture was rusted, the awnings were bleached and
tattered and the lawns were covered with weeds and fallen
dates rotting in the sun.

On the day after the incident at Sha'ar Hagolan, two men
walked in the garden. One was a small dapper fellow with a

round innocent face and mild eyes, who looked like a banker or a very senior functionary. His name was Idris Jarrah. He was a functionary of sorts, being the Director of Field Operations for the Palestine Liberation Organization. His nationality was uncertain, since he was by birth a Palestinian Arab, born in Jaffa, and his homeland was now occupied by a people whom he hated; a nation which, for him, had no legal existence and to whose destruction he had dedicated himself. Even in documentation he was an equivocal personage, since he carried a variety of passports: Egyptian, Greek, Syrian, Lebanese, Jordanian and Italian. His companion was an even more equivocal character; a tall, gray-haired man in his early fifties whose true name was buried in a carefully contrived obscurity but who was Head of the Planning Staff of the same organization.

The day was warm and languid. A low steady wind blew in from Africa, laden with an acrid smell of sand and the dank, familiar emanation of the Maryat swamp. Overhead the palm branches moved like fans in a low crepitant rhythm; and, as the two men paced the graveled walks, the dead leaves swirled at their feet in small dusty eddies. The elder man talked emphatically, punctuating his words with spasmodic gestures, like the fluttering of birds' wings. Idris Jarrah spoke softly and made no gestures at all, because he was a man who lived in a dozen different skins and had learned the need for control and anonymity. The nameless one said:

"This business in Galilee—a nonsense! A useless provocation which simply hardens public opinion in Israel and brings Syria into the limelight at a moment when we want her to stay out of it."

"Agreed," said Idris Jarrah mildly. "But these things happen. The mine had probably been there for months."

"When you get to Damascus, talk to Safreddin about it. Recall to him in the strongest terms our working agreement. Any future incidents must be confined to the Jordan border.

Impress on him that under the mutual aid treaty, Egypt is absolved from action if Syria provokes an Israeli attack."

"I'll do that. . . . In any case the new program calls for a concentration of our efforts in Nablus, Hebron and the Dead Sea sector. We'll have our hands full there. Safreddin will be kept busy with—the other matter."

"When does he expect to move?"

"Two weeks. He's waiting for me to get the money into Jordan."

"Is Khalil organized?"

"Safreddin says he is. But I want to check the arrangements myself, before I hand over any money."

"It has to work this time," said the nameless one with sudden anger. "Another purge in the Jordanian Army will set us back a year, perhaps longer."

"I know," said Idris Jarrah. "If there are any flaws in Khalil's plan, I am empowered to postpone the whole operation. Is that right?"

"Right. . . . Now there is the question of the money. We have deposited two hundred thousand sterling pounds to an account in your name in the Pan-Arab Bank in Beirut."

Idris Jarrah looked up surprised. "Pan-Arab? We've always dealt with Chakry."

His companion smiled, a small, inward, humorless smile. "I know. We've decided to make other arrangements. Your present balance with Chakry is fifty-seven thousand U.S. dollars. When you get to Beirut, draw it out immediately and deposit it in the new account."

"Is there a reason?"

"Many. The principal one is that Chakry has grown too big for his boots. The second is that the Lebanese have to learn that they cannot go on taking all the profits, while the rest of us take all the risks."

"And fifty-seven thousand dollars will teach them all that?"

"Hardly. But fifty million might do it."

"It sounds like an interesting month," said Idris Jarrah with thin humor.

"I hope you stay alive to enjoy it. When do you leave?"

"This afternoon at three o'clock. The ship is in the harbor now. I'll be in Beirut at eleven in the morning."

"Enjoy yourself," said the nameless one indifferently.

"Inshallah," said the moon-faced functionary.

BEIRUT

In his lighter moments—and a confident good humor was one of his most profitable assets—Nuri Chakry was wont to deliver a little speech describing himself.

". . . There's no such thing as luck. Character is destiny. We do what we are. We get what we deserve. I, for instance, am a Phoenician. I love money. I love trade. The haggle is a game to me; the risk is as heady as hashish. If I'd been here in the old days, I'd have sat in a little booth down by the mole, changing gold for silver, trading camel hides for ax heads and oil for the lentils of the pharaohs. I am—what do you call it?—a huckster. For me there is only one rule: never to do business with a huckster smarter than myself. . . ."

The statement was true. Everything Chakry said was true, because he made it a rule never to tell lies in business. The problem for those who dealt with him was to distinguish between the poetic truth and the actual, to remember that what was left unsaid was sometimes more important than what was expressed in the vivid and persuasive words.

Chakry was a Phoenician in the sense that he was an adopted citizen of what had once been a Phoenician city. However, the record showed—for those who could dig deep enough to find it—that he was a Palestinian Arab, born in Acre, who had fled the country in 1948 when the Israelis took over. There were others who claimed to have dug even deeper and to have proved that he was in fact a renegade Jew, who had more taste for the Trendex Reports than for the Talmud and who would rather chaffer in a free market than submit himself to the bourgeois socialism of the new Jewish state. But even his enemies were inclined to dismiss this as a calumny, spread by those whom he had trodden down the ladder in his swift and spectacular rise.

That he loved money was beyond question; that he loved trade was also an established fact. When he arrived in Beirut, he was almost penniless, but by begging, borrowing and bluffing, he had contrived to set himself up as a money changer in a back street near the docks. He was open for business day and night. His first clients were seamen, pimps, prostitutes, hotel doormen, nightclub touts, dockside dealers, smugglers, fences and traders in dubious antiquities. No currency was so debased that he could not manage to place it at a profit. No deal was too petty for him to act as go-between, provided the commission was adequate and paid by both parties.

He bought old coins from farmers who dug them out of their plowland, from workmen at the excavations at Baalbek and Byblos. He cleaned them and sold them at high prices through the columns of international collectors' magazines. He developed a canny eye for antiquities and a knowledge of their limited but profitable market. He was, in short, what he claimed to be: a huckster—with a taste for the good life and an intuitive understanding of the usages of power.

The first lesson he learned was that swift communication is the key to profit. A Phoenician gold stater in a dealer's tray at Byblos was worth, perhaps, a hundred dollars. In New York it would fetch four times that price. Thai bahts in Beirut were at a discount, but in Bangkok they would buy rubies and sapphires and belts of woven gold. A pound note from East Africa could be bought for five, and sometimes ten, percent discount in the European market, but if you could get it back to Kenya it would stand at a par with sterling. So, sitting in his dingy office, Nuri Chakry dreamed of ships and airlines and telegraph cables and telex machines—and a whole spider web of connections through which he might parley every day with the markets of the world.

He learned another lesson too, that money is a timorous creature and that those who possess it are more timorous still. They live in daily fear of tax collectors and social reformers and revolutionaries and politicians and deserted wives. For such timid Midases, Beirut was a happy haven: for the oil sheikhs of Kuwait and Saudi Arabia, for Syrian merchants in fear of expropriation, for Greek shipowners and Texan millionaires.

So, one day Nuri Chakry closed his office near the docks, buttoned his dreams into the breast pocket of a new suit and incorporated himself into the Phoenician Banking Company. Because he was able and audacious, because he was a careful hedonist who lent himself agreeably to the indulgences of his wealthy prospects, he prospered quickly. When the prospects, one by one, became clients, he was ready to go to fantastic lengths to confirm their confidence in him and his care of the wealth they entrusted to him. Once, in the Moorish Pavilion, which was an annex to his office where he entertained his Saudi and Kuwaiti princelings, he stacked gold bars four feet high upon the table and topped them with bonds and banknotes to prove that his clients' money was always at call and that nowhere in the world was there a safer custodian than Nuri Chakry.

By the time he was fifty—a sleek, black-haired, lively fifty —he had built himself an empire that stretched from Beirut to Fifth Avenue, from Brazil to Nigeria and Qatar; and he surveyed it all from an eyrie on top of the Phoenician Bank —a huge private suite of concrete and glass that looked westward across the Mediterranean and eastward to the mountains beyond which lay the oil-rich deserts.

In all of Lebanon, there was no one to match him for power and prestige, and the golden filaments of his web were tied to a multitude of enterprises. Through his clients and his employees, he could number one-tenth of the voting strength of the whole country, and twenty percent of its working capital was deposited in the vaults of the Phoenician Banking Company.

On his desk, encased in transparent plastic, was his private emblem and his good luck piece—a gold coin of Alexander the Great, which showed on one side the conqueror deified as the god Ammon and on the other the goddess Athena enthroned in triumph. The emblem proved him perhaps a vain man, but he was in no sense a stupid one. He knew that there were tighter limits to his empire than to Alexander's. He knew that his resources were spread thinly over bold but risky investments which, if he could hold out long enough, would double and triple in value; but which, if he had to liquidate, would cost him his right arm. He knew that the further his lines of communication were stretched, the less trustworthy they became. Above all, he knew that his very existence depended upon the precarious imbalance of Middle Eastern politics. The stronger the left-wing Baathists became in Syria, the more the Kuwaitis and the Saudis were troubled about the future of their wealthy autocracies. The more worried they became, the more they wanted to lay off their risks through that obliging bookmaker, Nuri Chakry. The more embroiled Egypt became in the Yemen war, the deeper she got into debt with the Russians, the more need there was of a friendly banker to discount her bills for working capital. With every clash on the borders of Israel, a little more funk-money flowed into Lebanon to be converted into European securities. Even the Russians kept a handsome six million dollars on deposit and that brought in the Americans as seesaw partners.

But to play the seesaw game, one needed strong nerves and a smooth tongue and a watchful eye for any straw that might tip the beam. This morning there were several straws floating in the wind and Nuri Chakry stood pensive at the window of his office, looking down at the sunlit sea and wondering where they would fall. After a few minutes he turned back to his desk, flipped an intercom switch and issued a summons:

"Mark? I'm ready for you now. Come in, please."

A moment later the electric doors of the office slid open noiselessly and Mark Matheson entered with a large leather folder under his arm. He was a bulky fellow in his middle forties with close-cropped hair and an incongruously youthful face. He was an American who had learned his business with the Rockefellers in New York and whom Chakry had lured to Beirut to serve as his lieutenant and his principal European negotiator. Many of his friends had warned him not to accept the appointment; but the rewards were high, Chakry's trust was flattering and he had accepted.

So far he had had no occasion to regret the decision. He had been startled at first by the dazzling intricacy of Chakry's manipulations, but the books were open, the record seemed clean and, if he did not always accept advice, Chakry never lacked respect for those who gave it. With those whom he trusted, he was brisk and forthright and his occasional bursts of temper were matched by moments of extraordinary generosity. He waved Matheson into a chair and plunged immediately into business.

"How are we holding this month, Mark?"

"We're tight," said Mark Matheson. "Tighter than usual. On Friday we need the usual ten million to meet the government salary checks. We can cover that. The week after, we're still OK unless we get any big withdrawals. . . . By the thirtieth of the month we're going to need some help."

"How much?"

"Six million. We might scrape by on five."

"I'll organize it," said Chakry firmly. "I'm lunching with the President tomorrow, we'll get the Central Bank to cover us. Now . . ." He tapped the small pile of newspapers which were stacked with mathematical neatness on the corner of his desk. "This means trouble. Four editorials this morning all attacking King Feisal. He's not going to like it."

Matheson shrugged. "It's the old Egyptian line. The papers are financed with Nasser money. Feisal must know that."

"Of course he knows it," said Chakry sharply. "But the papers are published in Lebanon. For Feisal they represent a large section of public opinion in this country. So . . ." He broke off.

"So?" Matheson prompted him gently.

"If I were Feisal—and I know him pretty well—I would ask myself why I should leave fifteen millions of my money in Lebanon where they insult me every day in the press, when I can transfer it to London and get eight percent from Imperial Chemical Industries."

"A good question," said Mark Matheson.

"A dangerous question—for us," said Nuri Chakry. "Now another thing. I had a call this morning from Ibrahim at Pan-Arab."

"Oh? How does he like the new job?"

Chakry shrugged indifferently. "He doesn't, but so long as we pay him on the side, he's prepared to tolerate it. He told me that the P.L.O. have deposited two hundred thousand sterling pounds with Pan-Arab to the account of Idris Jarrah."

"Jarrah!" Matheson was startled. "He's one of ours. Has been for three years. We're holding a substantial credit for him now."

"I know. My guess is that he'll arrive in a day or two, take the money out and close the account."

"Meaning what?"

Chakry picked up the small cube of plastic that enclosed his talisman and began to toss it idly from hand to hand. "Meaning that the Egyptians are expressing disapproval of Lebanese policy; that they want us more Arab and less Phoenician; that they want us more active against Israel; that they want us to call the Jordanians and the Kuwaitis into the UAR line. . . ." He held the cube up to the light, studying it like a crystal ball. "Meaning that when the Egyptians get nasty, the Syrians will get nastier still and the Russians will give us a slap on the wrist for good measure. . . . Meaning that two hundred thousand sterling pounds is a lot of money— much more than Jarrah needs for border sabotage. So something big is going to happen very soon."

"With two hundred thousand, he can buy every Palestinian refugee west of the Jordan—and part of Hussein's army as well."

"And he might just try to do it," said Chakry soberly. ". . . Tell me, Mark, if we needed some cover in a hurry, where could we get it?"

"Like how much—and for when?"

"Like fifty million in thirty days."

"Jesus!" Mark Matheson exploded. "In today's market that's like asking for a slice of the moon. When I.C.I. has to offer eight percent on a twenty-four million loan, that means money's tighter than a fish's ass."

Chakry gave him a swift mocking smile. "Scared, Mark?"

Matheson was not amused. "You're damn right I'm scared! We're three and a half percent liquid—which anywhere else but Beirut would be a criminal offense; and now you're talking of a run of withdrawals by major clients. Fifty million in thirty days! Where do we go for it? In London they're pasting Scotch tape over the tears in the pound note; we're in hock in Zurich and with the Rockefellers; which leaves us with Mortimer on the one side and the Jewish market on the other. Mortimer could cover us with a telephone call, but you know what he'll ask."

"The airline—and he'll get it over my dead body!"

"Precisely. And that throws you right back into the Jewish market. I can't see them breaking their necks to finance the Arab League, can you?"

"I'm not so sure," said Chakry softly. "Money has no race.

And the Jews have a taste for irony. Yes! I could see a situation in which a strong Jewish group could do very nicely out of the Phoenician Bank."

Matheson stared at him with skeptical admiration. "I really believe you've got gall enough to try it."

"It's not a matter of gall, it's a matter of survival, and if to survive I have to do business with Shaitan himself, I'll do it. Now let's make some notes."

AT SEA

Idris Jarrah, the mild-eyed terrorist, was a man who understood the why of things. He understood the personal *why*, the political *why* and the public *why*. And he understood that they were all different and mutually contradictory.

The personal *why* was the simplest of all. Idris Jarrah was a stateless Arab. A stateless Arab had no identity and no future. If he wanted a home, he could have it among the refugees on the Gaza Strip or in the hovel towns west of the Jordan. If he wanted work, he could have that too—as a street sweeper or a day laborer or a peddler of dates or a carver of trifles for the tourists. But if he wanted an identity—an official assurance that he was a person and not a nameless piece of flotsam—then he had to find a market in which he could buy one, at a price which he could pay.

Idris Jarrah had found such a market in the Palestine Liberation Organization—that family of dispossessed zealots which was vowed to drive the Jews into the sea, reestablish the old borders of Palestine and build an Arab hegemony across the whole of the Fertile Crescent. As for the price, Jarrah was able to offer solid coinage. He had worked first as an informer and later as a junior detective for the old Palestine police force. He knew the tricks of espionage and the usages of terror. He had learned from the British the value of system and method.

Because he had no illusions and no hopes beyond the Organization, he worked with a nerveless efficiency. Because he never promised more than he could perform, his work always gave satisfaction; and because he believed in neither God nor politicians but only in Idris Jarrah, he was beyond seduction —if not insensible to his self-interest. He spoke his mind, took his orders, delivered a night raid or a bomb explosion, collected his pay and slept happily with any available woman, while greater men tossed in nightmares of frustration or dreamed wild fantasies of empire.

The political *why* was equally clear to him. So far as the Arab world was concerned the State of Israel was like God. If you did not have it, you would have to invent it as a focus of discontent and as a rallying point for the sorely divided Moslem world. Without the Jew, what other scapegoat could you find for the slum dwellers in Alexandria and the beggars who scratched their sores in the courtyard of the Noble Sanctuary and the workless men in Damascus and the hundred and ten thousand lost people camped between the desert and the sea near the city of Samson? Without the Jew, how could you find a common cause for the wealthy Lebanese, the Kuwaitis and the Bedouin tribesmen and the Hashemite king and the Marxist Syrian and the Egyptian fellah fighting a meaningless war in the Yemen? Arab unity could only express itself in the negative: destroy the Jews! But without the Jews it could hardly express itself at all! As for the restoration of Palestine, Jarrah knew better than most that even if it were restored it would be dismembered overnight by its jealous neighbors.

So the Organization was dedicated to a fantasy, but fantasy was the stock-in-trade of politicians and they paid large sums of money to preserve it and to keep men like Idris Jarrah working for their rival causes.

And this was the public *why*. The Egyptians wanted Israel destroyed, but they lacked the money and the resources to do it. The Syrian socialists wanted to get rid of the little king of Jordan, who was a friend of the British and a symbol of outdated tribal monarchy. The Jordanians wanted a highway to the sea and a port on the Mediterranean. The Lebanese wanted money and trade and the Russians wanted a socialist arc from Baghdad to the Pillars of Hercules. For each of them, the Palestine Liberation Organization had a peculiar value. They could praise it publicly or damn it in secret and pay generously to keep it alive.

So at nine-thirty on a bright autumn morning Idris Jarrah stood on the deck of the motor vessel, *Surriento*—ten thousand tons out of Genoa with scheduled stops at Alexandria, Beirut, Limassol—and watched the mountains of Lebanon climb out of the sea and the golden city of Beirut take shape under the morning sun. He had spent a comfortable night—with a club singer of some beauty and considerable eagerness and he was bathed in well-being and the security of being a needed man.

After the drabness of Alexandria and the rasp of dealing with the Egyptians—a febrile, arrogant and unhappy people whom he heartily disliked—the prospect of two days in Lebanon was very attractive. His business there was simple and unexacting. He would lodge at the St. George Hotel, a pleasant place with a view of the sea and a concierge who knew his tastes and was eager to satisfy them. He would go to the Phoenician Bank, draw out his money and deposit it with the Pan-Arab Bank. He would confer briefly with friends and agents and then he would take a leisurely drive down to Merjayoun to see the local lieutenant who directed sabotage activities in the Hasbani thumb. There would not be much to do there, because the plan was to keep the Lebanon border quiet while attacks were mounted from Jordan along the Jerusalem corridor. He would pass out money and arrange for the distribution of the arms, which were being shipped in the hold of the *Surriento* in plastic pipes, which would later be sold to a drainage contractor in Beirut. After that, he would divert himself for an evening and take an early plane to Damascus to confer with Safreddin. It was there that his problems would begin; because Safreddin was playing many games at once and he wanted Idris Jarrah involved in all of them.

Colonel Safreddin was a soldier who had made a deal with the politicians. He would keep the Syrian army loyal so long as he was given power enough to control it and to satisfy his large personal ambition. He would build an officer class, trained in the doctrines of the Baath—the Arab Socialist Resurrection Party—and hold them always as an arm of enforcement for the political and economic policies of a one-party state. He would purge out the malcontents who still looked to Nasser and the Egyptians. He would keep constant watch upon the landlords and the merchants who were trying to bleed their capital out of Syria into Lebanon and the Mediterranean countries. He would keep the Russians friendly, while holding subversion in check or diverting it into the mold of Syrian Arab socialism.

His ambitions were larger yet. He wanted Syria and not Egypt to be the determining power in Arab politics. He wanted Israel wiped from the map. He wanted the Egyptians and the Jordanians involved as soon as possible in an all-out war against the usurping Zionists. He wanted the Hashemite king removed and a socialist government installed, so that the border blockade could be boosted into a full-scale siege. And Idris Jarrah was the ideal trigger man to start the shooting match.

Idris Jarrah would send saboteurs from Jordan into Israel; and when the Israelis retaliated, it would be against Jordan and not against Syria. The border populations would blame King Hussein and clamor for a new government to protect them against the Jewish Army. At the same time Idris Jarrah would pay out money to finance the palace revolution in Amman. Idris Jarrah would be responsible for the final operation—and if it failed he would carry the blame, as a paid agitator operating illegally inside the borders of a sovereign state.

But Idris Jarrah was a man who understood the why of things, and he had no intention of putting a noose around his own neck. So, as he sunned himself, sleek and innocent as a cat, and watched the mountains of Lebanon harden against the sky, he began to devise an insurance policy and to think of those who might underwrite it for him. . . .

His first underwriters were the members of his own organization in Lebanon and Jordan and Gaza. His money kept them eating; his arms gave them a sense of power and dignity; his promises of the restoration of their homeland gave them hope. Even the risks to which he committed them in their sabotage operations lent a glamour and a purpose to their otherwise pointless lives. They were not all heroes. Some of them were rank cowards, who had to be cajoled or threatened to perform their appointed tasks. But there were patriots among them too and, if their pride or hope in the lost homeland was destroyed, then they would be lost to him and to themselves. Without them he would be naked and powerless; with them he was a kind of prince—albeit a prince in a kingdom of mercenaries and outcasts.

So, he needed other and more potent backers. He needed a net to catch him if he stumbled and fell from his tightrope perch between the Syrians and the Egyptians. So he thought of Nuri Chakry, who was himself walking a tightrope and who might be willing to do a private trade on a matter of mutual interest.

TWO

Forty-eight hours after the incident at Sha'ar Hagolan, Brigadier-General Jakov Baratz was summoned to a meeting in the office of the Prime Minister in Jerusalem. The meeting was set for 1500 hours. A leisurely drive from Tel Aviv would take at most two hours; but Baratz chose to leave at sunrise. For his driver, yawning and sour-mouthed, it was a penance; for Baratz it was the purest of his Spartan pleasures.

At dawn, the sea was the color of opals and the mist trailed across it like a scarf over the breast of a beautiful woman. The land breeze was still stirring, small and chill, untainted yet by diesel fumes and the dust of the coastal traffic. The city had not yet begun to rub the sleep out of its eyes and the rare pedestrians had a plodding peasant look, as if they did not quite belong to this hustling, frenetic town that had mushroomed out of the sandhills north of Old Jaffa.

The flat farmlands were still damp with dew. There was a smell of orange blossom and turned earth. The long light shone green from the orchard leaves, gold on the mown stubble, pink and white and mottled brown on the limestone outcrops. In the folds of the eastern hills the pinewoods huddled, dark and somber still, but on the ridges they were tipped with fire like the spears of marching legions. . . . For

Jakov Baratz, this was the true face of the Land of Promise, clean and new with every sunrise—seen as a child would see it with a fresh wonder.

He had come to it as a child, son of a landless trader from the Baltic, and he had never forgotten the splendor of his arrival: the furnace blaze of the sun, the blinding sky, the mountains hewn as if by wild ax-men, the desert where the air danced and cities and palm trees swam upside down and vanished at a glance. As a youth he had farmed it, building rock walls with his bare hands, carrying baskets of earth on his back, planting the vine twigs and the lemon trees. As a man he had fought over it, using the military skills that the British had taught him, counting every bloody mile from Lydda to Ramle, to Abu Ghosh and the final foothold on Zion. And now his love for it was manifold: a dark passion that bound him closer to the soil than he had ever been bound to the body of a woman. He was jealous too, like all lovers; because his tenure in the beloved was always insecure —and no one knew better than he how strongly it was threatened.

In strict legality—if there were any vestiges of legality in the bargainings of nations—Israel had not even a border. Her frontiers were armistice lines, subject to ratification by the signing of a formal peace settlement—which now seemed far less possible than man's landing on the moon. Even the lines which she held were vulnerable in many places, because of the existence of demilitarized zones where no military traffic could enter and no man could carry a weapon to protect his life or his children or his tillage. Israeli trade was inhibited by sanctions imposed by the Arab States. The Suez Canal was closed to her shipping. Her communications were cut; so that it was impossible to make a telephone call from one side of Jerusalem to the other; and the road from Acre to Sidon was closed by minefields and barbed wire and armed men who would shoot to kill.

In spite of all, she had prospered and prospered still. But there was a little less fat under her skin and there were signs of a leaner time to come. After the first great ingatherings— from the wreckage of Europe, from Libya, Tunisia, Algeria, Morocco, from the Balkans, the Yemen, the South Americas, from Iraq and Iran and the Hadramaut—the flow of immigrants to Israel had dried up. Unless and until Russia opened her gates to let out her three million unhappy Jewry, Israel would be forced to rely upon her own natural increase to fill up the desert spaces and build an industrial economy and maintain her defense forces. The flow of brains and capital from the diaspora in America had fallen off; because the memory of the holocausts was growing dimmer and the trumpets of Zion sounded fainter and fainter in the ears of the affluent young. There were still those who came to share the life of the kibbutz for a season or two, but they were no longer a migration. Indeed they were hardly enough to replace those who were leaving the country for the abundant fleshpots of Europe and the United States.

Inside the frontiers of Israel too, history was beginning to repeat itself: in tribal tensions, in religious disputes, in social discontents and political rivalries. Israel had not yet decided —could not yet decide—into what shape it would grow: whether into an outward-looking western state, or into an inbred, impermanent Levantine community. So far, in spite of mass education and universal military service, there was no completely happy cross-breeding of western and eastern strains in the immigrant cultures.

The religious conflict was even more bitter. The *adukim*, the righteous ones, they of the Book and the old orthodoxy, would make no compromise with a secular state. They played with political power as ruthlessly as they imposed the rituals of purification; and, because of them, Israel still had no constitution and her social legislation was a tangle of anomalies and small abrasive injustices. Smoke a cigarette in Mear

Sharim on the Sabbath and it would be struck from your mouth by an indignant zealot; but members of the Rabbinate did not hesitate to plaster the walls with posters forbidding their people to exercise a legal vote—and for the most part they went unpunished.

There was no civil marriage in Israel. You were Christian, Jew or Moslem. But if you wanted to be a simple secular man and get legally wed or legally divorced—or even legally buried—outside a religious group, then you had to go to Cyprus to do it. A Moslem woman might be awarded a lower alimony than a Jew or a Christian, but she had no means of redressing the manifest injustice. The dietary laws fell as heavily on the nonreligious as on the orthodox and a Sabbath Day in the Carmel Hotel was as mournful as in Mear Sharim.

The political divisions had all the taint of personal vendettas. The great men of the fighting years were getting old and crotchety. They resented the young bulls who challenged their authority and their policies. Some of them were bitter enough to make family scandals in full view of a hostile world. They were still one nation; and it was the land that held them together. . . . But if they did not learn to hold themselves together they might, in the end, lose the land—as they had lost it before to the Assyrians and the Hasmoneans and the Romans and the Ottoman Turks. . . . As they climbed over the foothills and into the mountains of the Jerusalem corridor, the air was suddenly cold and Jakov Baratz shivered, as though a goose had walked over his grave.

When they reached Abu Ghosh, they turned off the highway onto the hill road that led to Habamisha and the Jordan frontier. It rose steeply at first, through hill farms and tufts of pinewood; then, abruptly, it broke out onto a big level ridge, from which they could see the desert hills of Jordan and the twisted ribbon of the Ramallah road, and the clustered hovels of the border villages: Beit Surik, Biddu and Qubeiba.

In the hard light of early morning, it was like the landscape of an alien planet. The contours were sharp and serrated as stone knives. The colors were strident: brown, yellow, crimson, purple, a dazzle of white limestone, craters of black shadow. At first glance it seemed too poor even for goat-cropping: but, down in the wadis, the Bedouin spread their black tents and grazed their herds, while the villagers scratched a painful living from the terrace gardens on the slopes. There was no inkling of violence. The land and the huddled hamlets seemed too parched of human sap to sustain it . . . until one reached the barbed barrier that cut the road and the two Israeli guards stepped out from the rock shadow, armed and watchful. They were very young but very soldierly. They did not open the barrier until they had inspected Baratz's papers and those of his driver. Then they saluted smartly and waved him up the last rise to the command post, which was hewn like a fortress into the side of the hill.

The commander, a thirty-year-old captain who spoke Hebrew with the glottal accent of the Yemenis, fed him black coffee and boiled eggs and yesterday's bread. Then they climbed on foot to the observation post, to look down on the landscape spread below them like a sand map. The commander rehearsed the situation laconically.

". . . You know the general disposition, sir. One company of the Third Battalion of the Arab Legion is based on Biddu. Their area extends eastward to Beit Surik and westward to Qubeiba. There are two companies in reserve at Ramallah. The reserve companies also perform police duties among the Palestine refugees in Ramallah and the surrounding districts. That's a trouble spot for them."

"For us too, Captain," said Jakov Baratz. "Our agent in Ramallah reports two new shipments of arms to the P.L.O. and a new spate of propaganda . . . mostly leaflets. I think you can expect trouble shortly."

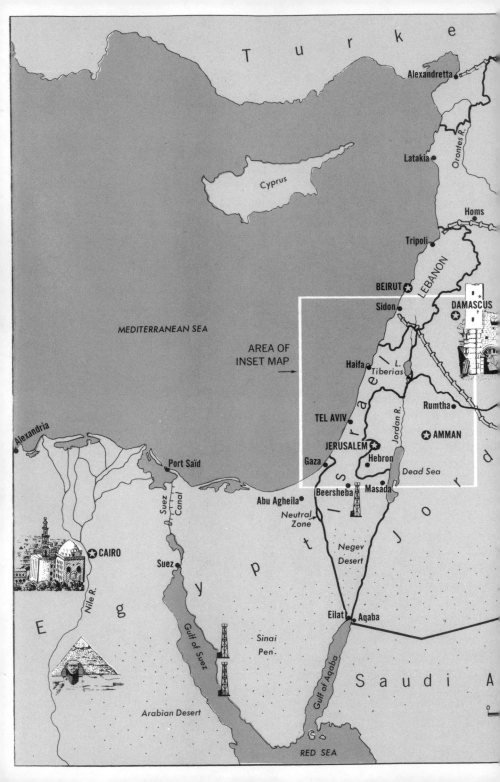

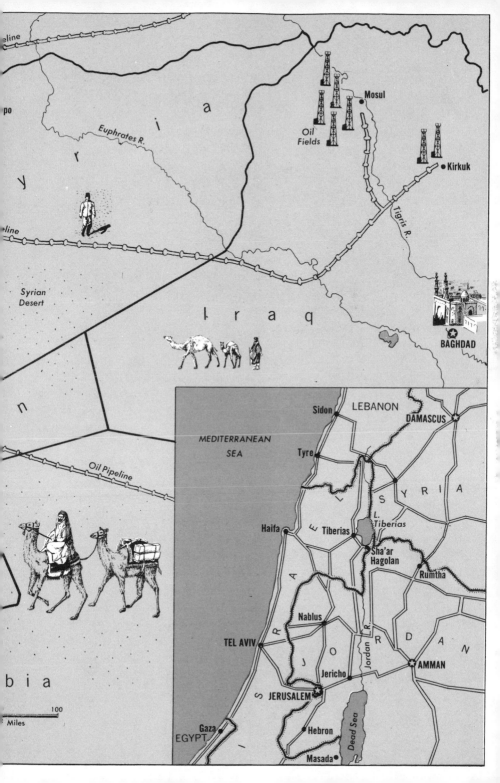

"We're ready for it." The young captain was very confident. "This has always been an easy sector to maintain. The contour works in our favor. We're two hundred feet higher than the nearest elevation in Jordan. There's little ground cover on their side and we have a clear field of fire for two miles either way. We've had no sabotage attempts for two years."

"I read your last report, Captain, that's why I'm here. You mentioned new convoy activity?"

"Yes, sir. For the past five days we've seen patrols moving east on the Beit Surik road and there are reports of similar patrols as far west as Beit Inan."

"How many vehicles?"

"Usually two trucks. Sometimes three. With a jeep in the lead. They make the outward trip between eight and nine in the morning. They come back about four in the afternoon."

"That makes seven hours between the outward and the homeward journey. . . . What's the maximum distance either way?"

"Twenty-five miles at most."

"It looks to me," said Baratz moodily, "as if they're more interested in their own people than in us. There have been no attempts to probe your sector?"

"Not by the Arab Legion. However, I did report that the Bedouin have been grazing much closer to our lines."

Baratz shrugged. "Who knows about the Bedouin? Winter's coming on, grazing is scarce. They take it where they can find it. Sometimes they'll do a job for the P.L.O. Mostly they mind their own business. Now . . . the wild asses. . . ."

The young captain laughed. "Two nights ago, half a dozen wild asses got in among the minefields. One of them stepped on a mine and was blown up. Another was shot. That was all. It hardly seemed worth reporting."

"Everything is worth reporting, Captain. Besides it's a

simple method of making a probe of the minefield and there's no risk to it."

"Except that you can't follow up the probe once you've made it, sir. And you can't plot the rest of the minefield."

"True," said Baratz with thin humor. "But you can load an animal with explosive and you can set a time fuse. And if he gets through the minefield into our sector he can cause a pretty piece of indiscriminate damage and diversion."

"I hadn't thought of that, sir."

It was Baratz's turn to laugh. "Neither had I until this moment, Captain. But, if you're fighting a nuisance war as the P.L.O. are doing and if the noise you make is just as important as the military effect, it pays you to be original. So I still like to hear about the wild asses and any other piece of local comedy that doesn't fit the pattern."

"I'll remember that, sir."

They spent another ten minutes in the observation post matching the living land against the symbols on the ordnance map. Then they walked back to headquarters, where Baratz made a telephone call to Dr. Franz Lieberman at the Hadassah Hospital in Jerusalem.

"Franz? This is Jakov Baratz. I'll be in Jerusalem in half an hour. I wonder if I could see Hannah?"

"If you want," said Franz Lieberman without enthusiasm. "If you prepare yourself a little."

"Will it be bad for her?"

"She will not see you, Jakov," said Lieberman gently. "She sees nothing, hears nothing. You can neither harm nor help her. You may hurt yourself."

"She's my wife, Franz. I love her."

"That's what I mean," said Franz Lieberman. "Call me from the desk when you arrive."

As they drove back to Abu Ghosh and through the last defiles to Jerusalem, he was tense and snappish and his driver handled the car with extra care, wondering, but not daring to ask, what had soured him so quickly.

They had a name for Baratz in the Army: *adish,* the man with ice in his veins and ashes where his heart should be. Like all nicknames it was half a compliment and half a jibe. He was too remote for their taste; precise as a surgeon in his profession, without mercy for slackers, devoid of tolerance for fools. Anger made him cold and deliberate and even his humor had a sardonic edge to it. What warmth there was in him was hidden jealously like a sacred fire; and though his friendships were deep, they were never effusive.

His habits were monkish. He drank little, smoked not at all and his name had never been linked with that of any woman but his own wife. It was a vanity with him that, however late his vigil or however early his morning appearance, he was always clean shaven and dapper enough to take a ceremonial parade. At conferences he delivered his information and his opinions with a flat confidence that provoked few questions and no opposition; then he sat back, placid as a stone Buddha, while the argument went around the table. When the time came to demolish the argument or challenge a conclusion, he did it with as little passion as a public executioner.

But there was a passion in him, a deep well of it. Friends who had known him in the days of the Haganah told stories of savage risks and wild conspiracies and exhortations to his men that had all the fervor of the ancient prophets. They remembered his swift romantic wooing of Hannah, who had come as a sixteen-year-old girl during the Aliyah Bet, the illegal migration of displaced Jews from Europe to Palestine. He had recruited her first as a messenger, exposing her to fantastic risks. Within six months he had married her, exposing her to even greater ones. Then, when the war was over, he had withdrawn with her into a domesticity that only his closest friends were permitted to share. His passion for privacy, which was the expression of his possessive passion for Hannah, had become the keystone which supported the whole arch of his public career.

A long time ago Franz Lieberman had warned him of the danger of this exclusive dependence on Hannah and of her dependence upon him. He had put it very simply:

"One of you dies, what happens to the other? For Hannah, you are a door slammed on her own past, so that she has never had to come to terms with the memory of it. For you, she is . . . Oh, hell! How do I know what she is . . . but too much already! You risk something, Jakov! A tragedy maybe."

Now Franz Lieberman was preparing him for the final act of the tragedy, which he had refused to foresee. Hannah was gone from him, probably for ever. The door had cracked and split and she was drawn back into the Bluebeard chamber of horrors, which was her childhood in the time of the holocausts. He himself stood at the edge of the dark well, looking down into depths that he had so long refused to contemplate. As they topped the last rise and came in sight of the Mount of Zion, he was suddenly and desperately afraid.

It was not only the loss that he feared; it was the mystery of the disintegration of a human person into something less than human. It had begun how long ago? Six months? A year? When, after the hour of love, Hannah had burst into tears in his arms and it had taken him half the night to calm her. Sometimes, afterwards, he would come home and find her still in her nightclothes with the housework left and the breakfast dishes unwashed. Sometimes she would play wild music and dance and sing and laugh immoderately. Sometimes in the night he would wake and she would be gone from his bed; then he would find her sitting, dumb and rigid, in the dark living room and he would need an hour, sometimes two, to coax her back into speech. Finally she had agreed to submit herself to treatment to Franz Lieberman and after a month she had come back, apparently recovered. After another month, the cycle had begun again, accelerated this time—the frenzies wilder, the withdrawals longer and deeper. How had it happened? Why? And if it had happened to her, could it not happen in another fashion to him, who had a different past but the same secret chamber at the center of himself?

At the hospital Franz Lieberman was waiting for him, gray, wizened and goat-eared like an ancient Pan. He wasted no time on courtesies but walked him briskly down the corridors to a large airy room that gave on to a garden bright with late flowers. There were perhaps a dozen women in the room with two young nurses in attendance. They looked normal enough. A small group was playing a card game; two were sewing; one was reading; others were sitting, gossipy as hens, around a coffee table. The nurses moved from one group to another like monitors at a children's playtime. Lieberman stood with Baratz at the door and explained the scene in his brusque, elliptical fashion.

"A community, you see. The commonest symptom of mental illness is retreat from the community into a private world. We try to draw the patient back into a community where the demands are small and the pressures reduced. . . . Simple, but complicated too."

"Where's Hannah?"

"Over there."

She was so small and withdrawn that she had created for the moment an illusion of invisibility. In the farthest corner of the room, where bookshelves made an angle with the wall, she sat perched on a stool, her knees drawn up under her chin, her hands clasped around them. Her eyes were blank, her face pinched and colorless. The bright ribbon in her hair made her look like a schoolgirl.

"You've seen her like this before," said Lieberman evenly.

Baratz nodded, not trusting himself to speak.

"There is no violence, no panic. She is locked in a time-womb from which she dare not emerge."

"It's a place as well as a time," said Jakov Baratz. "They

hid her for four years in an attic in Salzburg. There was no window, only a trapdoor. They fed her at night when the servants were in bed. . . . Can I speak to her?"

"If you want."

He walked to her slowly, the full length of the room. The other patients ignored him, all except one girl who laughed suddenly and obscenely. Even when he stood before her, she gave no sign of recognition. He laid a hand on her shoulder. It was warm but rigid as marble. He said, "Hannah, it's me, Jakov."

She made no movement, uttered no sound. He turned away and walked back to the door.

"Let's have a cup of coffee," said Franz Lieberman.

In Lieberman's office, with the coffee bitter on his tongue, he heard the old man deliver his verdict:

"You want a hope? I give you a small one only. Sometimes this spell is broken as it was for the princess in the enchanted forest. You want a medical prognosis? Negative. All the symptoms are regressive."

"I want advice, Franz. What do I do now?"

"Leave her with us. She will get no better care anywhere."

"I know that."

"Then . . ." Lieberman held a pencil between his fingers, flexing it like a bow until it came almost to the snapping point. "Then I would say you have to think of rebuilding your own life."

"Rebuild? Around what, Franz? . . . Around what?"

The pencil snapped in the old man's hands. He laid the two pieces side by side on his blotter and sat contemplating them for a moment as if stricken with regret for the small destruction. He said quietly, "I don't know, Jakov. I'm not God. I can't mend all the lives in the world. I wish I could."

Five minutes later Jakov Baratz stood alone in the driveway, breathing in the cool dusty air and looking across the valley to the ramparts of the divided city. With a sudden shock of guilt he realized that he was thinking, not of Hannah, but of Selim Fathalla in Damascus and of Fathalla's wife who lived in Jerusalem.

DAMASCUS

Selim Fathalla lay on his tumbled bed and watched the sunlight creep towards him over the tiled floor. After a night of love with Emilie, he was lapped in a pleasant languor; but his mind was clear and his pulse was steady. An hour from now, Safreddin would come to see him; and he wanted to remain calm and good-humored for the meeting. Safreddin was like a cat, sleek and comfortable when you stroked him; febrile and suspicious when you ruffled his fur. A strange man, proud as an ancient emperor, a cold intriguer, a Moslem mystic, fanatically faithful to his friends, ruthless and bitter to his enemies.

Thinking of Safreddin, he remembered Eli Cohen, the spy whose place he had taken in Damascus and whose body had hung, wrapped in a white sack, in Morjan Square, for a warning to traitors. Safreddin had stalked Cohen for twelve months, had monitored his radio transmissions, broken his network, arrested him in bed and tortured him for a hundred days before he brought him to trial. Safreddin had admired him and still told tales of his ingenuity and his daring exploits of espionage. Safreddin still laughed when he rehearsed the trial and the diatribes of the Moslem judges against an infidel, who had dared to pray in the mosque and recite "Allah Akbar" with the faithful sons of the Prophet. But under the laughter was a hatred, because Eli Cohen, too, had been his friend and he had felt himself doubly betrayed by this dog of a Jew. If Safreddin ever found out the double identity of Selim Fathalla, his vengeance would be doubly terrible. . . .

Perhaps he had already found out. . . . Fathalla's pulse beat quickened and a cold sweat broke out on the palms of his hands. Perhaps this morning's meeting was a cat's play with a mouse already doomed to die. But it could not have happened so quickly. There would have been warnings, signs and portents. Dr. Bitar, who had ears all over the city, would have sensed that something was amiss. Besides, Safreddin wanted a favor. A favor might mean a test of loyalty, but it could not mean a final sentence of death. Fathalla was Arab enough to understand the tortuous process of Safreddin's thought: trust no one; make one test and then another; and, the day after tomorrow, test again, because every man is a reed who will bend to the winds of change and break under the pressure of a hand. . . .

The Eli Cohen affair had damaged the whole fabric of Syrian society. Men of cabinet rank, merchants, bankers and high army officers had been found involved in Cohen's network. Some were willing agents of the Israeli: others were gullible friends; others again were well-paid mercenaries. When, finally, Safreddin had broken the network, he had found himself in the embarrassing position of having to censor the trial and make deals with men whom he would rather have hanged. So he was understandably suspicious and Fathalla was understandably cautious.

However, he had learned from Cohen's mistakes. Cohen had had flair and dash and a kind of contemptuous ingenuity in his operations; but in the end he had come to be afflicted by that mild paranoia which is endemic to men who take high risks and manipulate the passions of their fellows. Cohen had become careless. Even when they came to arrest him, he was sitting up in bed making a radio transmission, apparently oblivious of the fact that the detectors had pinpointed his location two months before.

Cohen had made an open display of wealth and talked freely of the funds available to him in Belgian, Swiss and

South American banks. His enterprises were always large and spectacular; and the fact that half of them were a fiction was in itself enough to rouse suspicion.

But Fathalla, the Iraqi, worked quite otherwise. His business was visible and legitimate. He had high friends, but he always managed to give the impression of setting himself below them, of being grateful for their patronage. He had only one foreign banking account—in the Phoenician Bank in Beirut—and he had been careful to declare its existence to the Finance Ministry and to report with moderate honesty on its operation. His gifts were generous, but never too generous. Eli Cohen had played the Arab, but he had played the part in so exotic a fashion that it excited attention. Selim Fathalla still had something of the demeanor of the bazaar trader who was always careful to look less rich than he was. . . .

So he would work on two alternate assumptions: either Safreddin's request for a favor was a genuine one, or it was a carefully contrived trial of his integrity as a Baathist sympathizer. If it was genuine, the granting of the favor would increase his credit. If it was a trial, he would accept it warily and make all the mistakes that an innocent man would be expected to make.

The door opened and Emilie Ayub came into the room. She was a small girl, but the long housecoat of Damascus brocade made her look taller. Her hair was dark and lustrous; her skin the color of honey. Her eyes, brown and limpid, seemed sometimes too large for her face, as if she were looking out on the world with a perpetual wonder. She spoke French with an Arab accent and Arabic with a curious languid lilt.

She bent over the bed, kissed Fathalla and told him, "Your bath's ready. Farida will bring breakfast when Colonel Safreddin arrives. I'd better dress and get down to the office."

He held her for a long moment, clinging with sudden need to the security and the warmth of her. Then he made her sit down on the bed beside him, locked her small hands in his own and asked her the question which had been plaguing him:

"When I was sick, Emilie, I raved a lot. I know that. Dr. Bitar told me. Did I say anything . . . strange?"

He felt her stiffen. He saw the faint swift fear in her eyes; but she recovered herself quickly and, after a moment's hesitation, she answered him.

"You said a lot of things I didn't understand."

"What sort of things?"

"I don't remember."

"Or you don't want to remember, Emilie?"

"That's right. I don't want to remember. I want to tell you something, Selim—beg you something! Don't ask me things—don't tell me things!—that have nothing to do with us." Her voice faltered and her eyes filled up with sudden tears. "I'm . . . I'm not interested. I'm not made to deal with them. So I don't want to know them—ever!"

"Are you afraid of me, Emilie?"

"No. I love you."

"You know that I love you."

"I know it."

"Trust me?"

"I want to, always."

"Then it's a bargain. No talk. No questions."

He drew her down to him again and they lay together for a long sweet moment. Then she left him. He got out of bed, walked to the window and stood a long time looking down at the fountain and the tamarisk tree, while the new fear crawled like a lizard on his skin.

Punctually at ten o'clock Colonel Omar Safreddin came to breakfast. He was an immaculate man: lean, hawk-faced, bland and amiable. He drank three cups of coffee and smoked one cigarette. He was solicitous for the health of his host. He talked circuitously of friends and acquaintances and made a brisk commentary on the news of the day. It took him nearly half an hour to come to the point of his visit. Then his whole demeanor changed and he became brusque and impersonal.

"Now, my friend, the matter we talked about. We need your help."

"You have it, Colonel."

"It's a simple operation—but quite confidential."

"Naturally."

"Your next consignment to Amman goes out on Wednesday. Correct?"

"Correct."

"How many trucks?"

"Two."

"What will they carry?"

"Flour, canned goods, manufactured cotton, a few miscellaneous items."

"What time do they normally leave Damascus?"

"Six in the morning. The trucks are loaded the day before. They stay in the warehouse yard all night. I go down just before six to get the drivers on the road."

"Who is on duty during the night?"

"Just the watchman."

"Good. Now this is what will happen. You will load the trucks in the normal fashion on Tuesday afternoon. At eight forty-five on Tuesday evening you will go to the warehouse and open up. Send the watchman off duty for two hours. My people will come at nine; one truck with an officer and a loading crew of four. They will unload part of your consignment, load our own stuff and then reload your trucks."

"And your stuff will be . . . ?"

"What I told you: guns, grenades and plastic explosive.

At six the next morning your drivers will take off for Amman as usual."

"They will know nothing about the new cargo?"

"Nothing. When they reach the Jordan border there will be the usual customs check. This time it will be a little more severe. The guns, grenades and the plastic explosive will be discovered and confiscated. Your drivers will be detained and questioned. They will then be released and will proceed with your cargo to their normal destination in Amman."

"And that's all?"

"That's all. Any questions?"

"One only. What about our future trade? I do a big business with Amman."

"There will be no problem. Border security will be tightened for a few weeks and then it will be relaxed again."

"But technically my company is the one shipping the guns."

"But the Syrian police will be making the report which will reveal the existence of the shipment. That report will absolve you and the company from any complicity. The Jordanians will ask us for a further investigation. We'll make it promptly and our supplementary report also will absolve you from blame. There are no complications, believe me."

Selim Fathalla permitted himself a small flattering smile. "I do believe you, Colonel. I have the greatest admiration for your efficiency. More coffee?"

"One cup, and then I must go." Safreddin leaned back in his chair, took a gold case from his pocket, selected a cigarette with great care, lit it and blew a series of perfect smoke rings. Then with a hint of patronage, he offered a compliment. "I admire you, Fathalla. You're a good businessman. You have excellent taste—and a quite splendid discretion."

Fathalla laughed and spread his hands in the age-old gesture of the bazaar huckster—humble, humorous and knowing. "I'm a guest in the house, Colonel. I try to mind my manners."

"Tell me," said Safreddin softly. "What do you know about Dr. Bitar?"

"Bitar?" The surprise was real. The shrug, he hoped, was sufficiently indifferent. "He's a pleasant fellow. Whenever I've been sick, he's always been very attentive. We play a game of chess occasionally. Apart from that I know very little about him."

"Is he a good doctor?"

"In my limited experience, yes. Why, Colonel?"

"He's been recommended to me as a family doctor. That's all."

Abruptly as he had come to it, he slid away from the subject and began to talk of the new measures for malaria control in the Euphrates valley. Three minutes later, he rose and took his leave. Selim Fathalla sat a long time, looking into the dregs of his coffee and trying to make sense out of a pointless piece of smuggling and an equally pointless question about Bitar's medical competence. But the solution to this puzzle would have to wait. He had to make his long delayed report to Tel Aviv and assure Baratz that he was at least alive. He climbed the stairs to his bedroom, locked the door, pressed the hidden spring that opened the faience panel and stepped into the stone womb, where he was transmuted into Adom Ronen, the Israeli agent.

BEIRUT

Nuri Chakry signed the check with a flourish and handed it across the table to Idris Jarrah.

"Fifty-seven thousand dollars, less bank charges. That closes the account of the Palestine Liberation Organization with the Phoenician Bank. A pity. We never like to lose a good client."

Idris Jarrah folded the check and put it in his breast pocket. He said with mild regret, "I'm sorry too. I'd never had any complaints about our dealings with the bank, but you understand that I am simply a servant of the Organization. I have no control over the disposition of its funds. I simply spend them at the direction of the Central Executive."

"I do understand," said Nuri Chakry. He picked up the small plastic cube with the gold coin inside it, and turned it over and over in his soft hands. "I do understand. It's just that the relationship between banker and client is a very special one. I felt—I still feel—that we might have had a little more notice of the intentions of the Organization. A personal discussion might have helped us both."

There was a small bleak silence. Then Idris Jarrah said:

"I would like to have a discussion with you . . . If you have time, that is."

"Of course. What can I do for you?"

"I should like a loan, a personal loan."

"In what amount?"

"A hundred thousand dollars."

Nuri Chakry laid the talisman down on the desk and looked up. His eyes were wide and unwinking as a bird's. "That's a very large loan, Mr. Jarrah. You have collateral, of course? Real estate, stocks, bonds?"

"No real estate. I'm a wandering man. I find it a handicap. Stocks and bonds? No. However, I do deal in commodities. Negotiable commodities."

"Such as?"

"Information," said Idris Jarrah.

"Information is only of value when it is exclusive."

"It is exclusive."

"Even then it is still a risk."

"I take risks to get it. I take greater risks in passing it on."

"You miss my meaning." Nuri Chakry was studiously polite. "The risk is that the information may be false, or that it may be doctored to make it appear true."

"I have learned to be very careful about the truth of my information, Mr. Chakry. My life depends on it."

"A good point, Mr. Jarrah. Please go on."

"Would you be prepared to make a test?"

"For how much?"

"This, you get free."

"Very well."

Idris Jarrah gathered himself for a moment. Then he leaned forward and, calm as a poker player, laid his cards, one by one, on the table.

"You are in trouble, Mr. Chakry. Your bank is in trouble. Your liabilities are somewhere in the region of a hundred and seventy million dollars. The face value of your assets, here and elsewhere, is about two hundred and fifty million, but a large part of these assets is in long-term investments, which cannot be realized quickly in the open market. At best you are five percent liquid, probably less, and this in spite of the fact that you hold about forty percent of the deposits of all Lebanese-owned banks. The Saudis are thinking of withdrawing their funds for political reasons. The Kuwaitis are under pressure from British interests to withdraw theirs, to bolster the sterling pound. Your American deposits amount to about three million dollars, but these could be frozen overnight because you are in debt to the same American interests in Switzerland and elsewhere. The crisis will come in thirty days. You have to cover yourself before then. You have an appointment with the Finance Ministry tomorrow morning; you hope they will bail you out from the Central Bank. They may promise to do so. On the other hand, you have a number of very powerful enemies. You foreclosed on Aziz and took over his apartment block. You refused a personal loan to Taleb when he was in trouble with a woman who had once belonged to you. There are half a dozen others I could name. Mortimer, who could get you out of trouble with one telephone call, is piqued because you wouldn't sell him the airline. . . . You can check every piece of that information, Mr. Chakry, and you know that if it were shouted in the streets at this moment, you would have to close your doors in forty-eight hours. The reason why my people have closed down their account is very simple: they cannot risk their working funds in a shaky enterprise."

He broke off and sat back in his chair, waiting. A conspirator himself, he was filled with admiration for the cold composure of the man who sat opposite him.

"Suppose . . ." said Chakry. "Suppose that this information were correct, you would have told me nothing I didn't know. . . . What else are you offering?"

"The test is finished, Mr. Chakry. Money on the table."

Without a word, Chakry stood up and walked out of the room. Jarrah, too, stood up and strolled over to the window that looked out on the dazzling sweep of the coastline—blue sea and golden beaches and new buildings piled like children's blocks along the headlands and the ribbon of the new motor road. This was the true trader's country. From the dawn of time, it had been the meeting place of raffish dealers who sat in the shadow of alien gods and forgot their loyalties to princes and satraps while they haggled over the price of girl slaves and frankincense. Bloody battles had been fought here, weird treacheries had been plotted; and the price of a man—or a woman—was still counted in pieces of silver.

Here they told the mocking story of the scorpion that came to the bank of the Dog River and could not cross because the river was in flood. He saw a fish, nibbling placidly among the weeds. "Please, fish," said the scorpion, "take me on your back and carry me across the river." The fish was unhappy about this. "If I carry you on my back," said he, "you will sting me and I will die." But the scorpion had an answer for him. "If I sting you and you die in the middle of the river, I will be lost too because I cannot swim." So the fish was reassured. He took the scorpion on his back and began to swim across the flooded river. Halfway over, the scorpion stung him. With his dying breath, the fish asked plaintively, "Why did you do it? Now we shall both die." To which the scorpion answered: "I wish I knew, little friend— but this is Lebanon! . . ."

It was nearly five minutes before Chakry came back. In one hand he carried a plastic satchel filled with fresh dollar bills, in the other a sheet of notepaper folded in half. He laid the satchel dead center on his blotter and held it there under his hands. Idris Jarrah sat down again. Chakry smiled.

"A hundred thousand dollars, my friend! Now talk."

"In approximately two weeks," said Idris Jarrah, "an attempt will be made by a group of army officers to assassinate King Hussein of Jordan. The officers will be led by a certain Major Khalil. As a prelude to the move, action will be taken to discredit the present commander of the Palace Guard, so that Major Khalil may be promoted and moved into his place. The whole operation is being planned by Colonel Safreddin in Damascus. I am flying there tomorrow morning to see him."

"And even if this information were true, how could it possibly benefit me to the tune of a hundred thousand dollars?"

"First, you have invested nearly a million in a new development project in Amman. In the event of a socialist revolution, you could lose it overnight. Second, you can sell this information for much more than you lend me."

"On the other hand I might offer it without charge to Colonel Safreddin. He's a powerful man. He would make a very good client for the bank."

"I doubt it," said Idris Jarrah placidly. "The Syrians are in debt up to the neck. You need stronger clients than that."

Once again there was silence in the huge sunlit room. Finally it was Chakry who spoke. "I regret, Mr. Jarrah, that I could not recommend your loan as a banking proposition.

However, as a personal investment I would be prepared to lend you the money myself, provided of course that you signed the usual acknowledgment and accepted the conditions of repayment."

"Which are?"

Chakry unfolded the notepaper and read from it:

"I, the undersigned Idris Jarrah, a stateless person presently employed by the Palestine Liberation Organization, acknowledge that I have received this day a cash loan of one hundred thousand U.S. dollars from Nuri Chakry, a resident of Beirut, Lebanon. I undertake to repay this loan on a sixty-day call at any time determined by Nuri Chakry. I agree that interest on this loan shall be at the rate of fifteen percent per annum on the full debt. I further acknowledge that, in return for this loan, I have given the said Nuri Chakry certain information of a business and political nature which has been recorded on tape in his office on this day. . . ."

Chakry pressed a button concealed in the fascia of his desk and a drawer slid open revealing a tape recorder on which the spools were still running. He switched off the machine, sat back in his chair and smiled with the utmost good humor at his visitor.

"Well, Mr. Jarrah? Is it a deal?"

"Of course," said Idris Jarrah pleasantly. "We understand each other perfectly. I hope that we may be able to do business again."

"We can always talk about it," said Nuri Chakry.

When he had gone, Chakry picked up his telephone and dialed an outside number. After a few moments a woman's voice answered, repeating the number which he had just dialed. Chakry said, "This is Mr. Chakry. Tell Miss Frances I shall be coming to have lunch with her at twelve-thirty."

The answer came back, stumbling and embarrassed:

"I'm sorry, sir. Miss Frances left for Tripoli this morning—with Mr. Aziz. Would you like to leave a message for her?"

"No message."

He put down the receiver and took out a silk handkerchief to wipe the sudden clamminess from his hands. Frances was a whore, a beautiful, intelligent and very exclusive whore. But when the whores began to leave a city, it was high time for the citizens to light the watch fires and look to the defenses of their walls. He made another telephone call, this time to a man who lived in a villa in an orange grove north of the Byblos promontory. The man's name was Heinrich Muller and he was a local recluse, who had a small but unproven reputation as a historian and archeologist. To him Nuri Chakry spoke, as always, amiably and with respect.

"Heinrich, this is Nuri. How is the work coming?"

"I'll be finished in three days," said Heinrich Muller.

"Can you do it in two?"

"At a pinch, yes." He heard Muller chuckle. "But I'll need a holiday afterwards."

"We may take it together," said Chakry. "A long holiday. Call me as soon as you're ready."

ZURICH

In a brown Gothic office in the sober city of Zurich, Mark Matheson talked banking business with Simon Lewisohn, a short, pudgy man with apple-bloom cheeks and twinkling eyes and a shock of white hair that made him look more like a retired opera singer than the head of a Swiss banking corporation. He was addicted to coffee and sweet pastry which he nibbled with childish enjoyment, while Mark Matheson spread his papers on the table and exposed the problems and the pressing needs of the Phoenician Bank. The exposition was long and detailed and Lewisohn listened in silence until it was finished. Then he brushed the crumbs of pastry from his shirt front, laid his hands upon his ample belly and smiled benevolently at his visitor.

"You have a good reputation, Mr. Matheson. I think you deserve it. If ever you should consider a change of employment, I should be happy if you would talk to me first."

"Thank you, Mr. Lewisohn. I'm not considering any change yet."

"I wanted only to put the thought in your mind. Now let me ask you some questions. The Phoenician Bank is, on your showing, about three and a half percent liquid at this moment. You think that's a good position?"

"Obviously not."

"But you are a personal assistant to Mr. Chakry. Why have you allowed the position to arise?"

"I do not determine policies, Mr. Lewisohn. I advise on them, when asked to do so. I execute them once they are decided."

"Have you ever advised against the present policies?"

"Sometimes. Yes."

"But the management has still pursued them?"

"For valid reasons, I believe. In the Middle East money is pumped out of the ground every day. There is no foreseeable end to the supply. To this moment we have been the major channel of investment for this money. There seemed no good reason to believe that this position would change."

"But now it has changed—is still changing?"

"Yes. There is pressure on the sterling pound. There is pressure on American gold reserves. There are political pressures exerted on Lebanon by other members of the Arab League. We believe that, given time to regroup our strength, we can counter these pressures. To buy that time . . ."

"You need fifty million dollars in a hurry."

"That's right."

"But the pressures will still continue."

"Of course."

"And there are others which you have not mentioned to me."

"I am not aware, Mr. Lewisohn, that I have concealed any pertinent information."

Simon Lewisohn smiled in his placid, childlike fashion and leaned forward, propping his elbows on the polished table. "Don't be angry with me, Mr. Matheson. I did not suggest that you had concealed anything. I simply stated as a fact that there were certain other pressures on the Phoenician Bank which you have not mentioned to me."

"And these are?"

Lewisohn numbered them one by one on his chubby fingers. "Item: even if you get outside help from us or anyone else, you still need the Central Bank of Lebanon to bail you out of the mess. There are important people in the Central Bank and in the Finance Ministry who dislike Mr. Chakry intensely. They would give a great deal to see him brought down. Item: there are people in Zurich, New York, Paris and London who question the honesty of Mr. Chakry. They would not be averse to making their questions public. Item: in the statement of assets which you have laid before me, there are certain, shall we call them, exaggerations."

"If there are," said Mark Matheson hotly, "I am not aware of them."

Lewisohn reached forward, picked up one of the large folio sheets and ran his forefinger down the list. ". . . This one, for instance: The Vista del Lago Hotel in Lugano. It is set down in this schedule at a value of fourteen million dollars. For my personal edification I had a private valuation made. It was bought for eight million. At the best possible appreciation, it is now worth eleven millon. With money as tight as it is today, you would be lucky to get ten million in the open market. So it is overvalued by at least three million dollars. Do you see what I mean?"

"I do. Of course I have no means of telling whether you're right or wrong."

"I can go further if you like. There are at least four other provable inflations on your list. I suspect there may be others."

"The only true proof of value will be made when we come to liquidate."

"And when will that be, Mr. Matheson?" asked Simon Lewisohn softly.

"Not for a long time, I hope. All we need is a little help from our friends and we are established for ever as the strongest banking institution in the Middle East."

"Chakry has no friends!" Suddenly the little fat man was not smiling. "Chakry is dog who eats dog. If he wants ready cash, let him sell his airline to Mortimer, and I'll make him an offer of eight million for the Vista del Lago, take it or leave it! But lend him money? Not in a million years. Let him rot in the ditch he's dug for himself."

"You're very vehement, Mr. Lewisohn." For a single moment, Matheson felt himself to be in control of the situation. "Do you mind telling me why?"

Instantly, like a mime putting on a new face, Lewisohn was cheerful again. "I do mind, Mr. Matheson. I do indeed. We're all entitled to our little secrets. But I'll tell you this. I've been a banker all my life. My father, my grandfather and my great-grandfather were bankers before me. You know what brings down men like Chakry and the empires they build? It's a little man who broods in a corner, because his pride has been hurt or his woman has been stolen. He waits and waits and waits. . . . He sees a whole covey of men stronger and richer than he nursing grievances much larger than his. Then our little man steps out of the corner and offers them a key to the floodgates. After that the deluge is inevitable!"

"Do you have a name for this little man?" asked Mark Matheson.

"I do," said Simon Lewisohn. "But it's too late to tell you. . . . Think about my offer, Mr. Matheson. And if you did join me, I'd love to hear why you went to Chakry in the first place."

As he walked out into the thin autumn sunshine of Zurich, Mark Matheson reflected bitterly that this was the one question he had never been able to answer honestly for himself.

JERUSALEM

The house of Yehudith Ronen, who was the wife of Adom Ronen the mirror-man of Damascus, was an old Arab dwelling perched on the top of the low hill of Har Zion. To reach it, one climbed through a straggle of dilapidated buildings to a high wall of whitewashed mud, broken by an iron gate. Beyond the gate was a garden full of olives and fig trees and tall cypresses. From the gate only the dome was visible, rising out of the greenery like a tomb of an ancient prophet. A strange silence hung about it, as if the distant murmur of the city and the shrill cries of the tenement children broke against its walls and were dissipated, like the ripples on a lakeshore.

It was exactly ten-twenty when Brigadier-General Jakov Baratz arrived at the gate and rang the bell. He was always meticulous to note the time of his arrivals and departures. And the habit was still there even though, after his visit to Hannah, time had become suddenly frozen into a blank and frightening eternity. Five seconds after his ring the electric buzzer sounded, the iron gate swung open to his touch and he walked into the garden closing the gate behind him. Under the dark canopy of fig leaves, the air was chill and he shivered. Then, as he turned an angle of the path, there was sunlight again and the house stood before him, squat, white and solid, with thick walls and dungeon windows and a low arched doorway, framed by a grapevine. The door was black and heavy, studded with iron nails forged a century since in a smithy of Old Jerusalem. It opened and Yehudith Ronen was there to greet him.

She was thirty-six years old: but, dressed in faded denims and a man's shirt, with her hair caught under an old scarf, she looked like a young girl full of sap and strength and contentment. In one hand she carried a pair of gloves and welders' goggles, the other she flung out in a greeting.

"Jakov! What a surprise. Come in!"

The room under the dome was as he had always known it: cool, shadowy, but lit by sudden and surprising splashes of color—the woven rug on the couch, the burnish of old copper hung above it, a flare of gold and purple oils from a wild landscape, a motley of dust jackets on the bookshelves, the dull gleam of Phoenician glass and the patina of her own bronzes on pedestals and wall brackets. It was a room without secrets but full of challenges. It was, like the woman who lived in it, brusque and exciting and restful all at once.

"What brings you to Jerusalem?"

"The Prime Minister's meeting this afternoon . . . and Hannah's back in hospital."

"O God!" Her concern was so poignant that it took him unawares and he felt himself suddenly close to tears. "You've seen her?"

"Yes. . . . She didn't recognize me."

"What does Lieberman say?"

"Prognosis negative."

"Did that surprise you?"

"No. I've seen it coming for a long time. I just didn't want to believe it."

"Now. . . ?"

"I'm damned if I know."

"Can you stay a while?"

"Of course. . . . I gave myself an hour. I needed to see you."

"Good! . . . Let's have some coffee."

He tossed his cap and his briefcase on to the settee and followed her into the small kitchen that opened off the vaulted chamber. He wanted to be close to her—close and companionable and absolved from the guilt which Hannah, all unknowing, had laid upon him. As he watched her bustling about the narrow bright room, he was reminded of her biblical namesake: "Yehudith was a widow in her house . . . of goodly countenance and very beautiful to behold. . . ." He wondered, as he had wondered many times before, what kind of union there had been between this swift, forthright creature and the subtle, restless fellow who lived in another skin in Damascus.

As if she had read his thoughts she asked him, "Have you heard from Adom?"

"Not for the last ten days."

"That's unusual, isn't it?"

"A little. He could be traveling, of course. He could be lying low during a security check. . . . I'll let you know as soon as I hear from him. You mustn't worry."

"I don't, Jakov." Abruptly she swung round to face him. "Understand that. I accept what he is—what he does. I have Golda and she's a sweet child. I have my work. I'm less—less lonely than when Adom was with me. I love him. In his own way I think he loves me. But we were never very happy together."

"I didn't know that."

"Dear Jakov!" She gave him a small somber smile and laid her cool hand for a moment against his cheek. "You're so clever in your job. So blind to other things."

"I've never been blind to you, Yehudith."

"Nor I to you. So where does it get us?"

"Nowhere! Nowhere at all."

"So relax," said Yehudith Ronen softly. "Let's be comfortable and truthful and not ashamed of the things we know together."

"It's a deal." He took her face in his hands, kissed her lightly on the lips and drew back. "Make the coffee and then show me the work you're doing."

They were over the thin ice and on to firm ground again. But they had both seen the dark water and, though they had drawn back, they knew that it would always be there, a deep and secret pool waiting to engulf them. They sipped their coffee and exchanged the gossip of Jerusalem and Tel Aviv, the follies of friends, the Yiddish comedies, the sometimes sinister tales of tricksters and jugglers who battened on the immigrant groups. Then Yehudith took his hand and led him through the shadows of the garden to her studio, a long whitewashed barn built against the eastern wall of the garden.

There was the usual distracting clutter of tools, wire frames, wax models, plaster casts, sketches pinned on walls, half-polished bronzes, tentative carvings in wood and stone. Most of it he had seen before; but there was a new piece, half the height of a man, covered with a sheet and standing on a low wooden bench, just where a broad beam of sun struck down from the fanlight. Yehudith made him stand a measured ten feet away from the piece and then took up her own position beside it. Then she played the necessary moment of self-mockery.

"So you don't like it, you don't buy it! . . . But there's no discount on this one, Jakov. I've put everything I know into it—and everything I am. I finished it yesterday. You're the first one to see it. . . . The title is 'Marriage.' "

She twitched away the sheet and stood watching his face as he surveyed the sculpture. A long rectangular strip of clear plastic had been bent into a double curve and set in a stone base. In the hollow of one curve was a female form, nude, strained into an attitude of climactic desire, reaching towards the male who stood, frustrated and agonized, beating against the side of the transparent wall. All the fury of passion was in their taut muscles, all the terror of solitude in their tormented faces; so that it seemed as if the wall must shatter under the impact of their need for each other. But the wall held firm and they were frozen in a limpid eternal hell.

The effect on the beholder was strange. There was a moment of detached curiosity, a moment of detachment within the composition itself, as if its parts did not match each other. This was followed by a shock as the detached parts fell abruptly into unity, and the observer was drawn willy-nilly into the action of the bronze mannikins. Then emotion welled up and spilled over into small inadequate words.

"It's beautiful," said Jakov Baratz. "Beautiful and terribly sad."

"Now you know about Adom and me."

"I wish I didn't."

"You have to, don't you? To protect him. To protect me."

"To protect us all," said Jakov Baratz.

Then she began to weep, quietly and with relief, as though she had survived an ordeal. When he took her in his arms she surrendered like a child, hungry for comfort and for simple tenderness; but he knew that the tenderness would never be so simple again and that, if the transparent wall were broken, it could never be repaired. So, as soon as she was calm, he made her cover the sculpture and walk back with him to the white house with the black door and the dungeon windows. There he made a telephone call to his headquarters and heard the news of the sabotage at Ein Kerem: a cottage wall blown open with plastic explosive, a child killed by the blast and a woman injured by flying masonry. He heard something else too: that Adom Ronen had reported from Damascus and a copy of his message was waiting in the cipher room in Jerusalem.

"Forty-one acts of sabotage in twelve months." The Prime Minister rehearsed the statistics in his gray, harsh voice.

"Seven deaths, two in the past week. We are here to discuss reprisals—their nature, their timing, their political and military effects."

He was a gray man all over, thought Jakov Baratz, gray-haired, gray-suited, gray of eye and skin and temper, a compromise candidate in a coalition government. He was the gray ruler following the bright zealots who had drawn the frontiers of Israel in blood. He was not weak. He had all the stubbornness of the professional politician, all the patient guile of the functionary. But he lacked presence and fire and the prophetic eloquence to hearten a beleaguered people.

". . . This morning's episode and the recent death of a tractor driver at Sha'ar Hagolan create a domestic crisis for my government. The people will demand to know—and they have a right to know!—what we are doing to secure their persons and their property against hostile incursions. That means a clear demonstration of our will and our capacity to resist aggression. More important still . . ." He splayed his thick hands on the tabletop and beat a slow tattoo with his thumbs. "If we do not take action now, our enemies will become bolder and we may find ourselves forced into a military adventure of great and dangerous consequences."

Baratz toyed with his pencil and tried to mask and master his irritation. The point was already made. Why embroider it with clichés and the stale rhetoric of the Knesset? You want reprisals; we'll arrange them. You want a list of possible consequences; we'll give you that too—and we'll quote you the odds on each one. But for God's sake, let's get down to business. And, when we've tidied this little mess, let's see what you make of my agent's report from Damascus. . . .

". . . Two separate kinds of sabotage." The gray voice droned on and on. "Direct attacks from Syria and forays across the Jordan border by members of the Palestine Liberation Organization. The mining of the tractor at Sha'ar Hagolan was the work of the Syrians. This morning's explosion at Ein Kerem is clearly the work of P.L.O. saboteurs based in Jordan. So, the first question: whom do we hit. . . . Syria, Jordan, or both?"

"Or neither." It was the Foreign Minister who completed the question and took the center of the stage at the same moment. "All incidents on the Syrian border are investigated by the Mixed Armistice Commission. If we ignore their investigations and make a direct attack, Syria can invoke immediately her mutual defense treaty with Egypt. If we attack Jordan, the Jordanians will say, quite rightly, that we are taking reprisals on innocent people for the work of illegal terrorists—to wit the P.L.O."

"So we sit and do nothing?" The Prime Minister was suddenly testy.

"I didn't say that, Aron. I simply point out that whatever we do, we are committed to a technical illegality, for which we shall have to answer in United Nations."

"And does United Nations answer to our people—for our dead?"

"No."

"So we are back to my question: Syria, or Jordan, or both?"

The Defense Minister uncoiled his long, serpentine body from the depths of the chair and delivered himself of an oracular decision. "Our policy towards Syria is determined by her treaty with Egypt. If Syria instigates military action, Egypt is not bound to intervene. If we instigate the action, Syria can and will invoke Egyptian aid. So, if and when they fire against us, we fire against them. . . . If they attack, we counterattack. We consider it dangerous to change this policy—at least for the present."

"And the Defense Ministry recommends. . . ?"

"A single strike against a single, well-defined objective inside the Jordan border."

"To demonstrate what?"

"That the Jordanians must police their own frontiers and get rid of the P.L.O. groups who operate there."

"It makes sense." The gray man nodded approval and

leaned back, folding his hands on his rumpled shirtfront. "Have you a particular objective in mind?"

"Not yet. If this meeting is agreed on the general principle, I should like to turn the matter over for immediate study by the Chief of Staff and the Director of Military Intelligence."

"How long would such a study take?"

"A week," said the Chief of Staff.

"I'd like two weeks at least," said Jakov Baratz. "Longer if possible."

The Chief of Staff frowned. The Defense Minister coughed, a dry warning. The Foreign Minister said bluntly:

"The longer we wait, the more the reprisal is divorced from the act which prompted it. Politically that's dangerous."

"There is more than one danger," said Jakov Baratz flatly. "We have to know and measure them all before we move." He fished in his briefcase and brought out the deciphered copy of the dispatch from Damascus. He spread it on the table under his hands and went on in the same detached fashion. "I received this morning an overdue report from our principal agent in Syria. He has been ill with malaria. This is the core of the message: 'Believe Safreddin preparing assassination plot against King of Jordan. He is using my transport for what seems decoy shipment arms to persons yet unknown. This shipment will be intercepted at Syrian border probably to throw suspicion on loyal palace elements. Will be present when shipment loaded at my warehouse. This may be decoy for me too. More when ready.' " He looked up and saw their faces, tense and questioning, all turned towards him. ". . . You see what I mean, gentlemen. If we attack Jordan, we are fighting a man who already has guns at his back."

THREE

BEIRUT

At seven o'clock in the evening Nuri Chakry, freshly barbered and bathed, sat in his apartment with a drink and a Picasso nude for company and gave himself over to a serious contemplation of his own future. It began with the establishment of a single, simple premise: that Nuri Chakry must survive in the state to which he had accustomed himself. Given this premise, it remained only to establish the best means of survival, the best manipulations of time and circumstance. He would like to survive in Beirut, in the sunny empire of bricks and concrete, stocks and bonds and mortgages and directorships and spheres of influence, which he had created for himself. If the choice were denied, then he would need a safe exit and a secure haven, where he could begin to build again.

The generality was simple; the problem lay in the particulars. If Nuri Chakry was to survive in Beirut, the Phoenician Bank must survive too. Survival was spelt in three words: fifty million dollars. If the Saudis and Kuwaitis left their deposits untouched, the problem was already solved. The chances were that they would pull them out within thirty days. The Finance Ministry and the Central Bank could save him too. They would put thumbscrews on him,

to be sure; but, once they were committed to a salvage operation, they could not easily extricate themselves from it. Thus,
Nuri Chakry would have the commodity he needed most—
time. There was a catch, however. The Finance Ministry
and the Central Bank were full of men who had been kicked
in the teeth or the tail by Nuri Chakry; so it was hard to
guess which way the votes might swing.

Eliminate these two hopes and you were left with the last
and least: Mark Matheson, still plodding round the mole
burrows of Zurich, in search of a reluctant friend or a gambler
bold enough to risk fifty million on Nuri Chakry. Matheson
had promised to call this evening, some time between seven
and nine. Until then Chakry had to possess his soul—if indeed he had such a thing—with as much patience as he could
command.

Reason a little further. All might fail and the bank would
fail too. What would happen then to Nuri Chakry? Firs'
there would be an independent audit. The audit would reveal what many suspected, but few knew for certain: that the
value of the bank's securities was grossly inflated for a tight
money market. It would reveal that large loans had been
made to favored persons, without security, or on documents
that were simply hope set down on paper. In the end—perhaps long before the end—Nuri Chakry would be called to
an accounting; his property in Lebanon would be distrained;
and, for all the laxity of the law, he might find himself in
prison.

Therefore, even though he might never have to make it,
his exit must be prepared. Time must be apportioned, punc-
tiliously; because he had only thirty days to save what he
could out of the possible wreckage of an empire. And here
was where Idris Jarrah, the venal agent, would be useful
to him, while Heinrich Muller would be absolutely essential.

Jarrah was not a fool, handing his head to an executioner
for dollars he would not live to spend. Jarrah was not afraid

of the recording tape or the incriminating document he had signed. Jarrah was a good gambler, betting all his chips on a man whose background he shared, whose motives he understood, with whom he had a common interest.

As he sipped his drink and studied the passionless curves of the nude, Chakry summed up the debits and credits on Idris Jarrah. Debit: one hundred thousand dollars. Debit: an uncomfortably accurate knowledge of the affairs of the Phoenician Bank. Debit: a strong position in a terrorist organization whose members would as happily knock off a banker in Beirut as they would bomb a pumping station in Battir. . . . Credit: a note of hand for a personal loan at fifteen percent. Credit: an incriminating tape. Credit: a set of signatures easy to duplicate. Credit: a piece of information salable in two or three markets at once. Summation: a good deal, with a reasonable profit to the client and a much bigger one to the banker.

Jarrah was a clever man; because he never tried to be too clever. It was obvious that he had been named the operations chief for the assassination in Jordan. It was obvious that he didn't like the job or its consequences. It was obvious that he did not trust Safreddin to protect him. The conclusion was equally clear: he was betraying the plotters in Syria and Jordan, while saving his own skin, keeping his organization intact and making a handy profit on the side. His only risk was that Nuri Chakry would betray him to Safreddin; but he knew that Nuri Chakry was on the side of kings and capitalists and he had nothing to gain from Syrian socialists and their Russian advisers and the cold men of the military junta. . . . So, a respectful salute to Idris Jarrah, blood brother in the hucksters' trade, who would never bet a cent on a man's honor, but would gamble everything on a nice calculation of his self-interest! A pity that, this time, he simply had to lose!

After the salute, a question: where best to sell the information which Jarrah had put into his hands? Two men sprang immediately to mind. Both were in Beirut. Both were business agents; the one, for the Royal House of Jordan; the other for a sheikdom in Kuwait. Each would be willing to pay largely for the opportunity of doing a personal service to the prince who paid him large commissions and whose favor was a guarantee of wealth beyond the dreams of simpler men. The Jordanian would pay promptly because he was intimately involved in whatever happened to the king. The Kuwaiti would haggle, but in the end he might pay much more, because he and his master had fingers in many dishes at once. A moment's reflection convinced Chakry that they would both pay, and together they would provide him with a quick profit on the hundred thousand he had laid out.

He put down his drink and made two telephone calls. The first one made him faintly unhappy. The Kuwaiti was at a cocktail party given by a representative of an American Trust Fund. The second was more encouraging. The Jordanian would be dining at the casino and playing afterwards in the private room. Which seemed as good a place as any to deal with kings and queens and knaves and the ace in the sleeve of the gambling banker.

The ace was Heinrich Muller, the minor scholar who lived in an orange grove near Byblos and published an occasional pale monograph on the Hyksos tombs and the development of alphabetic script from the pseudo hieroglyphs of Phoenicia. . . .

His first meeting with Heinrich Muller had been a moment of prime importance in the career of Nuri Chakry. He was still a money changer then; still hemmed in his rathole by the docks; still painfully building his courage and his capital to sally out of it. One day he received a telephone call from a petty trader who ran a tourist booth near the ruins of Byblos. The trader had coins to sell, and a set of seals. Arrived at the little port, Chakry found himself conducting his haggle under the eye of a visitor, a big ungainly fellow, shaggy and genial as a sheepdog. When the bargain was concluded, the visitor followed him outside and addressed him in passable Arabic:

"You are interested in old things?"

"I buy to sell." Chakry was brusque. His office was closed. He was losing business. He was impatient to be gone.

"You made a good deal," said the shaggy fellow amiably. "Except for the double ducat. That's a forgery."

"And how do you know that?" He smelled a rival and was instantly wary.

"It was offered to me. I tested it. Double ducats were minted over a period of about seventy-five years from the first quarter of the sixteenth century. This one weighs about one point two grams more than any known example. It is pure gold but it is a reproduction and not a minted piece. I would say it was cast about two hundred years ago. You won't lose on it. But if I were you, I wouldn't offer it to a good client as a real coin. An expert would identify it very quickly."

"Are you an expert?"

"An amateur." He chuckled and introduced himself in Teuton style. "Muller, Heinrich Muller. I live close by. I have a small collection which might interest you."

"Thank you. I'd like very much to see it." He was instantly agreeable. All his trader's instincts were awake. First rule in business: cultivate the man who knows; pay him for his knowledge; make him an ally—at least until you know as much as he does. . . .

His alliance with Heinrich Muller had lasted for seventeen years and had produced a handsome profit for both. They still traded together in coins, antiquities and exotica; and each knew enough about the other to ensure that the relationship and the profit would continue. For Heinrich Muller was not Heinrich Muller at all. He was a Swabian, born and baptized

Willi Reiman, and he had been one of the most expert forgers in the Third Reich—a maker of false passports, an engraver of counterfeit currencies, an expert on paper and inks and electrolytic plate; a man who buried the living in happy anonymity and kept the dead alive to protect them. He had a vast good humor, a staggering patience, a Levantine skill in the art of the possible. And for Nuri Chakry he was an expensive but comforting insurance.

The telephone rang and Mark Matheson was on the line from Zurich. His report was cryptic and depressing:

"No luck here. The 'J' groups are not interested. A couple of the others might help if they knew the Government was backing us. If not, they'll sit on their hands."

"How much do they know, Mark?"

"Too much."

"Active hostility?"

"No. Passive regret. They'll send flowers to the graveside. What do you want me to do?"

"Get back as soon as you can."

"Have you see the Ministry yet?"

"Tomorrow morning."

"With luck I'll be home in the evening."

"I'll call you. . . . And Mark . . ."

"Yes?"

"Have a pleasant evening."

"Thanks!" said Mark Matheson without enthusiasm, and hung up.

JERUSALEM

"You're asking us to stage a theater piece," said the Chief of Staff unhappily. "I don't like it at all."

"Politics is more than half theater." The Defense Minister had a taste for aphorism. "And this is essentially a political move."

"In theater," said Jakov Baratz, "the action is defined and limited by a prepared script. The reactions of the audience are already tested in dress rehearsal. And if the script calls for a gun, you use a plugged barrel and blank cartridges. In war you have only the script for the first act. You cannot predict how the second and third will develop."

"The guns are real too," said the Chief of Staff. "People get killed."

"So we drop the metaphor," said the Defense Minister blandly. "And confine ourselves to facts. It was agreed at today's meeting that we would mount a limited action against a limited objective on the best available terms. I think we three should attempt to define those terms clearly for ourselves. . . . Brandy, gentlemen?"

He got up from the table and went through the small ceremony of warming the glasses and pouring a careful measure of liquor for each of his guests. Baratz and the Chief of Staff exchanged a glance and a shrug across the candlelit table. They had played this gambit before. The Defense Minister was a canny politician, who knew exactly what he wanted and how to ensure that it would be proposed by his subordinates, who would then be saddled with the responsibility. It was a convention of the game, therefore, that Baratz, the junior, should make the first proposal:

"Let's take the middle term first: a limited objective. We have a list of the border villages from which the P.L.O. are known to operate. We choose one of these. We mount an attack in strength. We clear out the civilian population, destroy the village and then withdraw. Our point is clearly made. We are not concerned to inflict casualties. We demand that Jordan take her own action against illegal saboteurs."

"Excellent." The Minister brought the glasses back to the table and set them in front of his guests. "Which village would you suggest as the target?"

"None, yet," said Baratz deliberately. "The situation I have described is an ideal one. It assumes a location favorable to a surprise attack. It assumes that there are no Jordanian troops in the area. It assumes that we shall knock out police communications before they are able to call for intervention by the Arab Legion. Without further study we cannot make any of these assumptions. On the other hand, if we make any contact at all with the Arab Legion we shall have a pitched battle. I am sure that we shall win it. I am equally sure that we cannot guarantee to limit it."

The Minister cupped his hands around his glass, raised it to his long, sharp nose and inhaled reverently. Then, before he tasted the drink, he asked, "But you think that what you call an ideal situation might turn into a possible one?"

"It might, yes."

The Minister sipped his liquor, rolled it gratefully on his tongue and swallowed. He turned to the Chief of Staff. "And you, Chaim?"

"As always, I would have to decide on the basis of available information."

"And what does your present information tell you?"

"It is incomplete." Baratz answered for him. "And for two reasons. I presume, from the tenor of our talk today, that the information from our agent about an attempt on the life of King Hussein will be passed to Amman immediately, either through the Americans or the British. Once this information reaches Amman, it is clear that certain changes will be made in the order of battle of the Arab Legion. Second, there was news in today's press of an early visit to Jordan by Moslem dignitaries from Pakistan. The program for this visit includes a state visit to Jerusalem and to the Dome of the Rock. Inevitably there will be a concentration of combat units in the Jerusalem area. We have to know more about this before we make final plans."

"And if there is an attempt on the King's life," the Chief of Staff added a tart reminder, "we don't want it to happen while he's in Jerusalem and we're providing a diversion for the assassins."

The Minister sat for a long moment twirling his brandy glass in his hand and staring into the golden dregs of the liquor. Baratz and the Chief of Staff waited glumly for the next familiar move: the bright smile, the all-professionals-together speech, the cool presumption of agreement, the hasty good night. To their surprise the Minister did not make the play. He seemed to have forgotten his actor's gestures and his studious irony. When he looked up, they saw that his long bony face was gray and strained. He spoke haltingly on a note of deprecation:

"Look! I want to tell you I'm not any happier about this operation than you are. But I do honestly believe it has to be mounted. We're in bigger trouble than anyone wants to admit just now. In Cabinet yesterday, the Prime Minister presented us with a figure that shocked us all. Inside four months we're going to have eighty thousand unemployed . . . possibly more. Our shipping line's in trouble. At least one bank is going to go broke and the Government, to stave off a panic, will have to guarantee the depositors. If the unemployment goes on too long we're going to start losing just what we can't afford to lose—people! Now that adds up to high tension inside the community . . . a sense of frustration, insecurity, lack of confidence in public institutions. If you add another fear—that we can't or won't keep our frontiers safe—then we're up to our necks in bother. It's a brutal thing to say; but, for home consumption, we need a little war right now!"

"And for how long will we go on needing wars?" There was a dull anger in the voice of the Chief of Staff. "A democracy is supposed to be self-sustaining, otherwise what's the point? Self-defense—yes! But the army as a propaganda weapon and dead men to keep the living content . . . no thank you! If that's our future as a nation, let's call the whole thing off now. Let's have another dispersion and get it over with!"

"I agree, Chaim." The Minister seemed suddenly to shrink back into himself. "It's dangerous to say it too loudly, but that's the dilemma we're in. And, strangely enough, it's always been the dilemma of the Jew in the land of his fathers. We take it. We hold it awhile. We make it flower again. And then we lose it. Is it the land or ourselves? Is it the strange gods who seduce us, or the God of Jacob who is still jealous of His Chosen?"

"I don't know. I'm not a religious man. Sometimes I wish I were."

Jakov Baratz said nothing. His thoughts had suddenly struck off at a tangent. He was wondering what it was that sustained Adom Ronen in his lonely vigil in Damascus, and how he would sustain himself in the wintry years without Hannah.

As if disconcerted by his silence, the Minister put on his official manner like a mask. "So we're agreed. A reprisal operation to be planned and submitted for approval in the next week."

"Two weeks," said Baratz.

The Minister sighed theatrically. "You're an obstinate man. Two weeks then. But that's the limit."

It was still only nine-thirty when they left the Minister's house. The Chief of Staff suggested a stroll; so they dismissed the car and set out on foot for the King David Hotel. The night was chill. A small cold wind searched through the hills of Jerusalem; but the sky was clear and full of low stars and there was a curious domestic comfort in the huddle of apartments, the shapes of garden trees and the yellow home-lights between them. They strode out briskly at first, their heels beating a brisk martial tattoo on the pavement; then imperceptibly their pace slackened and the Chief of Staff began a moody, brooding talk.

". . . It's happening to all of us, Jakov. The day of the trumpets is over. Now it's politics and economic surveys and balance of payments and balance of power in the Knesset. It's the natural cycle, I suppose. But it worries me. We were the adventurers once—the plotters, the saboteurs, the gunlayers and the commandos. . . . Now we're the Establishment. Who takes over? Where will they take the country?"

"I wish I knew. I wish I had a son. Not so that I could tell him . . . but so he could tell me what's going on in the minds of the young people. In the army they're good. They like discipline. They have drive and purpose. Let 'em out, and they're lost again. I had a look at some figures the other day on juvenile delinquency in Tel Aviv. Frightening."

"Perhaps Yuval's right and we do need another war."

"And when that's over?"

The Chief of Staff made no attempt to answer the question. He was silent a moment, then, without preamble, changed the subject. "Something's been bothering me, Jakov. A phrase in your agent's report: 'This may be a decoy for me too.' What did he mean? Is he scared? Is he blown?"

"Scared? I imagine so. But that's no harm if it keeps him careful. Blown? I doubt it. He's probably under test, as all foreigners are from time to time. Safreddin's policy is to foment suspicion and fear while he consolidates the Syrian Army into an instrument of power." He gave a small wry chuckle. "Knowing the Syrians, that's a rough job in itself. But Ronen's a good man."

"What sort of a man?" asked the Chief of Staff.

"That's not easy to answer. I think you always have to start with the premise that a spy is a different sort of man from the rest of us. In a way I suppose he's like an actor. He's happier wearing greasepaint than he is in normal life. He has more convictions about himself, he imposes more conviction on others from the stage than from the sidewalk. Ronen's an Iraqi too, remember. He's not a European. I think he finds himself happier in an Arab ambience than in ours. That was part of the trouble with his marriage."

The words were out before he could check them. The

Chief of Staff seized on to them immediately. "Was his marriage unhappy?"

"Unsatisfactory—to both parties."

"Is he still married?"

"Yes. His wife's here in Jerusalem. I—my people—look after her and the child."

"What does he do for company?"

"He's always had girl friends. I imagine he has one now."

"Is that safe—from our point of view?"

"From our point of view," said Baratz slowly, "anything that keeps an agent contented and living a normal life in his area is an advantage. It's a matter of expediency and not of morals."

"Does his wife know where he is?"

"Yes."

"Is that wise?"

"Necessary, in my judgment."

"I don't question it," said the Chief of Staff mildly. "He's your man. You have to manage him. I'm just curious. What's his wife like?"

"Very intelligent. Very good-looking. She's a talented artist."

"Does she have a boy friend?"

"No."

"She must be a remarkable woman."

"She is."

"Does her husband communicate with her?"

"Only through me. We've arranged a code for simple messages. What he can't say, I invent."

"Like Cyrano de Bergerac, eh?"

"It's the wrong simile," said Jakov Baratz. "Cyrano de Bergerac was in love with the girl."

At which they both laughed; and the echoes rang loud and hollow along the empty street.

DAMASCUS

Colonel Omar Safreddin was a man of fixed and clear beliefs. He believed in Allah, the One the Merciful. He believed in Mohammed the Prophet—blessed be His Glorious Name! He believed in the Book and in the Reading which was the fountain of all knowledge. He believed in the People —the Chosen of God, the Sons of the Prophet, who had rolled like sea waves across the face of the earth and who, through the Book and the Prophet, must find again their identity and their brotherhood and their dignity among the infidel. He believed in the Land and in the Tribe, defined by borders and by possessions and by history and tradition. He believed in power, and its exercise by an elite who had prepared themselves to assume it.

In the Syrian Army, which was his own tribe and territory, he had set himself to create such an elite: a group of young officers, noble in body, enlightened in spirit and trained by education to be the first inheritors of the revolution and the resurrection. From the Russians, whom he admired but feared as well, he had learned the value and the method of cellular organization; and he had begun to apply it in his own training program.

The instrument of application was the Hunafa Club, a group of fifteen young men who met every week in his house in Abo Romana. The club took its name from that small group of Meccan believers, among whom Mohammed the Prophet first found inspiration and enlightenment. A hanif was one who had turned away from the crude idolatry which disfigured the original House of Allah. By extension, it meant a righteous man, who withdrew from corruption into the desert and who, in the Month of Heat, devoted himself to prayer and self-discipline.

Each meeting of the club began with prayer and ablution,

which were followed by a ritual meal eaten in common. After the meal, the members recited in chorus the Summons, which the angel Gabriel made to the Prophet at his first calling, and the Answers which he, terrified, gave to the angelic voice. It was, perhaps, symbolic that Omar Safreddin spoke with the voice of the angel while his disciples answered with the voice of the Prophet:

"Read!"

"I cannot read."

"Read!"

"I cannot read."

"Read!"

"What can I read?"

"Read: in the name of Your Lord who creates, creating man from a clot. Read: and it is Your Lord, the most generous, who teaches by the pen, teaching man what he did not know."

After the antiphon, the teaching would begin. Safreddin would read from the Glorious Koran, expounding the text and applying it to the life of the Chosen in the twentieth century.

"Give me pieces of iron. And when he had leveled up the hollow between the hills, he said: blow! Then when he had made it a fire, he said: bring me melted copper to pour on it. And Gog and Magog were not able to climb over it nor could they penetrate it. . . ."

Colonel Omar Safreddin explained the text as follows: "The words are old; but their message, like all the messages of the Prophet, is continually new. When we were a colony of the French, the colonialists lived on the hills and we remained subject in the valley. They made slaves of us and bled us dry; but the iron that was in us still remained. Now that the French have gone, we have begun to fill up the valleys with the iron of our own bodies. We have leveled out the differences between man and man. We have destroyed the merchant class and the foreign exploiters, who sent their money out of the country instead of leaving it here to better the lot of the people. We have burned the traitors out of their hiding places. We have raised fiery walls, so that they cannot come back to exploit us again. Gog and Magog have been rooted out forever from Syria; but they still flourish in the lands that surround us, in Iraq, in Israel, in Lebanon and in Jordan where a son of the Prophet has married an infidel woman and has made himself a willing tool of the British. . . . So we must make ourselves every day more strong, more watchful, more aggressive against our enemies. . . ."

There was a magic in his eloquence and he knew it. He exercised it with calm calculation, never surrendering himself to the frenzy which he felt sometimes mounting within him. He was a soldier; he must not make himself a dancing dervish or a wild besotted sufi, mouthing barren prophecies. Discipline, always discipline! Because the Prophet, himself, had been a disciplined man.

For this reason, after the teaching, there was always the exercise of manly arts. They would go down to the cellar of the house. There they would compete in pistol shooting, in fencing with saber and foil, in unarmed combat for which Safreddin had imported teachers from North Korea. Safreddin, himself, took part in the shooting and in the fencing but never in the hand-to-hand fighting, because he was older than his disciples and could not bear to be shown less strong than they. There was another reason too, which he did not care to examine too closely. He hated to be touched by one of his own sex; and if, in the normal commerce of the day, someone brushed against him, he found himself tingling and irritated like an animal stroked by an unfamiliar hand.

Finally, when the exercises were finished, they would go back to the dining room, where Safreddin would pose a problem for which, at the following meeting, each member of the club must present his own solution. . . . So it happened that while Nuri Chakry was sitting at cards with the business agent from Jordan, and Jakov Baratz was driving back from Jerusalem to Tel Aviv, and Idris Jarrah was diverting himself in his hotel room with a belly dancer from the Scheherazade, Omar Safreddin was proposing a riddle to the members of the Hunafa Club.

". . . We hanged the Israeli spy, Eli Cohen, in Morjan Square. We broke up his network. Was this the end of Israeli treachery among us? Obviously not. They must try again to establish a permanent agent in Damascus or elsewhere. They are not fools. On the contrary they are very clever and evolved people, so they will have learned from the mistakes of Eli Cohen, just as we have learned from ours. What is an agent? A spider who spins a web and waits quietly at the center of it, while unwary flies and mosquitoes are trapped in its sticky meshes. The center of the web is always in a shadowy corner. We do not come upon it quickly or easily. We see the threads first and the trapped insects, buzzing and struggling. . . . So here is your problem for tonight. Assume that, here in Damascus, there is a new agent. Assume that his character and his method will be quite different from those of Eli Cohen. Assume that his network will be different too. How and where would you begin to look for him? . . ."

ZURICH

In the bar of the Dolder Grand, with the lake and the lights of the city spread far below, Mark Matheson drank the last of a long series of whiskies, in a vain attempt to anesthetize his bruises. The lights were low. The music was soft and sweet. The women were elegant if not uniformly beautiful. The men were well groomed and prosperous if not uniformly sober. The place was perfumed with money— solid Swiss money, protected by stable laws, hedged with secrecy, managed with discretion according to the best banking rules. The whole scene was a reproach and a mockery to a man who once had come here honored among his equals but who now felt himself suddenly outcast. In forty-eight hours he had taken the worst mauling of his life. He had been affronted in his pride and in his most secret vanities. The shame of failure was like an aura about him. The stink of another man's discredit seemed to accompany him wherever he went.

It was a bitter experience, which he was determined never to repeat. Had he been less fatigued he would have been tempted to banish it all by a wild night with one of the international whores whose names were traded quietly among the rich and successful of Zurich, where the clubs closed at twelve-thirty and the life of the high half-world began at one. But he had used up all his strength in pleading, debating and defending the fading credit of Nuri Chakry; and his confidence in himself had been undermined by old Lewisohn's question: why had he joined Chakry in the first place?

Even now, in the time of whisky-truth, it was hard to give an honest answer. Opportunity? For a man in his middle thirties, it was no small thing to be able to break out of the slow, safe seniorities of American banking into the heady freedom of the Levant. In one leap he had accomplished what it might have taken him fifteen years to do in New York. Money? This too. Chakry paid generously and expected his personal assistant to maintain a style of life that did honor to the Phoenician Bank.

But there were other reasons, less creditable, less easy to admit. He knew that he had been hired to impose a character of sobriety, a character of confidence upon an institution which, for all its western form, still used the methods of the bazaar and the conventions of tribal traffic. He had done it. But in doing it he, too, had been seduced by the gambler's lure—money pumped up from the ground, spread fast and thin, sometimes for quick returns, sometimes for fabulous but future advantage. There was another reason also; but he always skirted it, sidelong, afraid to face the consequences of total self-knowledge.

Life was easy in Beirut. Pleasure was cheap and brought no moral censure, provided one enjoyed it with style and shared it generously with one's friends. To a puritan from Connecticut, it was a release into the world of the thousand-and-one nights, a ticket of admission to exotic intimacies which carried no penalty, except the slow realization that one could hardly do without them. It was only a formal truth when he claimed that the books were clean and the documents straight. He could swear it in court, and prove it by auditors' reports and still be clear of perjury; but only because he refused to inquire about what he guessed; because, if he spoke his guesses, he might lose the favor of the man who had put the sweet life within his reach. It was all written in the yellow surface of the whisky, and he hoped that only Mark Matheson could read it. What he wondered now was whether Mark Matheson could live with what he read. Then a nasal drawling voice spoke out of the air above him:

"Hullo, Matheson!"

He looked up startled and saw Lew Mortimer, standing beside his table. "Oh! Hullo, Mortimer." His greeting was less than cordial.

"I heard you were in town. I thought I'd find you here. Mind if I sit down?"

"Help yourself."

Mortimer eased his brawny body into the alcove and signaled a passing waiter. "Bourbon on the rocks. Double."

He was an incongruous man. His clothes were immaculate and made by the best Italian tailor; but always his big muscly body seemed ready to burst out of them. His face was smooth; his hair was trimmed every day; but his skin was burnt brown and hardened by exposure, as if he still worked on the oil lines, cursing the riggers to lay another pipe and another, because every foot was another dollar in his pocket. His voice still had the ring of command in it, the raw threatening humor of a man who knew what he wanted and wanted it delivered yesterday. He grinned at Matheson and drawled, "I hear you've been busy, boy."

Matheson shrugged irritably. "I've been around."

"And around and around and around. No luck, eh?"

"Some," said Mark Matheson.

"But not enough, boy. Not half enough. The Jews won't play, because they're going to have to step in and help the Israeli Government when the Wilderstein group goes bust next month in Tel Aviv." He was quick to see the surprise on Mark Matheson's face. "You didn't know that? Well, I guess you've had enough troubles of your own. It's true though. They were undercapitalized in the first place. Mr. Chakry, of course, made another kind of mistake. He had the capital, but he didn't know how to manage it. He didn't know how to manage people either." The waiter handed him his drink and Mortimer raised his glass in a toast. "Here's to crime."

Matheson drank in silence. Then Mortimer dropped his mocking tone and became friendly.

"This is a rough deal for you, boy. You've put in good work. I've admired you. If you want a job at any time, come to me."

"That's the second offer I've had today."

"And there'll be more. Good men are hard to find. Harder than money."

"You could help us, Mortimer."

"I could," said Lew Mortimer evenly. "I could do it right now. I could back you with a loan, take up your unissued capital or buy you lock, stock and barrel. But I won't."

"Because of the airline?"

Mortimer flushed. He was a man of swift angers, but he controlled himself and talked on in the same steady drawl.

"Not because of the airline, boy—though that's part of it. Because of Nuri Chakry, a son of a bitch who wanted all of the pie for himself and wouldn't give his old friends even a little bite. I loaned him money in the old days. You didn't know that, did you? But I loaned him money. Sure he paid it back, every penny with interest. But when he started to grow, when he started to issue shares—in the airline, in real estate companies, in hotels—suddenly I wasn't on the list any more. He knew I was as tough as he was and he didn't want competition. So he found other friends. Fine! Now he's stuck with them! I'll just sit around with the rest of the gang and pick up the pieces."

"So why tell me?" said Mark Matheson wearily. "I just work there."

"Because I want you to tell Nuri Chakry," said Mortimer with soft malice. "Because I want to know that he's squirming in that bloody great office of his. I want him to know that I know; that, when he goes to the Government tomorrow morning, they'll make him a whole slew of promises and keep none of them; that Feisal will be out in thirty days and the Kuwaitis will be out too and even the Russians won't like him any more. And you can tell him one other thing. He'd better find himself a country with no extradition laws because some of us have got enough on him to put him behind bars for the rest of his life."

"You're a good hater," said Mark Matheson with stale contempt.

"You bet I am!" Mortimer was suddenly savage. "I used to be a good lover too; though I'm getting a bit old for it now. And that's another thing. Tell Chakry to make a little list of all the men whose women he stole because he had to be the biggest cocksman from Istanbul to Cairo. . . . Then check the list of the men who are holding him by the short hairs today. That's where you'll read the true story." Abruptly he was calm again. "I don't hold anything against you, boy. You're a good servant—the best. But you'll never be a great man because you're soft in the center. The job's open any time you want to ask for it. I'll pay for my own drink."

He laid a five-franc note on the table and walked off. Mark Matheson gulped the rest of his drink and ordered another. He hated to fly with a hangover; but tonight, at least, he had to sleep soundly.

DAMASCUS

Dr. Bitar thrust open the door of the room and took in the whole scene at a glance: the woman huddled in the corner weeping, in a long monotonous ululation; the nurse, young and slack-handed, standing by the bed; the house surgeon cradling the tiny wasted body in his arms and trying to force liquid down its throat. Before he was two paces inside, the inevitable happened; the child gagged and vomited the liquid into the surgeon's shirtfront.

"Put him down, please." Bitar's soft deep voice brooked no contradiction. "Lay him flat on the bed."

The surgeon laid the child on the bed, and even as he did so the small, slack belly contracted and a stream of bilious fluid was voided on to the sheets. The child gasped and whimpered and his arms and legs twitched in a series of rigors. Bitar noted the dry lips and the waxen pallor of the cheeks and the eyeballs sunk back into the skull case. He opened his bag, took out a stethoscope and made a quick auscultation of chest and belly, while the woman wailed on and on hypnotically. Then he straightened up and gave a series of swift orders.

"Immediate intravenous feeding. Glucose and salines. Sterile instruments and sutures. Cardiac stimulant. Sterile water and a spoon. Urine bag and clean linen. Do you understand?"

The nurse nodded dumbly and then hurried from the room.

Bitar swung round to face the doctor. "How long has he been like this?"

The young man shrugged helplessly. "They brought him in only an hour ago. They said he's been sick since midnight."

"We'll be lucky if he's not dead before this midnight. Why the devil didn't you put him on intravenous immediately?"

Again the shrug and the spreading of soft hands. "We thought we'd try sedation and liquid feeding first."

"Allah!" Bitar swore unhappily. "What did they teach you in medical school? Look at him! Dehydration, desalinization, constant rigors. And you shove liquid down his neck fast enough to choke him. How old is he?"

"Two, they told me."

"Where's the father?"

"At some meeting or other. The woman brought him in."

Bitar threw a swift glance at the keening mother. She was lost to all reason, buried in a self-protective grief. He snapped an order at the house surgeon. "Get her out! Send her home! And then hurry that stuff up here."

The house surgeon hesitated a moment, resentful and stubborn; but the anger in Bitar's eyes subdued him instantly. He urged the woman to her feet and hustled her past the bed and out of the room. Bitar bent over the bed and bathed the child's forehead with a damp cloth, crooning a tuneless little song of comfort. He had seen hundreds like this one, in rich apartments and stinking hovels, the life draining out of them through leaking membranes and inflamed intestines, their skin dry as silk on the dyers' racks, their muscles knotted by electrolysis, literally dying of thirst because their parched gullets could not absorb a drop of water. Helpless and moribund they were the focus of all his anger—against demagogues and junta men and claptrapping theorists who made politics while their children wilted with trachoma and malarial spleens and intestinal parasites. Finally, with miraculous haste for Damascus, the bottles and the trays were wheeled in and he was able to scrub up and begin the simple overdue surgery. Below the child's left ankle he made an incision in a vein, then sutured in the hollow needle which would carry the life-giving fluid into the bloodstream. He connected the needle to the rubber tubing, tested the flow from the bottle. Then he injected a stimulant to boost the failing heart and, when he was sure it had taken hold, he ordered a transparent plastic bag hung over the child's shrunken penis, had the bed linen changed and the wounded leg strapped down lest the rigors wrench the needle out of the vein. Finally he straightened up.

"What now?" asked the house surgeon.

"We wait. When he has calmed a little we feed him sterile water, a drop at a time, from a spoon. We feed it to him as long and as often as he can retain it. After that we wait for him to pee. If he can't—if he doesn't—" His long elegant hands made a sign of resignation. "Inshallah. It is as God wills."

"If you like"—the house surgeon made a tentative bid for respect—"the nurse and I will take over now."

"No, thank you." Bitar's tone was curt. "I want to see the father. I want to know why an intelligent man leaves a child as sick as this in a houseful of hysterical women. If you'd like to do something for me, call my house and tell them where I can be found."

Crestfallen but not daring to be angry, the house surgeon went out.

Bitar turned to the young nurse and instructed her gently. "You must never let this happen again, to anyone. Always assume that the child has been sick too long before it is brought to hospital. The routine is simple. Intravenous feeding, glucose and salines. Slow but steady oral hydration. Use an eyedropper if need be, but never—like that fool—thrust water down a child's throat. He will vomit immediately and lose more than you try to put in. Look! . . ." Very carefully he spooned a few drops of water into the child's parched mouth. "Like this . . . slow and often. Cover him with a sheet, but check the urine bag every half hour. If the kidney function fails we have no way to reverse the chemistry. We lose him. . . ." He gave her a slow grave smile. "We old ones don't matter so much; but the little ones are too precious to lose."

"You're a good man, Doctor." There was gratitude and awe in her smile.

"And you'll make a good nurse—if you use your head and don't let the careless ones frighten you. Now would you get me a cup of coffee? This could be a long night."

When she had gone, he made another auscultation, spooned more water between the blue lips and then walked to the window, lit a cigarette and inhaled deeply. He felt suddenly old—too old for the angers that consumed him every day; too old for the hopeless battle against poverty and ignorance and disease; too tired for plots and counterplots against a regime which he hated, because his studies abroad had given him a taste for unattainable liberty and a faith in the free commerce of men and ideas. In his secret heart he knew that the battle was futile and the plots were barren. Only time and education would cure ignorance. There was no cure for death. And liberty was a state towards which man grew slowly, or reacted dangerously from the tyranny of the collective. But he could not abandon the fight, because to do so was to abandon himself. . . . The nurse came in with the coffee and, close on her heels, came Omar Safreddin, erect and soldierly, full of concern for the first son born to his name.

He stood for nearly a minute looking down at the shrunken twitching body, then he asked, "Will he live?"

"Inshallah!" There was open contempt in Bitar's shrug. "If he does, there will be no thanks to you."

"You have no right to talk to me like that!"

"I have every right! The child became ill twenty hours ago. He was brought here only an hour ago. You did not call me until he had left for the hospital."

"It seemed a simple illness. Many children get it."

"And many die of it! Gastroenteritis is the biggest killer of young children even in evolved countries, which ours— Allah take pity on us—is not."

A redoubtable man to friends and enemies, Safreddin was cowed for a moment by Bitar's anger. He stammered an apology and then asked with unaccustomed humility, "What causes it?"

"A virus. A virus that is carried by flies and dirty hands and unwashed food and dust and unpurified water. Sometimes in the belly of a child it goes mad and multiplies itself at a tremendous rate. We need a campaign on this. Call for the statistics from Public Health and you'll see why."

"We need so many campaigns. We have to cram fifty years into ten and we'll still be twenty behind."

There was a genuine pathos in the answer: the pathos of every man who finds that ambition outruns strength.

Even Bitar was touched. He smiled, a mite crookedly, and made his own apology. "I'm sorry, Colonel. I had a fright too, when I came in and saw the child. I'm still frightened. We may lose him yet. You have to be ready for that."

"Is there nothing more you can do?"

"Nothing. Except pray—if you can."

"I can pray."

He walked to the clear space between the bed and the window, turned his face towards Mecca, prostrated himself on the rug and began to pray in a low, murmuring monotone. It was such a simple thing to do, so direct and childlike that Bitar was shocked, and then strangely afraid of the raw primitive faith which prompted the act. He turned back to the bed and began to feed water into the child again. His pulse was steadier now, the rigors were less frequent; but the plastic bag at his loins was still empty and there was still no color in the dry yellow cheeks. A long time later, Safreddin rose from his prayers and came to stand by the bed.

"If you tell me what to do, Doctor, I'll take over for an hour."

Bitar shook his head. "Any change now is critical. I'll wait it out. Curl up in the chair and try to sleep. I'll call you if anything happens, good or bad."

"If you say so, Doctor."

Obediently he settled himself in the chair, stretched out his long legs, canted his military cap over his eyes and began to take long deep breaths. Within three minutes he was asleep. For all the tension of his vigil, Bitar felt the fear gnawing at him again. This was the method man, pure, without alloy. You see death hovering. You pray against him. You sleep; because you have done all that there is to be done. Death comes. You weep. You bury the body. You breed again. You live in watertight compartments. In each you are complete and self-sufficient. You have no regrets, no remorse. Today is complete in itself. Tomorrow is a different day. God help any poor devil who falls foul of such a one!

At two in the morning Safreddin was still sleeping and the night nurse came in to change the bottle. After three there were no more rigors and the child slept exhausted while a pale color crept into his cheeks. At four he urinated and Bitar woke Safreddin to tell him that the child would live. He wept for one moment and the next was calm and smiling. He held out his hand to Bitar.

"I shall never forget this, Doctor."

"All in a day's work—except this has been a rather long day."

"I must thank our friend Fathalla too. He told me you were a good doctor."

"My fees are high." Bitar grinned wearily. "And I charge double after midnight."

"I owe you a life," said Omar Safreddin.

As he drove home in the false dawn and smelt the desert dust in the air, Bitar wondered when, how and if he would ever be forced to claim payment.

In the same pale hour, Selim Fathalla woke from a dream into a new and strange reality.

The dream began in his own bedroom; whether at dawn or midnight he could not tell because there was light and yet no light; there were sounds and yet an overpowering silence. All he knew for certain was that he was lonely, trapped in a mortal sadness from which only the sight of another human face could release him. He wanted to go out into the streets and the bazaars. He could not. Wherever he turned there were blank walls and illusory doors with no locks and no handles. He was in despair until he remembered the mirror. His twin was there mocking but reassuring. He began to walk towards the mirror, but as he did so the room elongated itself into an endless tunnel, white and featureless. He tried to turn back. The tunnel receded into an infinity behind him. He went forward walking slowly at first, then breaking into a desperate run. Then the tunnel was not there any more and he stood panting and terrified, staring into the mirror. The glass was empty, like a flat lake seen from a great height. In the same instant he was aware of himself in a mode that was quite new. He was solid, whole. Alone, yes; alone like a tree in the middle of a great flat plain, but rooted like the tree in an earth no longer alien. Relief shook him like a great wind. He wanted to laugh and weep and shout for sheer senseless happiness. . . . The next moment he was wide awake, in his own bed, with Emilie naked and still asleep beside him.

The strangeness was that he was still happy. He knew exactly what had happened to him. He did not have to grope backward through mists and miasmas for an interpretation.

Miraculously, or by some slow subconscious mending of nature, the two halves of himself had been reunited. The mirror-twin was dead. Now there was only one man: Fathalla-Ronen, Ronen-Fathalla, it did not matter any more. One man to risk and reason and decide. One life to live. One love to enjoy—and the object of that love lay spent and placid beside him.

Carefully he eased himself out of bed and walked to the window. A faint pearly light brightened the sky behind the minaret. The garden was still in darkness but he caught the perfume of rose blooms and heard the small musical splash of water in the lion fountain. The unity which he had discovered in himself was a unity with the place too. The high walls held everything together: the man, the girl, the flowers, the water, the drooping tamarisk, the high-rising tower, the patch of dawn sky. Even the contradictions of his trade could be reconciled in the magic of the moment. He was a paid agent. Enough. It was not a noble trade, but it was not all ignoble either. He could serve his own people without a total rejection of those with whom he lived. He could put a term to his service; because that was part of his contract with Baratz. And when the term was out he could go away with Emilie and begin another life, in Europe perhaps, or even in Lebanon, where Jew and Moslem and Maronite rubbed along in a cynical kind of harmony.

As for Yehudith and the child, there was a contract there too and either was free to invoke it any time. On their last night together, after a bitter-sweet loving, Yehudith had told him plainly: "I don't know, Adom, how long I can take this. I suppose you don't either. I don't blame you. Somehow the chemistry never quite works with us. So, if it gets too hard—for either of us—let's be honest and call it off. Golda won't suffer, I promise you. Neither of us wants to make her a battleground. . . ." So, in all but the legal fact, he was free; and Jakov Baratz would arrange the legalities discreetly as soon as he was asked.

He turned back to the bed and stretched himself beside the sleeping girl. Then slowly and tenderly he began to solicit her, stroking her breasts and her flanks and the soft curves of her belly. She stirred and sighed, and then rolled over and clung to him, urgent and demanding until he possessed her in a oneness they had never known before.

FOUR

TEL AVIV

In the morning, early, Jakov Baratz assembled his planning staff in the headquarters briefing room. He gave them a brisk formal greeting and then plunged straight into business.

". . . The memorandum under your hands describes the operation which we are required to project. We have fourteen days in which to submit a final recommendation to the Chief of Staff and the Director of Operations. . . . I do not like what we have been asked to do. It has too many political qualifications. I do not believe that one can successfully qualify a military operation any more than a surgical one. However, our orders are clear. We shall do our best to carry them out. . . . We are asked to mount a reprisal raid. A reprisal must bear a clear relationship in time and geography to the acts which prompted it. The time relationship is already established. The geography demands that we should strike somewhere in the Hebron area, between these two points. Note the coordinates, please." He described with a pointer a long arc extending along the southern fringe of the Jerusalem corridor. He waited while the officers noted the coordinates on their own maps. "The objective must have a certain importance in itself. A hamlet will not do, or a scattered settlement. There are three large villages in the sector I have defined. They are marked A, B and C. Each has a police post, an infirmary, a post office, a mosque, a school and a population of between seven hundred and eight hundred inhabitants. None has any fixed military installations. We have to choose one of the three. Here are the terms which will determine our choice. There must be a good approach for tanks and armored vehicles, supported by infantry moving in two columns to execute a pincer strike. If we can have this together with some element of surprise, then we should try to do so. Next we must determine the distance of each village from the nearest known concentrations of Jordanian troops. A time factor enters here and a strength factor as well. How long will it take the Jordanians to move in troops? What routes are available to them? Will they be able to deploy armor? We have, then, to consider the villagers themselves. We are to avoid civilian casualties. Our plan is to move out the population and then destroy the village. However, the villagers must have some place to go. If there are caves and wadis where they can shelter, so much the better. We cannot have them caught in crossfire between the Jordanians and ourselves. . . . Finally there is the question of the strength in which we move. This must be impressive; because we are making a show. . . . Also because we must be certain of a total victory against any opposition which we may meet. Air support will be provided. Any questions?"

"The timing of the operation?"

"The earliest suitable date after our plans are approved."

"Night or day?"

"Day certainly. Dawn most probably. We have to see what we are doing and, with the men still in the village, we shall have greater control over the movement of the population."

"What kind of strength would you call impressive, sir?"

A laugh went round the table and Baratz permitted himself a thin smile of appreciation. "Tell me the maximum opposition we'll have to face; and we'll soon work out how impressive we have to be."

"What's the optimum time to break off the strike and finish the action?"

"If we could be in by 0600 and out by 0900, I'd say we were doing very well. Say 1000 at the outside."

"And no operations on the Sabbath, I suppose." This from a poker-faced wag at the back of the room.

"None on Friday either." Baratz chose to take him quite seriously. "That's another religious question—damned political too."

"Suggestion, sir."

"Let's have it."

"Medical services. In case there are civilian casualties, shouldn't we be able to provide prompt medical service?"

"So long as we're in control of the situation, yes. It's a good point. Make a note of it. Any more questions?"

There was silence in the room. Abruptly as he had begun it, Baratz closed the meeting. "Same time a week from today. I'd like a firm recommendation for private consideration by the Directorate of Intelligence. We'll need all of the following week to coordinate with Operations. That's all, gentlemen. Thank you."

As he walked back alone to his office he thought, as he had thought many times before, that it was all too spare and frigid and impersonal—a game played on a sand map, with no true knowledge, or even knowledgeable discussion about the human factors involved. Move out the civilian population! So simple! A roar on a bull horn and the human ants march out in orderly procession from the ant heap. But it was never like that. How could it be? It was something far more poignant and destructive, old women doddering in panic through the alleys, a confusion of men shouting and yelling in contradiction, babies snatched from the breast, children herded like frightened sheep to caves and cliffs in the hillside, the small hoards of seven hundred poor lifetimes buried under a pile of rubble. For what? To tell a harried princeling that he must police a hundred miles of desert border a little better. Medical services! God Almighty, how easy it was to say—how harsh the instant reality! A man with his eye gouged out by a bullet; a boy pushing his spilled guts back into his belly; the blank puzzlement on the faces of the dead. How easy it was to make political calculations—as if you could work out the whole human equation with a pair of calipers and a slide rule. Across the Atlantic the assembly of nations would sit in judgment on the act which, today, was being planned with such professional detachment. All round the spinning planet, men and women would read the news and wonder whether this incident or the next would trigger an atomic destruction. There were no bounds to the consequences of the simplest act of violence. One man dead meant thousands would never be born. One homeless man might one day tear down cities in mad vendetta against the human race.

You could push the monstrous logic to a point at which it would drive you mad. On the other hand you could affect to ignore it altogether and limit yourself to that area of action which was allotted to you by legal commission. You could inform, advise, protest and then submit yourself to the consensus with a clear conscience. . . . Or could you? He remembered Eichmann sitting in his glass box in the courtroom, and making the same plea in a hundred different forms. What beat Eichmann in the end was the sheer horror of the arithmetic; but it started with the first Jew beaten by the first bunch of bullies in the street. So, if because of what you have begun this morning, one child is killed in a Hebron hovel, where do you stand? You know it can happen. You know it probably will. You have already accepted this tacit probable. How do you plead, Jakov Baratz? Guilty or not guilty?

In point of fact there was no time even to consider a plea. The work on his desk was piled high as a mountain and there was a sealed envelope from the cipher room. The en-

velope contained a note from the officer in charge of the dog-
watch. "Damascus worked an emergency schedule at 0700 this
morning. We were puzzled by this decipher, but could not
call for recheck because operator went off the air immediately."

Pinned to the note was a copy of the decipher. It began
"For director" and then lapsed into a series of unintelligible
letter groups. Baratz recognized it immediately as the private
letter code which he had devised for Ronen to use in ex-
ceptional circumstances or for family messages. He would en-
code first and then put the code itself into cipher; and, at the
receiving end, only Baratz could unscramble the letters. Ten
minutes' work gave him a clear text:

"For director. Received telephone call from Bitar this
morning. My fears of Safreddin unfounded. Appears he has
high regard for us both. Therefore consider transport operation not repeat not decoy for me. Will report on completion.
Request personal service. Inform my wife she should seek
immediate divorce in terms our private agreement. She will
agree. Rely on you for appropriate handling. This resolution
my private problems essential for safe and efficient operation. Thanks. R."

DAMASCUS

At 8:40 on the same morning the Middle East Airlines
flight, which carried Idris Jarrah and his briefcase and his
meager personal luggage, touched down at Damascus airport. A military staff car and one of Safreddin's aides were
waiting on the tarmac. Idris Jarrah got into the car and was
driven immediately to Safreddin's office. There he was told
that the colonel had been in conference for an hour and
would be detained for some time yet. They served him coffee
to take the sting out of the implied snub, and left him to wait
in an anteroom for forty-five minutes.

He was not too unhappy. He understood the ploy because he had used it himself many times. It was intended to define his status as a very junior member of an important enterprise, to indicate that the Palestine Liberation Organization existed under patronage of legal Arab states and that, when Idris Jarrah rose to speak in council, he should comport himself with discretion and a proper deference.

The which of course he had no intention of doing. He had complaints to make—official complaints. The Egyptians were unhappy about the recent incident at Sha'ar Hagolan. They saw dangers in the constant forays along the Syrian-Israeli frontier. They had an unlucky war on their hands in the Yemen and they were far from ready for a worse one with a disciplined and well-equipped Israeli army. The P.L.O. had its own complaints. Safreddin had made his plans for the military coup with very little reference to the interest of the P.L.O. The original arrangement stipulated that P.L.O. irregulars would take over outlying communications centers and cooperate with rebel army units. The P.L.O. had agreed to contribute twenty-five thousand dollars to the expenses of the operation. In his briefcase Idris Jarrah carried ten thousand dollars for a down payment, but he had no intention of handing it over until he was satisfied with the arrangements. He was certain also that he would not be satisfied, because the whole operation was blown in advance by his own revelation to Nuri Chakry. So, he waited with patience and good humor until the great man was ready to see him.

Their first greetings were cordial. Safreddin was profuse in his apologies for having detained his colleague. His colleague was full of understanding and polite deprecation. Then, deviously, in the manner of the East, they arrived at the subject of their meeting. Jarrah conveyed the views of the Egyptians, dissociating himself from them, as a member of an independent political group.

As he had hoped Safreddin was immediately irritated. "The time is long past when the Egyptians can dictate the policies of Syria. We tried to work with them once in the closest cooperation. They were arrogant, overbearing and disruptive. Now we go our own way. If I say so myself, we are doing much better here than they are doing in the Yemen."

Jarrah lit a casual cigarette and nodded an equivocal agreement. "The P.L.O. has to live with everybody. We have private opinions but it is not always wise to express them. However, we do feel that Jordan is the place where we can all work most effectively—especially west Jordan. This is why we are so deeply concerned about the Khalil operation. What stage are we at now?"

"Let's begin at the letter alif, my friend—our objective. This is quite simple: to bring down the Hashemite monarchy by a military coup and establish a military government which will then develop itself along the socialist pattern, which we have evolved in Syria. This done, we have a united front along the whole eastern border of Israel. We have a common policy and a common political aim. In time we can mount an offensive which will roll the Jews into the sea."

"But the coup has to be successful."

"Of course. We think it can be. Major Khalil is a good soldier and a good organizer. He stands in high favor with the young officers on whom the operation depends. He is second-in-command of the Palace Guard, a key position for what we have in mind."

"Which is?"

"First to remove the present commander of the Palace Guard, so that Khalil will be promoted in his place."

"And how do you propose to do that?"

"Tonight two trucks, carrying normal merchandise to Amman, will be loaded with arms and explosives, packed in wooden cases. These cases will be clearly marked for consignment to the private address of the guard commander, which is a small villa on the outskirts of Amman. Tomorrow morning, at first light, the trucks leave Damascus. Acting on a tip from us, the customs officials at the Jordan border will search the trucks. They will find the arms. They will report their find to the Jordan security people. The report will be passed to the King. The commander of the Palace Guard will be suspended pending an investigation. Major Khalil will take over his duties. From that moment he will be in control of the situation. Quite easy. Quite foolproof."

"Too easy," said Idris Jarrah.

Safreddin flushed angrily. "Why?"

"It makes too many assumptions. It assumes first that the Jordan security service will accept in good faith a tip from Syria. The Syrian press—and the P.L.O.—have been calling for a long time for the removal of the Hashemites from the throne. The Syrian press is an official press. Therefore it speaks the mind of the Government. Therefore everything Syria does is suspect to the Jordanians. This move will be more suspect. The second assumption is that the King will remove a trusted man, simply on suspicion."

Safreddin allowed himself a small, sour smile. "Both the King and his commander were trained by the British. This is the British way of doing things. If the King doesn't ask for his suspension, the commander will offer it as a gesture of good faith. In any case suspicion is planted. The King has to cover himself by calling in Khalil."

"Unless he guesses at Khalil immediately and sends him to the wall."

"In this case we go one step down the ladder to the third man on the promotion list. He is a friend and supporter of Major Khalil."

"Which still assumes that the King and his advisers will follow the list. They might decide to scrap it altogether, and bring in another elite group from the Arab Legion; at least until the investigation of the arms shipment is complete."

Safreddin leaned back in his chair and surveyed his visitor with hooded hostile eyes. "I have the impression, Jarrah, that you disapprove of this whole operation and that, in fact, you are not prepared to support it."

"That's right, Colonel. And for a very good reason. I think the whole plan is already compromised."

It gave him a beautiful pleasure to see Safreddin's startled reaction. He thrust himself forward to the table and demanded harshly, "How do you know? When did you hear it?"

"In Beirut, yesterday." Jarrah was very calm. "I went to the Phoenician Bank to draw out our P.L.O. funds and deposit them with Pan-Arab. Chakry is shaky. We didn't want to be caught. I saw Chakry. I've known him a long time. I've done private business with him. He told me he had heard rumors of a palace plot. I pressed him for details. He wouldn't give any. He did say, however, that the information came from a Syrian source. If he knows that much, he knows more. If he knows, he has already passed on the information because he has investments in Jordan and because he trades in information as he trades in everything else."

Safreddin considered the proposition for a long moment. Then he shook his head. "I can't accept it. You said yourself a few moments ago that our newspapers and P.L.O. sources have been calling for a palace coup for a long time. I would say that's all Chakry has. It's all he could have. I'm not prepared to throw away months of preparation, and an opportunity that may never come again, on a piece of banker's gossip. It's too vague."

"It's too definite for me to risk P.L.O. funds and—much more important—our whole organization in west Jordan. My instructions are clear. I have the final word on whether or not the P.L.O. is to be committed."

It was a stalemate. Safreddin got up from his chair and began to pace the floor, angry as a caged leopard. Finally he turned to face Jarrah again. "There's the flaw! If the plan is known, why hasn't Hussein taken action?"

"He may be waiting for action; action that will publicly discredit Syria and the P.L.O."

Safreddin digested the answer in silence. Then he made a grudging admission. "That may be true. But it's still only conjecture."

"Agreed."

"So why don't we compromise?"

"How?"

"Let's send the arms through tomorrow morning as we arranged. You go into Amman yourself, make contact with Major Khalil, tell him what you know—or think you know —and see how he judges it. At least he'll be warned. If he seems optimistic, let him go ahead with his plans. You proceed to west Jordan, have your people in readiness; but don't commit them until you see what happens. Meantime I'll institute an immediate security check in Damascus to see if there have been any possible leaks. If I trace even a single one, I'll get in touch with you and Khalil immediately. Does that make sense to you?"

It made the best sense in the world to Idris Jarrah. It put him exactly where he wanted to be, straddling the fence, a dutiful servant of his own people, a careful friend of his allies —with a hundred thousand dollars in safe deposit with an American bank in Beirut. But he had to conceal his satisfaction. He worried the argument back and forth for five minutes longer and then said reluctantly:

"I see your point, Colonel. I have to admit it makes sense. I'll leave for Amman in the morning. At the same time I have a bad feeling about the whole business."

"It troubles me too," said Omar Safreddin. "But I'm in a position where I have to balance the odds and then act on the best information I have. Since we got rid of Eli Cohen, our security has been very tight. I'd hate to think we could have a leak as serious as this."

To which Idris Jarrah added his own private footnote: he

hated to think what would happen to any man whom Safred-din found guilty of treachery.

BEIRUT

Nuri Chakry looked down at the men gathered around the conference table and despised them all. The Minister of Finance was not there. He was, he said, preparing for a meeting of the International Monetary Fund in New York. However, he would give favorable consideration to whatever the representatives of the Ministry and the Central Bank decided. Nuri Chakry despised him most of all. Because this was his last stand and because he knew it, he pushed his argument down their necks without restraint. Let them swallow it or choke on it—he did not care.

". . . The Phoenician Bank wants help. No secret about that. We need it within thirty days. No secret about that either. But . . ." He thrust a folio of figures at them and waved it like a banner. "We need it as a solvent institution, a going concern. A house which has done more than any other to make Lebanon the financial heart of the Middle East. I do not ask you to accept my word. Each of you has a copy of the accounts, independently audited by a famous American company. Each of you has a copy of the letter which I requested them to write for this meeting. Their name and their seal is affixed. Read it! The Phoenician Bank is a solvent company which, through circumstances beyond its control, is suddenly in a difficult situation. . . . What are these circumstances? They are all political. King Feisal is affronted by the tone of articles published in the Lebanese press. The sheikdoms of Kuwait are being pushed by the British to invest in the sterling area. Good terms too! Nobody can offer better. Both know they can embarrass Lebanon. Each for a different reason wants to embarrass Lebanon. The Phoenician Bank is Lebanon! Cut the cards any way you like, the hand still deals the same way. Many of you don't like me or my methods. I accept that. But if I go, Lebanon, in banking terms, is put back ten years. Now . . . will you help me or not?"

He stood for a moment surrounded by silence. Then he sat down and waited to see who would make the first answer. He was only half surprised when Taleb opened the argument. Taleb had no money so he had nothing to lose. It must have been his women who gave him courage.

"You speak of circumstances beyond your control, Mr. Chakry. You specify them as political circumstances. Surely every banker has this problem, always? American banks, for example, invest in South America, in the new Africas and South Korea. They understand the risks of political instability. They provide against it. Why have not you done the same?"

"Precisely because we are not America. As a banking country we are quite new. Therefore we have had to bid for business. Therefore we have had to enter, at certain moments, into the risk market. Money is a commodity, Mr. Taleb. You have to sell it like refrigerators or vacuum cleaners."

"But you do not have to sell at a loss, surely?"

"We have never invested at a loss. Our audit proves that. We are solvent and in profit."

"But you have no ready cash?"

"If the Kuwaitis and the Saudis pull out—no!"

"Therefore you may be forced to liquidate assets in a hurry?"

"Yes."

"Therefore you may be exposed to loss?"

"Only if this country—which we have helped to build— leaves us at the mercy of our enemies."

It was Aziz who asked the next question. He lingered on it, tenderly as if he were testing the blade of a dagger. "Enemies? Surely that's an odd word to use, Mr. Chakry. In banking one talks of debtors and creditors, associates or competitors."

"For enemy read competitor—and you still have the same proposition."

"I wonder if you do." Aziz ruminated on the reply. "Your competitors have lent you money, have they not? Their terms have been quite moderate, quite normal. Why should you call them enemies?"

"Where money is concerned, there is no loyalty, only the legal advantage; because a man accepts your business, because he does not cheat you—this is not to say that he is a friend. If he sees a legal way to put you out of business, he will take it. That, in my dictionary, makes him an enemy."

"Then it seems to me, Mr. Chakry, you have been very imprudent. You have made more enemies than you needed— or could deal with."

"Grant that," said Nuri Chakry. "Though I could challenge it. You have a clear question to answer. Will my own country join the enemy and force the Phoenician Bank to default on thousands of small customers?"

It was his last card and he played it as coolly as he had played the first. But they were not prepared to bet against it yet. Aziz questioned him again.

"Would you be prepared to submit to a second independent audit?"

"Why not?"

"Would you be prepared to back the results of that audit with your private capital?"

"With every pound I possess."

"Would you sell your interest in the bank?"

"At a fair price, yes."

"Would you agree to an immediate liquidation of assets— including the airline?"

"No!"

"Why not, Mr. Chakry?"

"Because immediate liquidation means a forced sale. A forced sale means an inevitable loss. In justice to my shareholders I could not consent to it."

"But you may still be obliged to it?"

"If the Ministry of Finance and the Central Bank refuse us a temporary support, yes. In that case, they will take the full responsibility for—whatever may happen."

Still they would not bet. Still none of them would take the last responsibility and he despised them the more. He decided to force them.

"If you have any more questions, gentlemen, I shall be delighted to answer them. If not, I have one for you. Will you, or will you not, at any time within the next thirty days support the Phoenician Bank?"

Finally, after a long pause, it was the Deputy Minister who gave him the answer. "This meeting, Mr. Chakry, cannot give you the answer. The Minister himself cannot give you the answer. It is our job to consider your submissions and make a report to the Minister on his return from New York. The Minister will then make his own recommendation to the Cabinet, which will give the final decision."

"Within thirty days?"

"We must presume that, Mr. Chakry. We have not been otherwise informed."

"And meantime I have to run an international bank on presumption?"

"How else have you been running it?" asked Taleb with open malice.

"If you will excuse me, gentlemen," said Nuri Chakry, politely, "I have work to do. The Phoenician Bank is still open for business."

Forty minutes later he was driving furiously up the motor road, past Djouni and El Bouar, to the house in the orange grove.

Heinrich Muller, rumpled as always, was a tonic for his

jaded spirits. He shambled about the airy lounge, pouring drinks, showing off his latest treasures, making crude jokes about the sex life of Byblos. A cheerful voyeur, he had a pair of high-powered field glasses through which he made a nightly study of the mating habits of his neighbors. . . . "Better than the Scented Garden, my dear Nuri. Much better! So ingenious. So gymnastic." Chakry let him run on, happy to divert his own thoughts from the scarifying experience of the meeting. To hell with Aziz. To hell with that malicious little pup, Taleb. To hell with the whole boot-licking bunch! Give them a million apiece and they couldn't make it pay better than five percent! Bastards all of them.

". . . I have just told you of the most exotic perversion," said Muller reproachfully, "and you have not heard a word."

"I'm sorry, Heinrich." In spite of his ill-humor Chakry was amused. "Talk to me about money instead. I promise you I'll listen."

"Ah, money!" Muller made caressing motions with his hands. "Better than women. Better than boys across unfordable rivers. Let me show you money."

He trotted happily out of the room and, a few moments later, came back holding in his hands two pieces of thick paper. He handed them to Chakry with a flourish.

"There, my friend! One real, one my personal creation. For ten dollars—which is which?"

"Let's see them in full light."

He carried the twin sheets out onto the veranda and examined them carefully. They were bearer bonds on a well-known English bank, noted for its extreme precautions against forgery. The papers, so far as Chakry could see, were identical—the same curious grain, the same complicated watermarks. The ink was a perfect match, the printing and engraving were a masterwork of reproduction.

"Take your time," warned Heinrich Muller. "Take all the time you need. It could cost you ten dollars."

"Or my neck."

Minutes later, after examining both documents with a magnifying glass, he confessed himself beaten and paid over the money in Lebanese pounds.

"Now show me the difference."

"I cannot show it to you," said Muller proudly. "Because you could not detect it with a naked eye, or even with a reading glass. The ink is different but only a chemical analysis would show that. The paper is the same, because although you cannot buy it in commercial quantity, the makers always include a sheet in their catalogues for advertising. The engraving is different too. There is a fractional error in the depth of cut on my plate. But who's to know?"

"Who indeed, Heinrich? Who indeed? And the other stuff?"

"I'll bet on that too, if you like; but you'll lose your money."

"I'd still like to see it."

"I like a careful man."

He went into the house and returned with two small stacks of bonds of different origins and different denominations. He showed them in pairs, this time showing the true against the false. Chakry matched each pair with the same meticulous care and finally had to confess himself satisfied. But Heinrich Muller was not satisfied, he had a question of his own. He put it very precisely:

"Here, Nuri my friend, we have documents which have a face value of half a million sterling pounds. Convert that to dollars it makes near enough to a million and a half. Count in the duplicates and you double the figure. Now . . . what do you propose to do with them?"

"The originals belong to the bank."

"That doesn't answer the question."

"I know." Chakry chuckled happily. "The problem is, Heinrich, that there are two possible answers. I'd like you to tell me which you think is the better."

Muller gathered up the two stacks of documents and carried them back into the house. He mixed fresh drinks and then, comfortable as a cat, settled himself in a deep chair to wait for Chakry's proposals. Chakry took his time. He swirled the liquor, so that the ice tinkled musically against the glass. He lit a cigarette and contemplated the gray eddies rising towards the ceiling. Finally he said:

"A question first, Heinrich. Would you like me to pay you for this work, or would you like to ride with the money?"

"Depending," said Muller slowly. "Depending on where we ride and what risks are involved."

"Brazil. How does that strike you?"

"A pleasant country. Some political problems, of course; but an enormous potential for development."

"And for the right developers."

"Of course."

"I have a small company there, quite independent, quite profitable in a modest way. So, immediately, we have a business identity. To go further, we would need more working capital."

"And how would you get that?"

"We have it." He pointed to the bonds stacked on the table in front of him. "We have to choose which way to use it. The first alternative is to replace the forged documents in the bank and take the real ones with us—assuming that we are forced to go. If we ride out this storm, of course we stay in Lebanon and put the real documents where they belong."

"No." Muller was very firm. "No, and no again. It's a criminal act—fraud, grand larceny. Call it what you will, it adds up to police pursuit and twenty years in prison. I could not ride that horse."

Chakry nodded approvingly. "Good. In a desperate moment, I might try it. But I am not desperate yet."

"And the second choice?"

"We take your copies. We never negotiate them. We simply lodge them for safekeeping in a Brazilian bank. We make sure, of course, that our banker has seen the documents, inspected and listed them. Then, when we come to ask for current credit, how will he react?"

"Favorably, of course. But he will still ask for collateral."

"For which we give him a blanket document, pledging all our assets, including those held in safe deposit. But we never specify the individual items, nor claim that they have a value which they do not have. It's a neat point of law, but we have not committed any crime."

"Unless and until we default on the loan and the bank decides to call us on our note and cash the bonds."

"You agree that is the only risk?" asked Nuri Chakry.

"Yes."

"Then I will tell you it is no risk at all." A sudden fire blazed in him. He leaned forward in his chair, locked his hands together and launched into a passionate affirmation of all the things he had wanted to say at the meeting, but had left unsaid because he would not risk the contempt of his enemies. "Look, Heinrich! You know what I am. I know what you are. We are men who understand money and how it works. There are very few of us, you know. To eighty percent, ninety percent of the world, money is a mystery greater than God—because they've never had it and are never likely to have it. What is money? Confidence, trust. A balance of risks and chances. Look at this!" He picked up one of the bonds from the table and held it contemptuously between thumb and forefinger. "What is it? Paper and ink, nothing more. A pledge to pay, on demand, a given amount of other paper; which itself is a pledge to pay, on demand, a given amount of gold. Put it in a pulping machine and it disappears forever. But the thing it signifies still remains—metal torn out of the earth, wheat and corn and cotton, transmuted by the labor of men, distributed by men like you and me whose business it is to know where the need is that matches the surplus. *We* are money, Heinrich, you and I. And this is what those fools at the Ministry refuse to admit! We are money because we know. I drove up this coast this morning and saw twenty years of work—my work!—sprouting on the beach and on the hills, where even olives wouldn't grow. I did it once, I can do it again. And this time there'll be no mistakes. Do you want to come with me?"

"If we have to go, yes."

"Good! Then make me a new passport with a new name. Crate your collection and have it ready for shipment ten days before the end of the month. Five days before the end of the month, book two first-class seats on the best available international connections from Beirut to Brazil."

"You remind me of the Führer," said Heinrich Muller with ironic reverence. "You have the same magic."

"The Führer was a fool!" Chakry's tone was high and harsh. "He never understood money. He tried to exterminate the Jews. He was beaten before he began."

"And you, Nuri?"

"There's only one victory, Heinrich—survival! You survived when the men you worked for were hanged. The Jews survived and hung themselves round the neck of Islam. I'll survive too. One step back, two forward. If you're alive, you can always fight!"

He was still fighting so well that at three in the afternoon he sold a copy of Jarrah's tape and a copy of his promissory note to the Kuwaiti agent for a hundred and twenty-five thousand dollars. The Jordanian had already paid thirty thousand for the same evidence and Chakry had won five thousand from him in a poker game. Net profit, sixty thousand dollars—and not a cent of it was deposited in the Phoenician Bank.

DAMASCUS

After his talk with Idris Jarrah, Omar Safreddin was left with a pebble in his shoe. It frayed his flesh and his temper;

and there would be no comfort for him until he could prise it out. Little as he liked Jarrah, little as he was disposed to bend his own policies to the demands of an emigré plotter, he had to admit that Jarrah's fears of a security leak were well founded. If there was a leak, it had to be found and plugged immediately. If it could not be plugged, then it had to be turned into a political advantage. To find the leak presented the same problem as that which he had posed to the members of the Hunafa Club: assume the presence of a foreign spy, assume the existence of a Syrian traitor in a position of trust, where did you begin to look for him?

The most obvious places were already well covered by his regular agents. Every foreign embassy—the American, the Russian, the British—carried on some kind of intelligence activity. If the plot were known to people like these it would have had, already, clear and visible consequences. The Russians, for example, were at one with the Americans in wanting to preserve a political stability in the Middle East. They saw it, like the Asian rice bowls, as a pit from which a cockfight might explode into a world war. On doctrinal grounds, they hated monarchies and wanted in the long run to see the Fertile Crescent turned into a Marxist one; but they were far from prepared to risk a conflict for what might less dangerously be achieved by evolution. Had they heard a whisper of a plot against the Hashemite throne, they would have been probing weeks ago—and none too delicately—because Syria was a debtor nation and the Russians were her biggest creditors.

For a while he thought about the Egyptians, but the Egyptian interest was the same as his own. He thought for a longer while about the P.L.O.; but the P.L.O. in Jordan was so vulnerable that it had everything to lose and nothing to gain by treachery. The Israelis? To them he devoted a long and troublesome meditation. Ever since the death of Eli Cohen, he had been plagued by the unhappy conviction that sooner or later the Israelis would try to set up another network in Damascus. Against such a possibility, he had organized a special security group composed of those who had worked on the Cohen investigation, but so far none of them had turned up a single clue. Besides, if an Israeli had bought this information, he would have transmitted it directly to Tel Aviv. He would not have peddled it to a Palestinian Arab like Nuri Chakry.

He thought about Nuri Chakry and agreed with Jarrah that he would trade in anything—even the gold teeth of his aged grandmother. But Chakry as an information center? Hardly. Money had few allegiances and Chakry had none at all. He would pay tipsters. He was too shrewd to embroil himself with intelligence agents. If he had a tipster in Damascus, it must be someone who did business with him; someone who, in a quite legal correspondence, might pass a timely word—in return, perhaps, for a timely line of credit.

It was a long shot; but the long shots sometimes brought down quite surprising game. Eli Cohen had been hit by a long shot—a set of bank figures that did not match his trade balance. So he lifted the telephone, called the Finance Ministry and asked for a list of all those persons in Syria who had bank accounts in Lebanon, and especially with the Phoenician.

TEL AVIV

The cipher from Adom Ronen lay locked all day in Baratz's private safe. He needed time and reflection before he could deal with it; and, today, both were denied him. Intelligence work was like a jigsaw puzzle. The pieces were dumped in disorder on your desk and you had to sort them with infinite patience and concentration, matching and rejecting until the beginning of a pattern became visible. When you played it as a game, it was easy. The pattern lay in front of you, you had only to find the pieces to duplicate it. But, in the defense of a nation, the pattern changed from day to day, from hour to hour; and you had to construct the picture out of fact, conjecture and a very fallible imagination. The same piece of information could fit twenty different surmises; yet if you chose the wrong one, you ended in a sudden and total confusion and had to begin all over again. There were wild pieces too: happenings which looked profoundly important at first, and then, after long testing, were simply the result of chance or weird coincidence. According to the old proverb, a bear coughed at the North Pole and a man died in Peking; but if you related the wrong bear to the wrong man you made a nonsense; and, if you built a military plan on the fictitious relationship, you created a tragedy that might cost a hundred lives.

Adom Ronen belonged to a special sector of operations. He could not be allowed to intrude into other and more important ones. Yehudith Ronen had special places in his official life and in his private emotions. He dared not confuse the two. However, try as he might, he could not put either the man or the woman out of his mind. A report from the Mayor of Jerusalem called up a vision of the white house on Har Zion and a strange tormented sculpture. An account of patrol operations in the Hasbani Thumb set him wondering about the women in the life of Ronen-Fathalla and what risks they brought into an already risky espionage setup. A memorandum on radio security made him ask why Selim Fathalla had used his emergency schedule for a message that had no obvious urgency at all. A long piece on border smuggling between Arab families reminded him how little he knew of the physical circumstances of his agent's life in Damascus and how much less he knew of the intimate psychic adjustments which were necessary to live it.

Once, at the end of a quiet dinner, he had raised the question with Franz Lieberman, who was an inveterate addict of thrillers and espionage fiction. He had put it in a very personal form:

"Suppose, Franz, you sat where I sit, and you had to choose men to live permanently underground in an enemy country, what sort of candidate would you look for?"

Oddly enough, Lieberman dodged the question at first. He said evasively, "You'd know more about that than I, Jakov. You were an underground man yourself. You held a British commission, you wore British uniform; yet you worked in the Haganah. You were soldier, spy, saboteur, all rolled into one."

"It wasn't the same, Franz."

"Why not?"

"The ends we had in view were clear, definable, immediate. We had to win a war. We had to run guns, smuggle in people, carry out guerrilla operations. We were in brave company then. We were like the Mosaic tribes with the pillar of cloud going in front of us by day and the pillar of fire by night. The man I have in mind will have to live a solitary life, in a hostile environment. He will have to risk his life for information which many times will appear trivial. He will be separated from our community life. In fact he will know the worst part of it because he will read only what is presented by our enemies. And this is a Semite, remember— for whom a tribal support is especially necessary. He will not see and he will not profit from the results of his work. If he fails, he will have neither compassion nor a second chance. We'll regret him and write him into the Book of the Dead. . . . Now read me the sort of man who will take that sort of job."

"I can't," said old Franz stubbornly. "I've never made a clinical analysis of such a one. I know you're making these appointments and I'm not stupid enough to offer half-baked advice just because I've drunk three glasses of brandy. If you like I'll think about it and do some reading and see what comes out. No promises though."

"No promises."

Six weeks later Lieberman sent him a letter in which, without ever having met him, he had written a passable portrait of Adom Ronen-Selim Fathalla.

". . . You need an alienated man; one who is dissatisfied with the real which he has, and yet knows that the ideal to which he aspires is unattainable. In his youth he is a rebel. He may even become a revolutionary; but once the fruits of the revolution are in his hands they will turn to the apples of Sodom. So he will become, in a physical or spiritual sense, a wanderer, a seeker after the special and the exotic. He will become, perhaps, an adept in strange cults, a specialist in rare languages, an antiquarian, a trader in oddities, a chameleon who will take on the color of every tree except those in his own garden. Sexually he will be a man of strong appetites, whether for women or those of his own sex. His attachments will be passionate; but he will be at pains to keep them impermanent, because his security resides in alienation and not in identification. He will be brave to protect the private domain, in which alone he feels that he can remain himself. He will be more vulnerable to isolation than to torture because his reference points are very personal and he has therefore a special dependence on them. You must always manage him lightly. If you direct him too stringently he will become rebellious again and may be tempted to risks to affirm his challenged identity. . . ."

All of which added up to a clear prescription for the present case. If Adom Ronen wanted a divorce, Jakov Baratz, his master, had to bend his best efforts to procure it for him; even if, in so doing, he created problems for himself. So he picked up the telephone and ordered a call to Yehudith Ronen in Jerusalem. While he was waiting for it, he dialed the number of a senior member of the Rabbinate in Tel Aviv and made an appointment to see him at six the same evening.

When Yehudith came to the phone, he gave her a warning and a request.

"Yehudith? This is Jakov. We're on an open line. I'd like you to come down to Tel Aviv tonight and have dinner with me. Can you have someone look after Golda?"

"Of course. Has—has anything happened?"

"No. But there's a thing we need to discuss rather urgently. We'll eat at my place."

"Can you cook, Jakov?"

"Wait and see."

"It sounds intriguing."

"Don't expect too much."

"Prepare me a little, Jakov. Good or bad? The discussion I mean."

"Honestly, I don't know. I think you'll have to decide that."

"Till eight-thirty then."

He made one more call to order the staff car, folded Ronen's cipher into his breast pocket and then went out to keep his appointment with the rabbi, who was a man learned in the Law and an expert on matrimonial causes. When he had explained the nature of his problem the rabbi pursed his pale lips and lapsed into silent thought. Finally, with suitable deliberation, he delivered himself of an opinion.

"On the one hand, the need of secrecy is evident. On the other hand, the rights of both parties have to be protected. Normally the petitioner is required to set the reasons for his request for divorce in a formal petition. Provided the wife agreed, the court would probably accept the document which you have shown me as constituting such a petition. If, however, she did not agree, the court might require that you formulate the petition for him. Next the law requires that both parties submit to counsel by the court, so that they may have the opportunity to reconsider together their request for divorce. This is manifestly impossible. In my view this requirement could be waived by common agreement. . . .

Everything depends on the wife, you see. The court has discretion to override her objections; but I do not think they would be willing to exercise that discretion in the present case."

"Even in the interests of national security?"

"Even allowing for the most liberal interpretations, General, we may reach a point where we have a clear choice between the integrity of the law and public expediency."

"Or more bluntly, between the integrity of the law and the life of a secret agent?"

"True."

"And how would you choose, Rabbi?"

"There is no choice. Destroy the law and we are back to chaos."

"But if the law depends on the whim of a woman?"

"It does not so depend, General Baratz; and you know it. If two rights conflict, the law must decide which shall prevail. But it cannot deny that a right exists in each case."

"I wish it were as clear to me as it is to you," said Baratz —and wished he could put his own case as bluntly. . . . I want Adom Ronen free, because I need a satisfied and reliable agent. I want him free because, at night, I have guilty dreams in which I am David and he is Uriah— and it is no dream that I could send him to his death, more quickly and subtly than David sent Uriah to his. I want Yehudith free, because I cannot trust myself too long and, if I fall, I want no other guilts but my own. I want myself free too; but I am bound, by a faint hope, in a lifelong servitude to a child locked in a dark attic in Salzburg. . . .

". . . A difficult situation," the rabbi was saying, "for you and for both parties. However, with prudence and good will, we may be able to solve it."

"I'm having dinner with the lady tonight. If I may call you in the morning . . . ?"

"Any time, General."

"Thank you."

And so, back to a barren and empty house to prepare a bachelor's dinner for another man's wife. Mercifully, as he fumbled his way through the preparations, his sense of humor was restored to him and he was able to laugh at the spectacle of Brigadier-General Jakov Baratz, Director of Military Intelligence, tossing salad, slicing potatoes and carrots, laying a table for two and setting a suite of mood music on the record player. By the time Yehudith arrived he was seated, casual as bedamned, with a whisky—stiffer than usual—at his elbow and a copy of the latest edition of *The Chronology of Arab Politics* open and unread on his lap.

Yehudith was quick to see the contrivance of his staging and she made a cheerful joke of it, which carried them over the greetings and halfway into her first drink. Then she said:

"Jakov, I want to enjoy my dinner. Let's get rid of business first, eh?"

"Good idea."

He handed her Ronen's cipher and watched her face carefully as she read it. He saw her stiffen and grow pale under the first shock; but there were no tears and no outcries. Her first question was a calculated irrelevance.

"Who is Safreddin?"

"Head of the Extraordinary Military Tribunal, Director of Security Services in Syria. He's the man who caught Eli Cohen and had him hanged."

"And Adom deals with him?"

"Yes. We gather the relationship is constant and cordial."

"But a fearful risk."

"That, too."

"What does Adom mean when he says divorce is necessary for safe and efficient operation?"

"I don't know. I can only guess."

"Guess then!"

"Very well. But the guess is based only on my personal

experience. I met Hannah when I was working with the Haganah. I used her in all sorts of risky jobs—courier, spy, currency smuggler. I had no doubts, no fears. She was available and expendable. We all were. After I fell in love with her, after I married her, she was a handicap and an impediment. Every time I used her I was cutting my own heart in half—my brain too. I'd never do it again. I imagine Adom feels the same thing about you and Golda."

"You're lying, Jakov. Please don't."

"Then don't force me to lie, girl. You know. Adom says you know. You tell me."

"He's fallen in love with someone else."

"He's done that a dozen times before. At home and abroad. Why make it an issue now?"

"Do you care why?"

"You're damn right I care!" He was swiftly and unreasonably angry. "I need him working. I need him safe. He's got a whole network depending on him. I need to know everything about him."

She finished her drink at a gulp and then handed him the glass. "Give me another drink then."

He refilled the glass and handed it to her. She gagged on the first mouthful and put the glass aside. Then stumbling and hesitant, she told him:

"I know it like—like a child's first reader. I should be able to tell it in ten words. I can't. It's sad and dirty and we're both to blame and yet . . . you can't blame anybody. Adom's an Iraqi. I'm Polish. . . . For him marriage was one thing and love something else again. You know the way it is, Jakov. You know the way he was. As a lover he'd leave me drunk and spinning like a top. I . . . I had ecstasies with him. It was like living on champagne. We couldn't bear to be out of sight or hand's touch from one another. The girl he has now—I'll swear that's the way they are together. But when we married, it was immediately different. All of a sudden the

tribal man took over. I was the object—the breeder, the
mother. I was house and home and the social dignities—and
nothing else. Once I became pregnant he was impotent with
me. He couldn't help it, any more than I could help the
agonies of wanting him and not having him and knowing
that he was out hunting like a sad tomcat. . . . That's why he
went away to work for you. That's why he wanted to keep
the marriage and the home in the old tribal way. . . ."

"Then why does he want to destroy it now?"

"I . . . I don't know. Oh, what the hell! I've known a long
time already. He hoped it would happen with us. When
things were very bad he would beg me to make it happen.
He used to say: 'Somewhere, sometime, there has to be a
moment or a woman who lights up both parts of me at once.'
That was the horrible thing, Jakov, he knew what was wrong,
but he couldn't change it. I couldn't either. Now . . . I
think the moment's arrived, and the woman too."

"But if he married her, the pattern may begin again."

"Then I'm sorry for them both."

"I'm afraid for twenty people," said Jakov Baratz grimly.
"What would he do if you refused him the divorce—and if
I recalled him?"

"He'd hate us both. And he mightn't come back."

"And if you give it to him?"

"He has a chance to be happy as well as—what does he
say?—safe and efficient. But why should I? Tell me that,
Jakov! Why shouldn't I turn bitch and put him through the
wringer for a while? He put me through it, God knows!"

"Because you're not a bitch. Because you can come out
of it whole, even if Adom doesn't. Though I hope for everybody's sake he does! You're a grown-up girl, Yehudith. You're
too big for malice like that."

"Am I, Jakov? Am I?" Instantly she was on her feet, challenging him with savage self-mockery. "I'm a woman who
sleeps with a pillow between her legs and wishes it would

turn into a man. I sit home at nights with Golda and help her with her homework. I work in the studio till my eyes pop out. And all the time I want to stand at my gate and howl like a cat at the moon."

"I don't care." Baratz was as brutal as a hangman, masked and calm for the kill. "I don't care if you strip naked and run screaming down Allenby Street. I want to know now: will you agree to this divorce or not?"

"You're a bastard, Jakov."

"I'm paid to be a bastard."

"What do you want me to do?"

"Answer: yes or no."

"I need time to think."

"There's no time."

"You're not God."

"No. I'm a man with lives on his hands."

"I've never known you so cruel."

"You don't know me at all."

It was as if he had struck her in the face. All the fight went out of her and she stood wide-eyed and trembling, looking down at him. Then she surrendered.

"All right. I agree. What now?"

"I am a bastard," said Jakov Baratz softly. "And I hate the bloody work I do. Pour me a drink while I fix dinner."

FIVE

It was a quarter before nine in the evening when Selim Fathalla left his home to walk to the warehouse, which lay on the farther side of the bazaar. He threaded his way through narrow, odorous alleys, cluttered with vegetable refuse and animal droppings. He brushed against hurrying men and patient donkeys and veiled women and barefoot children. He lingered a while in the street of the coppersmiths, a long, shadowy cavern acrid with the smell of charcoal and hot solder, resonant with the rhythm of tapping hammers and ringing anvils. He was known here. Bright eyes smiled at him out of blackened faces, grimy hands were joined in greeting. Eager merchants displayed their newest wares, great burnished trays and fretted lamps and stoves of polished brass, salvers and coffeepots and ewers as tall as a man. He liked these people. They practiced their ancient craft with skill and dignity. They liked him, because he had a good eye and a respect for sound work and paid fair prices promptly.

In the street of the weavers it was the same. He knew good fabrics. He fingered the rich brocades with a loving hand. He paid compliments freely; yet was quick to see a bad run or a skimping of gold and silver thread in the design. He accepted gifts graciously—a scarf, a length of cloth—and he never forgot to make a return at the proper time.

In his new harmonious mood he felt a gratitude to these people on whom his trade was built, and a sudden sharp regret that he could not wholly identify himself with them. They were the salt of the earth. Their lives were harsh, their rewards pitifully small. They were caught up in events which they did not understand. They were led to destinies which they could in no wise control. Yet instinctively they reached upwards, groping for a better life, hungry for a promise of freer and more fruitful tomorrows. They saluted him as a friend, and yet he was the traitor in their midst. He wondered how he would answer, if this one or that adjured him to justify his treachery—old Hamid, the maker of filigree, almost blind from a lifetime at his bench, whose rough hands were ingrained with gold and silver and who yet had the dignity of an ancient patriarch; or Talat, the sculptor, who made the molds from which the smiths beat intricate designs into their silver dishes; he was a devout Moslem, who would not make an image of man, woman or animal, yet whose traceries were fluid and satisfying as tree patterns on moving water.

How would he explain himself to such as these? How would he make an intelligible tally of guilt and merit, he who shared their salt and still served a nation which they were taught every day to hate? They did not want to hate any more than he did; but the hatred blared from every cheap transistor; screamed from every headline, teasing them into insecurity, promising instant miracles, if only the enemy could be rooted out of the land of Canaan.

He was glad to break out of the lively, chattering alleys into the dark lane in front of his warehouse. He rang the bell and a few moments later the judas window opened and the grizzled aquiline face of the watchman peered out at him. A moment later the heavy bolts were shot back and he stepped into the courtyard where his trucks were parked, loaded and ready for the morrow's journey. As Safreddin had ordered, he dismissed the watchman for two hours, giving him money for a meal and a garbled explanation of his own presence at this unusual hour. Then he locked the gates again, went into his office and tried to prepare himself for his meeting with Safreddin.

For all his confident message to Baratz, he was still worried. It was his job to find out to whom the cargo of explosives was consigned. At the same time, he had to appear not only disinterested, but even unwilling to know about such secret and troublesome affairs. Safreddin was so febrile a man that the slightest untoward act or word would itch at him until he found an explanation for it. In spite of Bitar's encouraging telephone call and his confidence in Safreddin's gratitude, the only safety was in mistrust. The old desert code still applied: a guest was sacred while he ate your bread; once out of the camp he was again legitimate prey; and if there was blood between you, the blood price must still be paid.

Punctually at nine o'clock the bell at the gate sounded again and, when he looked out through the judas window, he saw two military trucks and a staff car, drawn up in the alley with their engines running. He swung the heavy gates open and the vehicles moved into the yard. He closed and locked the gates behind them. He pointed out the two trucks which were already loaded for Amman. Safreddin gave a swift series of orders and the soldiers got to work unloading the merchandise. Safreddin took his arm and led him back into the lighted office. He was elaborately casual. He offered Fathalla a cigarette and said:

"I want to thank you for recommending Dr. Bitar to me. He's very good, very devoted. Without him, my son would have died."

"I'm glad." Supple as a snake, Fathalla slid into Safreddin's mood. "I didn't know the boy had been sick until Bitar rang me. It must have been an anxious time for you."

"It was. Bitar was angry with me at first. He felt I had neglected the boy."

Fathalla smiled and shrugged. "He bullies me too. But he's the kind of doctor we need."

"He's not very proud of our Syrian medical services."

"Everything takes time. Bitar is an impatient man."

"No harm in that. We need impatient people, provided they are equipped to get things done. Do you think Bitar would make a good administrator?"

"I don't know. I've never thought about it."

"Would you say he was a political man?"

"Political?" Fathalla frowned over the word. "I don't quite know what you mean."

"It's a necessary question," said Safreddin calmly. "I had thought of recommending Bitar for a senior advisory position in the Department of Public Health. As we are constituted now, we need men who are not only good administrators, but who have a lively sense of the political aspects of what they do. This is something I've learnt from the Russians. The executive and the bureaucracy must work hand in hand. Is Bitar a Baathist?"

"I've always presumed so. I've never bothered to ask. I know he's very enlightened."

"He has contacts that could be of great use to us. He serves as medical adviser to a number of foreign embassies. He's quite a good linguist, I believe."

Before Fathalla had time to affirm or deny, there was a sharp cry from the yard and then a sudden clatter of voices. Safreddin moved swiftly to the door, with Fathalla close on his heels. As they stepped into the yard they saw one of the loading crews being helped from the tail of a truck. His right hand was streaming with blood. Safreddin hurried towards him, Fathalla only a pace behind him. The accident was simple but messy. The man had caught his hand on a coil of barbed wire which was part of the load and there was a long, deep gash in the heel of his thumb. While Safreddin was inspecting the damage, Fathalla had time for a swift glance at one of the packing cases stacked a few paces from the truck. The name and address of the consignee were stenciled in Arabic on the top and on the side. The one glance was enough. He pushed himself into the little group, helpful and solicitous.

"Here, let me look after that." He made a wad of his handkerchief, clamped it over the soldier's hand and led him into the washroom which adjoined his office. He cleansed the wound, disinfected it and then taped the lips together with adhesive bandage. Safreddin watched the operation with impatient approval. "He'll need stitches," said Fathalla.

"We'll get him to the infirmary as soon as we are finished here."

"He shouldn't use it again tonight. Otherwise it will break open. Would you like me to help with the loading?"

"No . . . there's no need." There was a faint edge of alarm in Safreddin's voice. "Besides there's something I wanted to ask you." He dismissed the soldier abruptly and waited until he had left the office before he put the question to Fathalla. "Did you tell me once—or am I imagining it?—that you have an account with the Phoenician Bank in Beirut?"

"I may have mentioned it," said Selim Fathalla with mild surprise. "It's no secret and it's quite legal. I use the Phoenician Bank as a clearing house for my foreign bills. They remit directly to my bank in Damascus. Why do you ask?"

Instead of answering the question, Safreddin asked another. "Do you keep any large amounts there?"

"From time to time the amount builds up, but I'm bound by law to convert to local currency within a reasonable time. Is there some reason for the question?"

"Between friends," said Omar Safreddin, "there's a very good reason. We hear from reliable sources that the bank is shaky. If you're holding any large amounts there now, I'd pull them out. I'd suggest also that you close your account and start operating with someone else—an Arab organization for preference."

"Thanks for the tip. I'll do something about it tomorrow."

But even as he said it, he was faced with another and more disturbing question: how was he to reset with an Arab bank the telltale arrangements that were necessary to finance himself and his network? The Phoenician Bank was geared to take care of the most eccentric clients and the most complicated transactions. No questions were asked, no explanations were expected. Nuri Chakry was the best banker in the world for a spy. How he would fare with another—and where he might find that other—was something Jakov Baratz would have to solve for him.

He must have lingered a shade too long on the thought, because Safreddin chuckled and said with faint malice, "You mustn't worry too much. We have good bankers in Damascus too. We know how to look after our friends."

"I've never doubted it, Colonel. It's just that it's such a nuisance to set up new payment procedures. When you do, you're always bound to lose money. Besides I can't understand why the Phoenician Bank should be so suddenly in trouble. They're one of the biggest organizations in the Middle East."

"Too big. Too much in the hands of one man. Tell me, have you ever had any correspondence with Nuri Chakry?"

"At the beginning, yes. Most of my later correspondence has been with his subordinates."

"I wonder if you would let me see it sometime?"

"You can see it now, if you like, Colonel. But, why?"

"We're looking for a man who, we believe, has been passing out confidential information in correspondence with the Phoenician Bank."

"And you suspect me?"

"No, my friend," said Omar Safreddin calmly. "If I suspected you I would not have trusted you as far as I have done tonight with that . . . that little affair out there. On the contrary I regard you as a friend. For that reason I want to be able to give you a clean bill with the Finance Ministry and with the Security Service."

"I want it too." Fathalla made no attempt to hide his anger. "I can't live under suspicion. My business is open. My books are clean."

"Good," said Omar Safreddin. "I'll move a man in tomorrow morning. He'll go through your files and make a personal report to me."

Fathalla flushed and demanded with heavy irony, "Shouldn't you search my house too?"

"That's being done now." Safreddin was bland as honey. "I expect a telephone call before we leave here. There's nothing personal in it, believe me. I know you are clean, but in any investigation like this I have to be impartial. Otherwise I cannot protect you or any other friend. I beg you to understand."

"I do! But it's a bitter thing to be investigated like a criminal. When does it end?"

"Never! Because who can swear that he will be the same man tomorrow as he is today?" He relaxed then and smiled in the friendliest fashion. "You mustn't blame me, Selim. I'm the watchdog who barks at friends and strangers alike. But I only bite the intruders and the traitors!"

"I hope your men have been polite to my people. I don't want my household upset. And I don't want gossip in the bazaar."

"If there's been any trouble, telephone me. I'll deal with the man who made it."

"Thank you."

"And when we've finished here, perhaps you'd like to have dinner with me."

"Perhaps another time." Fathalla was frigidly polite. "When you feel more confident in me."

Safreddin shrugged off the snub. "Of course. . . . When this problem is solved, we'll both be happier."

And on that equivocal phrase the conversation lapsed. Safreddin went outside to inspect the loading, while Fathalla smoked a restless cigarette and waited for the telephone to ring. He was angry with himself because he had let Safreddin shock him. He had dealt with him long enough to know that the man was incredibly devious and quite relentless. He was an adept in the classic technique of terror, which was to keep everyone in a constant state of tension and mistrust. Sooner or later the innocent would crack and offer the most intimate confidences in return for reassurance. Sooner or later the guilty would make one of two mistakes: he would accept a false statement at face value or would draw wrong conclusions from a true one. Either way he would entangle himself like a bird in a net.

Fathalla was reminded vividly of the old trick of the bazaar thieves, which was called finger dancing. Two of them would approach a victim in a crowded street. They would harass and jostle him. Their fingers, moving incredibly fast like gnats' wings, would flutter all about him—on face and breast and eyes until he became so distracted that it was easy for a third man to pick his pocket or even cut the watch from his wrist. Even if the victim struck out, he created another kind of confusion, a petty riot—and the result was always the same.

To Safreddin's technique there was only one answer: remain calm, even while you make a display of whatever emotion is appropriate, note all the points made and play with them later like chessmen, remembering always that the most obvious move might also be the most dangerous. At this moment, for example, Safreddin had men searching his house. It was a harassment, nothing more. Unless they found the secret lock that opened the faience panel, there was nothing to incriminate him. If they did, he was dead and damned beyond recourse. Then the thought hit him like a bullet. . . . They might not be looking for anything. They might well be an installation crew—putting a tap on his telephone and listening devices in his private quarters. The possibility was chilling. Even if you knew the bugs were there, they were still a trap. If you dismantled them, you were immediately under suspicion. If you tried to cheat them, the very artifices of your talk betrayed you. Ignore them as you would, you fell victim in the end of the psychosis created by living every hour exposed to the prying ears of your enemies. The telephone jangled at his elbow and he almost leapt from his chair. He picked it up. "This is Fathalla."

A male voice asked, "Is Colonel Safreddin there, please?"

"Just a moment, I'll get him."

But Safreddin was already back in the office and waiting for the receiver. "Safreddin speaking. . . . No, nothing else. Thank you." Safreddin put down the receiver and turned to Fathalla. "They've finished at your house, my friend. They give you a clean bill."

"I wish I could say I'm glad, Colonel. Instead, I find myself insulted."

"If you weren't insulted," said Safreddin amiably, "I'd be disappointed in you. . . . We're nearly finished outside. We'll get our vehicles out. Then, you can lock up and go home."

"Not yet. I have to wait for the watchman."

"Is he reliable?"

"For me, yes. For you, Colonel, I don't know. And to be honest, I don't care."

Suddenly and surprisingly Safreddin laughed, throwing back his head and slapping his thighs in mirth. "Good! Very, very good! I could arrange for you to be shot tomorrow and you would spit in my face. You test well, Fathalla. How would you like to work for me?"

He considered the question at length. He rolled it about in his mouth for taste and smell, while he calculated the gamble he was about to take. Then with great deliberation he laid down his answer:

"I might like that, Colonel. . . . I think! When I get my goods delivered in Amman, and my trucks back safe and my drivers home with their wives and the tap taken off my telephone and the microphones taken out of my house, I'll give you an answer."

"And how, Fathalla, would you know about such things as microphones and tapped telephones?"

"You'll find the answer in my dossier. I'm a Baathist, remember? I got out, one step ahead of the assassins, because I was warned about these little tricks. . . . Allah! To think I find them among my friends in Damascus! If you want my head, Colonel, just ask and I'll send it to you on a dish. But let us not defile the Resurrection Party with this sort of filth!"

The footsteps and the voices in the yard rang unnaturally loud; yet they seemed to belong to another plane of existence. There was a long and deadly silence in the narrow office under the naked yellow light. Safreddin sat, rigid as an idol, staring down at the tips of his fingers. Finally he raised his head. His eyes were bright, his thin lips smiled. He had the look of a man supremely satisfied with his own brilliance. "Very well, Selim. The equipment will be taken out in the morning. . . . But don't be too clever, will you?"

"I don't want to be clever, Colonel," said Selim Fathalla. "I want to buy and sell and sleep happy with a warm woman. For the rest—Inshallah."

"Inshallah!" repeated Safreddin piously. "Goodnight, my friend."

BEIRUT

In the rooftop restaurant of the Phoenician Hotel—which was, at this moment, richer and safer than the Phoenician

Bank—Nuri Chakry was entertaining Mark Matheson at
dinner. They sat at their customary table, private, by the
northward window, looking down at the dark sea and the
lights that ran northward along the littoral until the headlands lifted them against the low stars. The setting was luxu-
rious—soft lights, deep carpets, drapes of rich Thai weave,
snowy napery, shining crystal. The service was smooth as
silk, the food a sequence of exotic delicacies from all over
the world. The host was bubbling with optimism and good
humor.

". . . I tell you, Mark, things are better than I could possibly have hoped. These dolts at the Ministry—they were
like a bunch of schoolmasters, wagging their fingers and
trying to teach their grandmothers to suck eggs! Such lectures
they read me! But at the end it was quite clear. They'll come
to the party because they have to. The whole national credit
is involved. Oh, they'll hold off as long as they dare, just so
we'll be burned a little, but on the day before settlement
they'll deliver the cash."

"That's not what I heard in Zurich," said Matheson
gloomily. "That's not the way Mortimer read it to me either."

"You know why?" Chakry held up a spoonful of strawberries. "Because they want an atmosphere of no-confidence.
After you called from Zurich, I had a private tip that Mortimer was standing ready with an offer for the airline . . .
more than enough to get us out of bother, but not nearly
enough for fair value. Lewisohn told you he'd buy the Vista
del Lago, didn't he? And we've had nibbles about our real
estate in Paris and New York. . . . Even the boys at the Ministry asked me whether I'd consider an offer for my shares.
What does it all add up to? A concerted effort to depress the
market. . . . That's the real danger for us, lack of personal
faith. Not the Kuwaitis or the Saudis . . ."

"Faith isn't cash."

Chakry shoved the strawberries into his mouth and chewed

on them with relish, talking at the same time. "Don't worry about the cash. That's already on the line."

Matheson looked up, gaping in amazement. "The devil it is! When did this happen? Who's putting it up?"

Chakry grinned happily and dabbed at his lips with the napkin. He shook his head. "Not yet, Mark! Not even to you. This is going to be a little drama of my own. But to keep you happy I'm going to read you part of the script— the best part! We're going to let this crisis develop just the way everyone thinks it will. We can time it, almost to the day, as you know. Five days before they think we're going to the wall, I'm going into smoke—a little business trip. You're going to handle the final negotiations with the Ministry and the Central Bank. There'll be a lot of offers from the vultures too by then. You'll put everything together for my final consideration. Then, just before the Central Bank steps in for salvage, I'm going to appear and pull the rabbit out of the hat. Hey presto! And listen for the gasps!"

"It's a nice trick—if you can do it."

"I'll do it. Believe me."

"I'm happy to believe you. But you might have saved me the boot leather and the kicks in the tail I've been getting."

Chakry chuckled. "I'm sorry about that, Mark. Before you left, I wasn't sure I could bring this thing off. By the time I was sure, your trip had become part of the stage management."

"How much am I supposed to know about this—or talk about it? I'll have a lot of questions to answer in the next couple of weeks."

"Nothing. Except that there's every reason for confidence. . . . Excuse me a moment, I want to make a telephone call."

When he had gone, Mark Matheson sat, chin propped on hand, staring out at the lights of a coaster, distant and bright against the night sea. It was all too magical for belief and yet there came a moment when magic was all you could believe in—magic and the majestic conjuror with his sleeves rolled back and his tapping wand and his omnipotent smile. Besides, this was why you hired him: to suspend disbelief and make mock of the reasonings of lesser men. His assistant had another kind of job: to set the stage, to focus attention on the props, to lend dignity and authority to the great panjandrum. There were those who might carp at him and claim that he was party to a confidence trick. Yet there were moments in every performance when the assistant himself was subdued by the magic; and sometimes, he was surprised by a trick he had never seen before—a sudden fluttering of doves, a virgin, putative at least, popped out of a bridal cake. Besides what else was he to do—the good servant, the man with a marshmallow center? He was part of the show. He was hired for good coin. He had to stay with the act until it hit the top of the bill, or until the last rabbit was eaten and the silk hat fell apart. The Arabs had the right idea: squat on your hunkers while the thunder rolls overhead and let Allah look after tomorrow.

"Tonight, we play," said Nuri Chakry as he eased himself back into his chair. "Kamal Amin is giving a party. All our friends, none of our rivals and a whole ballet of new women. What do you say, Mark?"

"I say drink and be merry. We're rich again." He felt suddenly reckless and dizzy with reaction.

Chakry laid a warning hand on his arm. "Not too rich, Mark. That makes people jealous. Just rich enough to be confident, eh?"

"Faith, hope and love!" Matheson raised his glass. "Especially love! One of these days I must get married again."

When he got up to leave, he realized that he was a little drunk; but by the time they had reached the house of Kamal Amin, he was sober enough to see how carefully the party had been arranged and to recognize in its management the slim, practiced hand of Nuri Chakry. The men were all

his clients; associates and allies in one or another of his enterprises. They all had the sleek, comfortable look of success.
They all spoke the same sidling, cryptic language—the short-
hand of money and the stock market. They laughed readily
and lapsed as readily into whispered talk and gestures which
spoke more eloquently than words.

The girls were new, as Chakry had promised: a covey of
models from Rome, a clutch of starlets from the last festival
at Cannes, three dancers from the new show going into rehearsal at the Casino. Yet he had seen them all before—the
same clothes straight out of the fashion plates; the same
young-old faces from Rubinstein and Max Factor; the same
restless eyes, half wise, half puzzled, calculating the risks and
the profits in these new and opulent encounters. They came
first class, shipped in on approval when the summer began
to fade in Europe. They took up residence in the same apartments as their predecessors from last year. They stayed until
the winter snow began to fall on the mountains and then
they went back—first class if they were lucky—to Arosa and
Zermatt and St. Moritz, some a little wiser, a few richer,
all much older in the international trade.

They moved skillfully from group to group, carrying with
them a drift of perfume and a musk of sensuality. Their soft
hands touched wrist or cheek and then withdrew. They talked
melodiously with the high, vapid skill of geisha, sprinkling
their talk with names and places, making stale promises to
men who had bought fulfillment many times before and for
whom they represented not a conquest but an elegant con-
venience.

Chakry wove himself through the gathering like a golden
thread, caressing a bare shoulder, whispering in attentive
ears, drawing now this man, now that, into a private colloquy,
always breaking it off before he was forced to a conclusion
or a verdict. Matheson watched him with admiration and
envy, marveling at his toughness and the ease with which he

disengaged himself from talk when it became too particular. He was the perfect faith healer, calming fears, laying balm to financial wounds, full of promises too bright for contradiction. Scraps of his talk drifted across the room to where Matheson sat absently fondling the knee of the dancer who sat on the arm of his chair and chattered happily, unconscious of his boredom.

". . . Every one envies the autonomy and independence of Lebanon. . . . When they strike at us, this is what they are attacking. . . . The socialist state is the death of banking enterprise. . . . Periods of pressure are inevitable . . . even in the oil business you can get your throat cut. The trick is to find pockets of new money as we are doing. . . . American gold reserves are dwindling. . . . Always great promises from the British but their pound is in tatters. . . . Seven percent minimum annual increase in capital land value. . . . Air transport and hotels must grow together. . . . Don't sell, hold. . . ."

It was a virtuoso performance and Matheson knew that he himself could never match it in a hundred years. So after a while he surrendered himself to the liquor and let the talk roll over him, drowning the guilt of his own surrender, while he began to calculate hazily how long it would take him to cut out the dancing chatterbox and get her home to bed.

TEL AVIV

"I sometimes think there's only one great battle in all of us. . . ." Thus, Jakov Baratz in the last candle glow of his very private dinner party. "Once in our lives, the banners are bright and the trumpets are all silver and we conquer shouting or go down praying. After that, we know too much, and the best we can hope to be is loyal mercenaries."

"Is that what you are, Jakov—a mercenary?" There was no irony in the question; it was a simple polite request for information. Ever since her outburst of self-humiliation, Yehudith had been very subdued. She had talked freely enough during dinner; but her interest was remote, as if she had overspent her reserves of passion and must be quiet and withdrawn until they were replenished. Baratz was somber and brooding, needing to explain yet fearful of betraying himself.

"I don't know what else I am. I'm a permanent soldier. I collect my pay like any servant of the state. I like my job. I know I do it a little better than most—but that's a matter of aptitude and not of inspiration. . . . So I'm a mercenary."

"Do you care?"

"About the job—certainly."

"About what it means—the watch on the frontiers, the land, the tradition, the people?"

"That too. But I care in a different way. I don't have illusions now. I hear the bitter debates in the Knesset. I see men who plotted and fought together to found Israel, gibing at each other before the world. I watch the power play and the scrabble in the money market and I wonder if this is truly what we fought for."

"Yet you send Adom and men like him to risk their lives every day for it. You were happy tonight when I made a burnt offering of whatever small hopes I had. Why?"

"Would you like some music?"

"Do I get an answer too?"

"I'm looking for one myself."

"Then tell me at least where you're searching."

Baratz got up from the table, switched on the record player and a few moments later they heard Horowitz begin to play the Schumann concerto in C major, that rich tender poem of separation and longing. Yehudith curled herself in the corner of the sofa, closed her eyes and let the music sweep over her in healing waves. She looked so wounded, and so lost, so grateful for the momentary ease, that Baratz felt himself choked by a sudden surge of pity. He wanted to take her in his arms and soothe her unsatisfied body and calm her with tenderness and gladden her with a lover's passion and yet he dared not so much as touch her lest he stumble into treachery.

After a while, softly and without opening her eyes, she asked him again, "Where are you searching, Jakov? What are you looking for?"

"I want the lost thing—the thing you can believe in and die for, singing."

"Have you ever had it?"

"I thought I had once. Now I'm not sure."

"Why?"

"Why? Because of what I did to you tonight. Because the reasons for all the other things I must do get more and more confused."

"Are you a believer, Jakov?"

"In God, no. I wish I could be. You know, one day a couple of weeks ago I was in Jerusalem. I called in to the museum to get some information on a piece of Nabatean pottery I had bought from the Bedouin in the Negev. One of the guides brought in a group of old people from Safad. They were the real *adukim*. You know them. I don't have to tell you. I don't quite know why, but I followed them round. They were mildly interested in the antiquities, more interested in themselves and their outing. But when they came to that big room where the old Torah and the sacred vessels and the vestments are displayed, suddenly and quite strangely, they came alive. I saw men and women kiss their fingers and lay them against the glass cases. Some of them stood in a kind of ecstasy, eyes closed, their lips moving in prayer. I was so envious of them that I almost wept. For me it was simply history and tradition—a binding thing, yes, but not enough. Not half enough! It was the loving that escaped me. The loving that made the God of the Fathers real to them and permanently present."

"Maybe that's the answer already, Jakov—the loving."

"Maybe. If you know what it means."

"You love Hannah."

"I loved her. I possessed her. I destroyed her. Franz Lieberman told me it would happen. I would not listen. So what do I know about loving?"

She opened her eyes then and saw his face, gray and strained, half shadowed, half lit by the candle flames. For a moment his manifest agony shamed her; then resentment welled up and she probed at him again.

"And what do you do now, Jakov?"

"I work. I do what a believer does, without belief. I practice loyalty and impose discipline. I am paid to command. I command. I am trusted to give honest judgments. I render them as best as I can."

"And that's enough?"

"It's all I have."

"How long can you endure it?"

"For one day."

"And then?"

"There is another day."

"Is that all the hope you have?"

"It's all I count on. Hope is a different matter."

"And what do you hope for, Jakov?"

"What Goethe asked for before he died: 'Light. More light.' "

"It's dark where I am too, Jakov."

"I know."

There was no music now. There were no words either. They were two islands in a room full of shadows and silence. Somewhere in Damascus was a man whose absence divided them like a naked sword. Baratz got up from the couch and walked out of the room. A few moments later he came back and sat down beside Yehudith. He held out his right hand to her and she saw lying in the palm a small flat cardboard box. Soberly and gently he explained it to her.

"We've talked too long. We've hurt each other. We mustn't do it again. This is the most precious thing I have. I found it one day in a hole in the rock during the first fighting at Ramle. I want you to take it and go home; keep it, look at it sometimes and let it say all the things I can't."

Wondering, she took the box and asked, "May I look at it, please?"

"Of course."

She opened the box, unfolded the cotton-wool wrapping and held the small treasure between her fingertips: a square of ancient stone, flat, light green veined with silk and carved with the image of Venus rising from the sea.

"Jakov, it's beautiful! What is it?"

"It's emerald. Not very good, as stones go. The color's much too light. It's full of silk—that's the flaws you see all through it. It's Roman, probably carved in Alexandria about the time of Titus. At least that's what they think at the museum. They suggested it might have been a buckle ornament for a woman's waistband."

"I wonder who she was? Did she give it to her man before he went to the wars? Did he buy it for her and die before he could deliver it?"

"It was so long ago. Who knows? Who cares?"

"I know," said Yehudith Ronen softly. "I know and I care and I'm so grateful I can't even cry. Send me home now, Jakov. Send me home quickly."

DAMASCUS

In a shabby room, in a once grand hotel, Idris Jarrah lay on his bed and contemplated the fly-blown lampshade above him. He had eaten badly, spent a full two hours in a night-club where the girls were more rapacious and more ill favored than usual, and had decided, not for the first time, that Damascus was dead beyond any hope of resurrection by the Baath or anyone else. The streets were full of aimless soldiers and excessively vigilant police who had stopped him twice to ask for his papers. The merchandise in the shops was scanty and of poor quality. The buildings were seedy and run-down. He had not seen one elegant woman or a single well-dressed man. And, because public morality was now a matter of official concern, he had either to sleep alone in his hotel or risk his health and his wallet in a back-alley brothel. He had decided, without too much debate, that the dubious solace was not worth the gamble.

His only consolation was that tomorrow, at first light, he would be out of the place and on his way to Amman and Jerusalem. But even this was no balm against the doubts that were beginning to itch at his seasoned hide. He had come out from his interview with Safreddin elated and confident that he was, as he had planned to be, in control of the situation. Now, isolated in this cheerless box, in this suspicious and unhappy city, he was not half so sure. Safreddin had been too pliable, too complaisant. He had shown too much respect for the opinions of an interloper—even one who carried good P.L.O. money in his satchel. And when Safreddin stepped out of character there was always a smell of danger in the air. But what danger? A good question. A life-and-death question for Idris Jarrah, who had a hundred thousand dollars in the bank and wanted to enjoy them for a long time to come.

There were so many cross-currents in Arab politics, so many shifts and changes in the wind, that one needed to be a genius or a seer to divine them all. In Islam itself there were sects and sectaries and the sons of the Prophet were not at all a happy family. There were brawls and squabbles and tribal jealousies and ethnic tensions and national rivalries and political dissensions and sudden great oaths of friendship that would not survive the moment of common interest. Safreddin's professed interest was the removal of the monarch in Jordan; but a threat from the Israelis in Galilee would make him very chary of a civil war in the next garden patch. The whole plot might be a contrivance, to show Safreddin as a friend of the monarchy, unmasking traitors in the cause of Arab unity and the fundamental fraternity of Islam. As the kadi had pointed out centuries ago to Abu the Joker, there were more ways than one of copulating with a cat—and the luckless Joker had been beaten on the feet because he had claimed there was only one.

Safreddin had told him to make contact with Major Khalil. But Khalil was already compromised—might, even at this moment, be under arrest—because Jarrah had betrayed him to Nuri Chakry. To make contact with him would be to put his own neck in a hangman's noose. To refuse to make contact would make Safreddin suspicious, even if it did not expose the full extent of the treachery. . . . Quite clearly now, he saw how sharp and perilous was the blade on which he had balanced himself.

He had gambled everything on the belief that Chakry would not reveal the source of his information, that he would survive the financial crisis and stay in the market as a constant buyer of information. But if he did not, if his credit was already destroyed beyond repair, then how would he recoup the money he had paid to his informant? That he would recoup it was a certainty. Even if he had to squeeze it out in blood. What would a buyer do when a man, already discredited, offered him explosive news? He would demand proof of authenticity; and Chakry had it—a signature on a promissory note, a receipt for money paid, a tape with an identifiable voice. Jarrah had known other men killed in dark lanes or tumbled overboard from fishing boats because, after years of successful calculation, they had made one small error of judgment.

From this moment his life depended on *if*'s: if Chakry had sold out his informant; if the men to whom he had sold it had passed, or would pass, on his name to Safreddin. In Jordan he might survive a little longer because he had done a manifest service to the throne. At least he would have time to think and reckon the odds for and against him. In Damascus he was in deadly danger.

He made a swift calculation. From Damascus to the Jordan frontier post at Rumtha was two and a half hours by road. He could take a taxi and leave now, but that would mean hanging about the border town until transport for Amman arrived in the morning. So precipitate a flight would alert Safreddin; and his arrival in Rumtha at so late an hour would be noted with suspicion by the border guards. Better to rest on the *if,* risk the last, long night in Damascus and leave on schedule in the morning.

He got up from the bed and walked across the room to lock the door. There was no key. The chain bolt was broken. He wedged a chair under the handle. It would take only a few moments to dislodge it but at least he would have warning of any intruder. He rummaged in his suitcase and brought out a small, black automatic. Then he lay down on the bed, fully clothed, drew the soiled sheet over his shoulders and dozed uneasily, waking at every sound from the street and every footfall in the passage outside.

DAMASCUS

When Safreddin and his men had left the compound, Selim Fathalla made a telephone call to Emilie.

"Emilie? This is Selim. I'm at the warehouse. The watchman's gone off for a cup of coffee. Why don't you get the car and pick me up in about half an hour? We'll go for a drive."

"Where to?"

It was the question he had hoped she would ask. He answered it cheerfully, for the benefit of the agent who was listening on the line.

"Anywhere you like. I've been cooped up all day, I feel restless. If you feel like it we can have supper at Hakim's and then park somewhere and look at the moon. I'm in a romantic mood."

"Just as you like, Selim. I was worried tonight. Two men came from the security service. They said they had orders to search the house."

"I know about it," said Fathalla easily. "Colonel Safreddin told me. It's a routine investigation of people who have bank accounts outside the country."

"I wish you'd told me. I didn't know what to do. I just had to let them go through."

"You did the right thing. Don't worry about it. Meet me here in half an hour."

He put down the phone and gave himself over to a consideration of all the things which he must do immediately. First he must alert his whole network to the fact that some kind of security investigation was in progress. The alert itself would entail a risk—of panic, precipitation and the treachery of the weak. His operation was quite different from that of Eli Cohen. Cohen had made himself a very public man, with high friends in business, in diplomacy and in politics. Cohen had worked the old theater trick of the cloak of invisibility. He was so patently present that he was for a long time ignored. He was so obviously a suspect that he could not be suspected. But once the trick was revealed, his whole organization had collapsed like a card castle.

Fathalla's agents were humbler folk: clerks in the ministries, underpaid and unhappy; junior officers, disgruntled by slow promotion and the system of political preferment; dispossessed merchants, the victims of a socialist revolution; members of the Nasserite groups who had been purged from power when the Baath took over. They were spread all over the country and he himself had no direct contact with them. His network was based on the classic triad—the group of three—so that one agent knew only two others and could betray only those whom he knew. He himself dealt only with Bitar and another man in Aleppo, and neither of the two knew of the other's existence. So, in fact, he had two separate networks at his disposal and each functioned independently of the other. Tomorrow he must warn Bitar; and at the earliest opportunity he must go to Aleppo to deliver the same warning.

His next problem was more urgent. He had to get an immediate message to Baratz in Tel Aviv. Baratz must know the name and address of the consignee of Safreddin's arms. More urgently still, Baratz must know that the Phoenician Bank was in trouble and must send him an agent from outside, with whom he could set up new arrangements to finance his informers. But his own house was no longer secure as a communication center, nor would it be until Safreddin had removed his listening devices and he, himself, had checked every inch of the building to make sure that none had been left behind. There was a transmitter in Bitar's house, concealed in the panels of his X-ray equipment, but Bitar's house, too, might be compromised and, in any case, tonight was an unfavorable occasion to make contact.

Finally he had to think of Emilie and to make a critical decision; whether or not to admit her to his confidence. The more he thought about it, the more it was clear that the decision was already made. He loved her. He was sure beyond a shadow of doubt that she loved him. If he fell, she would fall with him; and her innocence would not protect her against the vengeance of Safreddin. So, he must arm her with knowledge, arm himself with her willing cooperation and repay her in the end with marriage and a safe life in a new country. She knew something already from his delirious babblings. Whatever it was, it was too much for safety and too little to protect her against indiscretion or a subtle in-

vestigator. He must commit her; but first he must make sure
that she was ready to commit herself. Once the revelation
was made, she would hold him and his whole enterprise in
her small hands. It was a terrifying risk. All his experience
as a plotter had taught him the danger of sharing secrets
with a woman; yet he knew with equal certainty that he
could not endure another division of himself to an unhappy
love affair. The self was a diminishing capital which needed
to be constantly restored by a relationship with another self.
He had spent too prodigally already and had seen all too
vividly the danger of personal destruction.

When the watchman came back, he left the compound
and stood in the shadow of the gatepost outside smoking a
cigarette. The lane was dark and deserted; apparently Safreddin was not yet worried enough to have him shadowed. He
strolled to the corner where the lane intersected a larger
street, stopped at a vendor's stall, bought a bottle of warm
orange soda and drank it slowly, looking up and down the
roadway for any loiterer who did not fit the scene. There
was still no one. Finally reassured, he walked back to the
gateway and waited for Emilie to come for him.

The desert moon rode low in a cold sky as they drove
through the time-worn city and out on to the Rumtha road.
The rocky hills reared themselves, gray and barren against
the faint stars. A small wind blew chill across the wasteland,
acrid with sand and limestone dust. Emilie huddled against
him for warmth and he drove with one arm around her
shoulders, her hair brushing his lips, her small soft hand thrust
inside his shirtfront. A mile from the last suburbs he turned
the car off the highroad and on to a narrow steep track that
followed the course of a dry and winding creek, back into the
hills. It was hardly more than a mule path and they bumped
and jolted over ruts and loose stones until, rounding a
shoulder of rock, Fathalla stopped the car outside a tiny
whitewashed church with a low stone wall and dilapidated

graveyard and a crumbling bell tower. He got out of the car and walked to the rusted gate.

Emilie followed him, puzzled and half afraid. "What is this place, Selim?"

"A church." He held her close to him and smiled down at her. "They say that in the time of the Crusades it was a famous shrine, with a well that gave healing water. Now, nobody comes here—except me."

She stared at him in surprise. "Why you?"

"I own it. I bought it from the Syrian Patriarch when I first came to Damascus."

"But there's nothing here."

"We're here."

"I know. But . . ."

"Do you love me, Emilie?"

"You know I do—so much!"

"Kiss me!"

They kissed, under the low moon, with the dead for silent witnesses. Then Fathalla took her hand, pushed open the gate and led her into the churchyard. He lifted a stone from a grave slab, dislodged a sleeping lizard and picked up an antique key. He opened the door of the church, led her inside and closed the door behind them. Inside the air was dry and musty; thin shafts of moonlight struck down on an empty nave and a tumbled altar and a broken font in the baptistery. Every vestige of furniture had been stripped from the place long since, every stick of wood had been burnt and every lead-light torn from the empty windows.

"Why did you bring me here, Selim?"

He laughed, softly, and the sound echoed round the stone shell. "Be patient. I'll tell you in a moment."

Standing on tiptoe, he reached up to the capital of a Norman pillar and brought down a flashlight. He switched it on and focused the beam on the arched ceiling of the sanctuary. There was a glitter of mosaic, gold, crimson and green; and

as the beam traversed the cupola she saw a motley of old
saints reaching up to the glory of a triangular godhead. Fathalla explained them to her, half seriously, half in mockery.

"They call them the holy martyrs of Nedjran. There were
three hundred and forty of them—count them if you want
—and their leader was Abdullah ibn Kaab of the tribe of
the Beni Harith. They were massacred by Dhu Nowas, who
was a Jew, and by Arab tribesmen, in the sixth century.
Even the Moslems venerated them and Mohammed mentions
them in the glorious Koran. . . . You see the child? They say
he followed his mother into the flames, lisping the name of
Christ. . . . I thought you'd like to see them."

"I've never heard of them before."

"I don't know anyone else who has either. So they're our
secret, Emilie."

"I don't like secrets. They frighten me."

"I want to tell you secrets tonight, Emilie."

"Please don't."

"I must. I want you to marry me."

"O God!" The words were a whisper hardly audible. All
the color drained from her cheeks and she stood like a stone
woman, staring in disbelief. The next moment she was in
his arms, sobbing and heartbroken. "I can't, Selim! I want
to but I can't! I can't! . . ."

"Why not?" He held her arms and shook her savagely.
"Tell me why not!"

"I don't know!"

"You must know. Tell me!"

"You're hurting me, Selim!"

He released her then and stepped back, watching as she
rubbed her bruised arms and struggled to calm herself.
Finally, in a very small voice, she gave him the answer:

"I can't, I daren't marry a Moslem."

"But you sleep with one. You love one."

"All that, yes. But marriage . . . marriage is different.

You can have four wives if you want. In my house I can't have rivals, Selim. I can't submit to the threefold dismissal when you get tired of me. I'm not that kind of woman. As we are now, I can take myself back any time I want. The other way, no!"

"And yet you say you love me!"

"I do. So let's go on as we are, until the loving is over."

It was so wintry and final, she was so strong, that he felt himself in the presence of a stranger. He found himself groping for words to touch her. The words came at last, but the voice that spoke them was not his own.

"Emilie, please listen to me."

"I'm listening."

"I brought you here to tell you secrets. Once I tell them, you can destroy me with a word. If I don't tell them, I am destroyed in another way. So, if you don't want the secrets, I'll drive you back to town, and tomorrow it's over—everything! We can't even work together."

"How can you be so cruel?"

"I'm not cruel—believe me."

"Why can't we go on the same way?"

"Because, even if you can endure it, I can't."

"I'm afraid of you, Selim."

"Why?"

"You're such a private man. I don't mind it now. Sometimes I rather like it, because I'm free to be myself so much of the time. But to be married and live half my life in a separate world . . . no!"

"But, don't you see, that's the point! I'm asking you to let me into your world. I want you to join me in mine—and then change it for me and with me."

"And what is your world, Selim?"

He had gone too far now to draw back. His own life, a hundred other lives were too small a counterweight for his need of her. He took her hand, and guiding her with the torch beam, he led her behind the broken altar and down a flight of steps into the crypt of the sacred well, dry now for centuries and void of wonders. In the wall of the crypt was an alcove where once a saint had lain under a slab of marble. The saint was gone, but the slab was still intact. He lifted her on to it and she sat, pale and dubious like some old pythoness looking down into his troubled eyes. Then he told her.

"I'm giving you my life now, Emilie. I'm not a Moslem. I'm a Jew. I'm not Selim Fathalla. I'm Adom Ronen. I'm an agent of the Israeli government."

"I knew. . . . Part of it at least." She said it very simply, but he was shocked to the marrow. "I knew and I didn't want to know. I kept telling myself it couldn't be true."

"And now?"

"I'm glad. I'm sorry."

"Are you still afraid of me?"

"I'm afraid for you. For myself too."

"I'm asking to be relieved very soon."

"Because of me?"

"Yes."

"You mustn't do that. When it is the proper time to go, when you can say, 'It's finished. There's nothing more I can do,' then we'll go."

"And you'll marry me?"

"If you still need me then—ask me."

"I need you now." He was urgent with her; a harsh note crept into his voice. "I have a wife in Israel. She is divorcing me so that I can marry you. If we are to survive together, we have to work together. Otherwise you can betray me and betray yourself, simply by not knowing."

"Is that the only reason why you want to marry me?"

"You know it isn't."

"Yes, I know. But you'll have to remind me all the time, Selim. It's a price you'll have to pay. You say you put yourself in my hands. I'm putting myself in yours too. If you drop me, I fall into a pit."

"I'll never drop you, Emilie. I promise it on my life."

She pushed herself down from the altar stone and they kissed and clung to each other in the darkness. Then he prised open the empty tomb and showed her the emergency transmitter. He lifted a small slab of stone from the floor and brought out a message block and a set of wavelengths and a book of ciphers. Then, while she held the flashlight and looked over his shoulder, he transcribed his signal to Jakov Baratz.

"Arms shipment consigned to Colonel Abid Badaoui 37 Kamouz Street Amman stop For reasons not known Safreddin conducting security investigation of all persons having accounts with Phoenician Bank Beirut stop I am included in investigation stop My house presently compromised by this investigation but Safreddin assures me no grounds personal suspicion stop He informs me Phoenician Bank financially unreliable and suggests immediate transfer my account to Arab institution represented in Damascus stop This entails immediate and essential reconstruction our finance channels stop Require urgent contact with agent from your end stop Request information personal matter already raised."

He hesitated a moment and then added a final sentence.

"View delicate security situation have appointed trustworthy person to make transmissions if I am unable to do so stop Signature Emil will indicate emergency conditions."

SIX

The message from Damascus presented Jakov Baratz with a neat irony, a rough dilemma and an unanswered question.

The irony lay in the fact that, at the very moment when Baratz was formulating plans for an attack on a Jordan village, he was passing out through the Foreign Ministry and its diplomatic channels information that might save the life of the King of Jordan. Even as he wrote the dispatch for the Ministry in Jerusalem, he could not resist the cynical thought that if you killed twenty common men, you had a border incident; but if you opened the veins of a royal man, you had an international crisis. The one you accepted as coolly as a risk in the corn market; the other gave you night-mares and diplomatic dyspepsia. And the sourest part of the joke was this: that while the King would not be in the least grateful for your warning, the border incident would pro-vide him with a grievance which he would exploit, most gratefully, in the forum of the nations. If politics was the art of the possible, it was also the chronicle of improbabilities which could never be matched in the wildest of fiction.

The dilemma had no humor in it at all. If he could not pluck Fathalla off its horns, he might lose an agent and a network. So long as the Phoenician Bank functioned normally, Fathalla's funds could be sent to him from half a dozen sources, each one of which would correspond with an entry in his trading accounts. But if every remittance—from Switzerland or Rome or Athens—was the subject of scrutiny by a government bank in Syria, Fathalla would be blown in a month. The only other alternative was to send money by courier—a risk for the money, the courier and for Fathalla himself, who seemed to be, even now, in a difficult situation. Baratz decided finally to send in an agent by way of Rome and provide Fathalla with a month's reserve of currency. These arrangements and a call to the Central Bank for information ate up half an hour of his time.

Which still left the troublesome question: who was Emil; and why had Fathalla taken the unprecedented step of handing vital radio and cipher information to an agent unchecked and unauthorized by headquarters? There was only one way to get the answer. He drafted his own signal for transmission to Fathalla when he worked his next schedule:

"Report fullest soonest identity Emil stop Your banking contact arrives in four days stop Identification comic opera stop Request urgent reports following matters personal and network security Syrian troop movements Galilee area ground plan and engineer specifications fortified positions Galilee hills information arrival new MIG aircraft and progress negotiations installation Russian ground to air missiles Iraqi participation Syria UAR defense pact stop Personal matter amicably arranged finality two weeks."

He sealed the message in an envelope, scribbled a note for Communications and called for a runner to make the delivery. Selim Fathalla was back in the files: a cipher in the accounts of a nation, a small variable x in the equation of survival. If only Jakov Baratz could discount him so easily in his own private ledger!

Fortunately, he had other matters to occupy him, at least during his working hours. The plans for the reprisal raid were taking shape. All his staff recommended the same target in the Hebron area. Operations approved. There were small disagreements about armored strength and artillery support and infantry deployment; but these could be resolved in conference. However, two questions still remained unanswered: the strength of Arab opposition and the political consequences of the act. In a sense the second answer depended on the first. If there was no major military engagement, the destruction of the village could be interpreted as reprisal, pure and simple. If there was a military action of any consequences, it would be read as an aggressive operation. . . . The irony again—and the terrible amoral folly of military and diplomatic judgments.

Today's order of battle for the Jordan forces showed two armored columns on patrol duty in the Hebron sector and two companies of motorized infantry in reserve ten miles from the target area. Their only approach to the village was a narrow mountain road which could easily be cut by shellfire. Their only air support was a squadron of Hunters which were no match for Israeli Mirages. But, by the time the raid took place, the whole disposition might be changed—by the threat of a palace revolution or the need to protect a group of visiting dignitaries. So, until the very eve of the operation, one would be working on changing quantities and very variable results.

The more Baratz thought about the whole affair, the less he liked it. The more progress he made in his estimates, the less control he had over the situation. The order of things was clear. Intelligence advised; Operations directed; the Defense Minister gave or withheld consent. Amen! God help us all!—provided He had not disappeared forever from the scheme of things.

The telephone rang. When he picked it up he heard the hurried but concise report of an action already in progress in Galilee. An Israeli fishing boat, trawling the Lake of Tiberias, had strayed too far towards the eastern shore. The

Syrians had fired on her. A patrol boat sent to her assistance had run aground on a sandbank and was now a sitting target for the gunners in the Syrian hills. Fighter aircraft had been ordered into the air to silence the gunpost. Baratz scribbled the notes on his desk pad, put down the phone and then sat frowning over the new information.

Galilee was the real trouble spot. In purely military terms that was where any strike ought to be made, to drive the Syrians from their commanding positions in the hills and make the lake and the Jordan valley safe for settlement and cultivation. But every engagement with the Syrians brought the danger of a war with the Arab states one day closer. Syria threatened, invoked Egypt. Egypt shouted holy war up and down the Mediterranean. This new action introduced another complication into the plans for the Jordan raid. It confused the political issue; since a gun duel always got more publicity in the world press than an isolated act of sabotage by the P.L.O. Once again he found himself beating his head against the walls which confined him. He was a soldier. He had to take note of political issues. He could not in any sense determine them.

In point of fact—and this was the true tragedy of the human condition—even the simplest relationship of *I* and *thou* was beyond the determination of any one man. Enlightenment was not enough because one man's light illuminated his own corner; his neighbor's lit up another; between them lay a dark wasteland, mined and treacherous. Goodwill was not enough. With all the goodwill in the world, it was impossible to render an absolute justice to every single human being who, by the act of birth, was made a victim of the human paradox. Six million Jewish dead were commemorated in the somber crypt of Yad Vashem; but three hundred and ten thousand living Arabs were camped in the hovels of the Gaza Strip and they would not renounce one jot of their claim to a place in their original homeland.

The all-knowing *I* and the *thou*, fully known and wholly

loved, might achieve a harmony. The sadness was that the knowing was never complete, the loving was never selfless, because at the center of every self was a walled area, like a sacred stone, which the self would defend even at the cost of self-destruction. The mystics of every faith saw truly that the moment of peace and perfection was the moment at which this wall was torn down and the last territorial possession was renounced, so that there was nothing to defend and, therefore, nothing to fight for. But even the mystics admitted that the perfection was visionary, to be found—if it existed at all—only in an afterlife. . . .

Which brought Jakov Baratz by a round turn, back to the task which he was paid to perform: the collage of incomplete information to make a picture, part true, part false; the balancing of risks and profits in the expenditure of human life; the making of battle maps with colored pins and paper flags; the matching of one threat with another because it seemed that men who were born of an act of love could only survive by the practice of terror.

RUMTHA

By a miracle—in which he did not believe—by an act of mercy—which he had learned never to expect—or by the simple good fortune of a bold gambler, Idris Jarrah found that he was still alive at sunrise. The discovery gave him confidence that he would make a safe exit from Syria, for he knew very well that security arrests were generally made in that autumn hour before dawn when the spirit is at its lowest ebb, and there are few witnesses to incite to violence. In spite of a restless night, he was refreshed enough to make clear decisions. The first was that he would use his Jordanian passport, a well-made document which had survived many inspections at several points of entry. The second was that he would not linger in Amman. He would head straight for

Jerusalem and find himself a safe foxhole in the Old City, where strangers were commonplace.

The decision made, he became calm and leisurely. He took off the rumpled clothes in which he had slept, bathed himself, shaved, taped his pistol to the inside of his calf, dressed himself in clean linen and a fairly well-pressed suit and checked out of the hotel. His car was waiting for him: a vintage vehicle owned by one of the tourist agencies which ran visitors from Damascus to Amman and Petra. He was happy to find that he had companions—an elderly couple from the Midwest of America and a dour-looking Briton in tweeds who chewed on an empty pipe and answered all questions with a scarcely audible monosyllable. Jarrah himself was in no mood for talk; so after a few abortive efforts by the Americans, a dusty silence descended on the ill-matched group.

The journey was a jolting progress through bleached desert and sparse rocky tillage and tiny Biblical villages stirring slowly into life under the rising heat. For half an hour they were caught behind a long convoy of military trucks. They breathed in sand and diesel fumes. Their ears were assaulted by the voluble curses of the driver. Finally, in a wild burst of speed, they passed the convoy and careered around rocky curves until they were slowed to a walking pace by a straggle of sheep. After the sheep they had clear going for another ten miles, only to be caught again behind two canvas-covered trucks laboring up a steep slope and holding relentlessly to the center of the road. No amount of horn blowing or cursing would force them to yield; and, when they topped the rise, they accelerated and ran fiercely downhill, leaving a cloud of blinding dust behind them.

At the Syrian border post, Jarrah had a moment of anxiety lest the long arm of Safreddin should pluck him back; but he and his little group were checked out of the country with the minimum of formalities. When they reached the Jordan side of no man's land, however, Jarrah's heart sank. The place was crawling with armed troops. Heavy vehicles were being shunted on to the side of the road; while cars and taxis were being directed into another lane, where police were checking documents and customs men were burrowing into every car and every piece of luggage. Remembering the pistol taped to his leg and the money stitched into the lining of his brief-case, Jarrah hoped desperately for a friendly face or a sloppy searcher. Remembering Safreddin's arms shipment, he felt faintly reassured; the whole thing could be the result of Safreddin's official tip to the Jordanian security service. If this was so—again the comfortless *if*—then he had little to fear. If not. . . . He composed his moon face into a patient func-tionary's smile and prepared to bluff for his life.

They were tenth in the line of cars and the movement of those ahead was fractional. Now that they were stopped, the air inside the vehicle was hot and fetid. Clutching his brief-case, Jarrah got out of the car and made a great pantomime of moving his cramped legs and breathing in the clean air of Jordan. As he had hoped, his companions climbed out too and they stood in a huddle watching the police and the cus-toms men at work, waiting for their own turn to submit to inspection. Jarrah was more interested in the trucks. These were being searched by the troops who were doing the job swiftly and efficiently, directed by a captain in the uni-form of the Arab Legion. They did not stop at labels and packing. They dumped the cargo like stevedores. They prised open cartons and wooden cases. They unscrewed the bungs of oil drums and thrust long metal skewers into bales of hemp and bags of grain. All the time, guards with automatic rifles blocked the entrance and the exit to the traffic lane, while a sergeant and a corporal made a body search of every truck driver. It was obvious they would take hours to search every truck. It was equally obvious that they were going to spend whatever time they needed.

The cars began to move at last. Jarrah and his party were

checked through passport control with more than the usual
fumbling and mumbling over their documents. Their car was
searched from trunk to bonnet. Even the seats were removed
by the diligent investigators. All their suitcases were opened.
As an afterthought one of the customs men demanded to
see Jarrah's briefcase. He opened it with every show of will-
ingness and even began to take out all the papers, making
voluble explanations as he did so. The official grew quickly
bored, gave him a thankless shrug and walked away.

Finally they bundled themselves back into the car and
drove off. They were half a mile down the road, rounding the
first curves, when they heard the explosions; a series of
thundering blasts that rocked the hills and sent the shock
waves slamming against the faces of the cliffs and the echoes
booming down the defiles.

"Good God!" said the elderly American. "What's that?"

"It sounds like blasting, dear," said his wife placidly.

The Briton took his pipe out of his mouth and uttered his
last words for the day:

"Nonsense, madam!"

But madam did not hear; because the driver had his foot
hard down on the pedal and was driving his rattletrap at
seventy miles an hour towards Amman. He was a Syrian, gun-
shy in hostile territory. Idris Jarrah heard, but said nothing.
He was an experienced saboteur. He knew what a mess you
could make with only one kilo of plastic explosive. He had a
shrewd idea what sort of shambles would be left at the
frontier post and he hoped desperately that he would not be
called to account for it.

DAMASCUS

When Selim Fathalla arrived at his warehouse with Emilie,
there was a surprise waiting for him. Two armed soldiers
stood guard at the gate; a rat-faced civilian was perched in

his office chair smoking a cigarette; and his watchman had disappeared. To his angry demand for an explanation, the civilian offered a shrug and an indifferent piece of advice:

"Why not call Colonel Safreddin? He made the arrangements."

Fathalla picked up the phone and dialed Safreddin's number. It was engaged. He waited five minutes and dialed again. A secretary answered and, when he had identified himself, held him on the line for another five minutes before putting him through to Safreddin.

Safreddin was suspiciously cheerful. "Ah, Fathalla! I was expecting you to call. What can I do for you?"

"I'd like an explanation, Colonel. My office is a private place. I find it occupied by a man whom I do not know. He claims you sent him."

"I did," said Safreddin, amiable as ever. "He should have had the courtesy to show you his credentials."

"I agree. Why the guards?"

"A security measure. We'll take them off this evening."

"That doesn't explain anything."

"I know. I was hoping we could meet this afternoon and talk more privately."

"Name the time, Colonel, I'll be there."

"Shall we say three-thirty? I have to make an important broadcast at two o'clock. You might be interested to hear it —for background."

"On what, Colonel?"

"Current events—and our interpretation of them."

"I'll be sure to listen. Another question—where is my watchman?"

"Oh, the watchman! Yes. I'd almost forgotten. He's being interrogated now."

"Interrogated? Why?"

"I'll explain that too when I see you."

"I'd like to know now. He's an old man, ignorant, almost illiterate. What can he tell you about anything?"

"That's what we're trying to find out, my friend. Perhaps we'll have the answer at three-thirty. You must excuse me now. I'm in conference."

And with that, for all his anger and the fear which it concealed, he had to be content.

The rat-faced fellow sat watching him with thin contempt. "Are you satisfied?"

"No!" Sudden fury blazed in him. He reached across the desk, caught the fellow by his shirtfront and hauled him to his feet. "Now get your backside out of my chair and do what you have to do. Over there in the corner!"

"You'll be sorry for this, Fathalla!"

"Are you threatening me?" His grip tightened on the shirtfront. "Are you?"

Sudden doubt showed in the close-set eyes. "No . . . not threatening. I just thought it was funny."

"It's a very bad joke," said Fathalla softly. "Remember that every moment you're here. Now what do you want?"

"Books of accounts, bank statements, files of orders and deliveries and all your correspondence."

"Give them to him!" Fathalla swung round to Emilie, who stood watching the scene wide-eyed and fearful. "Give him whatever he wants, and make sure that nothing is removed from this office without my consent. Is that clear?"

"Yes, Mr. Fathalla."

Fathalla turned on his heel, strode out of the office and walked into the long dark shed where his merchandise was stored. He was trembling in every limb. When he tried to light a cigarette, it slipped from his fingers. He ground it savagely into the earthen floor with his foot. He leaned back against a stack of hessian bales, closed his eyes and battled to control himself. Safreddin was probing at him now, a savage surgeon hunting for the soft spots and the exposed nerve ends.

He had to be calm. He had to be strong and calculate as cynically and as brutally as the adversary who claimed to be a friend and was acting in all respects like the bitterest of enemies. He looked at his watch. Nine o'clock; five hours to Safreddin's broadcast; six and a half to his meeting with the great man. It was going to be a long wait. He had to keep himself busy.

From a hook on the wall he took down a wooden clipboard and began to take stock of his merchandise. He wished he could make as simple a tally of the odds for and against his own and Emilie's survival.

AMMAN

(World Press International) "Shortly before nine o'clock this morning the Jordan village of Rumtha, a border checkpoint between Syria and Jordan, was rocked by a series of violent explosions. Twenty-three people were killed and eighteen injured, some of them seriously. Several buildings were wrecked by the blast and a number of civilian and military vehicles were destroyed. The border has been closed until further notice and a large security team from Amman has moved in to investigate the incident. The whole area has been sealed off by a roadblock ten miles south and newsmen have been forbidden to proceed farther than this spot. Official reports are vague but the following facts have been established. Acting on information received from an unnamed source that arms were being smuggled into Jordan in Syrian commercial vehicles, security men, customs investigators and a detachment of Arab Legion troops moved into Rumtha in the early hours of this morning. Traffic piled up and all vehicles passing through the checkpoint were closely searched. A consignment of suspect merchandise was found in two trucks marked with the name of a Syrian haulage contractor. It was packed in wooden cases. The officer in charge of the investigation ordered one of the cases to be prised open. There was an immediate explosion and the whole consignment blew up. Automatic rifles and other arms were found among the debris. When the first reports reached Amman, the Syrian Ambassador was summoned immediately to the palace and remained for more than an hour. No communique was issued from the meeting and no comment was forthcoming from either Jordan or the Syrian Embassy. More later. . . ."

DAMASCUS

At two o'clock in the afternoon with Emilie for company and the rat-faced one for hostile auditor, Fathalla switched on the radio in his office. First, there was a long passage of martial music; then an announcer called upon all Syrians to cease work or give over their play, to hear an important statement by Colonel Omar Safreddin, Director of Public Security. There was another burst of music; then Safreddin came on the air. His flat, harsh voice was pitched higher, into the eloquent Koranic mode which he used for all his public appearances.

". . . This very day, while the peaceful citizens of Syria were going about their normal business, two events occurred, almost simultaneously—events which concern the internal security of this country, the safety of its borders and its relationships with its Arab neighbors. There is a connection between the two events. They were both hostile acts. They were both planned by the same enemy and executed with the same ruthless disregard of human life and for the sanctity of national frontiers. . . . The first act was one of blatant aggression, cunningly planned and daringly executed. An Israeli fishing boat deliberately invaded Syrian waters on the Lake of Tiberias. It was followed by an armed Israeli patrol boat. Our gunners, ever watchful to defend our sacred soil, opened fire on the patrol boat which ran aground on a sandbank, again in our territorial waters. By obvious prearrangements Israeli fighter planes were immediately in the air, strafing our gun position, killing two men and wounding three others. Our Syrian fighters took to the air and two of them were shot down inside our frontier. Both pilots were killed. . . . But this is not the end of the history. At the very moment when these battles were in progress, something else was happening, much more sinister, much more bloody in its consequences. Three days ago one of our security agents discovered that an Israeli sabotage team had entered Syria by way of Lebanon and was preparing to begin operations in both Syria and Jordan. They had set up a secret arms dump in the city of Damascus itself and were preparing to ship guns and explosives across the border into Jordan. This was all the information we had. Immediately we sent warnings to the Government of Jordan and asked for their co-operation in uncovering the plot. Unfortunately we were too late to prevent a tragedy. This morning two trucks, owned by a general merchant in Damascus, crossed the border at Rumtha. They were searched and a large quantity of arms and ammunition was discovered. But the Israelis had been brutally clever. They had booby-trapped the packing cases and when they were opened, they blew up. Twenty-three of our Jordanian friends were killed and many more injured. In spite of our best efforts, we were unable to prevent the tragedy. This morning, however, we arrested the leader of the saboteurs. At midday today he was executed. The other members of the group are still at liberty; but we have their names and their descriptions and it will not be long before they are captured. . . . We urge all our citizens to maintain constant vigilance, to report immediately the slightest suspicious circumstances; because only by courage and watchfulness can we protect ourselves against imperialist colonialist aggressors, who have no regard for human life and who are dedicated to the destruction of Syrian independence and the unity of the Arab world. . . ."

There was more and more yet: the long, passionate peroration of a brilliant demagogue, who knew that belief could be imposed by the colorful repetition of a few simple catchwords. But Safreddin the demagogue was not half so brilliant as Safreddin the plotter, the double-thinker, the triple-talker, who had staged his own sabotage against the Hashemites, attributed it to the Israelis and, by a beautiful piece of virtuosity, tied it to a border incident in which the Israelis were at least half culpable.

As the tirade rolled on and on, Fathalla listened, stony-faced, not daring to look at Emilie, and conscious always of the secret amusement of the agent who sat thumbing through the files with contemptuous concentration. He had to think very clearly now. He had to work his way through the maze of Safreddin's thought process and try to determine the motive of his actions. A momentary propaganda triumph? Good —but not enough. A spy scare? Good, too. A suspicious public made an uncomfortable climate for foreign operators. But still not enough. A trap for himself? Not yet. But perhaps a strong inducement to make him a willing servant of Safreddin. The mention of a "merchant in Damascus" had not escaped him. Safreddin had him in a pincer grip. A simple accusation would be enough to hang him as an accessory to the death of twenty-three people. No proof would be needed beyond the fact that the arms had been carried in his trucks. The interrogation of his watchman would produce any kind of document that Safreddin desired. The nonexistent Israeli who had been shot at midday and the nonexistent saboteurs who would shortly be arrested were an obvious warning about his own fate if he refused to cooperate. But cooperate in what? He was still a long way from the center of the maze.

Then he remembered the message he had received the night before from Jakov Baratz. Baratz wanted reports on Syrian troop movements in Galilee and on the possible participation of Iraq in the Defense Pact between Syria and

Egypt. This was the constant key to Safreddin's stage management. He wanted to incriminate Israel as an aggressor, so that he could invoke the aid of the Egyptians, and through them, swing the rest of the Arab world into action against the Jews. . . . It made good sense—good enough at least to give a direction to his talk with Safreddin at three-thirty. But there were still a number of pieces that did not fit the pattern: the Phoenician Bank, the role of the P.L.O., the known desire of Safreddin to get rid of the King of Jordan, and why he had bothered to enlist the aid of an Iraqi like Selim Fathalla, when he could have had safer cooperation from one of his own people. This was the perennial problem of the spy: at a certain moment he was cut off from outside information and was deprived of the opportunity for free discussion with his colleagues. . . .

Safreddin's speech ended on a high, hysterical defiance of the aggressive Jews. The music surged up.

Fathalla switched off the radio. He looked up at Emilie and smiled. "I must say Colonel Safreddin is a very impressive orator."

Emilie nodded agreement. She was in command of herself now, and her answer had just the right tone of sober admiration. "I'm not a Moslem; but those passages from the Koran always touch me."

"A great man!" said the security man with sudden fervor. "The best we have had."

"I've always admired him," said Selim Fathalla. "Do you want any help with those files?"

"Not yet. I'll save my questions till later."

"Just as you like. Miss Ayub will give you any information you need. I'll be back as soon as I've seen the colonel."

"Don't hurry," said Emilie firmly. "I can deal with everything here."

He wanted to reach out and touch her in gratitude, but he dared not. He gave her a curt nod of approval, walked out, got into his car and drove past the two guards at the gate. When he reached the center of the city, he parked the car, slipped into a coffee shop and made a hurried telephone call to Bitar.

"Doctor, this is Ayub." Emilie's name was the codeword for an urgent communication. "I'm still getting those pains in the back. Could I come and see you?"

"Have you been taking the pills?"

"Yes. But they don't seem to be doing me any good. I can't walk properly."

"This afternoon then, at five-thirty. You know my address."

"I know it. Thank you."

Which meant that the meeting would be at four-thirty in the house of a bedridden Syrian priest, whose servant was in her dotage and with whom they sometimes played a harmless game of chess. The priest cherished two faint hopes: that he might convert at least one of his Moslem friends and that the good doctor might one day cure him of Parkinson's palsy. If occasionally they wanted to talk business, it was the least he could do to offer them privacy and a cup of coffee. . . .

Punctually at three-thiry, Fathalla presented himself at Safreddin's office. Somewhat to his surprise, he was ushered immediately into the presence of the great man, who greeted him with effusive courtesy.

"I'm sorry I had to be so short with you this morning. I had a great many things to deal with, as you can imagine."

"I didn't know how many, Colonel—until I heard your speech. Very impressive."

"I'm glad you liked it."

"I was puzzled, of course. I still am."

"By the speech? I thought that it was very clear."

"Perhaps I didn't interpret it the right way. Was I the contractor whose trucks blew up?"

"You were." Safreddin smiled and offered him a cigarette. "Does that distress you?"

"No." He took the cigarette and offered a light to Safreddin. "Except that I've lost two vehicles."

Safreddin leaned back in his chair and laughed immoderately. "You're such a cool fellow, Fathalla. I envy you. I'll have replacements delivered to you tomorrow, from army stores. Is that all that's worrying you?"

"There was only one other thing. My watchman."

"Oh, yes. I think they've finished with him now. You'll be able to see him shortly." He blew a series of perfect smoke rings and watched them drift slowly upwards to the fly-spotted ceiling. "Aren't you curious about what happened?"

"Naturally. But not too curious, Colonel." He leaned on the qualifying word. "You asked for my cooperation. I offered it willingly. If you remember, I told you I wanted a quiet life, with no complications. That's still what I want."

"I remember. I remember that I asked whether you would like to work for me."

"And I agreed to think about it—on certain conditions."

"I remember those too. Do you mind if I ask you a couple of questions?"

"Not at all."

"Do you remember the name of the man to whom the arms were consigned?"

"I never knew it, Colonel. You did not tell me."

"You didn't see it on the crates?"

"How could I? I was with you in my office when they were being loaded. I came out once to attend to the man with the cut hand."

"Of course. I'd forgotten. Anyway it doesn't matter. Another question. Where did you go after you left your warehouse last night?"

"Miss Ayub called for me in my car and we went for a drive out on the Rumtha road."

"Why did you do that?"

"I wanted some fresh air. And I wanted to make love."

Safreddin laughed again, but there was no humor in his eyes. "That's an odd place to make love, when you can—and do—sleep with the girl every night in your own bed."

"Not so odd, Colonel. You have listening devices in my house. I don't want my sex life recorded on tape."

Safreddin considered the answer for a moment, then relaxed and nodded agreeably. "A good point, Fathalla. I should have thought of it. The microphones were removed today as I promised."

"Thank you, Colonel. Now may I ask a question?"

"Yes."

"Do you suspect me of something?"

"Of what could I possibly suspect you, my friend?"

"I don't know. I want to know. That's why I ask."

Safreddin laid the tips of his slim fingers together and touched them to his lips. His answer was gentle, but measured out, parsimoniously, phrase by phrase:

"To me, Fathalla, every man is capable of treachery, if the price is right. I am investigating at this moment a leakage of information which is not unconnected with today's operation in Rumtha. You will notice that I call it an operation, because, although it was planned as something different, I was obliged to change the plans at the last moment. The leak was made through the Lebanon. You are one of a number of men with connections in Lebanon and beyond Lebanon— banking connections, trade connections, personal contacts. Therefore you were a possible suspect. As far as I know you are clean. But I still had to test you. You have a political history; therefore you are a political man. A man can change his politics as he changes his women."

"But you tested me very clumsily, Colonel. That's unlike you."

"And you were shrewd enough to see it, Fathalla. Which was part of the test."

"And what does it prove?"

"That you are sensitive and aware."

"You said yourself I'm a political man. If I weren't sensitive and aware, I'd have been killed in Baghdad. What else does it prove?"

"That you're bold enough to be angry with me."

"Or innocent enough."

"Agreed."

"So where do I stand now?"

Safreddin shrugged and blew more smoke rings. His answer was oddly indifferent. "I've taken the bugs out of your house. I think my auditor will find your files clean. The guards come off your warehouse tonight. Doesn't that speak for itself?"

"I told you, Colonel, I can't live under suspicion. I want to hear it from you."

"What?"

"An affirmation of trust."

"I'll give it to you. Come with me."

They walked in silence down four flights of concrete stairs into the basement of the building. At the end of a long flagged corridor, a soldier stood guard outside a heavy iron door, bolted on the outside.

"Open up!"

The guard shot back the bolt and pushed open the door.

"Come in, Fathalla!"

Fathalla followed him into a small cell lit by a single yellow bulb. On the floor was a pallet bed and, on the bed, a human figure covered with a stained gray blanket. Safreddin folded back the blanket to reveal the face. It was the watchman from the warehouse. He was dead. Fathalla fought back the nausea that choked him.

"Well?" Safreddin's bleak eyes searched his face.

"You tell me, Colonel." His voice was dry and bitter.

"We needed a traitor," said Safreddin calmly. "We found him: an old man with no family and no relatives and no one to care. Just so there's a real body to hang in the sack in Morjan Square, who asks which body it is? . . . You wanted an affirmation of trust. You have it there. We could just as easily have shot you—and we might have made more profit out of it!''

AMMAN

(World Press International) "This afternoon an official spokesman in Amman revealed later facts about Rumtha explosions. Automatic rifles and other weapons recovered from wreckage were identified as Russian, of the type supplied to the Syrian Army. Markings on wooden debris indicate they were consigned to Colonel Badaoui, Commander of Palace Guard in Amman. Jordanians reject Syrian claim, made over Damascus radio, that sabotage was work of Israelis. They claim to have absolute proof that arms shipment was part of complicated Syrian plot for assassination of King Hussein after removal of Royal Palace Guard Commander. Major Khalil, second-in-command of Palace Guard, is under arrest and interrogation for complicity. Strong note of protest delivered this afternoon to Syrian Government. Contents not revealed but understand diplomatic relations with Syria may be broken very shortly. Following for background from same official spokesman but not for attribution. First information on plot was relayed to Jordan by quote prominent banker in Beirut unquote to whom it was sold by member of Palestine Liberation Organization identified by same spokesman as one Idris Jarrah. Further confirmation of Khalil complicity and Jarrah involvement was sent to Jordan from Israel Foreign Office through British diplomatic channels. It is believed Jarrah is presently in Jordan and orders have been issued for his immediate arrest. End of background statement. Final information just to hand. Trucks which carried arms shipment belonged to Syrian merchant Selim Fathalla, who trades constantly with Jordan. Fathalla still at liberty in Damascus. Ends."

DAMASCUS

In the parlor of the Syrian priest, under the mourning eyes of a Byzantine Virgin, Dr. Bitar perched himself on a frayed divan and listened to Fathalla's story. Bitar looked ill. His long, smooth face was a muddy gray; there were heavy pouches under his eyes and lines of strain at the corners of his mouth; but there was still a fire in him, and, when he heard the tale of the old watchman, he burst out into a bitter invective.

"We have become savages again! We, who civilized the Mediterranean after the coming of the barbarians! We, who taught mathematics and philosophy and the healing arts! This is not Islam! Where, in all of it, is the mercy of Allah and the dignity of the sons of the Prophet? This is tyranny, brutal and bloody! It must be ended now!"

"It won't end today or tomorrow," said Fathalla wearily. "And we both know it. Did you hear Safreddin's speech?"

"No. I found two cases of typhoid today. I've been running round trying to dig up enough serum for inoculations, and fighting with the Public Health people to check the local water supply. If it spreads we're in real trouble. . . . What did Safreddin say?"

"It wasn't what he said: it was the genius with which he said it. He could raise an army in the street tomorrow."

"The holy war—a madman's dream! We're pouring out the national income for guns and aircraft and I can't buy serum for twenty people. How does it end? When?"

"I don't know. But there are things I have to know quickly. Why is Safreddin leaning on me? If he knew what I truly am, I'd be dead already."

"I'll tell you why. This is the madness of the old Moloch

who had to be fed with children roasted in his belly. A tyranny demands more and more victims. Not today perhaps. Not next week or next month. But sooner or later, yes! You are on the list, I am too—because each of us, for a different reason, makes a credible traitor. That we are traitors, in fact, has nothing to do with the case. You are an Iraqi, here by courtesy. You have a direct connection with the deaths at Rumtha. Safreddin can throw you into the furnace whenever he needs a spectacle. Me? I'm a known malcontent. I complain because too many children die and there's too much squalid misery in a country I love."

"But Safreddin talks of appointing you to the Ministry of Health."

"He'd be wise to do it. I'd do a better job than anyone they have now. But what would it signify? The higher they push me, the better victim I become."

Fathalla chewed on the thought for a few moments, tracing patterns with his finger in the dust of the tabletop. Then he straightened up. There was a wintry smile in his eyes and on his lips. "I think you're right. So we're at risk. We always have been anyway. At least now we're warned. We daren't have any illusions. Let's talk business."

Bitar levered himself up from the divan and sat bolt upright. His eyes were bright and full of professional interest.

Fathalla went on. "Pass the word to all contacts. We want full information on the present order of battle of the Syrian Army in Galilee and the north. We want constant reports on troop movement and new installations, especially of ground-to-air missiles. We want numbers and locations of Russian fighter aircraft. In the political sector, we need copies of current documents on the Syrian-Egyptian defense pact and the possible participation of Iraq in mutual defense arrangements. All contacts should be warned to tighten security and close any loopholes. Are you clear on that?"

"I'm clear."

"There's one other thing. . . ." He hesitated for a few moments before making the final revelation. "You have to know this. You may have to operate on the knowledge in case of an emergency. I am going to marry Emilie Ayub. She knows who I am and what I do. She knows that you are connected with me. She has the wave lengths and the code for my emergency transmitter. She will use it only if I am caught or immobilized."

There was a long somber silence in the faded room, with its grimy drapes, its tattered furniture and its sad Virgin who had seen the repetitious tragedy of centuries. Bitar sat very still, staring at the patterns which Fathalla had traced in the dust. When he spoke again his voice was rustling and remote, like the whisper of old silk.

"I think you have made a great mistake. I do not know what else you could have done; so I accept it. But the risk to us all is enormous."

"I know that."

"I wonder if you do. Have you thought what a man like Safreddin might do to a woman like Emilie?"

"I've thought about it."

Bitar gave a small despairing shrug. "Then there's nothing more to say. You pay the money; you name the music. Let's get to work!"

Had he been able to hear the judgment passed upon him in the house of the palsied priest, Omar Safreddin would have been vastly amused—and utterly contemptuous of the men who made it: a puling physician, tortured by ills he could never cure, and a rootless peddler from Baghdad who slept with a half-blood whore. What could they know of the high visionary enterprise of building a twentieth-century state on the ruins of a French colony and a province of the Ottoman Empire? What could they know about the vision—larger yet—of Islam restored and purified, of an Arab hegemony,

diverse but dominant, from the Euphrates to the Pillars of
Hercules? He was a prideful man but he had judged himself
more rigidly than any of his critics.

He did not find himself a cruel man; although he was
aware of the pleasures of cruelty as he was aware of the de-
lights of women and the subtleties of male friendship. To
know was one thing, to indulge oneself like a libertine was
quite another. Cruelty was a natural weapon of the ruler.
Women were a tool of the intriguer. Men were stones in the
hand of the strong builder.

He could not think himself a tyrant. He did not exercise
personal power for base satisfactions. But power must be
exercised; else its life-giving energy was dissipated, like water
poured on to the desert and swallowed by the thirsty sands.
The Prophet had forgiven his enemies and made a ten-year
truce with them, sitting under a tree at Al-Hudebiyal. But,
when the truce was broken, the Prophet had taken power into
his hands and mounted the campaign of Kheybar and brought
the Jews into subjection, in which they had remained until
the Caliphate of Omar. As for the exactions of the power
game, there was always a blood price to be paid, even in a
desert feud. He could demand the blood price from others
because he was prepared to pay it himself. He sat high because he was prepared to risk his neck. Even death was
glorious to a believer who understood the true meaning of
the *Surah* which is entitled "Victory." ". . . Say to those
wandering Arabs who were left behind: you will be called
against a people mighty in battle to fight them until they
surrender. If you obey, Allah will give you the reward you
deserve; but if you turn away as you did before, he will
punish you with a painful penalty."

This was his own mission. To fight the Jews, a people already proven in battle; to call together the wandering Arabs
—those who were left behind in the march of history—and
weld them into a mighty host eager for the rewards promised

by the One the Merciful. He had to bring them back to the tremendous simplicities of the Book. He had to teach them that the risk was worth the gain and that it was always expedient for a few to die for the ultimate greatness of the many. So he sat at the open window of his office watching the day descend through a peach-colored sky, and addressed himself to problems urgent and immediate.

On his desk was a memorandum from the Ministry of Foreign Affairs, listing all the accusations made by Jordan over the Rumtha affair. It was not necessary to answer them. No one would believe the answers anyway. In the propaganda game, he who shouted first and loudest always had the advantage. However, it was necessary to determine certain facts and to make swift decisions.

It was also clear that the Jews had prior knowledge of the plot against the King's life and of Major Khalil's part in it. Who had told them? Not Jarrah. Not Chakry. The Jews were too shrewd to do business with such as these. Therefore the information must have come from an agent, planted either in the P.L.O. itself or in his own service. He had had a momentary suspicion of Fathalla, because he had known of the arms shipment and because he had connections with the Phoenician Bank. But Fathalla was too vulnerable to be a spy. He was too clever a trader to sell his life for a few dollars which he would never spend. So? . . .

The thought of traitors working again in his own city, possibly in his own office, made his flesh crawl and set him burning with a slow rage. He was doing a dirty and thankless job. He had staked his whole career on success. If he failed, he could be toppled overnight, by venal politicians or army rebels; he too could end, hung in a sack in the public market. A vague thought stirred at the back of his mind. He forced himself to be calm and dream on it awhile. He smoked one cigarette and then another, sitting at the window and watching the sun go down over the rooftops and minarets of the city. He made a telephone call to the Russian Embassy and talked a long while with the Ambassador. He made a second call to the Director of the Syrian Bank and gave him a series of curt directions. Finally he summoned his secretary and told her to order him a seat on the first available aircraft to Beirut.

SEVEN

Jakov Baratz was at the end of a long and wearisome argument with the Chief of Staff. His patience was wearing thin; and he had to make an actor's effort to maintain his habitual air of detachment.

The Chief of Staff was not so restrained. He was terse and irritable. "For God's sake, man! You've set me up a copybook operation in Hebron. Now you want to confuse the whole issue again."

"Not confuse it, Chaim. To make clear what the issue is. Important things have happened today. We've had a land and air battle with the Syrians. That's headlines in the world press and a row in United Nations. The Syrians have tried to blame us for the massacre at Rumtha. Thank God the Jordanians blame it publicly on the Syrians. . . . Now we're talking of blowing up a Jordan village. . . . It doesn't make any kind of sense to me."

"It makes sense to the Prime Minister and the Cabinet."

"Then I think we've got to show them better sense."

"We're the military. They're the executive. We do as we're told."

"No!" The word came out in a small explosion of anger. "I've never bought that proposition. I won't buy it now.

We're all part of the same establishment. We fought the same battles for the same ends. We've got—for the present at least—what no other country has: a fraternity, a mutual commitment to Israel. The older we get, the bigger we get, the less we're going to have it. But I want to hold it as long as we can. The best way to hold it is to maintain the old Mapai tradition of free speech and communication on every issue—political, religious, economic, military. I don't want the Army to run the country. That makes us all Junkers. But I don't want the Army as a passive instrument of power. Neither do you. If we can't ask legitimate questions in council together, then you can have my resignation."

It was the bluntest statement he had ever made. He was surprised at his own vehemence.

The Chief of Staff was surprised too. He said, "I had no idea you felt so strongly, Jakov."

"Don't you feel the same way?"

"Not quite." The Chief of Staff ran his fingers through his thinning hair. "But I sit in a different chair. In a sense, I'm a politician too. I deal with the ministries every day. I suppose I've adopted some of their attitudes without realizing it."

"Not all of them." Baratz gave him a crooked, friendly grin. "You spoke pretty strongly at our first meeting in Jerusalem. What was it? . . . 'The Army as a propaganda weapon and dead men to keep the living content . . .'?" He relaxed then and threw out his hands in a gesture of apology and appeal. "Look! I'm not a rebel. I have no private ambition in the matter. But we both want the same thing—the best outcome for the country. All I'm asking is another talk with Yuval and, if possible, with the Prime Minister as well. After that we bow to regulation."

"It's a matter of how we ask for it." The Chief of Staff was still dubious. "I'd like Nathan there too. I'd like to present them with the Hebron plan, which would show

everybody that we're good servants. Then we can hit them
with the political arguments. Would you be ready for that?
And when?"

"I'm ready now. I'd like to talk tomorrow if we could—
while today's events are clear in everyone's mind. Could
you arrange that?"

"I think so. I'm leaving for Jerusalem in half an hour."

"I'll follow you up. If we're both on the spot, it makes
everything less formal. If it helps to arrange the meeting,
tell them I'm hoping to hear from Damascus on the Rumtha
affair. If my man reports on schedule, I should be able to
report at the meeting."

"Good!" He stood up and smoothed the creases out of his
tunic. "One other thing, Jakov. . . ." He broke off, doubtful
of the effect of his words.

Baratz prompted him. "What, Chaim?"

"I know you have a personal problem at the moment. It
doesn't show in your work. It shows in you. You're one of
the most controlled men I know; but it shows. I don't know
what I'd do if I had this kind of family situation. I do know
you can't bear it alone—forever. If you decided to make any
kind of—of adjustment, I wouldn't blame you."

"It hasn't come to that yet. I hope it won't. But thanks
anyway. I'll see you in Jerusalem."

They shook hands and Baratz walked back to his own
office with a social absolution in his pocket and the knowledge that he wanted desperately to use it. He looked at his
watch. Ten minutes to seven. His driver could get him to
Jerusalem by eight-thirty. He called Yehudith and invited
her to dine with him at nine. She was so eager that he felt
a sudden pang of guilt and added a rider to the invitation.

"I have to call in at the hospital to see Hannah and Franz
Lieberman. Would you mind if I asked Franz to join us?"

"Why not. . . . He's a darling old man. I love him."

"Where would you like to eat?"

"Why not here? It's a free meal and the service is good."

"Can I bring anything?"

"Yourself—and the drinks."

"It's done. See you at nine. Shalom."

Another call to Franz Lieberman and the threesome was arranged; the guilt was laid, temporarily at least, to rest. But as he drove, in the gathering dark, through the farmlands and the black clefts of the pinewoods, his conscience began to itch again.

Conscience? . . . A Christian word that had no place in the Mosaic tradition. There was Jahweh and the law of Jahweh, clear down to the smallest tittle of ritual and moral prescription. There was the one hand and the other hand, and the wise rabbi to show you how you might walk justly in between. But if, at a moment when you needed him most, when the ovens began to smoke, Jahweh was nowhere to be found, what became then of the Law and the Prophets with their empty promise and the Torah with its sanctions —so trifling against the sanctions imposed for the crime of being a man?

The sanctions were so horrendous that it seemed a madness to relate them to any kind of Divine plan. You were conceived without consent, wrenched whimpering into an alien universe, with your sentence already written in the palm of your helpless hand: a cancer will eat your guts; a fanatic with an ax will cut off your head; a tiger, escaped from a village circus, will devour you; a drunken fool will mow you down with an automobile; you will live, smiling and loquacious, until a dutiful idiot drops a hydrogen bomb in your backyard.

The sentence once passed, there was no mitigation, no commutation, no amnesty. There was only deferment. There was only time—'a time to plant and a time to reap, a time to weep and a time to laugh! . . .' There was all too little time to forget and all too much in which to remember.

. . . And in spite of it all, the miracle of man was repeated every hour of every day. Doomed man still managed to preserve the sacred illusion of immortality, cherishing it as Israel once cherished the Ark of the Covenant. Man, vilified by abject poverty, deformed by monstrous suffering, still managed to maintain a dignity, like a violated temple in a vast and barren desert. Man, debased by tyranny, still dreamed of justice; dispensed it, too, in faltering and uncertain fashion. Man, doomed to die, still planted apple trees, whose fruits he would never eat, raised giant cities for other men to live in, stretched upward to a cold moon and secret planets in a hostile space. Even the hedonist made his own defiance of the sorry bargain of life—sweet wine poured out to absent gods, soft kisses spent on golden girls before they withered into toothless crones. His own stern stoicism was another kind of defiance; but he had the uncomfortable feeling that it was the emptiest gesture of all. The believers were the lucky ones. They made a mockery of the death sentence, like the bull-leapers of ancient Crete, convinced that, one day, one last somersault would project them out of the fraying envelope of flesh into a pacific eternity of union with the One who was concealed under the mask of the Many.

But belief was a gift, like poetry or divination or the wonderful imagination of a happy child. If you had not the gift—or if you lost it—you were thrust back on reason. Noblest of the faculties, said the old Greeks; but no key to the mystery and the paradox and the tragedy of the human condition. On the contrary, reason could become the executioner's ax; reason could become an atomic trigger . . . unless the reasons of the heart were spoken to protest the tragic nonsense of human syllogisms.

Which left Jakov Baratz, lonely and troubled, riding the upland road into the Jerusalem corridor, a hungry lover, pondering the risks and the traps of love—for Yehudith, for himself, for Selim Fathalla, who was already a risk, and for Hannah, who might—just might—wake one day from her sad enchantment, and find no one there to greet her.

When he reached the hospital, she was asleep—drugged, Franz Lieberman told him, because she had taken to wandering at night through the wards and corridors, a blank-faced catatonic on a fruitless pilgrimage. Even in repose the marks of her affliction were visible. Her skin was dull. There was a coarseness in her features and in her slack hands. She was aging quickly, as an animal aged. An animal form was already imposing itself upon her once-beautiful face. When he kissed her, he felt a sudden revulsion that made him feel ashamed and unworthy.

He asked Franz Lieberman, "How long can this go on?"

Lieberman spread his hands helplessly. "Years, maybe."

"Is there any hope?"

"In my business you have to hope, always. I want to see how she might react to the lysergic acid group."

"Does she suffer?"

"Not too much. Total withdrawal is a total rejection of reality which includes the saving reality of suffering. It's a kind of induction of death, without the final mercy of dying. If I could find one thing that would make her react, even for a second . . . but I haven't found it."

"Let's have dinner, Franz."

"I hope your friend is a good cook. I'm sick of this diet."

"I guarantee it."

"That's already one mercy," said Franz Lieberman. "We should be grateful."

As they drove through the nighttime city towards the white house of Yehudith Ronen, Baratz felt a poignant need to open himself to the old man, so brusquely wise, so tender for the sick minds who were entrusted to him; but he could not find the right words to begin the revelation; he could claim no right to lay another burden on one who already carried so many. Franz Lieberman was a healer; to make him an arbiter of sexual morals would be to invite his contempt. Franz Lieberman had his own code, summed up in the old proverb: "Take what you want, said God. Take it and pay for it!" To which he always added an acidulous little tag: "But you have to pay with your own money. So check your credit before you pick up the banana." For the weak and the foolish he had a fantastic tolerance. For the selfish he had a brutal mockery: "Cry into your own pillow, friend! Cure your own bellyache! And the next time don't be so greedy!" . . . So there was no easy shriving for the guilts of Jakov Baratz; no salve for his self-inflicted wounds. For which cockeyed reason, he was gayer at dinner than Yehudith had ever known him. He told wild stories, played the mimic and the clown, sang the old sabra songs and flirted openly with Yehudith, while Franz Lieberman looked on, sage and smiling, hoping that something might be cured and no one too much hurt by the *kinderspiel*.

Their play ended, as children's games always do, in the soft bittersweet melancholy of fatigue. They were unwilling, as children are, to leave one another. They were reluctant to step out of the reassuring circle of light into the dark solitude of sleep. So they played another game: "It's early; don't go yet; hold back sleep; hold back loneliness; hold back the so-doubtful tomorrow." Their talk took on another color. It became a questioning, a tentative exposure of the fearful self to other selves who always seemed so much more confident. Baratz told them of the debate into which he must enter when morning came and of the doubts that plagued him, at a time when he must claim authority against those who had more authority than he. He summed it all up in a single question to Franz Lieberman:

"What is it, Franz . . . what is it that pushes us always to the point where our own life seems to depend on the death of another man, where our own trees will not grow unless we ravage the garden of the man next door?"

The old man seemed to absorb the question like a sponge soaking up water. He dilated with it painfully as if he were bursting with thoughts he could not express. The light shone like an aureole on his white hair and made dark shadows and high bright peaks on his troubled face. He did not speak for a long while. It was as if he were obsessed with visions, filled up with prophecy for which he was denied an utterance. At last he answered, slowly and uncertainly:

"I ask myself the same question every day. I lie awake wrestling with it. Many of my patients are sick because of the terror of it. There has to be an answer, else all man's life and all man's effort is reduced to a nonsense."

"That's the frightening thing," said Yehudith. "The absurdity of it all. You think you've made a sensible pattern, then it turns into an obscene jumble."

Franz Lieberman gave her a swift, shrewd look. "Why do you call it obscene?"

"Because that's what it is. One moment you see the human image clean and strong like a Greek statue—the next moment it's defaced and twisted out of all recognition. Walk two hundred meters from my garden and you'll step on a mine and be blown to pulp. But people put the mine there. People like us. We say we're builders, lovers, creators—but we're destroyers too, a pin prick under our skins. I get my name from a woman who made a man drunk and cut off his head."

There was so much self-mockery in her tone that Baratz was shocked; but the old man sat quietly weighing the bitter words and his own gentle answer. "I know what you mean. . . . Nobody has ever yet explained evil out of the world. I have patients who are literally mad with malice. It has become the focus of their whole lives, so that there is no room for the simplest decency to another human being. They make me believe in the old Biblical stories of diabolic possession— Saul striking at David with his spear in a repeated madness of jealousy and hate. . . . But there is good, too, child. I have a little nurse from Algeria who walks these same people in the garden and soothes them with her talk and her touch, as David soothed Saul with his music. Even though sometimes they have had to be restrained from hurting her, she still comes back smiling to try again."

"You make me feel ashamed."

"No. . . . There's no shame. Each one of us is a battle-ground between good and evil."

"I didn't think psychiatrists believed in evil."

Baratz said it with a grin, but Franz Lieberman chose to take him quite seriously. "Only the fools deny it. The ancients were right when they associated religion with the healing arts. It's one of the sad defects of modern medicine that we've become mechanics. Some of us are so specialized that we forget that the impact of disease on the human psyche is sometimes more lethal than the disease itself. . . . Illness like poverty can ennoble some. In others it breeds a destructive fear and resentment. . . ."

"And that's the evil you're talking about?" asked Yehudith Ronen.

"That's part of it. I can't define the whole. But I think that real evil consists in putting so high a price on the self that you will destroy everything else to satisfy it."

"So you equate evil with the will to survive?" It was Baratz's question and he pressed it strongly. "Don't we all want to survive—whatever the cost?"

"No!" Lieberman answered him strongly. "That's the difference between good and evil—how much you're prepared to pay for survival. Dishonor? Treachery? The killing of a child? A blasphemy against the dignity of man? A rejection of the God you worship—if you have one?"

"But who sets the price, Franz? Who draws the hairline? And why is one man's right another man's wrong? That's the real tragedy of the human condition. We never know for certain. Play all the rules, give homage to every commandment and every counsel in the Book, you still come to the point where you don't know."

"And you still have to decide," added Yehudith softly. "Otherwise you stop living. The minute you decide, you have conflict and dissension, because someone else—someone you love maybe—has decided the opposite. What happens then?"

"You compromise, if you can."

"How do you compromise," demanded Baratz harshly, "when you're looking down the barrel of a gun?"

"Unfortunately," said Franz Lieberman softly, "we never compromise until we realize that the man who presses the trigger and the man he kills are the same person."

"I don't understand that."

"Let me try to explain. I think—all my experience confirms me in the belief—that the root of dissension is the struggle of the individual to discover, affirm and maintain his personal identity against all that threatens or appears to threaten it. . . . The struggle begins at the moment of birth. The tiny human animal is set adrift in a strange and hostile ambience. He is no longer comfortable in the warm fluid of the womb. His nourishment is no longer automatic. He is subject to heat and cold, to hunger and pain, to the eccentric attentions of other human beings, whom he knows only by touch and smell, by the fact that they bring him comfort or discomfort. From that first tragic moment he finds that his desires and demands are thwarted, that he is forced, on the one hand, to accommodate himself and, on the other, to assert himself with his feeble resources against those who are stronger than he. Even before he knows, before he knows that he knows, he is in conflict. He has begun his dialectic with life, an argument that will last until the day he dies."

"Are you saying," asked Yehudith Ronen softly, "that he is doomed to go wrong always, without knowing?"

"I didn't use the word *wrong*." As he warmed to the subject he spoke more freely and confidently. "I say that he is doomed to conflict and that in every conflict there are a large number of casualties. A few end up in mental institutions. Many, if not all of the others, end with some kind of handicap; but in spite of the handicap they arrive at a reasonable equilibrium. The problem is that the earliest fight for identity centers upon the self, the weak self, the ignorant self, the vulnerable self. It takes a long time and much painful education before the *I* understands that it cannot survive without a *thou*. It takes a much longer time for the collective *I*—the tribe, the nation, the state—to recognize that the collective *thou* is necessary to it. Even in this age, when we are sending rockets to the moon, we do not recognize that when we upset a natural order, when we scatter insecticides, when we pollute the air with radiation and noxious gases, we are condemning ourselves to a later penalty. . . . Look at this city, Jerusalem! It is divided by a wall and on the wall are guns. We cannot pass freely from one side to the other. But microbes can pass and viruses, the germs of typhoid and cholera. So we are forced, in spite of ourselves, to cooperate on mutual sanitation. Why can't we extend the cooperation further? Because the *we* and the *they* still believe that other intangible things are necessary to our identity: sovereignty, possession of this or that shrine, occupancy of a foot of barren earth, religious or ethnic tradition. . . . We are still children, squabbling over an apple, tearing at each other, while the apple lies filthy in the dust." He broke off and turned to them smiling a little sadly. "It's late and we can't change the world tonight. Besides, why spoil a good dinner? I'm going home."

"I'll drive you back," said Jakov Baratz.

"No." He was very firm about it. "I like to walk. I like this time when the stars are out and children are asleep and even the sentries on the wall are too tired to care. It's a hopeful hour. We all need hope. Walk me to the gate and let me go."

They stood together at the gate and watched him striding down the track, through the tenements, past the barbed wire and up again on to the holy mountain. Then, hand locked in hand, they walked back into the garden and kissed in the shadow of the secular trees.

"I love you, girl," said Jakov Baratz.

"And I you, Jakov. Stay with me."

"I want to—God knows. But Golda is here. And Adom's shadow too. Let's wait."

"Are you afraid, Jakov?"

"Yes."

"Of what?"

"Myself mostly. I want to come to you whole—not split in pieces as I am now."

"I don't care how you come."

"You'll care later. And hate me. I'll hate myself."

"Because of Hannah?"

"And other things."

"You want love—and absolution too."

"If I can get it—yes."

"You ask too much, Jakov. What if there's no absolution?"

"Then I want time."

She thrust him away angrily and laughed in his face. "O God! The reluctant lover!"

He rounded on her, savage and bitter. "Don't bitch me, girl! Don't ever bitch me like this again. I can buy Rumanian whores in Tel Aviv for a bad dinner and a bottle of champagne. A couple of days ago you cried on my shoulder because you married a sad tomcat. You'll be quit of him soon. I want to marry you. Let's have a marriage that mends us both."

"Marriage or not, just love me! For the rest I don't care."

"But I care! Tomorrow and every day after men will live or die because of what I am and do. I made one mistake. She's up there in the Hadassah hospital, deaf, dumb, blind and turning into a cabbage! I daren't make another."

"Don't go like this, Jakov—please!"
"Then for God's sake let's not fight any more!"

DAMASCUS

When the servants had gone to bed Selim Fathalla with
Emilie at his side searched every room of his living quarters.
It took him nearly two hours to find the bug: a tiny transmitter, the size of a large olive, plaited into the knot of the
silken tassel which hung from the copper lamp above his
bed. It was a highly sophisticated piece of Russian equipment, which would pick up every word spoken in the large
room. He held it in the palm of his hand debating what to
do with it. He was tempted at first to send it back to Safreddin with a humorous note. The temptation was easy to resist.
Safreddin had a sense of humor; but he had no taste for
jokes directed against himself. To prove him a liar would be
an intolerable indignity. So he wrapped the transmitter in
an old shirt and stuffed it among his clothes in the lowest
drawer of his bureau. Later he might send it to Baratz, who
had a professional interest in such curiosities.

Now he was free to devote his attention to Emilie, on
whom the events of the day had had a strange effect. She
was no longer gay. In a night and a day she seemed to have
grown into a matron, so assured and calculating that he felt
vaguely patronized. She was tender, still; but the tenderness
was bestowed and not awakened. She sat on the edge of the
bed and began to undress, questioning him the while, like
an advocate whose rights in the court were no less than those
of the client.

"Why did you bring me into all this, Selim?"

"It was safer."

"For you or me?"

"For both of us."

"Why did you take on this work?"

"I used to like it. There was enough service in it so that I could respect myself. There was enough excitement so that I didn't have to think too much."

"About your wife?"

"And myself."

"What happened between you?"

"Nothing. That was the problem. Nothing happened. It should have. We were both in love. But it didn't."

"Are you still in love with her?"

"No. I love you."

"And what happens with us that's different?"

"Don't ask me to put it into words."

"I want to know, Selim. I must know."

"Why?"

"Because one day I'm a lover; and I'm very happy. Today I'm engaged to be married; and all of a sudden there's danger. The house is full of ears. An old man is killed in a cellar; an old man who used to bring me coffee when I arrived at work. I used to love this city. Overnight it's an enemy place. There has to be something to make it worthwhile."

"Just now, there's only me."

"And when we're alone and loving, that's enough. Truly it is. But when you are about this—this business of yours, I'm desperate. I don't care about plots and politics. I want a safe home and a garden and children and friends to talk to in the street. I want to know that tomorrow will be as calm as today. . . ."

"I'll give you that. I promise. Very soon."

"Did you promise it to your wife too?"

All of a sudden he felt deathly tired and sick of the sad persistent questioning. An angry retort rose to his lips, but he choked it back, remembering that he could no longer afford the luxury of anger in his own house. He turned away and walked to the window, throwing the shutters wide so that the moonlight streamed into the room and the dry cold air from the desert fanned his face. A calm tomorrow! . . . He had promised it so glibly out of an unendurable emptiness. And yet he had to keep the promise bright until the day came to fulfill it. He had to squeeze out a daily drop of comfort, lest love dry up and the lover regret the bargain to which he had committed her. Try as he would he could find no words to answer her and the old fear of impotence rose up to haunt him again.

She was still waiting, unhappy and resentful. "Why can't you answer, Selim?"

The words came then, sour with weariness. "The answer's yes. I promised it to my wife. I failed her. The day came when I couldn't even be a man with her. Then . . . it just had to end. But here, with you, I'm a man again. I do a man's work with my head laid on the butcher's block every day. . . . Now let's have some peace."

She came to him, running and clung to him, tense and passionate in the shaft of moonlight. "I'm sorry, Selim. Truly I am! I didn't mean to hurt you. I'm just so afraid!"

"Why not, little one?" His lips brushed her dark hair. "It's wise to be afraid. But you have to beat the fear. You have to spit in its eye every day. Otherwise you end huddled in a corner, screaming at shadows."

"Let's go to bed."

"Not yet. We have to call Tel Aviv at twenty minutes to midnight. They have to know everything that's happened today. They want a report on you too."

"Why me?"

"I've put you on the payroll of Israel. They want to know who you are."

"And what will you tell them?"

"The truth."

"When we marry, will I have to become a Jewess?"

"Only if you want it."

"What would you want?"

"Just a happy wife. . . . Now put on a dressing gown and let's draft the message."

"I'll make some coffee first."

"Good girl."

"But, Selim . . ."

"What?"

"Promise me one more thing."

"If I can."

"Don't ever let Safreddin take me."

"It will never happen, little one. That's one promise I *can* make."

Outside a tiny bat flew dipping and wavering through the silent garden; the water spilled musically from the wet mouth of the lion and the Crescent of Islam gleamed silver on the peak of the white minaret.

BEIRUT

At ten-thirty the following morning, Colonel Omar Safreddin paid a visit to Nuri Chakry at the Phoenician Bank. Because he was an important man, if not a very rich one, Chakry received him with more than usual urbanity and served him iced lemonade in the Moorish Pavilion. They chatted amiably for twenty minutes, sidling round a dozen irrelevant subjects, each as patient as the other in the rhetorical overtures. Then Safreddin began to stipulate the terms of his business argument.

"As I understand it, Mr. Chakry, the Syrian Bank and your own have a mutual arrangement to act as correspondents in transactions between our two countries."

"That's right. We find it a valuable and very pleasant association."

"We too. For this reason we are seeking your help in a matter of some delicacy."

"What can we do for you, Colonel?"

"You understand that Syrian citizens are permitted to maintain foreign bank accounts only with the consent of the Finance Ministry and subject to surveillance and control by the same Ministry."

"I understand that."

"The Directorate of Public Security and the Finance Ministry are now conducting a joint check on all Syrians with foreign accounts."

"For any special reason, Colonel?"

"For reasons of national security."

"Lebanon is a free market for currency transactions, Colonel. That market depends on confidence and secrecy. We do not like to be drawn into police matters."

"This is not a police matter, Mr. Chakry. Lebanon is a member of the Arab League. Her Government is pledged to support the League in mutual security arrangements."

"And this request comes under the heading of mutual security?"

"It does."

"If you could be more explicit, Colonel."

"We suspect that a new group of Israeli agents may be operating inside the borders of Syria. We have reason to believe that they may be financed through an account in the Phoenician Bank or in another bank in Lebanon. We should like you to permit an examination of all Syrian accounts on your books. I have the list here. It is not too long."

"And who would make the examination, Colonel?"

"I would. Today if possible."

Nuri Chakry pondered the proposal with theatrical deliberation. He poured himself a glass of lemonade and sipped it slowly. He put down the glass and dabbed at his lips with a silk handkerchief. Then he fluttered a regretful hand. "I'm afraid I can't do it, Colonel. It would be against the policy and interest of the bank. It would damage us with clients much larger and much more profitable than the Syrian Bank."

"I think you're already damaged, Mr. Chakry." Safreddin's admonition was very gentle. "You are about to lose two of your biggest depositors. I may be able to help you to hold a third who is already considering withdrawal. I may be able to do even more—persuade this client to tide you over your coming difficulties."

"*May* is not a banker's word, Colonel."

"I'll change it then. I *can* help you. I spoke last evening with the Russian Ambassador. He might be induced to recommend to Moscow a substantial support for the Phoenician Bank."

"And why would he do that?"

"Because the Russians have a vested interest in Syrian progress."

"But this is Lebanon, Colonel."

"Which is still committed to the Arab League."

"So we are dealing with high politics?"

"Very high, Mr. Chakry."

"That's a dangerous field for a banker."

"But you are already in the field, Mr. Chakry. Through a man called Idris Jarrah."

"I am out of it now. I was well paid for a service to friendly clients."

"You can make new friends—and be paid better. Call Damascus now. Speak with the Russian Ambassador. He'll confirm what I've told you."

"I'm sure he will, Colonel. But let's be precise. You're offering only good offices—not hard cash."

"It's hard to put a price on friendship, Mr. Chakry. But a man without friends is very poor. Your airline, for instance, flies into Damascus every day. It's a very profitable run. The goodwill of local authorities is very important to you."

"A sound point, Colonel."

"I'll make another one. Sooner or later—probably sooner —we shall be forced to a final confrontation with the Jewish State. On that day all true Arabs will stand up to be counted. If it were known that an Arab banker deliberately withheld information about Israeli espionage, he might find himself in an uncomfortable position."

"Bankers always survive, Colonel. And they never do business under threat."

"My banking experience is very limited. I'm a poor official. Forgive me."

"However, on the basis of friendship—and the good offices you described—we might bend our practice for you."

"Thank you, Mr. Chakry."

"If you don't mind I'll put you in the hands of my personal assistant, Mr. Matheson. He'll provide you with all the documents you need and assist you to analyze them. He's an American. It would be wiser therefore if your reasons for the check were phrased somewhat differently . . . if it were related only to the directives of the Finance Ministry and not to espionage."

"A good suggestion. Thank you."

When the request was put to him, Mark Matheson was startled. He was accustomed to the novel services which the bank rendered to wealthy clients, but a breach of secrecy— for the Syrians in particular—was somehow shocking to his confused conscience. He made a sharp objection. "I don't like this, Mr. Chakry. It looks like a direct breach of contract with our clients."

Safreddin answered for him, sedulously polite. "Mr. Chakry and I have already discussed this question, Mr. Matheson. We recognize the sacredness of the contract between banker and client. But your contract with Syrian citizens is a special one. They bank with you subject to government consent and control. What we are doing now is an exercise of our right of control."

"That's quite true, Mark." Chakry was disarmingly casual. "You don't have to worry."

He didn't want to worry either. He had made his point, like a perfect servant. He was absolved from further responsibility—even though he knew that Safreddin's answer was only half true and that Syria had no legal jurisdiction in Lebanon and that to allow her such jurisdiction was more than a breach of faith. It was in fact a diminution of sovereignty and it stank of conspiracy. But what was one conspiracy more or less in a town full of hucksters and percentage men? He submitted with a shrug and took Safreddin to his office to open the books for him.

When they had gone, Nuri Chakry sat at his desk fondling his imperial talisman and reviewing his own position. In the good days, before the rats began chewing at the roof trees of his house, he would have dismissed Safreddin with a shrug and a veiled insult. Now he must bend to him—for a worthless promise and an open threat—just as he must bend to Aziz and Taleb and all the other conniving fools whom he despised so heartily. But Safreddin had presented him with an interesting thought. The Russians might well bail him out; even if they would not do it for love of Safreddin and his threadbare administration.

A bank with full trading rights in Lebanon, an airline, majority holdings in key enterprises, these were interesting bait for a great power, committed already to a Socialist Arab bloc. If Safreddin had spoken the truth, they were already sniffing at the bait; but to hook them before the end of the month was another problem. A firm offer from American interests might turn the trick. But the Americans were playing a waiting game and it was always hard to set up an auction in a dull market. How to begin? . . . How to begin without committing himself and destroying the air of bold confidence upon which his final gamble depended?

Matheson might be the starting point. His trip to Switzer-

land had frayed him at the edges, but he still had presence
and respect. Pump a little more confidence into him and he
might be able to lay the groundwork for a competitive deal.
But Matheson was convinced, or had persuaded himself that
he was convinced, that there was already a white rabbit waiting to pop out of the hat. It would be dangerous to destroy
that conviction too soon. On the other hand. . . .

The intercom buzzer sounded. He flipped the switch and
answered, "Chakry. What is it?"

"This is Mark. Our friend Safreddin is asking for photostats of all these Syrian accounts. What do I tell him?"

"Let him have them."

"What?" A startled squawk from the box. "That's very
dirty pool. How do we justify it to the clients?"

"We don't. They're Syrian subjects."

"I don't like it at all."

"Do it, Mark. It's my decision. I'll explain later."

"It had better be a good explanation."

"It will be."

He cut the switch and sat back in his chair, smiling with
satisfaction. Matheson was angry. A weak man angry was
easy to manage. All he needed now was a well-constructed
story. He picked up a pencil and began to sketch the plot.

JERUSALEM, JORDAN

On the same morning, in the Intercontinental Hotel, in a
comfortable room that looked across the Hebron valley to
the huddle of old Jerusalem, Idris Jarrah ate a leisurely
breakfast and read the morning papers. He was in no hurry
to get up; he had, as yet, nowhere to go. The papers carried a
full account of the sabotage at Rumtha, accompanied by a set
of rather bloody photographs of the victims. There was also
a report of the arrest of Major Khalil and certain members of
the Palace Guard on charges of conspiracy against the throne.

His own name was mentioned too; and loyal citizens of
Jordan were offered a reward for information leading to his
arrest in connection with the Rumtha affair. There was fortunately no photograph and the description was vague. So
long as he did not circulate in the city, where a sharp policeman might recognize him, he was fairly safe. The Intercontinental Hotel was a new and modish caravanserai, built by
an American airline, to accommodate businessmen and pil-
grims from the Bible Belt, and sabbatical scholars and group
tours and peripatetic widows, none of whom could possibly
be interested in a moonfaced little man with a borrowed
name and a Greek passport. For a time at least he could
eat well and sleep soundly while he thought out his exit
arrangements.

These, unhappily, were a little complicated. He was not
short of money. He had ten thousand dollars of unexpended
P.L.O. funds in his briefcase. Once he was safely out of the
country he could call upon a hundred thousand more and
have it transferred immediately and secretly to a bank in the
country of his choice. There were only two ways for him to
get out of Jordan. One was by air from the Jerusalem airport. On the face of it this was much the simpler. He had
simply to buy a ticket, present himself at the passport barrier and have himself stamped out of the country like any
normal tourist. There was, however, a catch. The security
police were always active at airports. They had his description and by now they must have had a copy of his photograph
either from Cairo or through Damascus.

The safer way was to join a party of tourists crossing at
the Mandelbaum Gate into Israel. Neither Jordan nor Israel
wanted to bother the travelers who brought them goodwill
and foreign exchange; and, once an exit permit was granted,
the border formalities were minimal. A disapproving Jordanian checked you out. A smiling Israeli waved you in. And
there was a certain humor in the vision of Idris Jarrah being

welcomed back officially into the land of his fathers on a
Greek passport. But there was a catch here too. You had to
apply to the Jordanians for the exit permit. The application
had to be made either through your own consulate or
through a recognized tourist agency; and there was a manda-
tory waiting time of forty-eight hours. To apply to the Greek
consulate was manifestly impossible. Idris Jarrah spoke Arabic, good English and passable French. He had no Greek at
all. So he had to apply through the travel agency and try to
hook himself on to a tourist group, the larger and more
polyglot the better.

He finished his coffee and tossed the papers aside. He got
out of bed, shaved, bathed, dressed himself in clean linen
and a suit newly pressed by the valet. Then he flung the window open, breathed in the warm dry air and stood looking
out over the valley to the city walls and the vast cupola of the
Dome of the Rock.

A new thought presented itself to him. A new risk but a
comforting insurance. He knew this place like the palm of
his hand—every warren in the city, every defile in the hills,
every frontier post and patrol area. This was his own campaign territory and if all else failed he would be willing to
try the crossing on foot, at night, like any normal smuggler
or saboteur. He had plotted twenty crossings for the maraud-
ers of the P.L.O. He ought to be able to arrange a safe one
for himself. But this was all by way of last resort. So much
better to walk in, openly, to Israel, take a taxi for Lod airport and fly out in state to Athens, Rome or Paris. He amused
himself with a mental picture of Idris Jarrah, rich and secure,
sitting on the Champs Elysées watching the girls go by.

He heard a sudden clatter of traffic: the roar of motorcycles
at full throttle, the whine of jeep engines, the rumble of
trucks. He could not see the vehicles because they were hidden by the shoulder of the Mount of Olives. The noise grew
louder and a few moments later six armed cyclists in the

uniform of the Arab Legion swung into the drive of the hotel. They were followed by four jeeps, each mounted with a machine gun and manned by a driver, a gunner and a soldier with an automatic rifle. After the jeeps came two trucks full of infantry. Within a minute the garden and the entrance to the hotel were swarming with troops.

A cold hand closed round Idris Jarrah's heart. He stood, like a stone man, watching the soldiers disperse to their posts, until the whole hotel was surrounded with guns.

JERUSALEM, ISRAEL

"I like it. I like it very well." The Defense Minister smiled a benediction at his faithful servants of the Army and Air Force. "My compliments, gentlemen. It's a textbook exercise, beautifully documented. Wouldn't you agree, Aron?"

The Prime Minister agreed—in a gray and neutral fashion. Then he asked:

"When would you be ready to mount the operation?"

"Any time from now," said the Defense Minister happily. "On twenty-four hours' notice."

"The document says twelve hours, Yuval." The Chief of Staff corrected him mildly. "We have to be ready to move quickly if the disposition of Jordanian troops in the Hebron area changes in our favor."

"As of this morning," added Jakov Baratz, "it has changed. The King is making a visit to Jerusalem. He is due to arrive later this afternoon. The Pakistani delegation arrives tomorrow evening. The whole thing has been timed to reassure the West Jordanians after the Rumtha sabotage. Because of the presence of the King, the Arab Legion support company in the target sector has been withdrawn to Jerusalem. If you decide to strike, I suggest that tomorrow morning or the morning after would be the time to do it."

"*If* we decide? . . ." The Defense Minister overacted his

surprise. "I thought we were already agreed on the operation."

"Not quite." The Prime Minister slid into the discussion
like a great gray seal. "Nathan here quite rightly wants a
final examination of the political issues. These have been
complicated by the military action in Galilee and by the
sabotage at Rumtha, which the Syrians have loudly attributed
to us."

"Shouldn't we discuss these in Cabinet?" asked the Defense Minister pointedly. "And let the service chiefs get on
with their own business?"

"Now that we have them here, why not let us have the
benefit of their opinions?" The Prime Minister was beginning to be tetchy.

The Defense Minister submitted with obvious reluctance.
"Just as you wish, of course."

The Foreign Minister coughed, adjusted his spectacles and
shuffled his notes. He was a precise man and he hated to be
hurried. He had the air of a pedant, but he was a sharp and
quite ruthless debater with a whole armory of tricks and surprises. His opening was characteristic:

"A question to Yuval and Chaim. If we had a war tomorrow, or in three months' time with the Egyptians, the Jordanians and the Syrians ranged against us, would we win or
lose?"

"We would win," said the Defense Minister flatly.

"Provided," said the Chief of Staff, "provided we made the
first air strike and took out the enemy aircraft on the ground."

"Agreed," said the man from the Air Force.

"There's another proviso," said Jakov Baratz, "that we
fight a fast war and not a war of attrition. If we can't win in a
month, we're in trouble."

There was a murmur of agreement round the table. The
Foreign Minister put his next question:

"Given a fast and successful campaign, what does it get us?"

"In terms of territories?" The Defense Minister numbered them on his fingers. "All of Sinai at least. It could get us all of West Jordan, the Bethlehem-Hebron bulge, old Jerusalem and the hills of western Galilee. Maybe a little more."

"A lot more," said the Chief of Staff. "A million and a half Arabs against our own population of two and three-quarter millions. A social problem, a food problem and a police problem of the first magnitude."

"Plus the chance of a third world war." Baratz added the wintry afterthought.

"You're very cheerful this morning, Jakov," said the Defense Minister tartly.

"I'm paid to give answers," said Jakov Baratz calmly. "I can't guarantee that they're all cheerful ones."

"Which is my point, exactly." The Foreign Minister moved in swiftly. "Unless we can be sure of controlling the consequences of a victory, we have to be very careful about starting a war."

"It is we who are being provoked at every point." The Prime Minister slammed a thick hand on the table. "We have to answer strongly. Otherwise we begin to build a defensive mentality in the people. In the long run that could spell disaster."

"I agree," said the Defense Minister.

"I, too," said the Chief of Staff.

"So we have to choose between two horns of a dilemma," said the Foreign Minister deliberately. "Public resentment—the defensive mentality in Israel . . . or the trap into which the Syrians are trying to lead us: reprisal action which will enable them to invoke the aid of Egypt. Right?"

"Wrong, Nathan!" said the Defense Minister. "That's why we're striking at Jordan, which is not a signatory of the Defense Pact."

"But our aircraft were in action over Syrian territory yesterday morning, were they not?"

"Yes, but . . ."

"And the Syrians have claimed we organized the massacre at Rumtha?"

"But the Jordanians reject that."

"So we give away that advantage and blast a Jordanian village."

"We cannot sit and do nothing." The Prime Minister was angry now. "Our only strength is in national unity and national confidence."

The Foreign Minister was not abashed. "We don't live in a vacuum, Aron. Russia is fully aligned with the Arabs. But neither America nor Western Europe is fully aligned with us, however sympathetic they may be. We don't control the Suez and we don't control the oil that Europe burns and that America uses for the war in Vietnam. We don't control the Afro-Asian votes in United Nations. So let's at least add up the risk before we start shooting."

There was a short, uneasy silence. Every man had spoken his own truth and each was shrewd enough to know that it did not match the whole picture. Jakov Baratz spoke the next word:

"With permission, I should like to read part of a message received last night from our agent in Damascus. . . . 'Rumtha affair clearly a last-minute adaptation of first Syrian plan to discredit commander of Palace Guard in Jordan and introduce assassins into palace. Plan was leaked and security investigations under way. I have been involved in these investigations because my trucks were used to carry arms shipment. My opinion Safreddin booby-trapped boxes at last moment to create impression Israeli sabotage plot. Booby-traps fixed after I left warehouse. My watchman executed by Safreddin as quote Israeli spy unquote. No knowledge of who leaked information. Am tightening security precautions through network. We are still unblown otherwise Safreddin would have used me as authentic victim to prove Israeli plot. . . . View Jordan refusal of Syrian version believe we may expect more Syrian provocation to involve Israel. . . .' The rest of the message is an answer to other queries and does not yet concern this meeting. However I can add a couple more facts. A man named Idris Jarrah, member of the P.L.O., was named by the European press as being the source of the leak on the Rumtha affair. We have a file on this man. He has been directing sabotage operations in Hebron and West Jordan for some time. He has obviously defected and the Jordan police are looking for him. If I knew where he was I wouldn't mind buying him into Israel and seeing what he could tell us. The Western Press also mentioned a prominent banker in Lebanon. We're guessing it might be someone in the Phoenician Bank. . . ."

The Defense Minister interpolated a languid reproof. "I'm sure all this is very interesting from an Intelligence point of view, Jakov, but how does it affect the decision we have to make here?"

"It seems to me," said Baratz quietly, "that the sentence that concerns us most is this one: 'Believe we may expect more Syrian provocation to involve Israel.' It could be that in pursuing the Hebron Plan we are committing at least an irrelevance and very possibly an error of judgment."

"It *could* be an error of judgment. But *is* it, Jakov?"

"I believe it is."

"How then do you solve the problem which the Prime Minister has so clearly defined for us?"

"Not this way."

"That's an equivocal answer."

"I'll make it positive then. If we could hit the saboteurs, I would say hit them. We can't. We hit village folk who are involved, at most, in harboring the P.L.O.—often under threat. We hit the Arab Legion, who are trying to police the borders and not succeeding. It buys us nothing but a new enmity and a bad smell in United Nations."

"So what do we do?"

"Wait. Trust our own people a little further. Watch what the Syrians do. If they strike again, we hit them hard."

"And risk a full-scale war?"

"We risked it with our air strike."

"We haven't seen the full consequences of that yet," said the Foreign Minister moodily.

The Chief of Staff added his own comment. "Besides, Jakov, whatever the Syrians do we still have to cope with the P.L.O. If we can't reduce their sabotage, we'll have a whole rash of incidents from the Gaza Strip to Revaya."

"Any action is a risk." The Defense Minister moved in for the final blow. "Inaction is the greatest risk of all. It's like a nerve gas. It can reduce us to total paralysis. How have the kibbutzim survived? Not by sitting inside barbed wire but by sending patrols outside it. . . . Positive defense—not the psychology of the bunker and the rathole!"

Baratz felt the blood rising to his cheeks, but he controlled himself and asked with grim respect, "One question for the diplomats. How will it look to the world when two columns of Israeli tanks and two thousand infantry move in on an undefended village and blow it to bits?"

It was the Prime Minister who answered, a shapeless, unimpressive man, but stubborn and shaggy as an old mastiff.

"The world looks and sees what it wants to see. We have to live on the best terms we can make. Whatever we do can prove a costly mistake. It is right that we should know the price we may have to pay. I say we proceed with the Hebron Plan, at the best time recommended by the Chief of Staff."

"You name it, Jakov," said the Chief of Staff.

"O six-hundred hours the day after tomorrow," said Jakov Baratz.

"Amen," said the Defense Minister cheerfully.

"Not amen." Baratz's tone was suddenly edged with anger. "This time is set on the basis of present estimates of Arab

Legion strength in the target area. Any substantial buildup of that strength and we should call off the operation."

"Why?"

"You asked for a clean reprisal. Not a pitched battle."

"But there must be a point of no return. You can't call off the whole thing an hour before sunrise. That's a risk in itself."

"I agree with Jakov," said the Chief of Staff. "I agree with Yuval too. Name me zero hour, Jakov."

"Midnight tomorrow night. After that we're committed."

"And who makes the final decision?" asked the Prime Minister.

"I do." The Chief of Staff was very definite. "As at the close of this meeting, I must be in sole command of the operation."

"Agreed. Thank you, gentlemen. The meeting is closed."

EIGHT

Idris Jarrah stood at the window of his room, trying to interpret the scene below him. His first panic had passed, but he was still prickly and cautious. A man with money on his head could not afford to misread the omens.

The garden of the Intercontinental Hotel was like a film set. The backdrop was the naked sky, the lunar hills dotted sparsely with olive trees, the vast enclosure of the Dome of the Rock under which lay the threshing floor which David had brought from the Jebusites, from whence, so legend said, Mohammed had been lifted to heaven by the hair of his head, and behind the Dome, the piled rooftops and church towers of the Old City, a dazzle of white stucco and washed ocher and hazy pastels. The foreground was the garden enclosure, a semicircle of lawns and rockeries planted with yellow marigolds and bush roses, red and pink and white. On the driveway to the left the taxis and tourist cars were drawn up, their shirtsleeved drivers gossiping in the sun. Across the entrance, the military vehicles were lined out, the motor cyclists standing at ease beside their machines, the drivers and the gunners watchful in the jeeps. The rest of the troops were so disposed that they commanded the entrances to the garden and every door of the hotel itself. On the lawn some twenty or thirty guests strolled in pairs or stood in little groups, looking at the view, photographing the soldiers, comparing notes and guidebooks.

There was a knock at the door. Jarrah whirled at the sound. Then he composed himself and called:

"Come in!"

The handle turned, the door opened and an Arab scrub-woman, armed with brooms, pail and brushes stood framed in the doorway. Jarrah was so relieved, he could have embraced her. He asked:

"All those soldiers down there. . . . What's going on?"

"Oh that!" She shrugged indifferently and set down the pail. "The King is coming to Jerusalem today. Then, tomorrow, there are visitors from some other country. Lots of work. The whole place upset. May I do your room?"

He walked out into the corridor, turned left along the covered passageway that led to the main building, strolled past the reception desk where two Arab Legion officers were checking the guestbook, and turned the corner to the tourist office. To the elegant young man at the desk, he explained his needs in English. He would like to join a party crossing into Israel by the Mandelbaum Gate. He would like the agency to handle his clearance. The young man explained the procedures, helped him to fill out the application form, and offered a choice of diversions to fill in the forty-eight-hour waiting time:˙ a conducted tour of the Old City, a coach ride to Jericho, a visit to Bethlehem and Hebron, a trip to the Dead Sea and the Essene caves at Qumran. Idris Jarrah promised to take the offers under consideration. He signed the application form with his Greek name, handed it back, surrendered his passport, put on a pair of sunglasses and walked into the garden.

The guards at the entrance gave him no more than a cursory glance. A taxi driver made an eloquent solicitation, was rebuffed and went away grumbling. A leathery dowager

gave him the time of day in a Midwestern accent and asked
if he were traveling with the Church of Apostolic Reform.
Jarrah assured her politely that he was not. Had he been
to the Garden Tomb yet? Of course it wasn't authentic, it
couldn't be; but it was very beautiful and prayerful. Jarrah
was sure he would find time to visit it. Just now he was
tired from his journey. Where had he come from? Athens.
The lady had never visited Athens; but it was part of the
package and she was looking forward to the experience. Did
he know the Judsons by any chance? They were friends of
hers. They'd been living in Athens for five years now—or
was it six? He was something in oil—or was it shipping?
Anyway they were very charming people and they'd asked
her to call. Travel was always much pleasanter when you had
people to show you things, wasn't it? Much pleasanter—
much. If the lady would excuse him? She did, reluctantly.
He paced the lawn for a few minutes and then sat down on a
stone bench, a nondescript little man, inconspicuous as a
lizard on a rock.

He was beginning to feel the strain. An expert in underground warfare, he knew that the moles had a habit of
bobbing up in the most unexpected places. A professional
assassin, he knew that the victim was rarely safe against the
tortuous logic of the killer. The Jordanians were already de-
clared against him. The Syrians and the P.L.O. would soon
join the hunt—if they were not already in it. Each would
reason differently about his movements; but, sooner rather
than later, they would converge on him. Forty-eight hours
was a long time to sit, nursing anxieties. He needed a release
—the release of action or the release of sexual commerce.

There was a woman in the Old City who took care of his
sexual needs: a discreet widow who rented a number of
booths in the bazaar and was not averse from renting herself
to select and generous clients. However she practiced only at
night and it was necessary to telephone for an appointment.

If he telephoned he had to identify himself as Idris Jarrah and betray his presence in Jerusalem. Sex, therefore, might prove a disastrous indulgence.

Action? . . . He thought again of his emergency escape route: a journey on foot across the mined and treacherous no man's land between Jordan and Israel. It would do no harm to make a survey. Two routes, he knew, were open to him—one in the Hebron Bulge south of the city; the other in the north opposite Nablus. Each presented the same problem. The whole area west of the Jordan River was full of Palestinians, who, if they had heard from headquarters, might, even now, be on the watch for him. Next question: had they heard? They would know already that the Jordanians wanted him; but the Jordan police were natural enemies of the P.L.O., who would not betray one of their own to the Hashemites. There was at least a chance that they did not yet know that Idris Jarrah was a defector and a thief who had stolen ten thousand dollars of their funds. But how to be sure? . . . He pondered the question, sitting on the stone bench, while the Church of Apostolic Reform and the Talisman Tour group padded round the dry lawn and shared the charismatic mystery of Christian pilgrimage. Then he went into the hotel, shut himself into a public phone booth, dialed a number and talked through a handkerchief stretched over the mouthpiece.

"This is White Coffee."

"This is Black Coffee. Speak."

"Allah! We hear nothing from you. Our friend is to come from Damascus with money. He does not arrive. We hear strange stories in the newspapers."

"Allah! We hear nothing either."

"Where is the Coffee-maker?"

"He left this morning for Damascus. There was a message from his father."

"When will he come back?"

"When Allah wills—or when his father sends him."

"When he comes tell him White Coffee wants to hear from him."

"I will tell him. Khatrak!"

"Ma'assalameh!"

He put down the receiver, folded his handkerchief, dabbed at his forehead and tucked the handkerchief back into his pocket. So far, so good. So very good that he permitted himself a smile of satisfaction. The P.L.O. in Jerusalem had heard nothing of the defection of Idris Jarrah. Hebron was still in the dark. The people in Cairo were playing a careful game. They did not want to upset the local organization by a tale of treachery. They had called the local director to a conference in Damascus. Until he came back, or until he telephoned, Idris Jarrah would be safe among his own kind. Not that he wanted to mix with them any more. But he could risk a taxi ride and later, he might even be able to make a quiet visit to the widow. For a man halfway between death and lifetime riches, any reprieve was a singular mercy. He went back to his bedroom and took the pistol and the money from his briefcase. The money he lodged in a sealed envelope in the hotel safe. The pistol he kept in his trouser pocket. Then he went out again into the garden, hailed a taxi and, speaking now in English for the benefit of the driver and the doorman, asked to be taken on the tourist run to Bethlehem and Hebron.

BEIRUT

For Colonel Omar Safreddin, Beirut was a perpetual reproach. It was so sleek a place, so fat and complacent, so full of comfortable compromises that it angered him. Once, in the days of the great caliphs, this had been part of Syria, a maritime province of an Islamic empire that stretched from the Atlantic to the valley of the Indus, from the Cas-

pian Sea to the Nubian Desert. Once, the call of the muezzin
from the minaret of the Umayyad mosque in Damascus had
followed the sun westward, crying the name of Allah and
his Prophet, in Tangier and Cordova and Toledo, and up
to the peaks of the Pyrenees. The call was still heard; but
the empire had been corrupted and dismembered long since;
and nowhere was the corruption more evident than in this
bastard nation, carved out of the most fertile side of the
Fertile Crescent, where Moslem and Jew and Christian and
Druse paid lip service to a dozen loyalties and grew rich in
a base neutrality.

On every hillside the Christian Cross made a mockery of
the Crescent. The Chief of State was an Arab; the Chief
Executive was a Maronite Christian. The Jews were richer
here than they were in Israel. For the Lebanese, money had
no smell; whether it was pumped out of the sand in Kuwait
or smuggled across the border from Syria, or brought from
India as rubies and sapphires hung in a leather bag round
a man's crotch. Lebanon was a member of the Arab League;
but the only true service of the Lebanese was to the Golden
Alliance of bankers and traders.

For Omar Safreddin the zealot, Beirut was a great whore
of a city, perched on her hilltop, soliciting the trade of the
whole Mediterranean. For Safreddin the statesman, she was
the last and richest prize which, once the Jewish State was
destroyed, would tumble into the lap of a new Islamic Empire. For Safreddin the mystic, she was still the abode of
base gods and a marketplace for baser bargains between
the Sons of the Prophet and the unbelievers. And all the
baseness was summed up in Nuri Chakry, so vain in affluence and so pliable under threat.

Chakry was the symbol of all the sickness that debilitated
the Arab world. His only faith was in the power of money.
His only brotherhood was that of the bourse. The unity of
Islam was a threat to him because he battened on division

and dissension. The funds which he channeled into Europe and America could make the desert blossom, could rebuild Damascus into the shining city which even the Prophet hesitated to enter because he wished to go into paradise only once. But Chakry's dreams were all of profits and percentages, of the manipulation, but never the ennobling, of men. For him the Arab Resurrection was an academic dream. His Mecca was in the West, where the sun of capitalism was already declining. In the East he saw no dawn, only a twilight of past glories and a gaggle of jealous princelings enthroned over a bottomless sump of black oil. He would shout any creed you pleased, provided you left your purse in his safe. He would bend to every wind like a reed rooted in a festering swamp. Open the highway from Tyre to Haifa and he would be the first to ride along it, his pockets stuffed with bonds, bursting to do business with the Jews who had cast him out of his homeland. If the Americans played money music, he would dance to the happy tune. If the Russians beat the drum he would march, submissive to the martial beat, a happy camp follower ready to bolt at the first boom of the guns. He and his kind would be the first to be rooted out when the day of reckoning arrived. Until then they had their uses.

As he sat in a private corner of the terrace of the St. George Hotel, killing an hour with coffee, Safreddin examined the photostats which Matheson had delivered to him with such bad grace. It was extraordinary how much you could read about a man in two columns of figures, extraordinary how vulnerable he was to a simple addition and subtraction. In a couple of hours a good accountant could write you a passable history of his works and days, and a horoscope of his future. Selim Fathalla for instance. His history began with a large deposit of twenty-five thousand sterling pounds. Not a bad capital for an Iraqi on the run. Not too large though for a shrewd trader from the bazaar in Rashid Street. He had a backer too, which was news to Safreddin. There was a notation in the accounts authorizing a constant credit of twenty-five thousand pounds sterling—or a dollar equivalent—guaranteed by the Societa Inter-commercio Bellarmino of Rome. Why would an Italian company guarantee an Iraqi trader to establish himself in Syria? Where and how had Fathalla made so friendly a con-tact? Interesting questions. More interesting still to see how Fathalla's answers matched with his trading records. Safred-din hoped they would match well. He liked the man. There was a hard, abrasive quality about him that commanded respect. If only he had a little more ambition, were a little more eager for favor, it would be easier to deal with him. It was the faint air of mockery, the hint of contempt of the Baghdadi for the Syrian which was bothersome. Perhaps, now after the death of the watchman, he would be a little less arrogant.

As he leafed through the bulky folder of bank documents, Safreddin pondered the shape of a personal problem. Secu-rity depended on rigid documentation. Documentation was useless without an efficient system of controls and communi-cations within the administration. A modern socialist state needed a large and growing pool of trained administrators; and these were as rare as rocs' eggs in most parts of the Arab world. Politicians grew like weeds in every garden patch. A man who could set up a department and keep his files in order and dispatch his business within a measurable time was a jewel beyond price. Even one who could write a legi-ble hand or find a cross-reference between breakfast and lunchtime was to be treasured.

What was the point of a frontier check if you did not know who had crossed the border until he was out again? Or if you could not read the scrawl on the checklist? How could you monitor the telephone system if the operators could hardly speak their mother tongue correctly? If the tax collector was venal and the merchant studiously bad at arithmetic, how could you stay solvent and pay the Russians for guns and tanks and MIG fighters?—and what was left for schools and universities when the arms bill was paid? Education was the only answer, and Safreddin knew it better than most. His problem was that revolution and unrest drained the brains out of a country as they drained its money.

A blaring radio and an eloquent television announcer were no substitutes for the disciplines of the classroom and the dedication of skilled educators. But how did you find them and how did you keep them? Send a man to school in Beirut and he came back a malcontent, with a taste for the sweet life and better clothes than he could afford. Send him to Cairo and he came back a Nasserite. In Moscow they stuffed him so full of the Marxist dialectic that you had to purge him roughly before you could set him to the service of Islam and the Arab resurrection. In America they taught him computers and adding machines and when he came home he despised the primitive tools of pencil and paper.

Once again his irritation focused itself on Nuri Chakry, the prodigal, who had dissipated a fortune among the infidel when it might have helped to build a new caliphate for the believers. He had risen so quickly to the bait of Russian help that he must be in desperate straits. If a little help from Omar Safreddin would sink him more quickly, Safreddin would be happy to give it. As he drove out to the airport through the prosperous bloated city, he diverted himself with a vision of Chakry tormented by all the plagues of Egypt and crying for help to a laughing world.

All unaware of the malice which he provoked, uncaring too, Nuri Chakry paced his sunlit office and reasoned tolerantly with Mark Matheson. Matheson was still angry. His heavy handsome face was flushed. His hands made large indignant gestures. He was eloquent and righteous.

"Look, Nuri! We're in a jam. You say we're going to get out of it at the last moment. You don't tell me how; but I accept it. Still there's one thing you're forgetting. This crisis has hurt us. It will go on hurting us. We've lost a lot of confidence and goodwill. We'll lose more before we're out of trouble. . . . You don't help us by a blatant breach of faith like this. Don't think the news won't get round. Don't think Safreddin won't trade on our weakness! He will! And little Mark Matheson is going to be trotting round town for months trying to explain it away!"

"Mark, my friend!" Chakry halted in the middle of the field of carpet and threw his arms wide. "You're right in every word you say. I know the rough things I ask you to do. I know half of them don't make sense in New York or Zurich or London. But here they make the only possible sense. We need a Western framework. We can't do without it. You've given it to us. And I'm grateful for that. I've tried to show my gratitude. You admit that, don't you?"

"Of course, Nuri. But . . ."

"Wait! Wait! Let me try to explain. We are not the West. We are the Levant. We modify but we do not change. You've been here long enough to learn that much. But you still have the illusion that we can or want to change over- night. We don't want to change. We can't. You think a tribal prince is going to give up the power of life and death just because it's not exercised in Connecticut? In a pig's eye he is! You don't like preferential investment. You say the small- est client of the bank has the same claim on our money management as the man who trundles up in a Cadillac with a million dollars in the trunk? Come on, Mark! One's a prince. The other's a beggar! The prince demands to be treated like a prince. First offer of a new issue, best discount rate on his bills, cut price for bank services. They don't do this at the Chase Manhattan? Maybe they don't do it the same way. But they do it, little brother. They do it! Except that I do it the Arab way."

"But even the Arab demands confidence and secrecy."

"Do you mean to say you can't run a credit check on a rival with any bank in the United States?"

"It's a question of the method!"

"So it's the method we're talking about—not the principle!"

"Well, if you put it that way . . ."

"I do put it that way, Mark; because you and I have to understand each other. Do you know the real reason for Safreddin's visit today?"

"He wanted information. He wanted it pretty badly too."

"He wanted it so badly he made a whole opera out of it. Remember the Arab mind, Mark! The thing you really want is hidden in your sleeve."

"So? . . ."

"So we gave Safreddin what he said he wanted. Face was saved on both sides. What he really wanted was quite different."

"And that was?"

Nuri Chakry stopped his pacing and came close to Matheson. He propped his fists on the desk and bent lower. He dropped his voice to a somber undertone. "This is a high secret, Mark. I want your word that you'll keep it so."

"You don't have to ask."

"I know. Forgive me, Mark." He sat down, put his feet on the desk and picked up the talisman. "This will make no sense, Mark, unless you understand what's going on. Safreddin's a powerful man, as you know. He's also very ambitious. He's the puppet master in Syria. He pulls the strings that make the politicians dance. He makes the voices that come out of their mouths. Now . . . Safreddin's ambition is to become the new Nasser. He wants to be the prophet of the Resurrection. He can't compete with Nasser. He knows that. He doesn't have the magic. . . . He doesn't have oil and he doesn't have the Suez Canal either. So he can't bargain and he can't persuade. But he can organize and he can plot. And his plot is to create a situation which will mass the whole Arab world against Israel. . . . He wants war. Nobody else—especially Nasser—wants it just now. But if Safreddin can bring about even a massive confrontation, then he's a bigger man than he looks. He's especially big with the Russians who pay the bills. I don't think they want war either. But they want every bit of tension short of war . . . the Russians always make a neat distinction between the mouthpiece and the executive. Just now they're leaning to Safreddin as the future executive of the Pan-Arab movement. . . ."

"I still don't see where we come in."

"You will, Mark. And it makes a lot of sense. The Russians want to buy out the Phoenician Bank. If they buy us, they buy the biggest single stake in Lebanon, which is the only democratic state in the Arab League. But the Russians are shrewd. They won't make a blunt offer. They send Safreddin to sound me out. Safreddin's shrewd too. He can't make himself an obvious agent of the Marxists. So he cooks up this little scheme to come to Beirut and goes out with a set of photostats to prove he was doing a normal security job. . . ."

"Well, I'll be damned!"

"You see why I had to play the chess game, Mark?"

"I do indeed. Did Safreddin bring a firm offer?"

"Firm enough. But of course without the numbers. The way he put it was this: if we want to sell, the Russians want to talk business."

"My God! That's dynamite."

"It is, indeed."

"What are you going to do about it?"

Chakry sat in silence for a few moments contemplating the image of the gold emperor. When finally he spoke, he was frowning and remote. "I have to be honest with you, Mark: just as I expect you to be honest with me. At this

moment I'm prepared to consider any offers. I feel betrayed
—by men whom I made, by a country that I have done more
than anyone else to build. I don't have to sell. You know
that. But I'm tired, Mark. I'm tired of the backstairs battle
and the daggers in the dark. I wouldn't mind making a
killing and getting out. I know it shocks you to think I'd
sell to the Russians. You're an American. You have very
special loyalties. But I don't have any special loyalties to
Lebanon. Especially not now. I'm a Lebanese citizen; but
at bottom I'm still a stateless man. And people like Aziz
and Taleb never let me forget it. Fine! . . . I wouldn't be too
unhappy to cash my chips and buy myself another citizen-
ship. . . . Can you understand that?"

"Very well," said Mark Matheson quietly. "I don't blame
you at all. But even from a business point of view, wouldn't
you do better with an auction?"

"I might. I'm not sure I want the trouble."

"Would you let me try to organize it?"

Chakry pouted and frowned in obvious indecision. "It's
kind of you, Mark. But I'm not sure what you could do."

Matheson was suddenly eager. "This is a political situation of immediate interest to the State Department. If they
got interested—and they'd have to be interested to keep the
Russians out of Middle Eastern banking—they might do
overnight what we couldn't do in six months. It's worth a
try. Why don't you let me talk to the Ambassador?"

"Do you care so much, Mark?"

Matheson stared at him in surprise. "Well—yes. I guess
I do care."

"Why?"

"You've been good to me. I'd like to see you come out
well."

"But that's not the whole reason."

"No. . . . I suppose the rest of it is that I am an American,
that I do have certain fundamental loyalties and—and I'd
like to discharge them."

"In that case, go ahead. But keep me out of it for the present. You have the information. Use it anyway you want. I'm neutral."

"Fair enough. I'll call the Embassy after lunch and try to set up a meeting with the Ambassador. Anything else, Nuri?"

"Not for the moment, Mark. . . . But thank you."

When he had gone, Nuri Chakry lay back in his chair and chuckled happily. The old plot never failed. Offer a Westerner a clean woman for an honest price and he spat in your eye and called you a dirty Arab. Give him soft lights, sweet music, the glamour of the mysterious East and he would pay double the price for the same merchandise. Haggle with him over a copper tray and you were a cheating son of a camel. Clap your hands for coffee, throw in a paste scarab and a clay horse baked in a backyard kiln and you were a noble fellow bred to the courtesies of the black tents. All Americans wanted to be loved and respected; and when they died they wanted to be wrapped in the Stars and Stripes and buried to the sound of tin trumpets. They never understood that if you were born in a mud hovel and nursed at dry breasts and grew up as a donkey boy, kicked awake and cuffed to sleep, your only loyalty was to the one who offered the next meal. Mark Matheson could afford the luxury of an itchy conscience. He could not come to terms with it half so honestly as the meanest beggar in the bazaar.

DAMASCUS

On the same morning, while he was sitting in his office checking the bills of lading for a shipment to Istanbul, Selim Fathalla had a telephone call.

The caller spoke in heavily accented French. "Mr. Fathalla? This is Sergio Bellarmino from Rome. I've had a comic opera journey. But I am finally arrived in Damascus. When can we meet?"

"Now, if you are free. Where are you staying?"

"At the Hotel des Caliphs."

"I'll be there in ten minutes. And there are beautiful things to show you. New fabrics and some goldwork to knock your eye out."

"Splendid. I'll wait for you."

As he put down the receiver, Emilie looked up from her typing and asked, "Who was that?"

"One of our Italian clients. You'll meet him at lunch. Can you get Farida to prepare something special?"

"Of course. Were you expecting him?"

"I thought we might be hearing from him about this time. He's from the Societa Intercommercio Bellarmino. You've seen the name on our invoices. Be nice to him. It's a rich account."

"How will you explain me?"

"The Italians are very cultivated people, Emilie. One doesn't have to explain the things of the heart."

He said it with a laugh, but as he drove to the hotel, he knew that the explanation would be demanded and that he would have to make it good. The men of Baratz G2 Intelligence were a very professional bunch and they gave short shrift to fools and bunglers.

Sergio Bellarmino was an excessively handsome young man in his early thirties, beautifully turned out in a blue silk suit, shoes of black crocodile and a Battistoni shirt. In the foyer of the hotel he was eager and deferential. He was bubbling with simple pleasure at this first visit to Syria. He had a whole briefcase full of plans for the development of future trade. . . . In the privacy of Fathalla's house, he became suddenly brisk and businesslike. He talked rapidly in Hebrew with the accent of the Italian rabbinical school.

"We are secure here? No bugs? No servant problem?"

"Today we're clean." Fathalla grinned at him. "Yesterday we had problems."

"What sort of problems?"

Fathalla told him, at length and in detail. The young man asked few questions, but they were pointed and barbed. On the subject of Emilie Ayub he delivered a Draconic verdict:

"I think you've made a bad mistake. But it's done now. You have to live with it. So do we."

Fathalla was nettled. "Baratz bought me as I am. If he's not happy, let him pull me out."

"He may decide to do that. I'm just the messenger boy. I brought the money." He delved into his briefcase, brought out a thick parcel of notes and tossed it to Fathalla. "There's enough for a month on your present scale of payments."

"And after that?"

"How often do you ship out of Aleppo?"

"There's a monthly run that goes to Istanbul and the Greek ports. We usually use that."

"How often do you go there?"

"Every six weeks or so."

"Call at the office of the Arkadia line. Ask for Mr. Callisthenes."

"Is he safe?"

"Very. By the way, where will you keep this stuff?"

Fathalla showed him the faience panel and the young man nodded approval.

"Excellent. Quite ingenious."

"We do some good work," said Fathalla dryly. "And we have to make our own decisions. It's different in Tel Aviv —and in Rome."

Sergio Bellarmino was young enough to be put out of countenance. He flushed and stammered a little and then made a grudging apology. "I wasn't trying to teach you your job."

"Don't!" said Fathalla coldly. "And when my girl comes in be nice to her. We all need her now."

"I apologized. I meant it. . . . Let's talk about general security."

"It's hard to be precise about it." Fathalla was the professional again. "We work on the triad system as you know. One link in the chain can be broken, but you can't break the whole network overnight. Besides, the small operators believe that they're working for a Syrian organization and not a Jewish one. The most vulnerable people are Bitar and myself. . . ."

"And the girl?"

"She is myself," said Fathalla.

"Tell me about Bitar."

"A doctor. A very good and dedicated one. His weakness —and his strength—is that he's a humanist and an internationalist. His wife is dead. His only son was run down by an army truck while he was crossing the street. Bitar was in Lebanon at the time. The child died in hospital. Apparently the Army were pretty callous about the whole affair. Bitar has never forgiven them."

"He's a Moslem, of course?"

"And a good one."

"So how does he square that with working for us?"

"It's a complicated reasoning. I've never quite worked it out. Partly it's a personal vendetta against the Army who now control the country. Partly it's a private crusade against poverty and sickness. All the money he gets from me, he spends on a private clinic for poor people in the city. For the rest . . . it's a French education, I suspect. Liberty, equality, fraternity—and a shame at being segregated by a new nationalism that he doesn't believe in. He sees peace with Israel as a means of projecting the Arab world into a permanent and profitable relation with the West. But . . ." Fathalla shrugged and grinned. "It's always the same with the Moslem. You reason along happily together; and then, all of a sudden, you're standing on the edge of a dark pit and he's asking you to jump off with him." He chuckled and added an ironic afterthought. "Of course the Moslem feels the same way about the Jew."

Bellarmino was definitely not amused. "But you trust Bitar?"

"With my life and a lot of others."

"Read me Safreddin."

Fathalla shook his head. "I'm still trying to read him myself. He's a puzzle box, full of surprises. He uses everybody, trusts no one and yet has a childish need to be admired and even loved, I think."

"And where is he heading?"

"Politically? He wants Syria to run the Arab League. As long as Nasser is alive, he'll never bring it off. So he's playing the power game, trying to involve the Egyptians in a war with us."

"How does he stand with the Russians?"

"Very well, I think. They understand this type of man."

"And with the Iraqis?"

"They're scared of him. They know he can cut their pipeline any day he wants. They don't like him. But they try to live with him."

"You got our last questions from Tel Aviv?"

"I did. I haven't the answers yet."

"We need them quickly."

"We'll do what we can. I expect a fairly quick answer on the aircraft. One of our agents is a contractor who supplies the Army and the Air Force. He has access to bases and airfields. The missile question? Difficult. If they're here—which I doubt—they're under wraps. They certainly haven't been installed near any airfield. The Iraqis? . . . That's a matter of documentation. It will take time. I stay away from the Iraqis as you can imagine. My cover's pretty good; but I don't want to meet a man who knows Rashid Street better than I do."

"And Galilee?"

"Our last battle order for Galilee was filed four weeks ago. We've seen nothing to indicate major changes in that time. However, we have a fairly good agent in Quneitra. His identifications are usually accurate. He's on the job now."

"Let's come back to the missiles. We know the Egyptians have them. Why do you conclude the Syrians haven't?"

"First, there's no evidence of installations or even mobile units. Second, the political situation here is much less stable than it looks. The Army's in effective control, but there's a great deal of economic hardship and underground discontent. Third, the Russians are strong wooers and so are the Chinese. Syria has had more delegations in China and more delegations from China than any other Arab country. They've been clever enough to exploit the friction between China and Russia without ever coming down on either side of the fence. . . . But the Russians want a full commitment. And they won't hand out pretty presents like SAM missiles unless they get it. That's my reading at least. But we're checking as requested."

Bellarmino seemed satisfied with the answer. He was obviously embarrassed by the next question he had to ask.

"About the young lady, Fathalla. . . . What are your plans for her?"

"I'm going to marry her."

"Here? In Damascus?"

"Obviously not. She's a Christian. I'm known publicly as a Moslem. I'd lose face and friendships if I married her here."

"So? . . ."

"As soon as Baratz can conveniently replace me, I want to get out and take Emilie with me."

"Would you consider another alternative?"

"What?"

"Let us get the girl out. We'll establish her wherever you want. We'll maintain her and look after her. You stay on and work here for, say, another twelve months."

"Did Baratz make that suggestion?"

"No. He asked me to inform myself about your personal situation and make recommendations."

"I'd have to think about that. And talk to Emilie. At first sight, I don't like it. I don't think she'll agree either."

"If you leave, Fathalla, we'll have to start building a new network—just when we need a well-run organization."

"If there's something I don't know," said Fathalla slowly, "you'd better tell me."

"There's a reading on our present situation which goes like this. Provocation from the P.L.O. in the Gaza Strip and in West Jordan is increasing. Provocation from Syria is increasing too. We're being pushed inevitably into a military confrontation which, equally inevitably, will include Egypt and very probably the whole Arab world. Damascus is the best listening post we have—for the Russians, the Chinese, the Syrians, the Iraqis and all the rest. If you pull out, we're badly hurt, at a critical time. There's no coercion in this sort of job. There can't be. But . . ."

He left the rest of the thought unspoken; but the meaning was louder than trumpets to Selim Fathalla. Loyalty was being invoked. He had to specify what his loyalties were, at what points they contradicted each other and how he would choose between conflicting interests. Sergio Bellarmino watched him with shrewd cold eyes. He was one of the new Maccabees; critical, calculating, quite ruthless in their determination that never again would the Jews be herded to a slaughter like sheep. He was the voice that shouted at Eichmann's trial: 'Why didn't you do something?' He despised the ghetto man. He had no pity for the divided heart. No understanding of it either. Fathalla decided he would not give him the satisfaction of knowing his indecisions. He said curtly, "I'll think about what you've said. I'll let Baratz know."

Bellarmino smiled and shrugged. "Take your time. I'll be around for a few days."

Fathalla gaped at him. "A few days?"

The young man grinned and spread his hands eloquently. "Why not? I'm a legitimate trader on an Italian passport. I'm looking for merchandise. I want to talk to the commercial people in the Government."

"That could be dangerous. You'll be very conspicuous."

"It could be more dangerous if I didn't make myself conspicuous. You're a government trading agent. Intercommercio Bellarmino is one of the big clients on your books. . . . I'm looking for trade wherever I can find it. By the way, have you told your girl about me?"

"Not yet."

"Don't."

"Is that an order?"

"A request."

"You'll have to leave it to my discretion."

Bellarmino shrugged. "As you choose. . . . There's a piece of personal news for you. Baratz told me to tell you the divorce case will be heard on the twenty-fifth. You'll be free the day after."

"That's good news. What else is happening at home?"

"The Wilderstein bank's going bust. We're selling two ships because they cost us too much to run. Unemployment's going up and there'll be sixty or eighty thousand out of work in a month or so. Money's tight. The Government is fumbling and the tourists aren't spending as much money as they used to. We need some excitement to liven the market."

"Safreddin's doing his best to oblige."

"I'm anxious to meet him."

"If you do," said Fathalla soberly, "watch every word.

And don't try to be clever. The stupider you look, the safer you are. . . . And while we're about it, let's go over the cover story on my association with Intercommercio Bellarmino. That's one of the first questions Safreddin will ask you."

They were still rehearsing when Emilie came to summon them to lunch. She had changed out of her office clothes and was dressed in a housegown of Damascus brocade, caught at the waist by a belt of filigree gold. She wore no other ornaments, and, with her hair tied back from her face and her attitude of demure respect for Fathalla and his guest, she looked like a character from an exotic Eastern fairy tale. Bellarmino was at first surprised and then voluble with Italianate compliments, which she accepted so calmly that he was put out of countenance. She would not eat with them. She took no part in the talk. She served and listened and, when the coffee was brought, she was about to withdraw.

Fathalla held her back. "Sit down, Emilie. We have things to talk about."

"Shall I get a notebook?"

"It won't be necessary. These are private matters." Bellarmino gave him a sharp, warning look. Fathalla ignored it and went on. "As you know, our friend is from Rome. He's one of our more important clients. He wants to extend his trade with us and with other people in Damascus. He'd like to meet some of the more important people in the Government. After lunch, take him down to the warehouse, go through our lists with him and handle his telephone calls. He will speak only Italian and French. If he needs an interpreter, you go with him."

"There's no need for that! I can speak Arabic."

"There is need." Fathalla was very definite about it. "You should not speak Arabic in this city. You are the innocent European fumbling in a foreign situation. Much safer for you—and for us." He turned to Emilie. "You should know that Mr. Bellarmino is also an agent of the Israeli Government. He will want to ask you questions too. Answer them if you can."

The young man was obviously irritated but he controlled himself. He said pointedly, "Perhaps Miss Ayub has an answer to the question I put to you."

"What was that, Selim?"

"Whether you would consent to leave the country and wait for me in some safe place for a year or so."

"Is that what you want, Selim?"

"Mr. Bellarmino thinks it might be advisable."

"I'm not marrying Mr. Bellarmino. I will stay where you stay. I will go where you take me."

"We might have to stay another twelve months."

"Then we stay together."

Bellarmino cut into their talk. He was surgically precise. "I'm sorry to say it, Miss Ayub, but in my view—and I have to report my view back to Tel Aviv—you're a risk to Fathalla and a greater risk to us."

"Then get rid of us both." She was very cool and very strong.

"That's a decision for Tel Aviv."

"No!" said Fathalla sharply. "It's a decision for us. I'll make it now. I can't survive as a man without Emilie. You feel we're too great a risk to keep in Damascus. Let's decide here and now that we're out. Let's work out a way to maintain the network and move another man in to control it. We'll stay as long as we're needed. But Tel Aviv is on notice as from now."

"You must be very flattered, Miss Ayub," said Bellarmino acidly. "A woman weighed against a country. And the woman wins."

"You're a fool!" said Fathalla with soft anger. "You're a witless fanatic. You're offered the service of two lives and you throw it back in our faces." White-faced and trembling he stood up, showering a low bitter invective on his colleague. "You live in a comfortable apartment in Rome and you run messages round the Mediterranean! What the hell do you know of a job like this? What do you know about me and how I feel and what it takes to endure the simple bloody solitude of a Jew among his enemies? When I was sick I talked in my sleep. Emilie heard it all and could have betrayed me in an hour and guaranteed herself safety and reputation for a lifetime! To her, Israel's just a name on a map. To me it's a place I love and can't live in. I'm her country. She's mine. What more do you want of us? The last stand of the Zealots on Masada?"

"I want to know what you'll do if you're asked to make it," said Sergio Bellarmino.

"I'll tell you," said Emilie Ayub. "We take the little pills that Selim keeps in his secret room. And we go to sleep in silence. Did the Zealots do any more?"

Sergio Bellarmino did not answer. He drank his coffee, set down his cup and reached for a cigarette from the silver box. Watching his unhurried movements and the lines of his face set hard under the sleek skin, Fathalla in a bleak moment of truth knew that he was a very dangerous man.

NINE

The old road from Jerusalem to Jericho had been cut a long time ago and was now mined on both sides of the armistice line. The new road made a detour of eleven miles past Bethany and Bethphage and the fortress-tower of Queen Melisande. It plunged down among the ancient tombs where David the King was thought to be still buried—although no one had found his resting place. It climbed up the Hill of Evil Counsel where, unconscious of the irony, the Chief of the United Nations' Mixed Armistice Commission had his residence. It sloped downward through Sur Bahir and up again to a ridge from which the spires of Bethlehem could be seen and, eastward on the edge of the desert, the mountain tomb of Herod the Great who, after the coming of the Persian kings, had ordered the massacre of the men-children.

Idris Jarrah had seen it all a hundred times before. He cared not one whit for the tale of the shepherds and their angelic visitors, or the Christian Messiah or the Crusaders who had done murder in His name. He was preoccupied by a new experience—a sensation almost sexual in its intensity and satisfaction. The moment he rode out of the confines of the hotel he had felt the onset of it. He was at risk again,

wholly and completely, as he had been in the days when
he had scurried round the Judean hills, fighting a rear-
guard action against the Jewish usurpers.

In cold logic his taxi ride into the territory of the P.L.O.
was the wildest folly. He was risking his life on the one assumption that the rank and file of the Palestinian guerrillas
had not heard of his defection and would not hear of it for
at least twelve hours. But, if the assumption was correct,
and they accepted him still as director of their operations,
his word would be mightier for them than the law of the
Medes and Persians; and they could have him across the
border and walking a free man in Israel before the next
dawn.

Old Hamid, the candlemaker in Bethlehem, had a son
who knew of a way through a dry gully where there were no
mines, where the wire could be cut, and an hour's careful
walking would see him safe into New Jerusalem. Abdul, the
herdsman, had told him of a tunnel that began as a cave on
the Jordan side and wound through the hills to a safe exit
in Israel. There were a dozen such men between Bethlehem
and Hebron, but he had dealt with them always through the
man whose code name was White Coffee, the guerrilla leader
in the southern bulge, who worked by day as a teacher in a
Hebron village and, at night, trained gunners and demolition
crews for the P.L.O.

White Coffee was an amiable man, well educated, well
behaved and always serviceable. He had made good friends
among the Armenians and the Orthodox and the Romans
who tended the Christian shrines. He cared for his own
people too. He lent them money, arbitrated their disputes,
acted as broker for their marriages. No one had ever seen him
angry. But there were tales, whispered by candlelight—an
informer beaten to death, a reluctant saboteur knifed and
thrown into a dry well—which made his name feared and
kept his authority unquestioned. Idris Jarrah had found him

a friendly and competent colleague. He hoped now to find him a willing collaborator in his private designs. But he would ask questions first. Why did Idris Jarrah chance his neck in a border crossing? He had never done it before—why attempt it now? Why alone? What target justified the risk of a senior operations man who, if the Israelis caught him, would be a mine of information on the P.L.O? Idris Jarrah would have to answer the questions, promptly, clearly and with such conviction that there could be no doubt of the urgency or authenticity of his mission.

So, when he came to Bethlehem, Idris Jarrah dismissed his driver, paid him double for the journey so that he would not hang about in the square, walked into the Church of the Nativity, seated himself, like any soulful Christian, in a dark corner and gave himself over to meditation. The meditation was fruitful. It stilled the sensual excitement. It humbled him so that he would not discount too readily the serpent wisdom of Safreddin, or the subtleties of the Nameless One in Cairo, or the animal cunning of the Coffee-maker. It made him prudent, so that he would not blow up one escape route before he had ensured another. It brought him to a series of sober conclusions.

First he would buy himself a room in the pilgrim hostel in Bethlehem. That he would not sleep in it made no matter. He would be registered there. His hideout at the Intercontinental Hotel would remain safe. Next he would avoid a face-to-face meeting with White Coffee, he would telephone him from Bethlehem. He would demand a guide and a rendezvous for an unnamed agent who had to cross the border the same night on an unspecified mission. If White Coffee wanted to know more, Jarrah would invoke the authority of Cairo and threaten to withhold the funds which White Coffee knew he was carrying. If there were more objections he would break off the talk and hie himself back to his bolt hole in the Intercontinental Hotel. . . .

The more he thought about it, the better it looked. At best he would be in Israel before dawn, armed with yet another of his passports. At worst he would have revealed to the P.L.O. that he was lodged somewhere in West Jordan—an assumption which they would have made in any case. He had exhausted the resources of piety. He walked out into the dusty sunlight of the square and plunged into the narrow lane that led to the pilgrim hostel. They balked a little at registering him without baggage or passport, but two days' rent and the promise to present himself, documented and respectable, before nightfall made them reasonable. He scrawled an illegible signature in the book and headed for the post office.

It took him half an hour to raise White Coffee in Hebron and ten minutes to identify and explain himself in the jargon of the guerrilla underworld. But—Allah be praised!—White Coffee was amenable and efficient. He accepted Jarrah's story at face value. He was full of regrets that he would not be able to superintend the operation himself. He had to leave for Nablus as soon as school was finished. However he would make all the arrangements. The traveler should present himself at the house of Hamid the candlemaker an hour before midnight. After that he would be passed from hand to hand and delivered into Israel before dawn. White Coffee inquired discreetly after the health of his brother. Jarrah assured him that his brother's health was excellent, in spite of the heat. White Coffee chuckled and expressed the pious hope that he would meet his brother very soon. He needed money. Jarrah chuckled too and told him that his brother was waiting only for a suitable moment to discharge all his debts. They invoked a mutual blessing and the thing was done—no questions, no problems, a routine job.

Idris Jarrah sat in the fetid phone booth and laughed until his sunglasses misted over. When he took out his handkerchief to wipe them his hands were trembling so violently that the glasses fell upon the ground. It was a mercy that they did not break. He would have felt very naked without them.

BEIRUT

The Ambassador of the United States of America to the Republic of Lebanon was, by nature, a cordial man. He smiled readily. He listened patiently. He was full of small courtesies that made the most casual visitor feel cherished and important. He had spent a long time in the Arab world and he understood the uses of obliquity. He never said yes and he never said no. He encouraged eloquence in others; he was never guilty of it himself. It was easy to underrate him, as many a blunter colleague had found to his discomfort. He dispensed favors readily—especially when they cost nothing. When he had to perform a diplomatic execution, he did it with such delicate regret that the victim suffered for the headsman and died with a blessing on his lips.

For Mark Matheson he had a professional respect, clouded only vaguely by a personal doubt. The man was a sound banker. He was well educated and well informed. He understood and could interpret intelligently the monetary equation of politics, even if he was sometimes naïve about the tribal and charismatic overtones of Middle Eastern relationships. He was socially polished. He lived his private life with sufficient discretion; and, if his loyalties to his country had never been strongly tested, at least they had never been called in question. The doubt about him was instinctive rather than reasoned. If you had to write it down, you would have to express it by negation. There was no drive in him. There was no discernible direction. You were conscious of his charm, but you had no clear impression of his character. He raised neither malice nor enthusiasm; and even his women —of whom there were many—described him in terms of rather indifferent affection.

Today, however, there was a subtle change in him. He told his story of the Russian bid for the Phoenician Bank with great vividness. He argued the case for an American takeover with a passion that had a hint of desperation in it.

"Let's make no mistake, sir, if the Russians did take us over they would be in a position to manipulate the investment program of the bank to give them an enormous political advantage. They could control the institutions in which they invest. They could build alliances which would otherwise be beyond their power to forge. They could buy friends and discriminate against enemies. They could exercise a disproportionate influence in Lebanese politics and in oil politics too. . . . I'd hate to see it happen."

"Are you convinced, Mark, that it is going to happen?" The Ambassador put the question without emphasis.

Matheson weighed it for a moment and answered it very precisely. "I know that the approach was made this morning. I know that Mr. Chakry is in a mood to enter into discussion."

"As I hear it, he's under a good deal of pressure just now."

"He has been. And he has been both disappointed and disillusioned by the conduct of those whom he regarded as friends. I think he's in a mood to sell."

"And you think an American interest should buy?"

"Yes."

"But the Government of the United States is not a banking institution. It's a political one. I don't see how we can or should intervene."

"The Russian interest makes it a political situation, Mr. Ambassador. That's why I felt I should discuss it with you."

"I'm very glad you did, Mark. I'm not sure, though, what you are suggesting that I do."

"I'm not sure either." Matheson was sedulously frank. "I thought perhaps you might be disposed to report the fact to the State Department, who might then recommend an examination of the deal by an American banking corporation."

The Ambassador frowned over the proposal for a few moments and then shook his head. "That's a ticklish one in a free enterprise society. I don't think any of our people would go for it."

"As a banker and as a private citizen, I think they should be given the opportunity to consider it—at a political level."

"That's a good point, Mark. However, as a diplomat, I would put it rather differently. I would say we should inform the State Department of the Russian interest and let them decide whether they want to take the matter further. That way we are both absolved from a direct recommendation which might, in the end, prove a mistaken one."

"That makes sense. Provided the Russians don't move faster than we expect."

"If there are no other bidders, Mark, why should they move fast? And how quickly could they set up a transaction like this anyway?"

"Very quickly. The audit figures are available."

"Would the Russians accept them?"

"I don't see why not. They might haggle over the goodwill."

"That's pretty low at the moment, isn't it?"

"On the trading figures, no. The most one can say is that the goodwill figure might be clouded somewhat by the politics of the present situation. It would clarify itself very quickly in a final negotiation."

"Does Chakry know you've come to see me, Mark?"

"Yes. I asked his permission. I had to do that."

"Did he oppose the idea?"

"No, he seemed indifferent about it."

"That's a little strange."

"Why, Mr. Ambassador?"

"An American bidder would mean an auction. An auction might force the price up. Chakry could hardly be indifferent to that."

"That's the way I put it to him. His answer indicated his state of mind. He said: 'I'm not sure I want the trouble.' "

"And you believed him?"

"I did. I do."

"It sounds out of character to me. Although I don't know Mr. Chakry as well as you do."

"In one way it is out of character. In another, perhaps it isn't. Chakry's clawed his way up to the top. He has to fight to stay there. It's reasonable to believe that he's come to the moment where he wants to take his profit and the easy life as well."

"Another question, Mark. Wouldn't it be easier to make a direct approach to an American bank and sound out their interest—without a political play?"

"I'm not in a position to do that until Chakry asks for it. I'm a servant of the bank. He's the major shareholder. I asked his permission to approach you because I'm an American citizen and my loyalties are involved."

"And now? . . ."

"You have the information, Mr. Ambassador. You must make the decision how to use it."

The Ambassador leaned back in his chair and began probing at his blotter with the tip of a steel letter opener. For the first time, he seemed ill-at-ease, unwilling to end the talk, yet not knowing on what note to continue. Finally he said:

"You've given me frank answers, Mark. They do you credit. I'll try to be frank with you. Chakry's a big man with a bad name. The more we hear about him, the less we like him. He plays too many games on the side . . . games that have nothing to do with banking. In the last week we've had some very surprising intelligence reports in which his name is prominently mentioned. I don't want to quiz you about them because you're a servant in a position of trust. I don't even suggest you know anything about them. However I'd like you to answer me a question: yes, no or maybe. In the job you do with him and for him, do you trust Mr. Chakry?"

"In the job I do—and that's the only one I know—I do trust him."

"Put it another way then. You are recommending to me that American interests should buy the Phoenician Bank. Would you recommend they buy it on Chakry's figures?"

"If I were advising any buyer, in any enterprise, I'd say get an independent audit before you sign the contract. That's only common sense."

"Would the figures stand up?"

"What do you want me to say, sir?" Matheson made a proper show of irritation. "We're solvent and profitable. The auditors, who are one of the most reputable firms in the world, have signed the accounts. I can't go further than that."

"No. I guess not." The Ambassador stood up and held out his hand. "Thanks for the information, Mark. I'll discuss it with my commercial people, then I'll send a minute to Washington. After that it's out of my hands."

Two minutes later, he was standing in the sunshine at the embassy gates, wondering whether he had made a fool of himself and knowing quite clearly that, finally and irrevocably, he had made himself a liar. The odd thing was that he felt no guilt about it, only a sharp resentment that he had been forced to adopt this last and most primitive device of survival. He resented the Ambassador who had so quickly reduced his cloak of virtue to tatters. He resented Chakry who for years had framed the lie for him and added enough truth to make it palatable when he spoke it. He resented the shabby soft fellow who lived under his skin and tempted him to small ignoble follies, but never to the big and risky enterprises of his master. A horn blast sounded at his back, so loud and startling that he stumbled against the iron railings of the fence. He swung round angrily to see Lew Mortimer grinning at him from the window of a large limousine.

"Hi, Matheson! Jump in. I'll ride you back to town."

"For Christ's sake, Mortimer! You frightened the wits out of me!"

"You needed it. You looked like a man with a monkey on his back. Come on, let's have a drink!"

He lacked the energy to refuse. He could not tolerate a curbside argument with this bawdy buccaneer. He climbed into the car.

Mortimer chuckled. "Things getting rough, eh boy?"

"No rougher than usual."

"I hear different. I hear Chakry's playing 'I spy.' He's peddling information now—like to the Kuwaitis and the Jordanians."

"I don't know what you mean."

Mortimer gave him a swift sidelong look. Then he nodded. "I believe you. You're the kind of guy who does his homework on the stock market and then goes out looking for broads. But you should read the news pages too. Very interesting! A former client of yours is on the run, because Chakry sold him out. Name of Idris Jarrah. Works for the P.L.O. He sold Chakry some inside dope on their operations in Jordan. Chakry peddled the tape and a note of hand. The word is he made a handsome profit."

"Where the devil did you hear this?"

Mortimer chuckled again. "It's all over town. The press has it—although they didn't print Chakry's name. The C.I.A. has it. The Ambassador has it. I was talking to him before you came in. Strange he didn't mention it."

"He didn't."

"I wonder why?"

"How the hell should I know? The subject wasn't discussed."

"Have you given any more thought to my proposition?"

"No."

"I think you should. You're still clean, boy. I know it. Most other people still know it. But if you hang around too long, some of the dirt's going to rub off on you. Then your value goes down. Even in Lebanon, it goes down. If they don't say you're dishonest, they'll say you're dumb. And that's a hell of a lot worse in our business."

"You never let up, do you?"

"I told you. I'm a good hater. And you're a good banker. So long as you're clean I can still use you."

"I can use a drink," said Mark Matheson wearily.

"I'll buy you one," said Mortimer easily. "And if you don't fight me, I'll read you chapter and verse what's going to happen to Mr. Nuri Chakry in the next three weeks."

He did read it. He read it in the bar of the Phoenicia Hotel with such an abundance of factual detail and so much chilling logic that Matheson was stupefied. He ended with a summation that read like a death sentence:

". . . So Chakry's only got one place to go—out! He's got two bolt holes and they're both in South America where he's got enough stacked away to let him live comfortably. One of them might extradite him. The other can't. I know because I've had my lawyers do a private study. But in Lebanon and Europe and the Arab world, he's finished. This little caper with Jarrah has put the lid on him. So ask yourself, where does Mark Matheson go after the funeral?"

"According to Chakry," said Mark Matheson slowly, "there won't be any funeral."

"And you believe that?"

"Why should he lie to me?"

"Because he needs you, boy. He needs you like a corpse needs an embalmer—to keep the stink down. He needs your nice honest-Joe face in the front office, while he slides out the back door one jump ahead of the sheriff. Come on, Matheson! Get wise to yourself! He wants fifty million at least to get him out. Why doesn't he produce it now?"

"He says he has it."

"Where and from whom?"

"I don't know."

"Have you asked him?"

"Yes. He just grins and says he has it. And he'll produce it at the right moment."

"He's selling smoke!"

"Maybe he isn't."

"Do you want to prove it?"

"Of course I want to prove it."

"Then this is what you do. Tomorrow morning confront him in his office. Tell him you've had another offer. That's the truth. You've got it from me. Tell him you want to stay with him, but you need tangible evidence that you have a future with the Phoenician Bank. Ask to see the color of his money. And tell him something else too. I'll match it, dollar for dollar in seven days."

"Would you?"

"Given effective control of the investment—yes!"

"He wouldn't accept that."

"No skin off my nose. But it gives you a chance to test him. It may take a little guts. Still . . . what have you got to lose?"

"Nothing."

"Then it's your play, boy!"

Mortimer grinned at him over the rim of the glass; but whether the grin was a mockery or an encouragement, Matheson was too confused to care. The dancer was waiting to be taken to dinner and then to bed; and there at least Mark Matheson would be wrestling in his own class.

JERUSALEM, ISRAEL

The Israelis' observation post was a concrete bunker set high on a naked hilltop overlooking the Hebron valley. North, south and eastward it commanded a view of the stony plain, the toy villages shimmering in the heat, the wadis and defiles of the low hills beyond them. On the sandbagged platform in front of the bunker, Jakov Baratz stood with the Chief of Staff and their aides, watching the helicopter that cruised, black and bumbling, against the dazzle of the sky. The helicopter carried an observer who was plotting the movements of traffic along the Hebron road and calling the coded coordinates in Hebrew to a radio man in the bunker. They could hear his toneless voice crackling in the dry air, they could see his directions translated into symbols on the plastic face of an operations map.

It was a strangely static scene, like a lighting rehearsal on an empty stage. There was no sense of urgency, no hint of danger. The actors stood, silent and relaxed, listening to the clatter of the helicopter and the unhurried call of the observer. The plain was bare and deserted save for a Bedouin shepherd who stood like a tiny black statue leaning on his staff and watching his drowsy cropping flock. The villages were dead as graveyards, huddled behind their stone walls. The airspace was a shining vacuum where the black bug trundled along unhindered and unchallenged. The illusion of theater was so strong that Jakov Baratz had to make a physical effort to bring the reality into focus.

The village was not dead. There were children in it, chanting their numbers in a classroom. There were women beating their laundry at the well. There were laborers and artisans, and farmers tending the sparse earth in the folds of the wadis. There was a police post where professionals like himself were watching the helicopter and trying to read a meaning into its aimless flight. There were armed men, too, the shabby irregulars who were dedicated to the overthrow of Israel and the recovery of their own expropriated garden patch. Westward behind the hills there were fighter planes dispersed on secret airstrips. Tank men were checking their vehicles, truckloads of troops were being assembled, armed and briefed for an operation which would make the bare valley flower into fire and raise a thunder that would echo round the spinning planet.

He looked over the shoulder of the officer who was recording the coordinates called by the aerial observer. There were no significant changes in the battle order on which the operation had been projected. Unless any such changes took place within the next thirty hours, they were committed to the strike. He was glad to be committed. He was glad to be dispensed from argument and contention, to be once again the clear-eyed mercenary who took his pay for a job well done and slept soundly afterwards. He was grateful to share again the simple unquestioning comradeship of those who kept watch and ward on the hills of Judah.

The Chief of Staff asked him a question. "Anything new, Jakov?"

"Nothing significant. Convoy movements fit the regular pattern. The rest is civilian and tourist traffic. No change in aircraft dispersal."

"Good! Let's call in the helicopter. Same routine tomorrow morning and tomorrow afternoon."

The signaler relayed the order and, a few moments later, the helicopter turned homeward. They talked for another ten minutes over the map and then Baratz and the Chief of Staff walked down the hillside to their vehicle.

Baratz said; "I'll come down to the assembly point with you, Chaim. Then I'll go back to Tel Aviv. Unless there's anything special. I'll come up here tomorrow afternoon."

"No need even for that, Jakov. It's an operations matter now."

"I'd like to be here," said Baratz.

"Just as you like."

As they drove through the rocky defiles to the assembly point, the Chief of Staff asked lightly enough, "How do you feel now, Jakov?"

"Better. It's almost out of my hands."

"But still not convinced?"

"No."

"It's too easy, isn't it?"

"Much too easy."

"I couldn't help thinking how different it would be if we'd decided to push the Syrians off the heights in Galilee. That could be a very bloody one."

"We may still have to do it—sooner than we think."

"I know."

"I've been studying that area again. We've called for more information from our man in Damascus. He's kept us fairly up to date on the order of battle, but there's one dangerous gap in our information."

"The same one?"

"Yes. We have no detailed plans of the Syrian fortifications on the heights. They have to be complicated because we know the Russians have been working up there as engineers and advisers. But we have no plans. The Syrians aren't usually good at keeping secrets. In this case, however, their security has been watertight."

"We still have our own battle plan though."

"Based on blanket bombing and napalm. I don't think it's good enough. The first wave of infantry could be murdered."

"Can't your agent help?"

"It's on his list of projects. I know he's working on it. I know it will take time. I haven't pressed him because we had time too. At least we seemed to have. Now I'm not so sure."

"I'm not sure either, Jakov. You'd better put a priority on the Syrian project. Let's stop here a moment."

They were on the saddle of a high ridge that fell away sharply into a wide saucer valley, timbered with young pines. After the naked contours of the desert hills, the greenery was rest to the eye and to the spirit—until, after the first moment of pleasure and surprise, one saw that the forest was alive with men, bivouacked under the trees, that every clearing was a parking place for tanks and armored carriers and mechanized fieldpieces, a zoological garden full of deadly monsters.

"Impressive, isn't it, Jakov?"

"A steamroller to crush a gnat," said Baratz dryly. "Have we invited the press?"

"No. Maximum security—maximum surprise. The press can arrive when it's over and garble the story any way they like."

Baratz lifted his fieldglasses and scanned the valley with a professional eye.

"Good deployment. Sloppy camouflage in a couple of places. Is this the lot?"

"No. The rest come in at nightfall. It's a good exercise in night traffic control. Let's go down and talk to Zakkai and his boys."

"Before we go, Chaim . . ."

"Yes?"

"A personal thing. I'd like to tell you about it."

"Go ahead."

"Our man in Damascus is getting divorced. His wife has agreed. I've arranged it quietly with the Rabbinate. He's in love with a girl in Damascus.

"Not a good thing from our point of view, Jakov."

"No. But unless we pull him out immediately—which I don't want to do—we have to wear it and see how it works."

"You said it was personal, Jakov."

"It is, very. I'm in love with his wife."

"Oh. . . ." A small surprise. A small silence. "What about Hannah?"

"Lieberman tells me there's no hope. I'll wait long enough to be sure."

"What do you want me to say, Jakov?"

"Nothing. I thought you should know."

"Thanks for telling me. It's a rough deal. I'm sorry. It doesn't make any difference between us—professionally or personally."

"It has made a difference to me," said Baratz quietly. "Professionally it has made a difference."

"How?"

"You asked about the plans of the fortifications. I haven't pressed for those because I had another reason as well."

"Which was?"

With a soft and bitter irony, Jakov Baratz quoted him the words of Samuel the Prophet:

" 'And David wrote a letter to Joab saying, Set . . . Uriah in the forefront of the hottest battle and retire ye from him that he may be struck and die. . . . And Uriah the Hittite died. . . . And when the mourning was over, David sent and fetched Bathsheba to his house and she became his wife. . . .' I couldn't risk that, Chaim. I just couldn't risk it."

"Can you risk it now?"

"Yes. He asked for the divorce. Yehudith had nothing to do with it. And she's not my wife, or my lover—yet."

"It's a knife-edge kind of morality, isn't it?"

"So's that!" Baratz flung out his arm and pointed down into the valley encampment. "And there are no prophets any more to read us the will of Jahweh Elohim."

"I'm not blaming you, old friend," said the Chief of Staff gently. "You don't have to justify yourself to me."

"To whom then?"

"Only to yourself. But we do need to know about the emplacements, don't we?"

"Yes. We need to know."

They walked back to the car and drove down through the grateful shadows of the pines into the garden of monsters.

DAMASCUS

On the night of his return from Beirut, Colonel Omar Safreddin presided at a meeting of the Hunafa Club and chose for the text of his discourse the Surah which is called "Al-Mujâdilah": She who makes dispute:

"Oh you who believe! When you conspire together, do

not conspire together for crime and evil deeds and disobedience towards the messenger, but conspire together for righteousness and piety and keep your duty to Allah unto whom
you will be gathered. . . ."

He read the text twice to fix it in their minds. Then he
began to embroider it, crisply and passionately:

"In the name of Allah, the beneficent, the merciful. . . .
You will notice first, my brothers, that in this revelation the
prophet makes clear distinction between the uses of conspiracy. He does not say that conspiracy itself is an evil act.
On the contrary he commends it when it is put to good ends.
We here are conspirators, because we meet in private to
discuss what, publicly spoken, might raise mistrust and dissension. We are those whom the Prophet invokes . . . 'All
you who believe!' We are believers. We believe in Islam, we
believe in the unifying mission of Islam. We believe in the
Baath as its political instrument. We believe in the right of
the enlightened to counsel and the strong to lead. The conspiracy in which we are engaged is a conspiracy of enlightenment, a conspiracy to test our strength in secret before we are
called to exercise it openly. But there are others, here and
elsewhere, who conspire in the contrary fashion to crime and
evil deeds. . . . These we must root out of the land before
they become a plague in our midst. . . . At our last meeting
I put a question to you: assuming that there is a new Israeli
agent in Damascus, how and where would you begin to look
for him? If you have answers, I should like to hear them
now. . . ."

There was a short, uneasy pause which made Safreddin
impatient.

"Speak in order of rank and seniority. You, Major!"

The major was a short, stocky man, built like a wrestler,
but his voice was soft and deep. "I would look for this one,
Colonel, in a low place. Eli Cohen lived high and conspicuous.
This one will be very ordinary. He will deal with low people."

"And how will he get information about high matters, Major?"

"From the same low people of whom I have spoken—clerks, typists, functionaries who will do anything for a little extra money, a waiter who serves food in an embassy, a truck driver in the Army, a switchboard operator. Such people see and hear much more than we realize."

"Will he be known to such people?"

"No. He will be always removed. He will have learned from Cohen's mistakes; because Cohen was always in direct contact with his sources."

"So he needs a network?"

"Exactly."

"How does he control it?"

"By the group system . . . the group of three, the group of five."

"And where does he find the group leaders?"

"He looks for the man in need of money. The man in need of a friend. The man with a grudge. The woman who wants a lover. He never treats with them directly but always through another."

"What sort of other?"

"Someone who can dispense favors. An official who issues licenses and permits, a shopkeeper who gives credit. A doctor, a customs officer."

"Can you draw me a portrait of our spy?"

"No, Colonel, I cannot."

"Captain Shabibi?"

It was a younger man this time, slim and studious, faintly nervous under the scrutiny of the great Safreddin.

"I do not think, Colonel, that a portrait helps us at all. A man can change his face in ten minutes. It helps very little to know whether our man is high or low. I think we come closer if we ask ourselves how he communicates his information to his masters."

"Good!" Safreddin nodded a wintry approval. "Please go on, Captain."

"He will rarely use the mails because they are censored and"—he added a tentative afterthought—"in Syria they are, unhappily, not too reliable."

There was a faint ripple of laughter in the room; but Safreddin's frown quelled it instantly.

The young captain went on. "Eli Cohen used couriers from time to time. But couriers mean a coming and going of persons, or contacts in odd places. An agent must send regular information. Sometimes it will be urgent. So he must use radio. We have a monitoring system. We have also direction-finding equipment. I have studied both. The equipment is not wholly adequate for police work. The personnel are not well trained."

There was no laughter this time; but Safreddin smiled. "Could you illustrate your point, Captain?"

"I can, Colonel. Last night I was in the monitor room. We picked up an unidentified station transmitting locally in figure groups. We called the direction-finders. One truck was out of action. Before the other could give us a vector, the station went off the air. All we got was thirty groups . . . useless for deciphering. You'll find a copy of the signal and my report on your desk."

"I've seen it already, Captain. Very clear, very concise. My compliments."

"Thank you, Colonel."

"And from tomorrow we'll have four direction-finders operating in the Damascus area. . . . You have a point, Captain Kasem?"

"My point, Colonel, is money. An espionage network means a lot of money, available all the time. It means a lot of people have spending cash which they can't account for. . . . That's where we might get our first break."

"But we haven't got it yet."

"No, Colonel."

"Have you thought why?"

"Yes. There is control on money going out of the country. There is no control on money that comes in. Under the new —under our government—there is a certain mistrust of the banks. People are hoarding cash so that they will not become too conspicuous."

"Do you think our policies are wrong, Captain?"

"I do not question them, Colonel, but . . ."

"Then you should question them like a wise brother. If there are defects we should try to remedy them by fraternal criticism. You were saying? . . ."

"That from an intelligence point of view, we are handicapped by our own restrictions on the money flow."

"Agreed. But we have other problems as well. Intelligence work is only a small function of national life. If we begin to demand declarations at the border on how much money the tourist imports, we lose the tourist. He says, quite rightly, that if he is prepared to spend in Syria, he should not be exposed to harassment. . . ." He relaxed and sat down on a leather cushion among the men. "But the point is still well taken. This very morning I was examining the accounts of those who operate foreign banking accounts. Some interesting facts emerged. Two well-known citizens have been cheating the Government by holding foreign currency abroad instead of repatriating it as the law demands. They are not spies. They are, however, criminals. They will be dealt with severely. A third—and this may prove an interesting exercise —has done nothing illegal; but I did discover that he was financed by a loan from an Italian enterprise. By the merest chance I checked the list of those who entered Damascus by air in the last two days. The name of this friendly financier is on the list. A further check revealed that he is staying at the Hotel des Caliphs, and that he has come to do more business in Syria. Nothing suspicious in that. On the contrary, we welcome foreign investment, provided it does not become foreign exploitation. So we have a foreign investor and a man to whom he has already lent money. It is dossier information, nothing more. But the man to whom he lent the money is an Iraqi who does business as a government contractor. So I want to know more about the association. My question is how do I proceed?"

"Question the Iraqi." This from a junior officer on the outer circle of the meeting.

Safreddin gave him a benevolent acknowledgment. "I know the Iraqi. I have a complete file on him. He will answer my questions and shrug and tell me that if I want him to do business for Syria, I must not frighten the traders. He will be right too. . . . I think we need something better than that."

"With respect, Colonel"—the studious Shabibi was on his feet again—"we fail in this matter too. There is no normal channel through which a friendly visitor, or friendly trader, can be drawn into our society, so that we may get to know him."

"There are channels, Captain. We never fail to offer the courtesies of trade and diplomacy to our visitors."

"These are not enough, Colonel. They are tainted with formality. Everyone wears a public face and hides his private one. In this we are becoming like the Russians and the Chinese, who have so much influence in our country."

A whisper of shock went round the circle of initiates. All eyes were turned on the unlikely fellow who made so bold a challenge in public. Safreddin sat, blank-faced, measuring the young man and the implication of his complaint. He should be proud of him and yet the shame of jealousy diminished the pride. He should commend and yet he was tempted, violently, to mock him for his indiscretion. There was a pit opening under his own feet and he could very easily fall into it unless he mastered his own vanity and his fear of potential rivals. Captain Shabibi was still on his feet, waiting. Finally Safreddin began to speak, quietly and persuasively.

"Sit down please, Captain. . . . First let me say that your frankness pleases me. It is not easy to say an unpopular thing even in this—this conspiracy of the righteous. I would like nothing better than that we should be able to present ourselves, full grown and proud and strong among the nations; so that every stranger would feel honored to enter our house and share the intimacy of our lives. But Syria has been sick for a long time. We have purged out the disease, yes. But the patient is still in convalescence. There is still the atmosphere of the hospital and the humiliation of continued treatment. Our private face, as you call it, is still pale and shrunken. So we cling strongly to our stronger friends: those who have suffered the same sickness, who have undergone the same harsh remedy of revolution, who are prepared to aid us to recovery with money, arms, trade and political support. They have given us new blood. They are helping us to build strong bone and muscle against the day of the last battle. Do you understand?"

"I understand, Colonel. But . . ."

"Let me explain the *but* for you, Captain—for all of us here. We do not like all the manners of our friends. We do not share all their ambitions for us. Just as we could not share the plans of the Egyptians when we had a joint command with them. But we do not rupture our friendship on this account. We are more subtle than that. We bend like the reeds of the Tigris to the wind. When the wind dies, we are upright again. We let the Russians teach us organization and management. We let the Chinese teach us how to preserve a political unity while we carry on an internal struggle. All the time we remain ourselves . . . rooted in Islam, rooted in this land which once was the throne of Islam. Now. . . ." He broke off and surveyed the small gathering with affection and authority. ". . . Now let us come back to our question which you have answered in part, but not in full. How do we catch our spy and break his network? How do we catch the rat who is nibbling at the cornsacks? I will tell you. A spy works for one thing only—information. How do we tempt him out of his hiding place . . . with the bait of information! To you, Captain Shabibi, if you were a Jewish spy, what would you most want to know about us?"

Selim Fathalla had had a bad day. Ever since lunchtime he had been fretting over his quarrel with Sergio Bellarmino —a quarrel which had introduced new risks into a situation already perilous enough. Emilie had felt herself insulted by the argument and had spent the afternoon in a state of such tearful tension that he had sent her home early. Bellarmino had refused her as a guide and interpreter: instead he had trotted off to do his own errands among the traders and the officials of the Ministry of Commerce. Either the man was an arrant fool, or he was playing a private game under instructions from Tel Aviv. . . . And yet this was not Baratz's way at all. Baratz chose his people with care and then trusted them to the limit, nursed them through their crises and took the final responsibility on his own back. Every courier he sent brought an affirmation of confidence and a word of encouragement. But this fellow was not content to be a messenger; he was acting like an inspector as well. He was offering moral judgments—an expensive luxury in a trade essentially amoral. He was asserting an authority he had no right to exercise. He was too prone to anger, too sure of his own rectitude to be let loose among a people long noted for their suppleness and subtlety.

He had been on the loose now since early afternoon. He had telephoned once to say that an official of the Ministry of Commerce had invited him to dinner on the following night and that Fathalla too was invited. After that, nothing. In desperation Fathalla had driven round to his hotel at nine in the evening only to be told that the gentleman had hired a car to go to Aleppo and that he would not be back until the evening of the next day. There was no sense at all in such conduct; unless . . . a new thought struck him and he wrestled with it for a long time while Emilie tossed in uneasy sleep, muttering and moaning.

Israeli intelligence was not handled by a single organization. There was the Military G2 which was run by Jakov Baratz. There was the Research and Analysis division of the Foreign Office. There was also a service dealing with counterespionage which was under the direct control of the Prime Minister. Like everyone else in Israel, the three departments worked sometimes in harmony, sometimes at odds with each other. It was not impossible that Baratz, worried by his breach of security with Emilie, had called in a man from counterespionage to check him out. It was an ugly idea; and it itched like a burr in his skin; but he could not discount it. It would at least explain the extraordinary brusqueness of Bellarmino and his obvious desire to set Emilie and Fathalla himself on the defensive. There was only one way to get the true answer: ask Baratz. He looked at his watch. Ten forty-five. Tonight's schedule with Tel Aviv called for a transmission at thirty-five minutes after midnight. He locked the door of the bedroom, opened the faience panel and settled down to draft and encipher his report.

He had been working for nearly twenty minutes when his doorbell rang. The sound startled him. Night visitors were rare in Damascus. He climbed out of his box in the wall, closed the faience panel and struggled into a dressing gown. The bell rang again, a long impatient sound that echoed through the house. He hurried downstairs and unbolted the heavy wooden door. A truck, full of vegetables, was parked across his entrance and the driver was standing on his doorstep, a shabby truculent fellow who stank of arrack. Clinging to him like a punch-drunk boxer was Sergio Bellarmino; his clothes were torn and filthy, his face was scarred with scratches and bruises and his head was bloody under a soiled bandage.

"Allah!" the driver swore unhappily. "I thought you would never come."

"What's happened?"

"An accident. Sixty kilometers north. A taxi was hit by a truck. The driver is dead. This one was thrown out. He seemed all right at first. He gave your name. I brought him back. Then he went stupid on me. The police will want to see him in the morning . . . Allah! Get him off me, will you! . . . And there's money to pay."

"Help me get him inside first."

They carried Bellarmino upstairs and laid him on a couch in the bedroom. He was quite bemused and he threshed about, babbling incoherently, while a small bloody foam gathered about his lips. Emilie woke and sat up, wide-eyed and startled, drawing the sheets about her naked body. The driver stared at her with drunken approval. Fathalla thrust a handful of notes into his palm, hurried him out of the house and locked the door.

When he reached the bedroom again, Emilie was already busy with warm water and towels. She gave him a brisk order. "You should get Dr. Bitar. He's very sick."

Fathalla dialed Bitar's number and waited a long time until Bitar answered, irritable and heavy with sleep. He told him the news.

"A business associate of mine arrived today. He's been in an accident. There's a head wound and other injuries. It looks serious. I'd like you to see him immediately."

"Best call an ambulance and deliver him to the hospital. I'll see him there."

"I'm not sure we should move him yet."

"Give me fifteen minutes. I'll come."

Bellarmino was quieter now, so that they were able to

cleanse him and strip off his torn jacket and keep him covered with blankets. While Emilie sat beside him, Fathalla went through his pockets. He found small change, a bloodied handkerchief, an Italian passport, an international health certificate, a wallet stuffed with Syrian notes and a book of travelers' checks in denominations of fifty and a hundred dollars. There were seven visiting cards, identifying Sergio Bellarmino as a representative of Intercommercio Bellarmino, Rome. There was a notebook full of addresses and telephone numbers and, sewn inside the lining, a small hard rectangular object. Fathalla slit the lining and took it out. It was a gold plaque, engraved in the center with the Star of David; on the reverse side, inscribed in Hebrew characters, were the names of the European concentration camps, and under each, the number of the victims who had died there. Fathalla uttered a very dirty curse.

Emilie looked up, startled. "What did you find, Selim?"

"Enough to hang us all. Bellarmino is a fool and a fanatic as well. To carry a talisman like that makes nonsense of every rule in the book. A wonder he didn't wear it around his neck!"

He riffled through the addresses. God only knew how much they might reveal! There was no time to examine them now. He locked the book and the plaque behind the panel and shoved the wallet and the documents back into the jacket.

Emilie felt Bellarmino's wrist. "His pulse is very weak."

"I hope he dies."

"Don't say that please, Selim."

"I'm sorry."

"What happened to him?"

"I only know what the truck driver told me. An accident. Apparently Bellarmino was well enough to get himself a ride back. He collapsed on the way. Allah! If they'd taken him to hospital! . . ."

"Please, Selim, be calm. Dr. Bitar will tell us what to do."

"We'll have the police on our necks in the morning."

"That's tomorrow. Just let us get through the night."

Bellarmino began to stir and mutter again. This time the words were clear—four words uttered over and over again, as if they were recorded on a loop of tape—*Barukh attà Adonai elohenu . . . Barukh attà Adonai elohenu . . . Barukh attà. . . .*

Emilie looked at Fathalla; his face was grim and strained. "What's he saying?"

"It's Hebrew. The first words of the blessing: 'Blessed be thou, O Lord our God!' Why the devil doesn't he shut up!"

The doorbell rang. Again Fathalla turned away and ran clattering down the stairs. Bellarmino's head rolled from side to side on the pillow and the words tumbled out monotonously as a water fall. *"Barukh attà Adonai elohenu . . . Barukh. . . ."*

A moment later Dr. Bitar was in the room with Fathalla at his back. He made a pulse count and an auscultation. He peered into eyes, ears and nostrils, he stripped off the bloody bandage and palpated the skull case while the words still poured from the frothing lips. Finally Bitar straightened up and announced, "Depressed fracture and hemorrhage. There's nothing we can do here. Call an ambulance and then I'll telephone the hospital and have them prepare for us."

"Wait!" Fathalla held him with the high harsh word. "How long will he babble like this?"

Bitar shrugged. "Until the pressure is removed either from the fracture or from the blood clot."

"Would he talk again?"

"He might. Who knows?"

"Do you understand what he's saying?"

Bitar listened a moment. "It sounds like Arabic, but it isn't."

"It's a Hebrew prayer. We can't risk him in the hospital."

"You can't risk him here either," said Bitar firmly. "He would die on your hands. He may die anyway."

"Then kill him!" said Selim Fathalla. "Kill him now!"

They gaped at him, speechless. The only sound in the room was the steady, insistent voice of Sergio Bellarmino pronouncing his barren blessing.

"You can do it." Fathalla's voice was cold and impersonal. "Adrenalin straight into the heart—a big dose. You must do it. Three lives, twenty lives, fifty—against one. Do it!"

Without a word and very slowly, Bitar hoisted himself to his feet. From his bag of medicines he took a large syringe, a long needle encased in sterile plastic and an ampoule of clear liquid. He fitted the needle, filled the syringe and held it out to Fathalla. There was not a tremor in his hand or in his voice.

"You do it, Selim. I'll show you where to inject. He's a Jew. You have family rights. I'm an Arab. If what I do and what I risk means anything, it means an Arab should not kill a Jew. . . . You inject here."

He parted Bellarmino's shirtfront and marked the spot with his forefinger.

JERUSALEM, JORDAN

The preparations which Idris Jarrah made for his flight into the Promised Land of anonymity and affluence were very simple. He put two hundred dollars' worth of currency in one pocket of his trousers. In the other he put his pistol with a spare clip of ammunition. The rest of his ten thousand dollars he folded in a clean handkerchief and taped to his body with an adhesive bandage. Then he put on his shirt, knotted his tie, buttoned his passports, his health documents and his new American checkbook in the pocket of his jacket —and was ready for the road.

He had thought everything out very carefully. His suitcase and briefcase would remain in his room. He was still in residence at the Intercontinental Hotel. If there was any hitch in tonight's plans, he could always come back, reclaim his Greek passport and get his exit permit for the crossing at the Mandelbaum Gate. Once inside Israel he would buy himself a suitcase full of new clothes and use his Italian passport to identify himself as a tourist and ensure a safe exit from Lod airport. He had one bad moment when he remembered that his Italian passport would have no entry stamp to show that he had been legally admitted into Israel. Then he recalled that, because of the Arab boycott, the Israelis were prepared to admit their visitors without marking their passports so that they might be free for later travel to Arab countries. So he had nothing more to worry about. Israel was a peaceful place, and who would question a respectable fellow taking an early morning walk in the suburbs.

He felt so pleased with himself that he would have liked to pay a short visit to the widow in the Old City; but it was already twenty-five minutes to eleven and he was expected, on the hour, in the house of Hamid the candlemaker. He took a final look at himself in the mirror, and saw a relaxed round-faced fellow with twenty years of good living ahead of him. Then he walked down to the lobby, summoned a taxi and set off on the road to Bethlehem.

Tonight—Allah be praised—there was no moon. The sky was full of stars that hung almost within hand's reach. There was a chill in the air and soon, on the uplands, the desert wind would begin to stir. It was a perfect night for his enterprise. Step ten yards away from the yellow lights of a village and it was impossible to distinguish a man from a rock. The cold kept the border guards on the move and, once the wind rose, it swirled and eddied through the time-scored hills so that it was hard to know the true direction of a sound.

Yet, as the lights of the Old City fell away behind him Jarrah felt a faint pang of regret. There was always the tendril root of the self that clung tenaciously to the native soil. There was always the folk memory that stirred painfully at a trick of the light, a scent of dusty flowers, the lilt of a phrase spoken in the mother tongue. But when you traveled long enough and far enough you became like the Bedouin, a sand dweller, living without encumbrance, loving without permanence, building nothing, because tomorrow the sand would bury it anyway. And after a while the memories that tied you to a birthplace became faint and tenuous, like a song piped by a shepherd on the hillside, half heard and quickly forgotten.

The house of Hamid the candlemaker lay halfway along an alley wide enough for a camel, but too narrow for an automobile. The cobbles were fetid with refuse and donkey droppings and the slops thrown from tenement windows. At this hour the windows were shuttered and the only light came from the low stars and the faint gleam of yellow lamps behind the wooden slats. Idris Jarrah picked his way among the rubbish until he came to a low door set in a Norman arch. Two steps led down to the door. In the center of the door was a judas window, curtained on the inside and protected outside by bars of rusted iron. Jarrah knocked at the door, once, twice, then twice again. The curtain was drawn aside and a pair of old eyes inspected him. Then the curtain dropped again, there was the sound of heavy bolts being drawn, and the door opened. He walked down three more steps into a cellar room heavy with the smell of wax and incense and Turkish tobacco and stale coffee.

The cellar was stacked from floor to ceiling with candles: slim tapers, white and yellow, squat cubes molded with the figures of Byzantine saints, long curlicues green and yellow and red, white Paschal candles studded with nails, the Three Wise Men with cotton wicks growing out of their crowns, the Wise Virgins and the Foolish One, painted in the garish colors of childhood round a spiral as thick as a pillar.

In the midst of them all stood Hamid himself, gnarled as

an ancient olive tree, gray as a biblical patriarch. He joined his hands in greeting and asked, "Are you the man who is expected?"

"I am he. You know me, Hamid?"

"I am not asked to know you. Only to set you on your way."

He clapped his hands. The curtains at the rear of the cellar were drawn aside and a young man dressed in sandals, slacks and a greasy sweater stepped forward. The old man presented him without ceremony.

"This is Yussuf. He will take you."

"Where are we going?"

"To Hebron first." It was Yussuf who answered. "I have a truck. I carry hides for the tanners."

"And after Hebron?"

"The others will look after you."

"How much do I owe you?"

"Nothing. We are paid from Hebron. You settle with them."

"Let's go then. Thank you."

"Tikram. . . . You are welcome." The old man turned away, indifferently.

Jarrah followed his guide through the curtain into a yard where the wax vats stood lined out under roofs of corrugated iron. At the end of the yard was a gate that opened into another lane, wider this time, but filled with the stink of fresh hides. The source of the stink was a battered truck piled high with sheep and goatskins. Jarrah coughed and spat.

The youth laughed. "You get used to it after a while. Lucky you don't have to ride under the skins. That's happened to some people!"

Jarrah climbed into the cabin; his guide swung the starting handle, scrambled in beside him and coaxed the coughing engine into life and took off with a breakneck jerk. Yussuf drove like a maniac on the downhill slopes and nudged the ancient vehicle up the hills with curses and bawdy invocations. He hung wide out on the curves so that it seemed as if the load would tear loose and be scattered in a foul mess all over the valley. He charged relentlessly at oncoming vehicles pounding his horn and shouted with delight as he swung aside at the last possible moment.

When Jarrah remonstrated with him, he laughed happily. "We go slow, you get the stink. We go fast, you lose it. Make up your mind!"

Jarrah decided against the stink and endured the rest of the bone-shattering ride in silence. Finally they turned off the main road and headed downward over deeply rutted tracks into the Hebron valley. They passed one village and another, and then halted a hundred yards from the outskirts of a fairly large settlement.

The young man pointed through the cracked windscreen. "I leave you here. Walk straight ahead. The fifth house on the right. Knock four times."

"Why don't you take me in?"

"I have to deliver this stuff. Have you got a cigarette?"

"I don't smoke."

He climbed out of the truck and flexed his cramped muscles. The youth drove the truck around him in a wide circle and headed back to the main road. Idris Jarrah began to walk towards the village. The lights were sparse. There was no movement of people. His footsteps sounded uncomfortably loud on the loose gravel of the track. As he passed the first house a tethered dog barked at him and went on barking until a muffled voice cursed it into silence. Jarrah counted off the houses. At the fifth one he stopped. It was dark and silent. He stepped up to the door and rapped sharply, four times in quick succession.

There was a long pause, then the door opened. A voice said: "Come in, friend."

He stepped forward into darkness.

TEN

At ten-fifteen in the morning, Nuri Chakry received a telephone call from the manager of a Swiss bank in Beirut. It was a gesture of courtesy, to inform Mr. Chakry that the Swiss were holding a post-dated check for fifteen million dollars drawn on a Saudi account with the Phoenician Bank. It would be presented for payment in ten days. Nuri Chakry acknowledged the courtesy with appropriate gratitude and assured his colleague that the check would be met promptly. At ten-thirty precisely, a similar courtesy was offered by a British banking agency. They would present three Kuwaiti checks within ten days in a total of thirteen million dollars. Nuri Chakry offered the same assurance of prompt payment and put down the telephone.

His hands were clammy. There was an empty space in the pit of his belly and his whole body seemed to be contracting around it. He was not surprised. He knew he had no cause to be shocked. This was the way they announced your execution in the small world of money. They sent you an engraved invitation to the ceremony and gave you adequate time to enjoy your nightmares before they cut your heart out. They were not brutal; they were not even unfriendly. They were mechanically precise about the whole business. A check was a document payable at sight, but decent practice required seven days' notice for the payment of a large capital amount. They were giving him ten. How could they possibly feel guilty? How could he possibly feel aggrieved?

He would pay, of course. He was still three and a half percent liquid. But another large call would clean him out—and the call was certain to be made. Who in his right mind would continue to trust his money to a man who already had the mark of death on him? In ten days, unless the Government stepped in, he would have to close his doors and leave thousands of his smaller depositors screaming for their money. No use then to explain that their funds were temporarily converted into a Manhattan skyscraper, into a shipyard and an airline, a dozen hotels and a hundred other impressive but uneatable assets; no use to show them the assets growing like mushrooms on a piece of graph paper. He had made a bargain with them which he could not fulfil. The bond was written thus: "Deposit your money with me and I will deliver it back to you any time within banking hours, six days a week." If he did not deliver the money, they would yell for his blood—and there was every chance that they would get it.

For a long time, he had been insulated from violence; but now the memory of it rose up to haunt him: a cheating card-player kicked to death in a lane near his dockside office; a pimp who had sold tainted girls, beaten to a pulp by the crew of a Dutch merchantman; the massacres in West Jordan when he was still a donkey boy; the bloody violent days of the Stern Gang and the Palestine Police. He had seen what a mob could do with brickbats and bottles of petrol. He could hear them already chanting and raging and smashing the plate-glass windows of the dream palace which had been built with their money.

Then, with equal vividness, he saw that the very threat of violence might be his salvation. Faced with civil disorder,

with the destruction of public confidence, with the deface-
ment of the image of Lebanon as a safe harbor for money,
as a tourist paradise, the Ministry of Finance and the Central Bank would have to help him. No matter that they would
happily see him boiled in oil, they would have to hold him
safe and respected. The tension in him relaxed. He dried
his damp hands and mopped his forehead and breathed long
and deeply, and his pulse beat steadied. Then he dialed out
on his private line and spoke with Taleb.

"Taleb? . . . This is Chakry. I've been waiting to hear from
you or from the Minister. I've had nothing."

"No decision has been made yet." Taleb was brusque and
unfriendly. "The Minister has only been back a few days.
He's been very busy."

"Has our problem been referred to him?"

"I'm not sure. I'd have to look at the files."

"Don't hurry," Chakry told him pleasantly. "I know
you're all very occupied. But I thought you'd better know.
In ten days we pay out twenty-eight million against sight
documents. The next day we're out of business."

"What!" Taleb squawked like a startled parrot. "You told
us. . . . We thought. . . ."

"You didn't think at all!" said Chakry with thin malice.
"You were so busy sharpening the knives for me, you didn't
give a curse what else happened. Well, little brother, it's
going to happen in ten days. We're solvent, but we're out of
cash. No government wages, no money for small traders,
nothing in the till at all. It's all yours now!"

"No, wait!" Taleb was desperate. "If you could send us the
figures . . ."

"You've had them. They're in your file too. What you
haven't got is a decision. I suggest you get it."

"It's going to take a few days."

"You take as many days as you want. We close the doors
in ten."

Taleb was still spluttering unhappily when he put down the phone.

Chakry picked up his golden emperor, tossed him high in the air, caught him and held him and talked to him like a happy brother. ". . . They never understand, do they? Show them the jeweled temples on the other side of the river and they cry because the water's cold. Put 'em in a pack and they howl like wolves; snarl at them and they're jackals. They're carrion eaters and they want to feast with kings! But we've got 'em now, haven't we? You and I, we've got 'em! A month from now they'll be selling us their daughters and their sisters to show what good friends they are. . . ."

The golden emperor sat silent in his prison and stared at him with one godlike eye. Chakry set him down on the desk and walked to the window where he stood a long time surveying the capital of his threatened empire. He was quite calm now: calm and exalted and contemptuous of the machinations of his enemies. He was on the eve of the last battle. To judge from Taleb's terror, he had an even chance of winning it. Even if he lost, he would still survive. But, from this moment, everything he did and said was of a critical importance. He could not afford a false or timid move because the jackals would be pacing round the encampment, sniffing for the smell of fear. Every act must be calculated to create doubt and confusion among those who held him under siege and yet were afraid that he would outguess them in the end.

This was the strange chemistry of the casino: you played best when you knew you would walk out a prince or a pauper; and you had a heady contempt for those who would fawn on you if you won and refuse you a cup of water if you lost. Irrelevantly, he thought of Idris Jarrah, harried and in hiding. Jarrah was of the same breed as himself, a good gambler with the deck stacked against him. It would be pleasant to know that he had managed to beat the house.

Matheson? . . . Matheson was one of the nothing-men for whom you need neither weep nor cheer. Matheson you could buy under twenty names in as many countries. He would serve any paymaster, as he served himself, without distinction and without commitment. This was his prime value: you could always trust him; you were never obliged to respect him.

Matheson had asked to see him at eleven this morning. He wanted to report on his interview with the American Ambassador. He wanted to discuss what he called a "personal matter of some importance"; which meant that his feathers had been ruffled and he wanted them smoothed by a firm and friendly hand. So be it. Just so he stayed happy for the next fourteen days, Chakry was happy to massage his vanity every hour on the hour.

Matheson had prepared for his interview with considerable care. First he recited his interview with the American Ambassador. He concealed nothing. He leaned rather heavily on his own embarrassment at the questions he had been forced to answer, and on his own stout defense of his master. He offered a blunt opinion that the Americans would not be one whit interested in a takeover until a Russian offer was firm and public.

Chakry nodded a smiling agreement. "Naturally, Mark. I knew that from the beginning. But you seemed so anxious to salve your conscience, I had to let you do it. As I told you yesterday I don't really give a damn about the Americans. You've done your duty. Forget them. . . . Now you had something personal to discuss."

Matheson had rehearsed this part of his story with considerable care. He told it glibly and confidently. Lew Mortimer had offered him a job. The money was better than he was getting now; but he had deep personal loyalties to Chakry and to the Phoenician Bank. He was happy to stay where he was —provided Chakry could assure him that the bank would stay in business. Lew Mortimer had said just the opposite. The bank would be closed in a month. He had laughed at the idea that Chakry or the Finance Ministry or any banker in the world could save it. Of course, Mortimer was a sworn enemy; but Matheson needed, and felt that he had a right, to provide for his own future.

Chakry heard him out with practiced sympathy. He asked just the right questions to keep Matheson embarrassed. He was solicitous enough to make Matheson feel valuable and valued. When the recital was over, he lapsed long enough into silent thought to give weight and importance to everything Matheson had told him. Then he leaned forward in his chair and began to talk, earnestly and quietly.

"Let me tell you, Mark. I wouldn't blame you at all if you accepted Mortimer's offer. You've been carrying a heavy load these last weeks. You've shown a loyalty and courage which is all too rare in our business. If you want to go, you'll have my blessing and a bonus as well. I'll be hurt; I have to say that. I'll be damaged at just the wrong moment; and it will take me a long time to replace you. But I won't blame you."

"I don't want to go." Matheson was obviously unhappy. "But you understand, Nuri, I do need clearer and firmer information than I have now."

"Agreed. And this morning I'm in a position to give it to you. Let's start with the worst news and then I'll show you how it works for us. The Swiss have called—and the British. Ten days from now the Saudis and the Kuwaitis pull out their money. In theory we put up the shutters the next day. In fact, we won't. But that's the story I've told Taleb at the Finance Ministry; if they don't help us we'll have a run on the bank. Taleb is scared. They're all scared. Which is exactly what I want. It's my guess that, right at this moment, Taleb is pouring out his heart in the Minister's office. Today's Tuesday. Our deadline is Thursday week. That means they'll have to come to the party by Monday at the latest. Otherwise we can't pay the government wages next week. So, unless I'm very much mistaken, they'll be in touch with us just before the close of business on Monday. They'll let us sweat until then . . ."

"But you told me we don't have to depend on the Finance Ministry."

"I told *you*, Mark. I didn't tell them. I want them committed. It works better that way."

"But if they don't commit?"

"Then here's what happens. I leave tomorrow morning for Paris. I spoke with Moscow last night. They're serious about this offer. They're sending two men to meet me in Paris. I've told them they have forty-eight hours to make up their minds about the general principles of a sale agreement. In that same forty-eight hours I shall be making arrangements for a fifty-million-dollar financing by a French insurance company. . . . That's one side of the market which I've been exploring quietly on my own account."

"Which company?"

"The Société Anonyme des Assurances Commerciales. The deal is that they will take up our unissued capital to the tune of twenty-five million and make us a loan of another twenty-five million at six percent, repayable in three years."

"How the devil did you get a deal like that?"

"By promising them all our new insurance business and all our renewals."

"You're a genius, Nuri!" Matheson's relief was almost comical. Chakry grinned cheerfully. "Never twist the old tiger's tail, Mark, he's liable to bite. . . . So here is how we play the comedy. I leave tomorrow, as I told you. You stay here and deal with Taleb and his boys. At close of business on Monday, I'll call you. If the Finance Ministry has agreed by then, well and good. If not I'll sign either with the Russians or the insurance people before five o'clock and I'll be

back in Beirut on Tuesday morning. Then we'll see whose
face is red."

"A question, Nuri. Suppose the Russians take us over, what
about my job?"

"They either keep you on or buy out your contract. My
guess is they'll want to keep you on because they're anxious
to preserve the present administration."

"That's fair enough. What do I tell Taleb to explain your
absence?"

"Nothing. I'm in Paris on business. I'll be back on Tuesday morning. That will give him another headache. . . .
Anything else?"

"Well, there was something else. I wasn't going to mention it because I thought Mortimer was trying to call your
bluff. He said that if you could raise the money you needed,
he'd match it, dollar for dollar, provided he could take control of the investment. Do you want me to tell him anything?
I'll have to give him an answer this evening."

"Tell him to go sleep with his mother," said Nuri Chakry.

"A pleasure," said Mark Matheson.

"And don't mention the Assurances Commerciales."

"Of course not."

HEBRON, JORDAN

Idris Jarrah, the moonfaced mercenary, was hung like the
Prophet's coffin between heaven and hell. The heaven was a
tiny sliver of daylight, far above his head; the hell was a black
and bottomless pit below his dangling feet. He knew that he
was alive because every nerve in his body was inflamed with
pain. He knew that he would soon be dead because last night
he had walked into a snare—ten men all armed waiting for
him in the fifth house on the right. White Coffee had been
there too, unarmed and smiling, ready to welcome his faith-
less brother at the judgment seat.

They had not been too unkind to him at first. They had stripped him of his clothing and confiscated his pistol and peeled the ten thousand dollars off his chest and sat him naked on a chair with a gun pressed against the back of his neck. Then they had told him the story of his own mistake. When he had telephoned Black Coffee from the Intercontinental Hotel, White Coffee was sitting in the same room with him, discussing how best they might carry out Cairo's order to hunt down and kill Idris Jarrah. Thereafter everything had been simple. If he had not made contact with the Organization, they would have killed him in the hotel or shot him in a taxi on the way to the Mandelbaum Gate. They would still kill him, of course; but if he wanted to die comfortably, he must pay for the privilege. He was to write them a check to clean out his personal funds from the American bank in which he had deposited them.

This Jarrah had refused to do. He reasoned that with patience and endurance he might be able to strike a bargain: fifty thousand dollars for his life and fifty thousand dollars left safe to begin a new one. White Coffee reasoned differently. Given time and ingenuity he could break any man. He was sure he could break Idris Jarrah, whose white and shivering body was obviously very sensitive to discomfort. So they had beaten him and burned him with cigarettes and played all sorts of agonizing games with him until, just before cockcrow, he collapsed. Then they had trussed him like a fowl, stuffed a greasy rag into his mouth, looped a rope under his armpits and hung him in an ancient silo where, two thousand years ago, the Romans had stored their grain. They had covered the silo with a wooden lid and left him swinging like a lead weight at the end of a plumb line.

He was there still, drifting in and out of consciousness, gasping for air as the gag stifled him, moaning helplessly against the ache of his wracked muscles, the pain of his festering burns, the rasp of the rope against his bare flesh.

He had lost all sense of time. He knew only that it was day because, when he found strength enough to lift his head, he could see the strip of sunlight and feel the heat building up around him. He could feel his body drying out too, and he knew that by nightfall he would be ready to grovel for a glass of water and that by the end of another day he would be dead.

For a while he went mad, gnawing on the gag, twisting his tortured body this way and that, trying to swing himself against the walls of the silo and beat himself to death; but the chamber was too broad and, after a while, the pain drove out the madness; so that he hung, twisting and turning, half stifled by his own mucus.

After that he began to experience the separation of himself. There were two of him now, perhaps three, or even four. There was the seeing Jarrah who clung like a bat to the walls and looked down upon the bloody bundle suspended in the still, stale air; there was the suffering Jarrah, conjoined with the bat and the bundle, mewing and gargling in an intolerable diversity of dolors; there was the fantasy Jarrah, coupling with a bewilderment of women, counting out piles of banknotes, sleeping on silk, waking to the sound of heavenly music. . . . And then there was no Jarrah at all, only a core of anguish at the dark center of nothing.

DAMASCUS

Colonel Omar Safreddin was enjoying an unfamiliar experience: the sudden flowering of friendship with an intelligent and handsome young man. In a night and a day, Captain Shabibi had become a personage in his life—a personage so vivid and various that all others receded into a gray background. In a night and a day Safreddin had become aware that his own life had been, for too long, very poor in personal satisfactions. He had dedicated himself so rigidly to ambition that he had become almost insensible to the sterility of his existence. He had protected himself so closely that it was a keen pleasure to find himself still vulnerable to affection. He had married late—and so traditionally that even his most knowing friends had whispered behind their hands, asking how so public a man could content himself with such a domestic woman. He had been content, because she gave him everything he needed from a wife: solicitude, the service of a strong body, the comfort of an obedient household, fidelity, freedom from the harassment to which men who married more educated women were constantly subject. She had given him a son, a mirror in whom one day he would contemplate the extension of himself and the renewal of his powers. Her humility elevated him. Her respect made him gentle and her gratitude for his condescensions made him generous and forgiving for her obvious shortcomings.

But there were moments, more frequent when he was under stress, in which he felt himself strangely solitary and naked to the malice of his many enemies. There were times when he saw clearly how prodigally he was spending his reserves of strength and intelligence and how hard it was to renew them. Often, when he played with his infant son, he wished passionately that he could grow up overnight and fulfil immediately the promise of continuity and participation, in the old tribal way. It was in these hours that Safreddin felt the dangerous tension building up inside him and the feline fearful cruelty tingling under his skin.

The Hunafa Club provided a release for the tensions. The contests of physical skill purged out the fears that might otherwise have poisoned him. The patent admiration of his pupils provided a partial illusion of a paternal relationship. It was enough to hold him steady and strong on his chosen course; but never quite enough to fill his solitude or rid him of the fear that haunted his private hours: the fear of secret animosity and public scorn when his strength should fail, and the usurious exactions of the power game in terms of bodily and mental resources.

Now, in a night and a day, everything was changed. After

the meeting of the Hunafa Club he had walked in his garden
with the young captain. He had been tender with him, a
happy master with a brilliant and eager pupil. He had drawn
him into a confession of his hopes and uncertainties, a cata-
logue of his career, a revelation of his private affections
which, it seemed, had centered themselves for a long time
on Safreddin himself. He had given him sage and careful
counsel, which the young man had accepted with a quite
touching thankfulness. He had invited him to work as his
own assistant and had been deeply moved by the passionate
expression of loyalty which the offer had evoked. He had put
his arm around the young man's shoulder and felt, not revulsion, but a strange relief in the bodily contact. They had
parted late and he had felt empty but curiously happy as if
he had consummated an act of union. They had met early in
the morning, before the office staff reported for duty and the
harmony of the evening had hung over all their hours of
work together, so that even the sinister affairs upon which
they were engaged took on the aspect of a mutual adventure.

Captain Shabibi had too much courtesy to thrust his
opinions at his superior; he insinuated them, quietly and
shrewdly, unfolding his reasons tentatively, with much deference, arguing them subtly but always with great respect. He
never sidestepped an uncomfortable fact and his guesswork
had at moments a touch of inspiration.

By three in the afternoon they had disposed of an enormous amount of paperwork and narrowed their discussion
to three items: the presumption of an Israeli espionage network, the illegal transmitter, and the curious affair of one
Sergio Bellarmino delivered by ambulance to the hospital
and found to be dead on arrival.

Captain Shabibi was sure that the first two items had to be
considered together. ". . . I reason this from our own activities, Colonel. We have an open frontier with Lebanon. We

had, until the Rumtha affair, an open frontier with Jordan.
We have telephone and telegraph communication with these
countries and with Iraq and Egypt. Our agents have no real
problem in keeping in touch with us. But the Israelis are cut
off. They have to use radio. We know that there is a transmitter, somewhere in Damascus, that operates on variable
frequencies, to a constantly changing time schedule. Last
night at forty-three minutes after midnight the monitors hit
the new wavelength. Figure groups again. This time, however, we got only eleven groups before they went off the air.
There was too little time for the direction-finders to operate.
Shortly after, we picked up a foreign station also sending five
figure groups. We got nearly a hundred groups of that. I'm
just guessing that this was an answering signal to our fellow
here, whoever he is."

"I agree, Captain. So we keep working until we strike a
lucky night. I've asked the Russians to help us on the cipher-
cracking problem. They have much more experience than
we have. We'll send them whatever we pick up. . . . What
interests me more is your proposal last night to bait a trap
for our Jewish friends. We still haven't decided what to use
for bait and where we plant it."

"The *where* I think is easy, Colonel. We have to work on
the assumption that information is being sold out of our own
ministries by venal or disaffected employees. As for the bait
itself . . ." He opened the linen envelope on his lap and
took out a bulky set of blueprints. "I suggest these. The first
engineering drawing for the emplacements on the Galilee
heights. They've been altered considerably during the con-
struction so they wouldn't do us too much harm if they got
into the wrong hands. But they do have the advantage of
being authentic documents. Normally they are kept in the
safe. I'm new here. I'd like to file a requisition for them so
that I can study them for a few days. I'll be rather careless
and leave them on my desk and in my drawer which does

not have a lock on it. If there is a mouse in the woodwork, we may tempt him out. . . . That is if you approve, Colonel."

Safreddin approved; but he tempered the approval with a question. "And if you do tempt him out, what then?"

Captain Shabibi put the documents back in the linen envelope and demonstrated how it was sealed by closing a metal clip. "The documents are delivered to me like this. I hand them back, closed in the same way. No unauthorized person is permitted to open the envelope. We treat the blueprints with ninhydrin. It's a powder the Russians use and the Americans too, I imagine. The powder is reddish brown. When it touches human skin it reacts with the amino acids and stains the skin purple. It can't be washed off; it has to wear off—and that takes about four days. So, anyone tampering with these documents will be easy to identify."

"You console me, Captain!" Safreddin laughed happily. "You prove my work is not wasted! We'll do big things together, you and I. Now . . . let's talk about the late Mr. Bellarmino." He opened the folder on his desk and passed the documents one by one across the table to Shabibi. "Police report on the accident. . . . You'll see I've penciled a request for a disciplinary inquiry into the conduct of the two officers who permitted a seriously injured man to be brought back to Damascus in a truck instead of delivering him directly to hospital. It is possible that money was passed. . . ."

"Then why was it offered, Colonel?"

"The explanation could be just what is written there. The man is in shock, dazed and frightened. He is in a strange country. He will trust himself only to the friend he knows. Rather than struggle with him, the police let him go, knowing that they can always pick him up the next day. He is delivered to Fathalla's house. . . . There's Fathalla's statement. It checks with that of the truck driver. . . . Fathalla calls Dr. Bitar. Bitar makes his examination and calls an ambulance to take the patient straight to hospital. Before the ambulance arrives, the patient begins to sink. Bitar gives a cardiac injection. The patient fails to respond. He dies. Bitar's statement is confirmed by the report of the surgeon who made the autopsy. Simple and straightforward. . . . Until you start to ask questions and get answers that don't match. Bellarmino and Fathalla were business friends—so intimate that Bellarmino's first thought after the accident is to get back to Fathalla's house. But the desk clerk at the Hotel des Caliphs reports that at nine o'clock last night Fathalla came to the hotel to see Bellarmino. Bellarmino had left for Aleppo without telling him. Fathalla claims that Bellarmino spoke only Italian and French. The police officers —and they speak only Arabic—say that Bellarmino spoke to them fairly well in their own language. Bellarmino's company guaranteed Fathalla a constant credit of twenty-five thousand sterling pounds, but Fathalla's books show an average yearly trade with Intercommercio of something less than eighteen thousand sterling pounds. Fathalla says Bellarmino came in from Rome. His air ticket shows a BEA flight to Athens, a one-day stopover, a flight to Cyprus with another stopover and then a flight to Beirut with a four-hour connection to Damascus. There is no return ticket, which is rather odd for a businessman, who would normally be concerned for travel discount. Two other things. The police recovered Bellarmino's belongings from the taxi. There was a traveling bag made of nylon fabric which contained clothing and toilet things. There was a briefcase which contained only two order books, some business stationery and a bunch of catalogues of merchandise handled by Intercommercio. Fathalla handed the police a wallet, travelers' checks, a passport and health certificates which he had found in Bellarmino's pockets." Safreddin spread the articles on his desk like a cardplayer laying down his hand. He looked up at his pupil with a smile of affectionate challenge. "Now tell me what's missing."

Captain Shabibi studied the pathetic little array for nearly a minute and then shook his head. "I don't know, Colonel."

"Think about it," said Safreddin, genially, "and we'll see if your answer's the same as mine. Another question. What do you make of the contradictions I've given you?"

Shabibi frowned and shook his head. "They're not necessarily contradictions, Colonel. Bellarmino may have been just a close man. It's a good trick in business to conceal your knowledge of a language and to force the other fellow to speak in a foreign tongue. The air ticket doesn't say too much. Bellarmino might easily have told Fathalla he came in from Rome without specifying his full itinerary. The high credit guarantee might be explained as a provision against trading emergencies. There's no question that Fathalla used it for private purposes, is there?"

"Not yet. We're still checking his figures."

"So what bothers you about Fathalla?"

"The answers you've just given me. I can hear Fathalla saying the same things in the same way. I've had a lot to do with him lately and I just can't shake him. I've tried hard to, because I do like him and yet he always irritates me and I'd like to make him eat a little dirt. But there's something about him that I can't . . ." He broke off. He stood up and began pacing the floor while the young man waited in discreet silence. Abruptly as he had begun, Safreddin stopped his pacing and swung round to face his pupil. There was a flush of excitement in his sallow cheeks. "That's it! I said you were good for me. You are! I know what bothers me about Fathalla. He reacts like a professional."

"A professional what?"

Safreddin waved the question aside. "A professional, like you or me. A man who knows the answers because he's guessed what the questions will be."

Captain Shabibi meditated on the idea for a while and then rejected it. "If you're saying he's an agent, that's a long guess, Colonel. Unless you have evidence to support it, you can hardly move against him."

"There's the evidence!" Safreddin moved back to his desk and rearranged Bellarmino's possessions so that the wallet and the check book lay together and there was a significant gap between them and the passport. "A man goes out to do business—any business!—what does he need first of all?"

"Contacts."

"And contacts mean names and addresses and telephone numbers. No one keeps those in his head. Where are they? Not here. Not in his briefcase either. The police found nothing else at the scene of the accident. There's the inventory under your hand. Conclusion?"

Captain Shabibi was still reluctant to come to it. "Not yet, Colonel. We have too many questions to answer ourselves. If Bellarmino was a legitimate businessman—and we can check that very easily through our contacts in Rome—then his address book has no significance for anyone but himself. Why would Fathalla want to take it?"

"Where is it then?"

"Bellarmino could have mislaid it. He could have dropped it out of his pocket when he took his coat off in the heat. There are twenty explanations."

"Then let's test them all, my friend. And while we're about it, let's not forget the other question we've never been able to answer: who gave the Israelis the name of Major Khalil so that he was arrested in Amman on the day of the Rumtha explosion? We know the Jordanians got it from Tel Aviv. But who passed them the word? Fathalla was in that little affair also."

"But you questioned him and got no satisfaction."

"We put a bug in his house too. And the bug hasn't worked. Either it was defective or he found it and took it out."

"And if he found it?"

"That makes him doubly professional."

"So question him again."

"No! Not now." Safreddin relaxed and smiled as if at the contemplation of a secret pleasure. "This time we let him think we are finished with him. We'll ask him to make arrangements for Bellarmino's funeral and to tidy up his business here. Then we leave him in peace. But we watch him, day and night. We watch him until we can draw a map of his dreams."

"I can draw that now," said Shabibi with soft contempt. "The Iraqis are great womanizers."

"Are you a womanizer, Captain?" The question was casual and good-humored.

Shabibi laughed. "I cannot afford it, Colonel."

"You're a wise young man. I build great hopes on you. Have dinner with me tonight—and then we'll spend an hour or two in the monitor room. Maybe our talkative friend will be on the air again."

"I'd like that, Colonel. I'd like it very much."

"You killed him," said Emilie Ayub.

"You don't know that," said Selim Fathalla. "You passed out, remember? When you woke, he was dead."

They were sitting in the garden where the last, late roses spread their perfume and the stone lion made his plaintive water music. They were sipping iced lemonade and basking in the last warmth of the day before the desert cold invaded the city. A calm like the calm of the wastelands had taken possession of them both and their talk was a dialogue of actors remote from reality.

"Why did you kill him?"

"Why do you ask, girl?"

"I have to live with you, Selim. I have to feel your hand on my breast and my belly. I need to love it. I want to love you."

"I'm a trader. I have been all my life. I do arithmetic in my head. One life is in my right hand. In my left are—how many more? Yours, mine, Bitar's—all our operatives spread over Syria. I hear a hurt man babbling a death sentence on all of us. What am I to do?"

"I don't blame you, Selim. Don't ever think I blame you. But the last thing I remember is that Bitar was hating you so much."

"He wasn't hating me, Emilie. He was testing me. He had to know whether I had enough courage to do what I demanded of him. He serves me to serve his own cause. He cannot do that unless he respects me."

"So you kill a man to win respect?"

"I carry a dead man on my back to spare the living."

"Right or wrong, Selim?"

"I'm not a Christian. I don't know."

"Don't the Jews have right and wrong too?"

"We have it, girl. Six million dead is a wrong . . . yes? Two and a half million living is a right, no? A little enough right—God knows! One man dead is how much of a wrong? You finish the mathematics. I can't. I'm just too tired."

"Bitar wouldn't destroy even one man."

"Wouldn't he?"

"That's what he said. It's the last thing I remember."

"He said he wouldn't kill a Jew. But a Jew is a man. And a Moslem is a man. And you're a Christian woman. You know what Bitar said to me when it was done? He said, 'Now I know you're my brother, Selim. Now I know we can live in peace—all Semites, all believers in the One, the Merciful!' He took my hand and kissed it and there were tears in his eyes. He said: 'You killed a Jew to save a Moslem!' It was a kind of sentimental madness; but there was a truth in it as well. I had absolved him from something. He was grateful. He knew he couldn't absolve me. And yet he wanted to. . . . Can't you do the same? You're my woman. Can't you try to forgive me?"

"I'm trying to forgive myself, Selim. You needed me and I wasn't there. I flew away."

"What would you have done?"

"I don't know. A woman doesn't really have a country. She doesn't have a religion either. She's the life-carrier. It's the only thing she understands. . . . Give me a child, Selim. Give it to me tonight. Here, now if you want!"

"I'm a dead man tonight, Emilie."

"I can make you alive again."

"Can you?" His face was haggard in the long pale light. "Last night, while you were still asleep, I took a message from Baratz in Tel Aviv. He's going to marry my wife when our divorce is through. He's so honest I can see him bleed in every word. He wants the plans of the Galilee emplacements. There's war in the wind and he wants them urgently. He knows the risks. He's honest about those too. He leaves the decision to me. If I can't face the job, he'll pull me out—pull us both out—now. I have to answer him tonight."

"And what will you say, Selim?"

"What do you want me to say, girl?"

"What does your heart say, Selim?"

"My heart? God! My heart says the plain thing plainly. Pack and go! Tonight! Over the hills into Lebanon and out by the first plane in the morning to Cyprus. We could do it. I've planned it a hundred times over. And yet . . ."

"Say it truly, Selim. Truly."

"I can't put it into words."

"Try."

"Why won't you let me be?"

"I can't. I'm you, Selim. You're me. Apart we're dead leaves blowing in the wind."

"So this is the way I think, Emilie. Some day—soon, late, who knows when?—there will be a war between Israel and the Arabs. Boys will come climbing up the Galilee hills to silence the Syrian guns that have been firing on their farms for years. If they don't know what I may be able to tell them, they will die, with their bellies spilling over the rocks. So many boys, Emilie. So many. . . ."

"And if they do know, Selim, Syrian boys will die by their guns. . . . So many of those too."

"You fight with your brothers," said Fathalla harshly. "Whom else do you know?"

"When you sleep with me, do you ask what I am? When I woke last night and saw Bellarmino lying on the bed, he was just a dead man. Arab or Jew, who cared? Who cares now?"

"Do you have to torment me, woman?"

"If we have to die, my dear one, shouldn't we ask why?"

And then, as the sun went down, they heard the muezzin crying to all who would listen, "There is no God but God. . . ."

The incantation still lingered in the air when old Farida ushered Dr. Bitar into the garden. For a man so prone to melancholy he was in high humor. He gulped a glass of iced tea, stretched his long, gangling legs and delivered a minor oration:

"Everything goes in threes—good or bad. I should be in bed early tonight because there is a woman who is sure to go into labor after midnight and call me out to hold her hand. She won't give birth for at least ten hours, but what does she care? But I don't want to go to sleep tonight. I am so happy I could sing. Last night was bad, Selim. This morning with the police was bad too. Today everything changes. Listen! Everything goes in threes as I told you. Before I leave my house to come to you, I have a telephone call from the police surgeon. He's an old friend. I've patched up some of the bad jobs he has done and I have never charged him anything. He told me the case is closed. Accidental death. No more inquiries. Good, eh?"

"Very good." Fathalla was skeptical. "As far as it goes. The police are one department. The security service is another. Let's not be too confident. Our friend Safreddin will be burrowing into the files like a rat in a sack of rice."

"No, Selim. Safreddin had the files, sure. But he sent them

back. The word came from him. That's the first of the three good things. The next you have to pay for."

"How much?"

"A little more than usual. But I think it's worth the money." He fished in his pocket and brought out a grubby piece of paper scrawled in cursive Arabic. He held it out to Fathalla. "It's a copy of a letter filed today in the Ministry of Foreign Affairs."

"Authentic?"

"Absolutely. We've never had any trouble with our man there. That's why I like to pay him well. Read it and then cross the question off your list."

Fathalla scanned the letter hurriedly and then read it again, slowly searching for the false notes and the concocted phrases. He found none. The content was impressive and important. In return for a year's guarantee of safe passage for their oil along the Syrian pipeline, at a regularly scaled price, the Iraqis would commit themselves to military cooperation with Syria. The terms of the cooperation were precise. The agreement was to remain secret and no demand for a treaty was to be made. The commitment of troops and arms would be made in the event of a direct attack by Israel on Syrian or Egyptian territory, or, alternatively in the event of joint defensive action undertaken by Syria and Egypt acting in concert. The agreement would be enforceable from the date of the letter.

"Well?" Bitar poured himself another glass of tea and sipped it with noisy satisfaction. "Is it worth the money, Selim?"

"Yes. I'll pay you before you go." He grinned at Emilie. "This will keep Baratz happy too. At least he'll feel he's getting reasonable service. I hope the third item's as good as this, Doctor."

"Not quite as good, Selim. So you don't pay as much. It comes third-hand from the man who duplicates the minutes of Defense meetings, through his girl friend, to the lover she keeps on the side, who happens to work for us. Twenty Syrian technicians leave at the end of the week for training in Russia on ground-to-air missiles."

"So they're going to get them . . . if they haven't got some already."

"It looks like it. . . . Are you happier now?"

"We're in business again. That always makes me happy."

"So now you'll give me a baby, Selim?" Emilie was suddenly willful as a schoolgirl. "Every woman needs a baby, doesn't she, Doctor?"

"Of course she does." Bitar folded his long hands on his shirtfront. "Why not give her one, Selim? She's healthy. She's got a good pelvic structure. I'll do the delivery myself—free of charge."

"I'll buy you both a dinner instead."

"Let's have dinner here, Selim. I'll make it myself. We're comfortable. Why move?"

"I want to get out for a while, girl. I'm sick of this rat-hole life. We've had it for a week now and it's bad for us all."

"I agree." Bitar was delighted with the idea. "Let's go to Abu Nowas. His food is pretty bad; but it's still the best in Damascus. Make yourself beautiful, young woman, and I'll see you get your baby. Even if I have to give it to you myself."

When she had gone, Bitar turned to Fathalla and chuckled. "So what do you do now, Selim? When they get like this, there's only one cure."

"You're very bright tonight, Doctor. And much too clinical."

"Do you know why?" Bitar leaned forward and laid a bony hand on his wrist. "I've defied the Prophet. I'm a little drunk —on two glasses of whisky."

"Another could be dangerous, Doctor."

"I know it. But sometimes you need a lift to get you over the fence into tomorrow. There's another piece of news I didn't want your girl to hear."

"Good or bad?"

"Bad. A patient of mine came to see me today. I've been treating him for a mild heart condition. This time he wanted a certificate to excuse him from night work."

"So?"

"He told me what the night work was. He's been cruising the streets in a radio van looking for an illegal transmitter."

Fathalla said a very dirty word.

JERUSALEM, ISRAEL

An hour after sunset, Jakov Baratz received his last intelligence report for the day: the King of Jordan and the visiting dignitaries had left Jerusalem and were driving back to Addan; there was no significant change in the disposition of Arab Legion troops; the order of battle in the Hebron area remained unchanged.

The report disappointed him. He had been clinging to the hope that at the last minute the dispositions would be changed and the operation, with all its dubious consequences, would be called off. There was still time, of course —five hours to midnight; but there was no more hope. The Mandelbaum Gate was closed. The most vigilant watcher on the hills could not identify small bodies of troops moving at night. So, for all practical purposes, the argument was over. Gunfire would begin at dawn.

The Chief of Staff was conferring with the Operation Commander. Baratz telephoned his report, made a rendezvous for five in the morning at the Hebron observation post and then drove to the white house on Har Zion to have dinner with Yehudith Ronen. A black depression hung over him. His whole world had taken on a sinister aspect, like a landscape too calm under the clouds of a coming tempest.

The news from Damascus was bad. A key agent and a vital network were in jeopardy because of the indiscretion of a courier. The courier was dead, killed by his own colleague. At a moment when he was required to procure strategic information, Selim Fathalla was being forced into a defensive attitude to keep himself and his own organization alive. If, by mischance or miscalculation, the organization was broken, the Syrians would have a beautiful propaganda piece to prove the aggressive intentions of Israel and rally the divided Arabs to a holy war. There was no legality in the hidden politics of the half-world; but an open illegality like espionage, or like tomorrow's operation in Hebron, was a potent weapon in the hands of an enemy.

When he came to Yehudith's house he called his office and gave them the telephone number for emergency contact. Then he followed Yehudith into the garden and walked with her in the cool darkness watching the sickle of the new moon climb over the walls of the old city. The dark mood still clung to him like the cobwebs of a nightmare, but Yehudith was patient with him. She plied him with the small gossip of her day: her plans for an exhibition, a new work which she was sketching to express the beginning of a new life for them both, her idea of keeping the old house in Jerusalem even after they had established themselves in Tel Aviv, the work of a young painter from Mali who was studying on a scholarship in Jerusalem.

Baratz let himself drift with the flow of her talk, touching now a beach, now a promontory of a country which, for too long, had been alien to him. This was the problem of the underworld trade, indeed of the whole military life: you were a member of a small separate brotherhood, you spoke in dialect, you used strange weights and measures, you calculated in the currency of crisis and disaster; you forgot so quickly the varied simplicities of common life—wooings and weddings and children's bellyaches and men who caught fish and girls who embroidered handkerchiefs and happy wives haggling over the price of apples.

There was a great danger in the esoteric existence of the specialist, a fatal fascination in the backstage intimacy of the puppet theater. After a while you lapsed into a subtle contempt for the happy ignorance of the herd. You despised the innocence of those who had no knowledge of iniquity. The mother tongue became strange to you and you ended, perched like a stylite on a pillar, surveying a desert and wondering where the people had gone. He was not conscious that he had put the thought into words; so he was shocked when Yehudith answered it for him.

"Isn't that what marriage means, Jakov? Two doors to two worlds, and a coming and going all the time. Isn't that why we need marriage—or whatever we can get instead of it? So that we don't go crazy locked with ourselves in a room full of mirrors?"

"I suppose so, yes. Looking back now, I'm sure that was my mistake with Hannah. I forced her to live a one-room life. I locked her into my private world. The only way she could escape was to retreat into the past. I can't forgive myself that."

"You have to forgive yourself, Jakov. Otherwise there will be no happiness for us either."

She said it so vehemently that he was startled. He looked at her and saw that her face was tight as the skin of a drum, ivory-pale in the moonlight. He answered her lightly. "Come on, sweetheart, relax. Two weeks from now the past is dead. We begin again."

"No, Jakov. That's just the point. The past doesn't die. It remains part of us. We have to accept it and try to be grateful for it, if we can. If we don't, it becomes a poison working inside us. . . . I talked to Franz Lieberman about this the other day. He said the same thing in a different way."

"Why did you talk to Franz?" He was resentful now, and wary.

"Because he's a wise and gentle old man. Because I needed some help."

"For what?"

"For myself—and you. He took me in to see Hannah. I cried, Jakov. She's so changed. So pathetic and remote. Franz was very kind to me. He took me into his office, made me drink a cup of coffee and talked to me for a long time, about myself and Golda and Adom—and you too, Jakov. He didn't preach. He didn't make any judgments. He just explained things. He said that the only way to stay human is to say three things: 'I'm guilty. I'm sorry. I want to make amends.' Then he laughed in that pawky way of his and said: 'Of course, liebchen, we all know we're only half guilty and we're only half sorry, and the best we can do with a broken pot is patch it and put it on the shelf. But even that's a beginning, nicht?' He's right, Jakov. It is a beginning. It stops you hating other people. It stops you hating yourself."

"But we still go on breaking pots, don't we? I have to tell you this, Yehudith. I've given Adom an assignment that may put him in danger of his life. I've offered him a way out if he wants to take it. I don't think he will."

"Do you feel guilty about that too?"

"A little, still. I told him about us. He had a right to know. If he thinks I'm asking too much, I've offered to pull him and his girl out of Damascus immediately."

"Could you have done any more?"

"I don't think so."

"Then why the guilt?"

"Because I'm here with you, safe in this garden, while he's in Damascus with daggers all around him."

"Is he well?"

"He's having a rough time just now; but he's well."

"I wonder what he'll do when it's all over."

"Do you care?"

"Of course I care, darling. He's my past, just as Hannah is yours. He's my present too, through Golda. We're in the same boat, you and I, Jakov. That's why we have to be careful for each other. . . . Let's have some drinks before dinner?"

"Please. But not too many. I have to be up at four in the morning."

She kissed him lightly on the lips and went into the house. He was calmer now. He had submitted himself to the sedative rite of confession and received the customary counsel: "Relax, friend! We're all in the same galley. We try and we fail. We can't forget. We can forgive and be forgiven. You be tender to me and I'll be tender to you. God knows it all—even though He's too busy to tell us. It isn't enough? It's all you have, friend! Make do with it or go blow your addled brains out. . . ." So tonight he would drink and eat and be a little merry with a loving woman. And tomorrow he would watch a stone village blown to powder. Who, he wondered sourly, would be careful for the poor devils sleeping tomorrow night in the caves and gulleys along the Hebron valley?

ELEVEN

Nuri Chakry had prepared for his evening with considerable care. It might be his last in Beirut; it might be the prelude to a triumphant return. Either way it was an occasion to be marked.

Just before the close of business he drew a check for the balance of his personal account in the Phoenician Bank; he would have to leave a great many things behind—real estate, furniture, automobiles, a speedboat, clothing and a few quite satisfactory women. He had no intention of leaving a cent of hard cash. Then he called for his safe deposit box, emptied it of every negotiable item and sent it back to the vaults. He stuffed the cash and the documents into his brief-case, dropped the golden emperor on top of them and drove home to his apartment.

There was little to do here. His suitcase was packed. His half a dozen valuable pictures had been taken from the frames and rolled into cardboard tubes labeled "Architectural Draw-ings." The frames were filled with expensive prints so that the rooms still had an inhabited look. He bathed and shaved and made a telephone call to Heinrich Muller at Byblos; then he poured himself a drink and sat down to review his travel arrangements.

These had been made in a very normal fashion by his secretary, except that he had discussed them with emphasis and detail to fix them in her mind. He would leave at eight o'clock in the morning on a direct flight to Paris, where a suite was reserved for him at the Lancaster Hotel. His return was also booked and confirmed for the morning of the following Tuesday. The documentation was very simple; but it proved—if ever proof was called for—an important fact: a legitimate businessman was making a legitimate business trip with every intention of returning to his duties on a fixed date. No question of defalcation, subterfuge or escape.

Heinrich Muller, on the other hand, had prepared a different set of documents: a new passport, a new certificate of vaccinations and inoculations and a one-way ticket from Paris to Brazil. So, come closing time on Monday afternoon, Nuri Chakry was prepared to jump in one of two directions: back to Beirut, if the Finance Ministry and the Central Bank moved in to help him; across the Atlantic to a new life, if they didn't.

Which left him with an evening and a night to fill. He was determined to enjoy them both. He would drive out to Byblos for a drink with Heinrich Muller, who also would be packed and ready to move as soon as the bank issue was decided. He would take delivery of his personal documents and Muller's collection of valuable forgeries. He would drive back to the Casino, play the tables for a while and then have supper with the long-legged chanteuse who owed him her job and her beach apartment at Djouni. After supper he would take her home and drive directly from her apartment to the airport in the morning. A comforting schedule of diversions for a man who was just a little tired of walking the high wire without a net. So, a drink for the road, ten minutes of music and a last contemplative interlude before he stepped from one life into another.

Whatever happened now, life would be changed. There was

only one true arrival, one high, drunken moment when you scrambled up the last rise and stood on the peak and saw the patchwork of the world spread below you. After that the staleness began, the more-of-the-same sensation that tempted you to wilder risks for less profit and far, far less satisfaction. There were other peaks; but when you had climbed them you saw the same old world in a slightly different pattern. Time was when you wanted to embrace it all, feel every one of its sensations in your flesh. But you couldn't do it, because the body could not tolerate so much variety. Try to drink all the wine in the world and you ended with a hangover. Try to love all the women in the world and you were committed to a vast monotony.

In one way he would like to come back to Beirut. This was the womb out of which he had been born again, from donkey boy to merchant prince. But subjects grew envious of their princes and princes, too, came to the moment when they wished all their subjects had only one neck to put on the block. So, in another way he would be glad to go adventuring again, testing his mature self against new challenges before his sap dried up and his aging heart cried out for repose. It was not a bad way to begin a festal evening—a libation to the old gods, in case you needed them again, an offering to the new ones to make them benign towards the stranger. And if both failed—Inshallah! At least he would never again be a donkey boy. He finished his drink, carried his baggage into the elevator, locked the empty apartment and rode downstairs to the car park.

The sea road was clogged with evening traffic and it took him nearly forty minutes to reach Muller's house. Muller was sitting on his veranda with his field glasses and a mug of cold beer on the table before him, a perfect picture of Teutonic contentment. He waved Chakry to a chair, poured him a drink and made a toast. "So. . . . Der Tag, eh? Good luck, my friend!"

"It's not Der Tag yet." Chakry grinned. "That's Monday. I'll be waiting in Paris for the news. If it's good, I come back. If not. . . . You've got my stuff ready?"

Muller set down his glass and wiped his lips. "Everything. The passport's a very pretty job. I'm proud of it."

"And you, Heinrich? Are you ready to move?"

"I'm not going, Nuri."

Chakry stared at him, surprised and angry. "What the devil do you mean? We agreed that . . ."

"I've changed my mind," said Heinrich Muller placidly. "I called the movers to take a look at my things and give me a quote for packing and shipping. When they'd left, I came out here and looked at the sea and the town and I asked myself why in hell I should go trotting round the world because my friend Nuri Chakry wants to build himself another empire. I asked myself what I would do in Brazil which is full of old comrades I don't care if I never meet again. Money? I've got money and this house and a whole coast-line full of beautiful things waiting to be dug up. Just down there, the second house on the right, there's a girl who undresses in front of her window every night, just for me. She knows I watch her. She wants me to watch her. And I feel at home. I am at home, Nuri. I don't want to move."

"But we've always made money together. I need you, Heinrich."

"I know you do, Nuri." He poured himself another beer and blew the foam at a buzzing night beetle. "But you don't need me so much that you can't do without me. All you want is someone on the other end of the seesaw to bounce you up into the air. It's a one-sided game. You have to be up all the time. I don't blame you. I don't envy you either. After the war, I had to keep my head down. After a while I learned to enjoy it. It's like looking up a girl's skirt from the bottom of a ladder. A free peepshow and you never get your face slapped. . . . You mustn't be angry, Nuri. You want any little job done with documents, you can always count on me—once your check is cleared. We know we'll keep the other's secrets. So what's to fight about?"

"Nothing." Nuri Chakry spread his hands in a gesture of resignation. Then he grinned. "But who's going to teach me about whatever kind of antiquities they have in South America?"

Heinrich Muller threw back his head and gave a great spluttering laugh. "Teach yourself, Nuri! Make friends with a museum curator and do everything legally this time. That way you don't have to pay commissions to rogues like me—and you get twice as rich in half the time."

"I like rogues, Heinrich. That's part of the fun."

"I know you do, Nuri. . . . That's why you owe me twenty thousand dollars."

"You're joking!"

Heinrich Muller fixed him with a humid and affectionate eye. "No, Nuri. For a perfect set of bearer bonds with a face value of a million and a half dollars, for a beautiful passport and an ironclad secrecy, it's a very reasonable price. . . . And I know you can afford it."

"You're a bastard son of a camel, Heinrich."

"I know. . . . I'm ashamed of myself every day. But what can I do about it?"

"Call it ten thousand and I'll give you a check right now."

"Call it twenty and I'll take cash. You're carrying a lot of it tonight, Nuri."

"Fifteen, then."

"Twenty. Think of the service you've had."

"Seventeen and a half. That's my final offer."

"Eighteen and I'll take it." Muller chuckled. "You get the cash, I'll get the papers. And I'll throw in another bottle of beer for good measure."

"I'll miss you, Heinrich."

"I'll miss you, too, Nuri. Send me some dirty postcards from Brazil."

Then they both laughed, a pair of hucksters, looking down

on the ruined port where the hucksters of an antique world
had haggled while empires rose and fell.

HEBRON, JORDAN

Late in the evening, while simple folk were supping by
lamplight or preparing themselves for sleep, they hauled Idris
Jarrah out of the silo and carried him down a hundred yards
of hillside to the house where White Coffee was waiting.
Jarrah was in a bad way, feverish, dehydrated and comatose.
They took off his bonds, laid him on a bed and poured water
and raw arrack down his arid gullet. He revived long enough
to see them standing over him, then he drifted back into
unconsciousness. They fed him more water and a little more
spirit and when he woke again, he saw only White Coffee,
relaxed and amiable, sitting on the edge of the bed. He turned
his head painfully. The others were sitting at a table playing
a card game. He struggled to speak. His tongue was too big
for his mouth. The silly, irrelevant words issued from his
mouth in a dry croak.

"What time is it?"

White Coffee looked at his wrist watch. "It's twenty
minutes after nine. That was a long day, wasn't it?"

Jarrah tried to nod, but his neck muscles were stiff and
strained. He closed his eyes.

"Tonight may be even longer. And tomorrow will be
worse. I've known men to last three days in the silo. Would
you like another drink?"

"Please."

White Coffee lifted him, not ungently, and held the cup
to his lips. Every muscle in his body cried out at the movement. He gagged on the liquid and then lay back, sweating
and exhausted.

White Coffee talked on softly and relentlessly. "If you like,
we'll let you sleep for a while. You wouldn't be able to write

a very good signature now. But you will write it later. Do you agree?"

"I agree."

"That makes it so much easier, Brother Jarrah. Easier for us. Certainly easier for you. Sleep now. We'll wake you in an hour or so."

Grateful as a child for such solicitude, he closed his eyes and tried to hypnotize himself into forgetfulness of the pains that pervaded him and the cramps that knotted his stretched muscles. Death would be a mercy now; a light at the end of a long tunnel, which when you reached it, would switch itself off and switch you off, too—switch off the pain and the fear and the voices and the accusing eyes and the mocking memory of riches held once in the palm of a hand and then snatched brutally away. He could see the light, a tiny pinpoint, like the eye of a black target, very far away. The target, they told you, was a man's chest. The eye of the target was his heart. You aimed at the heart. You squeezed the trigger. The bullet plowed into the heart. The man died instantly. Instantly. . . . That was the consoling word. No waiting, no feeling, no afterwards. Or was there afterwards? Was there a real Eblis, salted with fire, peopled with eternal accusers who wore the same faces as those who accused him now? Was there a real Paradise from which languid houris threw pomegranate rinds into the fiery pit below? It would be useful to know. The small flame beckoned and he was following it, or was he falling backwards into the silo? He was spinning now, endlessly downward, waiting for the jerk and rasp when the rope brought him up short. But there was no rope and the light was following him down, an avenging fire pursuing him like a live creature. He screamed—a long, agonizing, soundless cry. And woke to find White Coffee smiling into his face.

"Are you rested, Brother Jarrah? Are you ready now?"

"I think so."

As they hoisted him off the bed and half-dragged, half-carried him to the table, he had a brief, wild notion that he could fight them still; but he knew that he could not sustain another assault on the poor relic of his person and he closed his mind to the foolish thought. They propped him in the chair and set in front of him a fountain pen and a sheet of blank paper. Beside him they laid a letter, one of those which he had written to the Organization in the days of his authority. It was signed in his own hand.

White Coffee leaned over his shoulder and pointed to the signature. "Is that the signature you gave the bank?"

"Yes."

"Write it again, on the blank paper."

He tried it a dozen times, but his hand was so shaky that the writing degenerated into a scrawl.

White Coffee was not impatient. He studied the sheet of paper and then nodded. "It's getting better. You'll do it in an hour or so. Would you like something to eat?"

"Yes."

They brought him stale bread and harsh cheese and an apple and a bottle of warm soda water. They stood around, watching him eat, as if he were an animal in a cage. He almost vomited the first mouthfuls and White Coffee had to admonish him to be more careful of himself.

"Take your time, little brother. Eat slowly. Chew well. That way you will hold it down."

As he munched the niggardly food, Idris Jarrah felt a small strength seeping back and, with the strength, a faint, faint whisper of hope. Until they had cleared his check at the bank, they would never be absolutely sure that he had given them the right signature. They saw him now, cowed and broken. All of them would be happy to put a bullet in his belly; all except White Coffee, for whom a life was an incident in time and only the Cause was a permanence. White Coffee knew about checks and banking. He knew about men too; and, for a hundred thousand dollars in operational funds, he would be very long-suffering. White Coffee was talking again. Jarrah raised his throbbing head and tried to listen with respect.

"Tell us, Brother Jarrah, why did you leave us? Why did you try to steal our money? Why did you sell us for more money? Are we camels or asses that you could think to trade us? I don't understand. I would like to understand. Why?"

Jarrah let his head drop almost to his soiled plate. His hair brushed the cheese crumbs and the core of the tasteless apple. "What does it matter now?"

White Coffee thrust a hand into his scalp and jerked him upright. "It matters, little brother! Tell us! Why?"

The sudden pain infused a new strength into him. He forced the words out contemptuously through his broken lips. "Because we *are* camels and asses. Palestine is as dead as Babylon! We'll never go back. But the Egyptians pay us and the Syrians pay us to believe that we will. We're men without a country. But will they give us a new one? Never! The Jews have a wailing wall. We're the wailing wall for the Arab . . . but when they've finished crying, they piss on us!"

"Enough!" White Coffee slammed his face down against the table. A hive of bees began buzzing in his skull case. When the bees went away, he pushed himself upright in his chair and tried to mock them again.

"You want the money? Bring me the checkbook and I'll sign. Then kill me and finish this stinking game."

White Coffee laid the checkbook on the table, thrust the pen into his hands and set the specimen signature beside it. "Write."

He managed a passable signature.

"Another."

The writing was a trifle firmer.

"Sign six more."

When he had finished, he tossed the pen on the table and

leaned back in his chair, facing his executioners. The small fire that the food had built in him was still burning. He licked his lips and turned his face from one to the other, challenging them. "You promised me a decent killing. Get it over."

"Not yet, Brother Jarrah." White Coffee was amiable again. "You must be patient awhile longer. Tonight, if you are sensible, we will tie you and let you sleep here. In the morning I will take the first plane to Beirut and cash your check. If your signature is good, we'll give you what you want. If not . . ."

"The signature is good."

"I'm almost sure it is. I'll be quite sure tomorrow."

Then they tied him to the bed and jammed the gag back in his mouth and left two men on watch while the others dispersed to rest. As they filed out of the room, each man paused by the bed and spat in his face.

DAMASCUS

In the pavilion of Abu Nowas, who claimed, a little bombastically, the best kitchen east of Paris, Colonel Omar Safreddin drank coffee and nibbled sweetmeats in company with Captain Shabibi. They were languid with food and the pleasures of a companionship that promised good things for each of them. Perched on their cushions under the fretted woodwork of the alcove, they had fallen into that brooding rhetorical talk which is the traditional exercise of noble Arab minds, a poetry of volubility and immobility, a dialogue of contemplation without which the monotony of action would become intolerable. Safreddin was well launched on his favorite theme.

". . . Never, my boy, never confuse the means we use with the ends at which we aim. If you do this, you are like the gardener who pulls up a weed and imagines he has created

a rose garden. Security work—this hunting of spies and disaffected people—is like pulling up weeds and thistles. Even
the war for which we are preparing is simply a plowing and
a harrowing in order to plant for the new harvest. Let me tell
you something. . . ." He laid a strong hand on Shabibi's
shoulder, pressing it till his fingers bit into the young muscle. "Let me tell you a treason! I could as easily be a Jew as
an Arab. My people came from the region of the great
rivers, as the people of Abraham did. We are all Semites.
We believe in one God. We have rubbed along together for
centuries. We are more like the Jews than we are like the
Egyptians, who have been bastardized since the time of
the Pharaohs. We are more kin to the Jew than we are to the
blue-faced Touareg or the black slaves who came north from
Africa. And yet we are enemies. Why? I will tell you. The
Jew is always a separate man. He gives only to his own. From
all others, he takes. Right from the beginning he took and
held and lost and came back to take again. He will not lend
even his God, while we spend Allah like an alms upon the
world. This little land which the Jew holds—we can live without it. But we cannot live with it, while the Jew is there, a
separate man, a separate tribe, a separate God. . . . You see?"

"I think I see," said Captain Shabibi cautiously. "But I'm
not sure. We root out the Jew. We restore Palestine—or we
remake greater Syria. What then? We are still separate tribes.
If anything we are more jealous of each other than we are
of the Jews. Look at the Iraqis and ourselves. Look at what
happened when we had a joint command with Egypt. Look
at the Kuwaitis and what is happening in the Yemen."

"Give me your hand."

Shabibi thrust out his hand. Safreddin held it a moment,
lingering over a touch which, with another, would have re-
volted him. He spread the fingers wide and laid the hand
palm upwards on the table. He took a knife, laid the point
of it against the center of the palm and pressed it against

the skin. Shabibi's fingers contracted towards the blade. Safreddin chuckled.

"Now do you understand? First there were five fingers and a thumb. Now there is a fist clenched against danger. This is what the Jew means to us. He is the dagger pricking our palm."

"But afterwards, Colonel." Shabibi was a very stubborn young man. "When the dagger is withdrawn. What unites us?"

"Afterwards?" said Safreddin with sober emphasis. "Afterwards there is Islam. Islam rearmed with book and sword. Islam alive with new teachers . . ."

"Good evening, Colonel."

He looked up, startled to see Selim Fathalla standing by the table with Bitar and Emilie Ayub. It took him only a second to compose himself and make the introductions.

"Gentlemen, Miss Ayub, this is my new assistant, Captain Shabibi." After the polite murmurs, he said, "I was very sorry, Fathalla, to hear of the untimely death of Mr. Bellarmino. It must have been a great shock to you."

"It was, Colonel."

"He died in your house, I understand."

"Yes."

"How very distressing. I imagine you've had a lot of formalities today."

"Enough. There'll be a few more when we come to bury him."

"If you have any problems," said Safreddin politely, "don't hesitate to call on me. I'm sure we'll be able to help you."

"You're very kind, Colonel."

"Not at all. . . . I hope you're well, Doctor?"

"Overworked as usual. But well, thank you."

"I think you may have some good news shortly."

"Oh? . . ."

"I was asked to endorse a certain recommendation for a

high position in the Department of Public Health. I was very happy to do it."

"Thank you."

"Enjoy your dinner. I recommend the stuffed peppers."

He watched them as they moved away and settled themselves in an alcove in the opposite corner of the room. When he turned back to Shabibi, he was frowning. "That's odd."

"What, Colonel?"

"That little bunch. Last night they were all together at a death. Tonight they're dining together."

"Is that significant?"

Safreddin relaxed again. "Probably not. But it always pays to ask a foolish question. . . . Now what were we talking about?"

"Islam, Colonel. Islam and the new teachers . . . that interests me. Who are these new teachers? Where are they? Not in the Ulema in Damascus, certainly. In Cairo? If they are there we do not feel their influence. And we should feel it, as we feel yours at the Hunafa Club. . . ."

"You have to understand something. . . ." Safreddin was eager now. The intriguer was thrust back behind the zealot. "Once, and once only, every great religion unites its followers so strongly that they will march or die like a multitude of brothers. The Christians took over the Roman Empire like that. Islam in its glory was like that. Buddhism was the same. Marxism was the same in our own time—though not in yours. It is the special, explosive magic of the fresh idea, the new vision of renewed man. . . . Then the vision is clouded. The philosophers move in, the theologians, the dividers and distinguishers who will split a man in two to prove a doctrine. You ask what is a Moslem . . . you will get twenty answers from as many sects. The Christians are split. The Jews are split. The Marxists too are fragmented. And you will never put any of them together with a cartload of scholars. . . ."

"How then, Colonel?"

"You go back to the thing all the prophets understand. The bald statement. The great simplicity. Every man who says, 'There is no God but God and Mohammed is his prophet,' is a brother Moslem. Every man who honors Christ, is a Christian. . . . Look what Ben-Gurion did in Israel. He was a genius, too. Any Jew who came, whether he wore the caftan or a sweatshirt, was immediately a citizen. . . . We have to do the same. The single formula, the long, strong shout and the banner of the Crescent is unfurled again through the world."

"It sounds so easy, Colonel . . . and yet. . . ."

"I know." Safreddin was still caught in the glow of his own prophecy. "Yet it is not enough . . . something is still missing. What? Tell me—you whom I see like a son at this moment—what is still needed?"

"Blood on the flag," said Captain Shabibi.

Selim Fathalla's dinner party was something less than a success. The presence of Safreddin was a constant reminder of the danger in which they lived. The food was indifferent, the service in the half-empty restaurant was haunting, as though the underworked waiters had all been recruited as spies for the Security Service. Bitar, sober again, was tired and a trifle portentous. Emilie quickly gave up trying to be gay. Fathalla was moody and preoccupied with the new and urgent problem which Bitar had dropped so casually into his lap. They finished early. Dr. Bitar took himself home. Fathalla and Emilie drove out to the edge of the desert and sat listening to the late music from Damascus Radio. They were silent for a long time, each withdrawn into a private world, hesitating even to embrace lest the other should be unready for affection.

Finally, Emilie asked, "What is it, Selim? What's troubling you?"

"Things are turning sour all at once. That's the time to go underground. We can't. I'm not sure that we shouldn't take Baratz at his word and pull out."

"Together?"

"Of course."

"Then let's do it, Selim. As quickly as we can."

"Let me think about it. If we could keep the network intact and hand it over to a new man I'd feel much better. If only Bellarmino hadn't been such a pigheaded fool! A notebook full of names—and this crazy trip to Aleppo. I'd like to have ten minutes with the man who trained him! Anyway, he's dead, and I'll have to bury him and make a whole ceremony of sending the sad story back to Rome. That means more contact with the police, just at a time when I'd like them to forget me. I'll have to send word to Baratz—and that's another kind of problem. I don't know the answer to it, yet."

He explained how an illegal operator might work undisturbed for months until one night direction-finders pinpointed his hiding place. He explained the risk he must still take. . . .

"So, for a while at least, I daren't transmit from the house, or from Bitar's place either. I've got two choices: either I put a transmitter in the car and make myself mobile, or I send from the Church of the Martyrs and take my chance. But, either way, there's danger. If my car were searched, or if I had an accident, like Bellarmino, I'd be finished. On the other hand, if they moved in on the church while I was there, I'd be trapped. That mountain track is a dead end and there's no other place I can hide my car. . . . And yet, somehow, I've got to get my stuff out to Tel Aviv."

"I could drive you out to the church, leave you and come back for you. That way you wouldn't have to worry about the car."

"But, if they moved in on me, you could be caught on the

road. . . . No, wait!" He fished out a notebook and began to make a series of rapid calculations. "Take everything at its worst. My longest transmission is ten minutes. The Church of the Martyrs is seven, eight minutes from town. Suppose they hit me right at the beginning of the transmission—by the time they call out the police and mount a search, I've got at least five minutes to close down and head back into the hills."

"But you can't do this every time."

"I'm not thinking of every time. It's now. Tonight! . . . What's the time?"

"Twenty-three past eleven."

"Right! Drop me back at the church. I'll start coding immediately and I'll begin sending at twelve-fifty. You can expect me home round about three . . . even later, if I strike trouble."

"I'm afraid, Selim."

"One night . . . just one! With luck it may be the last. Then I can be Adom Ronen again."

"And I can have my child?"

"It's a promise."

They kissed under the desert moon and Fathalla turned the car back on to the Rumtha road. When they reached the turn-off, he got out and stood watching until Emilie had turned the corner, then he scrambled up the rocky path towards the Church of the Martyrs. The sound of his footsteps was very loud in the still air. A thing to remember: sound carried far and clear in the hills. A scatter of shale or a loose rock bouncing down a slope could betray him in an instant. A turned ankle would be a death sentence.

He skirted the wall of the cemetery and climbed the low, jagged hill at the back, scouting his line of retreat. On the farther side of the hill, a narrow path led downwards into a dry creek bed which divided itself round a spur of white rock. One arm of the creek turned northward, back to the city. This was the path he would take to lead him back to town. The other pointed westward, towards the hills of the anti-Lebanon, thirty kilometers away. Once around the spur there were caves and crevices by the hundred, where you would have to hunt a man with bloodhounds before you found him. But the hills were cruel, too: in summer all the wadis were dry and a pool of water was as rare as a diamond; you bleached by day and froze at night, and the Bedouin told weird tales of djinn who rode the wind over the sawtooth saddles.

He heard a sound behind him and swung round defensive and alert. A black and bearded old goat bleated at him and scampered away up the hillside. He laughed uneasily and turned back to the white church nestling among its faithful dead.

BEIRUT

"Listen, boy!" Lew Mortimer was opening his heart to Mark Matheson over the fifth drink in the bar of the Phoenician Hotel. "You're an American, right? You play it straight down the line—right? You believe in God. You believe in honest auditors and a fair day's work for a fair day's wage, rah-rah-rah, right? What the hell are you doing in a cartload of monkeys like this one, eh? Oh, I know! You like the life. So do I. You want to get laid on request and paid without Uncle Sam skimming off the cream. So do I. But, Jesus, you don't have to do it this way. What does Chakry pay you? Thirty thousand? Thirty and a half?"

"Forty."

"Call it fifty and work for me. For chrissake, you're ten thousand better off and you don't have some goddam Arab groping you every time your zipper's undone."

"It's a tempting offer," said Mark Matheson. "I'd like to work with an American outfit again. But you know the way it is. You build something, you like to stay with it and see it grow."

"Sure you do." Mortimer was as relaxed as a great brown ape swinging from his favorite tree. "You trowel the mortar, you lay the bricks, you carry the roofbeams on your shoulders. You've got a right to be proud and say 'I built that.' And you have built, boy. You've built well. But look! These goddam people don't think the way we do. They squeeze all the juice out of you and then stick you in the balls. What's yours is mine and what's mine's my own, and up you, Jack! Look at Chakry! Brother! Has he given you the runaround. Go to Switzerland, talk to the Jews—as if they'd lend you a wooden nickel!—see how the State Department feels. Shit! This isn't banking, Mark. This is touting. And Chakry's made you do it."

"I don't know, Lew. I like the guy. He's got a lot of gall. But he's got guts, too. I admire that. Anyone that can fly off to Paris and present an ultimatum to the Russians. . . ."

"The Russians? Jesus, Mark! You bought that horseshit? You think the Russians have got so much *valuta* they're going to pay out a hundred and fifty to a hundred and seventy million for a card castle in Lebanon? You think they work as fast as that? By the time the Central Committee authorizes a shipment of paperclips, the model's out of date."

"He's very sure about it, Lew."

"Chakry's been sure of everything since he peddled his first three-dollar bill to a blind whore. He's making you the fall guy, Mark. Can't you see it?"

"Lew, you don't know this man like I do. He's got a magic."

"I've seen the magic before. Three thimbles and a pea . . . carny stuff."

"It's easy to say. But just think about it. We can close our doors in ten days and he flies off to Paris in the morning and, if the Russians don't play, he'll be back on Tuesday with a fifty-million-dollar loan."

"Say that again."

"He flies off to Paris in the morning."

"I heard that bit. Go on. He comes back with what?"

"A fifty-million-dollar loan."

"Who's giving it to him?"

"I know, but I can't tell you, Lew."

"French money?"

"Yes."

"I don't believe it. The French are so damn short of capital, they're pulling it out of grandma's stocking. I'm dealing with them all the time. Believe me, Mark!"

"I tell you he has it, Lew."

"You're not kidding me?"

"Why should I kid you, Lew? He pays me forty. You offer fifty. I should kid you for that?"

"What sort of money is it, Mark? Bank money?"

"No."

"Mutual funds?"

"No."

"Insurance?"

"Yes."

"Now I'm damn sure I don't believe it."

"He gave me the name of the company and the terms of the deal."

"I think I need another drink. Join me?"

"Why not?"

Mortimer snapped his fingers at a passing waiter, gave his order and then sprawled in his chair, legs stretched, thumbs hooked under his lapels. His rugged, walnut face shone with benignity and admiration. "Mark, I love you. I love you because you're as honest as southern fried chicken and so damned innocent I bleed internally when I talk to you. I know every son-of-a-bitching French insurance man from Alsace to the Midi. If you can prise more than two million dollars out of any one of them just now, you're a better man than I am, Gunga Din. Chakry's conning you, Mark. He's flying the coop. And if the Central Bank doesn't bail him out next Monday—which they won't—he's going west, brother! A long way west! You don't believe me?"

"I want to . . . and I don't want to, Lew. It pays me to believe you, but. . . ."

"What's the *but*, Mark?"

"I don't know."

"Then I'll tell you, boy." Mortimer unhooked one ham of a hand and thrust it across the table at Matheson. "You're a nice guy, Mark; but you're a baby. Somebody offers you a warm, sweet titty to suck and you don't want to let it go. Grow up, boy! Mummy's tucking it back into her dress and going out whoring again."

"Cut it out, Lew!"

"I'm sorry—I don't want to hurt your feelings. But I don't want to see you left with Chakry's night soil either. One answer will prove whether I'm right or wrong. What's the name of the insurance company?"

"That's a rough one, Lew."

"Sure, it's rough. It'll be rougher still when the Finance Ministry puts you up on a collusion charge to cover the fact that they don't have a decent banking law in Lebanon."

"They wouldn't do that. They couldn't."

"It's your neck, boy . . . not mine."

It was funny how you came to it—the last betrayal, with all the excuses ready made for you. It was funny how little it mattered with a man like Lew Mortimer. Lay a broad or lay a pipeline, it was all a matter of muscle and confidence. He hesitated just long enough to save his rather flushed face. Then he gave the answer:

"Strictly between us, Lew . . ."

"Of course . . . of course."

"It's the Société Anonyme des Assurances Commerciales."

"Oh, brother!" Mortimer gurgled with surprise and delight. "Oh that sweet, smiling bastard. If I had a hat, I'd take it off to him. He owns that goddam company and one decent claim would put 'em out of business!"

"You mean? . . ."

"I mean you'd better resign tomorrow, Mark. You're on my payroll a month from now. Fifty a year flat—right?"

"Right, Lew. And I can't tell you how grateful . . ."

"Don't, boy. Just do an honest job and I'm happy. I'm going up to the Casino to shoot some craps. Like to come?"

"No, thanks, Lew. I've got a dinner date."

"Does she pay off?"

"Sure. But she talks too much."

"One way to fix that, boy. Simplest trick in the world. Fun, too."

Whereat Mark Matheson laughed so immoderately that the waiter had to come and slap him on the back. By the time he had recovered, Lew Mortimer had paid the bill and was already on his way to the door.

In the Casino de Liban, perched on its cliff top like a monument to Midas, the sheep had already been separated from the hardier goats. The sheep were the tourists, herded into the tiered auditorium to eat an overpriced dinner and be stunned by an extravagant spectacle of jugglers, acrobats, dancing boys, singing girls and a ballet of bare breasts. The goats were gathered into the private gaming room where all gamesters were alike in the sight of the money-god, provided their capital was sound, their income assured and their credit rating unspoiled.

Nuri Chakry was among the gamesters, because his chanteuse had two numbers and a grand finale, and he had no intention of sitting through the whole elaborate boredom again. Besides, he was an actor himself and he felt the need to give one last public performance and make one final, mocking exit. He liked to play the tables but he played modestly and to a predetermined limit. It was not the risk that bothered him, it was the odds that were stacked so securely against the player. The house had to win in the end and Nuri Chakry had no taste for such a foregone conclusion. It was the atmosphere of the place that pleased him; musky with smoke and perfume and the odor of human excitement; the faces lined out above the green baize like portraits of all the passions; the constant traffic of the watchful and the wishful; the parrot cries of the croupiers and the dealers, the click of counters and the hypnotic spin of the wheels.

He did not settle down to play immediately, but strolled about, sleek, smiling and superbly confident, watching the pattern of the play, exchanging a word or a smile with the regular clients. He knew that he was under scrutiny. He could almost hear the questions they were asking themselves but would not dare to ask him in this sacred temple where every devotee was rich by presumption so long as he held a member's card. Some of them were his enemies, a few were his friends. None but the transient strangers was indifferent to his presence. Everyone knew that he had helped to build this place, and that, by whatever equations you calculated, Nuri Chakry still functioned as X the Unknown, which might prove out at either zero or infinity.

Finally, he bought himself a handful of chips—half of the stake which he might ultimately allow himself—found a chair at the end of a roulette table and settled down to play. He used no system; he would not hedge his bets but played the numbers straight, committing himself to the longest chance and waiting to follow his luck when it began to run. He lost steadily for fifteen minutes. Then he won on a seven. He let the stake lie and moved it to seventeen. He won again. Again he let the money ride and moved it to twenty-seven. When he won again, there was a gasp around the table.

The croupier grinned, encouragingly. "Again, m'sieu?"

Chakry shook his head. The croupier pushed all the money off the table. Chakry tossed him a tip and gathered up his winnings.

"You're a piker, Nuri," said Lew Mortimer, behind his chair.

"Would you like my chair, sir?" Chakry was frigidly polite.

"You're a piker," said Mortimer again. "Why don't you let it ride? You may never be so lucky again."

Chakry ignored him, stuffed the chips into his pockets and moved away from the table towards the cashier's cage.

Lew Mortimer's bulky body blocked him. He was rolling on his feet. His face was flushed and his eyes were puffed and bloodshot. "Don't go yet, Nuri. I'd like to talk to you."

"Excuse me, please."

"Just a little talk, Nuri. And one drink for the road. Then I'll kiss the back of my hand to you."

"I'd rather not talk to you. I certainly won't drink with you. Please let me pass."

There was silence in the big room now. The attendants were moving in warily.

Lew Mortimer thrust out a big knotted hand and grasped Chakry's shirtfront. "Don't brush me off, little man! You can't afford it. You can't afford to brush anyone off any more."

"Please, sir!" A muscular but polite young man moved into the group. "If you have business to discuss would you mind doing it outside? And take your hand off the gentleman."

"Mind your own goddam business!" Mortimer was savage now. "You know who this is? This is Mr. Nuri Chakry. He's a business friend of mine. He wants to drink with me, don't you, Nuri?"

"I do not."

There were three young men now, and they wrestled Mortimer away and held him, while Chakry straightened his shirtfront and headed for the cash desk. But they could not stop his shouting and the drunken words rang through the room.

"You're running out, aren't you, Nuri? You've used all the

broads and you've used all the dough and you're running out
to South America. Who's going to pay the depositors, Nuri?
Who's going to clean up the mess? Look at him! Cashing in
his own chips. But what about yours? What about all the
rest of it? . . . Tell 'em, Nuri . . . tell 'em about the great big
insurance loan you're never going to get. . . . Tell 'em you're
out of business next week."

They then had Mortimer out through the service entrance
and all the table men were chanting at once to start the
games again. But no one was listening. Everyone was looking
at Nuri Chakry as he counted the last of his cash, folded it
into his wallet and walked the long, solitary stretch of carpet
to the door.

It was not a bad exit. It was even a kind of triumph. Publicly humiliated, he still held them at bay. His smile gave the
lie to his drunken accuser. His contempt cowed the most
malicious of his enemies. He left them like a prince with a
gesture of ironic farewell.

None of them would ever know how easily they might
have stripped him back to donkey boy between the cash
desk and the door.

TWELVE

There were four operators in the monitor room, each equipped with a receiver and headset, tuning slowly around the shortwave band, looking for a station sending out five figure groups. There were four other operators in the vans cruising the city and each of the vans was tuned in to the monitor station so that, as soon as any one hit the pirate channel, the others would know it instantly and could lock the direction-finders on to the transmitter. It was a work that called for patient ears and sensitive fingers because the channels were so busy that the signals drifted into one another and some, sent from far away, skipped a whole continent and came in loudly as if from a local transmitter.

Captain Shabibi had drilled his men well. He had started them all at the same time, each at a different point on the band, and shown them how to tune at a regular rate, so that there were eight chances of picking up the transient operator. Shabibi, himself, talked constantly with the cars, making sure that they were always far enough apart to give four separate vectors of the transmitter—provided, of course, that it was working tonight and that they managed to hit it.

Colonel Omar Safreddin sat, relaxed, in his chair smoking one cigarette after another. His attention was divided between

the technical details of the operation and the young man
who had moved in so swiftly to control it. Look at Shabibi
in one light and you were tempted to crush him with a blow
before he grew too big. He was the perfect young careerist,
supple, apt to the arts of flattery, intelligent, obstinate and
well informed. See him in another glow and all your hopes
were instantly justified: the hope of honest administration
and industrial advancement and political maturity. His was
the hand that would build the towers high and plant the
crescent flag and spill his own blood to make it glorious.
Look at him by night-light, and you felt the stirrings of
strangely mixed passions, brotherly, fatherly, comradely, all
of them noble, none of them quite free from the urge of
sensual contact. The urge was noble, too; the great poets of
the caliphate had celebrated it in song and verse a hundred
times. But for a man who had just accomplished a revolution, and was still trying to build it into permanence, the most
noble affection was touched with the hint of danger. No bath
was private against the assassin's dagger, no wine was proof
against venom and many a catamite had spat in the face of
his dead patron.

This was the weakness in himself for which he had found
no cure. So long as he could hate, he could stand alone; he
could never commit himself to the risky liberty of the lover
or even to the community of equal spirits. Always at the
moment of surrender he would draw back, despising himself
and venting his self-contempt in cruel contrivances upon the
beloved object. Tonight, he wanted Shabibi to win. Tomorrow, he would humble him, clawing at him delicately until
he began to bleed. And when he had tasted the blood, he
would be generous again, full of tolerance and healing pity.

He saw one of the operators stiffen, adjust the tuning dial
and clamp the headset harder against his ears. The operator
listened for a few moments, then turned, excitedly. "I've got
him, Captain. Low on the band . . . four point two . . . four
point three. . . "

Shabibi snapped an order. "The rest of you tune in and start copying."

He turned back to his own set and began calling the direction-finders to lock on to the wavelength and send him the vectors which would point to the exact position of the transmitter. As they were repeated to him he scribbled them down and passed them to a junior officer who plotted them on the map of the city. The vector lines ran off the map and Safreddin cursed angrily until they found the matching sheet and projected the convergence to a point south on the Rumtha road.

Three minutes were gone already and it took another five to make his orders clear to the police and to the duty officer at security headquarters: two roadblocks, one south and one north of the map reference; a police party, fully armed, to close on the search area; the direction-finders to move south towards Rumtha, plotting as they went. Then he raced downstairs with Shabibi, shouted at his sleepy driver and headed off to the rendezvous.

When they reached the edge of the city, where the foothills began and the road took a wide swing around an escarpment, they found the first roadblock already set up. The radio vans were there, too, parked on the grassy verge. They were useless now; the transmission was finished. Safreddin and Shabibi drove slowly down the road looking for a reentrant that would take them back into the hills. By the time they found it, the armed police party was already cruising behind them. They turned together on the rutted track that led to the Church of the Martyrs.

Safreddin was all professional now. He dispersed his raiders swiftly round the sheltering wall of the cemetery, then moved them in, cautiously, through the weed-grown tombs, until they were flattened against the wall of the church itself. The door was locked. They blew off the rusted lock and burst into a moonlit emptiness. Safreddin held them in a small, tense group, just inside the door and shone a torch

beam down the paved floor of the nave. The track of footmarks was clearly visible in the thick layer of dust. Safreddin
knelt to examine them. And then he beckoned to Shabibi. He
traced two outlines with his forefinger.

"A man and a woman. The man comes more frequently
than the woman. We can have tracings made of the size and
shape. Move the men forward by the walls. Tell them not to
disturb these marks."

It was Safreddin who led them down into the crypt. He
cast the light about the empty chamber noting the wellhead
and the alcove tomb and the scuffle of footmarks around it.
For a long while he stood silent, sunk in thought, then he
turned to Shabibi again.

"Let's get a police team down here before we disturb
anything . . . fingerprint men, photographers. . . . I want them
to plumb that well and open the grave there and tap the
floor and the walls. We're not equipped and we might miss
something important. Get them out now and have them scout
the hills. I don't expect they'll find our man but let's go
through the procedures. Have them report back here in an
hour. Leave a guard detail of four men in the church."

After the first excitement of the find, it was an odd anti-
climax. Shabibi was tempted to comment, but when he
looked at Safreddin's face, he thought better of it. He led the
troops outside and sent them scrambling up the moonlit
hillside in extended order. He sent out a radio call for the
police experts and then took up his post by the car and waited
for Safreddin.

It was nearly five minutes before he came out of the
church and walked through the graveyard, head sunk on his
chest as though he were returning from a funeral.

Shabibi reported briskly. "The search parties are out, sir.
The investigating team is on its way."

"I couldn't find the key," said Safreddin absently.

"Colonel?"

"I know this place." Safreddin talked on in the same withdrawn fashion. "I know it. I think I remember why . . ."

"I don't understand, Colonel."

Safreddin gave him a wintry, ironic smile. "You're a very bright young man, Captain. Tonight you've come ten steps nearer to promotion."

"And you, Colonel?"

Safreddin laid an affectionate arm about his shoulder. "You wait many years, boy. You wait and work and study like a miser building up treasure he will never spend. Then, one day, someone walks in to your life on whom you are willing to lavish it all. To me, you are that someone. We shall finish here. We shall wait for the tradesmen and let them do their work. Then I will show you the rewards of patience and a long memory."

Scrambling along the tortuous defiles, Selim Fathalla had heard the sound of the vehicles far away on the Rumtha road. It was ominous but inconclusive. It could have been a military convoy heading south to the border posts; less probably it could have been a string of commercial vehicles northward bound to the Damascus market. The sound was distorted by the contours of the hills and it was hard to be precise about direction. Then he had heard the gunfire, one burst that echoed and reechoed round the empty mountains. He hurried forward, heedlessly, until he stumbled and barked his shin against a rock. The pain sobered him swiftly. Another panic might cripple him. He moved forward cautiously now, picking his footholds, moving from shadow to shadow along the flank of the valley, stopping occasionally to draw breath and listen to the silence that followed the echoes.

He was crouched in the mouth of a shallow cave, panting and rubbing his injured shin, when he heard the new sounds, faint but clear in the dry air; the scramble of heavy boots on shale, the voices of men calling to each other as they topped the rise and scrambled down into the wadi behind him. A new terror threatened to engulf him again. He fought it down desperately, clamping himself to the rock until he was calm again. Then he moved off, furtive as a fox, trying to outdistance the hunters.

He had lost all sense of time, all sense of human identity and relationship. The feral instinct of survival possessed him utterly. The earth was his only friend—the nodules of sheltering rock, the animal tracks where he could trot safely for a few moments, the pits and pockmarks where he could crouch and draw breath and listen for the sounds of pursuit. They were fading now. He could not hear the footfalls, only the occasional voices, sparse and attenuated. The defile was widening and soon it would break out into the open space on the outskirts of the city.

A new fear caught at him: what if they had sent men to outflank him and take him at the valley mouth? Above him, twin horns of rock reared themselves black against the moonlit sky. If he could reach them, he would command a view of the road, northward to the city and south along the first curves of the highway. The valley wall was steep here and he had to grope his way up the transverse slope, testing every foothold and handgrip lest he tumble or start a noisy rockfall. The sharp granite tore at his hands and his clothing, and there were moments when he hung spread like a fruit bat in the moonlight, an easy target for any sniper. He was drenched with sweat, his heart was pounding inside his rib cage. Dust fell into his gasping mouth and he had to choke down a coughing spasm as he dragged himself up the last twenty feet to a tiny plateau under the shadow of the horns. For a full minute he lay retching and exhausted. Then he crawled into the cleft between the horns and looked down.

Four radio vans were parked on the grass at the foot of the hill. Their crews were lounging against them, smoking and gossiping. Two police cars were drawn up, nose to bumper, blocking the deserted highway. Twenty yards away, two men with flashlights stood ready to halt oncoming traffic.

His approach to the city was cut off. He was too weary to attempt another long scramble through the hills to the west. Nothing to do but wait, and hope they would call off the search before daylight, and try to plot the next precarious campaign to save his neck and his network. It was clear that they had found the church and probably the transmitter. They would probably not find fingerprints because he had wiped the instrument clean in the hurried moments after his transmission and had swept the top of the tomb. They would find footprints and the marks of his occasional presence, but these would be hard to identify so long as he himself was at liberty.

One small mistake bothered him. He had locked the door of the church and put the key in its usual place under the rock on the tombstone. A subtle investigator might argue that possession of the key implied a tenancy. He would inquire from the Patriarch to find out who held the key. The Patriarch would inform him that the church had been deconsecrated long since and sold. If he did not remember the buyer's name—and the chances were that he would not, being old and preoccupied with maintaining a fearful Christian community in a Moslem state—he would consult the records. The records would reveal that the present owner was one Selim Fathalla. And then there would be a trouble which he flinched to contemplate. So . . . perched on his rocky refuge, dry-mouthed and shivering, he made a decision.

As soon as the roadblock was lifted he would head for home, warn Bitar to close down the network, bundle Emilie into the car, and drive by the back roads, towards the Lebanese border. They would abandon the car before daybreak, lie up in the hills during the day and strike out round the Hermon foothills during the night. This was a friendly border, lightly policed. With luck, they would be in the valley of the anti-Lebanon before dawn of the next day.

A sudden commotion down on the road woke him from his reverie. He looked down and saw the police cars being pulled off the highway to make way for a staff car and a truckload of police coming from the south. When they rounded the bend they, too, pulled off the road. He saw Safreddin and Shabibi get out of the staff car and summon the police and the drivers to a hurried consultation. He strained to hear what they said, but their voices reached him as faint, confused murmurs. After a few moments they dispersed to their vehicles, started the engines and drove off. Three minutes later the road was deserted.

Fathalla waited another ten minutes, then scrambled down from his hiding place and began to walk back to the city.

It was a nerve-tingling experience. Once he had to dodge into an alley to escape a patrolling policeman, who, finding him adrift in the city, tattered, dust-stained and without papers, would inevitably have pulled him in for questioning. When he paused to drink at a fountain, he was nearly surprised by a patrol car. When he plunged into the network of alleys that led through the shuttered bazaars, a pair of ruffians followed him for a hundred yards until he turned and confronted them and threw a handful of bank notes in the gutter. While they were still groping for the money, he took off at a run, his footsteps echoing against the leprous walls. A beggar dozing on a pile of straw thrust out a leg and sent him sprawling against the opposite wall. He turned, cursing, to see the gleam of a knife. He kicked out and the knife flew into the air while the beggar yelped with pain. He ran on, not pausing for breath, until he came to the end of the lane which opened into his own street. He leaned back in the shadow of an archway, trying to compose himself for his meeting with Emilie.

Then the cars came, three of them, screaming past the mouth of the lane and skidding to a stop in front of his own doorway. He flattened himself against the wall and saw Safreddin and Shabibi stride up to the door and ring the bell, while the escorting police, guns drawn, bunched up behind them. He saw the door open and Emilie, pale as a white moth, peering out. He saw them thrust her backwards into the house and slam the door shut behind them. Then, sick with despair, he turned away, sidling like an alley cat back into the darkness of the slums.

It took him ten minutes to work his way back to the center of the city, to the only spot from which he could communicate to anyone—the public telephone booths at the central post office. He was very vulnerable here, but he had to take the risk. He fumbled in his pockets for a slug and dialed Bitar's number. It rang and rang for a long time and then an alien voice answered.

"This is Dr. Bitar's residence. Who is calling, please?"

He put down the phone. They had taken Bitar, too, and by now the police would be prowling the city looking for Selim Fathalla. He hurried away from the lights of the post office and back into the shadows of the mean streets behind it. All of a sudden he was desperately weary, shocked almost into immobility by the incredible collapse of all his calculations. That Emilie should have been snared, brusquely and brutally, while he stood helpless in the shadows, was a paralyzing shame. Had a policeman passed by at that moment and found him, drunk with fatigue and wretchedness, leaning against a shuttered booth, he would have surrendered without a murmur and begged to be taken to her.

The sound of an approaching car startled him out of the syncope and he ducked behind the booth until the sound receded into the distance. He looked at his watch. It was nearly three-thirty. In an hour at most the false dawn would brighten over the city. In the light and the stir of people he would be more naked and helpless than he was now. Emilie

and Bitar were as good as dead. He could do nothing to
ease the torment that would attend their going and he knew
that if he dwelt on it too long it would drive him crazy.

He gathered his last strength and set off, staggering through
the nightmare streets towards the shelter of the western hills.

"I am sorry to have disturbed your rest, Doctor." Safreddin was sardonically polite. "But, as you see, we have a
patient in need of your attention."

Dr. Bitar stood near the door with his little black bag
dangling from his hand and surveyed Fathalla's bedroom.
Every drawer had been ransacked, the faience panel had been
smashed and all the secrets behind it laid bare. Emilie Ayub
sat slumped in a chair, her clothing stripped from her
shoulders, her face and her breasts scarred and bloody. They
had been very professional with her. They had assaulted her
swiftly and savagely, trusting that the shock would break her
before she had time to stiffen into outrage and obstinacy. It
was all too evident that they had succeeded.

Two men stood behind her chair, two others were ranged
with Shabibi and Safreddin in the window alcove. Two more
stood between Bitar and the exit.

Bitar turned slowly to face Safreddin. His deep voice was
charged with a bitter and weary contempt. "You are barbarians!"

Safreddin smiled amiably. "You will wake her up, please,
Doctor. We have more questions to ask her."

"Put her on the bed."

The two men lifted the lolling, doll-like figure and laid
it on the bed. Bitar sat down beside her and opened his bag.

Shabibi moved forward quickly and took the bag from his
hands. "May I see that please, Doctor?"

Bitar ignored him and lifted Emilie's wrist to make a
pulse count. He held out his hand for the bag. Shabibi
handed it back without a word. Bitar rummaged in the

inside pockets and brought up two tiny glass capsules. He held them out for inspection.

"Nitroglycerin inhaler. It's the only cardiac stimulant I have."

"Use it," said Safreddin.

"Before I do," said Bitar, with the same arid scorn, "understand something. There will be no more torture."

"I think, Doctor, you misunderstand your position. You, too, have questions to answer. Questions about an address book taken from the pocket of a dying man in your presence. Many, many questions about your association with Selim Fathalla and where he is hiding now."

Bitar looked up at him, weary but unmoved. "You know the answers. Why bother to ask. . . . Besides, you owe me a debt. I claim it now."

"I owe you nothing!" A sudden anger blazed in Safreddin's eyes. "There is no reward for treason."

For the first time, Bitar's long, melancholy face creased into a mocking smile. "A noble Arab! Who will not pay a life for a life! Fathalla, the Jew, was more honest than that!"

There was one suspended moment in which Safreddin stood immobilized by his own fury, while Shabibi and the others stared in shock at his contorted face. Then, hand upraised to strike, he moved towards the bed.

In the same instant, Bitar crushed one capsule under Emilie's nostrils and the other under his own. They were dead in two seconds, in a perfume of almonds.

HEBRON

At five in the morning the sun rose and waves of gold and crimson and purple rolled over the land. It was a short, miraculous moment of transfiguration, in which, so the legend said, the angel with the flaming sword swung back the gates and allowed mankind a glimpse into the lost garden of Paradise. Then the waves receded and the magical land became a desert again, seared and scarred under the naked light.

In the assembly area, in the valley of the pines, the troops were swilling out the dregs of their canteens and checking their combat equipment and turning over their engines, waiting for the order to move out. Thirty miles away, the Mystères were being fueled and armed while the pilots straggled out of the mess hall and waited for the final call to the briefing room. The flurry was minimal, the excitement muted; the jokes had a stale aftertaste, as though the lions of Judah were being summoned to do battle with conies.

In the observation post, overlooking the Hebron valley, Jakov Baratz ate breakfast with the Chief of Staff and waited for the war game to begin. They were relaxed and almost cheerful, a pair of competent technicians who had fed all their facts into the mechanical brain and who had nothing to do but wait for it to deliver a predictable solution. Their responsibility was reduced to a minimum. They were inspectors watching the performance of junior men, who now must carry the burden of action and decision in the field.

In essence, the Hebron plan was very simple and there was little room for mistakes. At 0600 hours the fighters would be in the air, and the ground troops would be right on the Jordan border. They would drive five kilometers into Jordan territory and surround the village. The villagers would be moved out and a mixed company of infantry and engineers would move in to clear out stragglers and set demolition charges in houses and public buildings. The charges would be exploded, the company would withdraw, the operation would be over. The tanks were there to protect the infantry, provide a massive show of strength and bar the road to any approach by troops of the Arab Legion. The only probable opposition would be small arms and sniping from armed irregulars of the Palestine Liberation Organization.

The Chief of Staff turned to Baratz and laughed. "You should have stayed in bed, Jakov. There's nothing to do here."

"I might have, Chaim. Except that they woke me at three to take a decipher from Damascus. After that, there was no point in going back to bed."

"Anything new?"

"A couple of things. The Iraqis have agreed to take part in any military operations initiated by Syria and Egypt under the Defense Pact. The price is open traffic on their pipeline across Syria."

"That means Jordan is locked in now."

"Geographically, yes. They've got Hussein in a trap."

"Anything else?"

"A Syrian missile team has been sent to Russia for training. So they'll be getting the hardware very soon."

"No word on the Galilee emplacements?"

"None. And we may have to wait awhile before we get it. Fathalla's afraid he has been compromised. He wants us to pull him out with his girl. He's willing to stay to hold the network together, but I'm not in favor. I'm going to see what can be worked out when I get back to Tel Aviv today."

"So the girl was a mistake?"

"We made a mistake, too, Chaim. We sent a bad contact from Rome. He was a fool. He's dead now. But he made some stupid mistakes."

"Like what, Jakov?"

"A quarrel with Fathalla over the girl. A side trip to Aleppo to contact our paymaster. He had no right to make it without consulting Fathalla. He was injured in a road accident and died later."

"Is that the true story?"

"It's the most convenient one," said Baratz. "I'm happy to accept it."

The Chief of Staff was silent for a few moments, then

went off on a tangent. "When this little duck shoot is over—and it won't be finished this morning, as we both know—I think we ought to discuss a mobilization exercise and another rehearsal of the Abu Agheila plan before winter comes."

"There are other things to talk about, too, Chaim. Stockpiles, for instance. We're down below the agreed minimum of six months' reserves. That bothers me."

"It bothers me, too, Jakov. I've made a note to discuss it with the Minister when I see him today. . . . Make me a guess—what happens next and when?"

"I don't like guessing games, Chaim. But there's one foregone conclusion. The Syrians will keep hacking away at us in Galilee until they force us into a confrontation. Then they'll yell for the Egyptians. If the Egyptians move troops into the Sinai, the game is on. When? . . . Who the hell knows? How *can* you know? You read the files. You read the daily news. It's a mad world—a' tower of Babel, where we all shout gibberish and die raving in a wilderness of apes."

"How does it feel, little brother?" White Coffee stood over the bed mocking his painful waking. "How does it feel to look at your last morning?"

"I want to piss," said Idris Jarrah.

"Untie him. Take him outside."

They loosened his bonds and jerked him to his feet and when he staggered and fell on the floor they laughed and let him lie there until he found strength and balance to get on his feet again. They led him outside into a small stone enclosure and held their guns on him and made crude jokes while he relieved himself against the stone wall. They gave him no time to enjoy the sunlight or the clean taste of the morning, but hustled him back into the house and sat him at the table. They gave him a mug of stale water and a crust of bread. Then White Coffee sat at the opposite end of the table toying with a loaded pistol. There was no humor in him this morning. He was sour and menacing.

"I dreamed about you last night, little brother. I dreamed that you had left us and walked across the border. I saw you sitting down with the Jews to tell them all our secrets and collect more money. I woke up then; so I don't know how the dream might have ended. I'd like to know now."

Jarrah stared at him out of bloodshot eyes. Something was wrong. He was too confused to think what it might be.

"I don't know what you mean. I've told you everything. You'll have the money by midday. What else do you want?"

"Who was your contact in Israel?"

"I had no contact."

"You're lying."

"Why should I lie now?"

"That's what the dream was about, Brother Jarrah. Expound it to me."

"There's nothing to expound. I had money and passports. I was making for the airport. I was going to fly out to Paris."

"But you had a lot to sell to the Jews, didn't you? Much more than you sold to Chakry in Lebanon. You could have sold them a complete plan of our organization in West Jordan. You could have sold a list of names and the position of the arms dumps and where our money is lodged. Once they had that they could trade with the Hashemites and break us in a month!"

"Then why didn't I sell to the Jordanians?"

"Oh no, little brother! The Jordanians wouldn't have paid you a pinch of camel dung. They'd have put you in a cellar and beaten it out of you in twenty-four hours. You knew that. That's why you made contact with the Jews."

"I didn't make contact. How could I?"

"Do you know what broke my dream?" White Coffee held the pistol in two hands and pointed it across the table at Jarrah's breastbone. "It was a telephone call from the Coffeemaker. At four this morning he had a telephone call from Safreddin in Damascus. They cracked a Jewish spy ring there last night. Safreddin thinks you had some connection with it.

He thinks you told the Jews about Rumtha and the palace plot and Major Khalil—and lots of other things, too. . . . Well, little brother?"

"I never knew they existed. How could I tell them any-thing?"

"Let's try some names then. . . . Selim Fathalla."

"No."

"A woman called Emilie Ayub."

"No."

"Dr. Bitar."

"No."

"You're lying."

"What have I got to gain?"

"Time! You're valuable to the Jews. You're hoping they're going to get you out of the mess you're in now."

"No!"

"I have no time to waste this morning, little brother. The plane for Beirut leaves at eight. So think for a moment and . . ." He broke off, listening to the high ominous sound of approaching aircraft. He pushed back his chair and snapped an order. "You two—watch him!" Then he hurried outside, with the rest of the band at his heels.

Jarrah sat holding his head in his hands as the wave of planes swept over the house. He was in total confusion now. There was no way he could reason himself out of the wild unreason of White Coffee's accusation, no way to escape a renewal of torment. They would dismember him slowly in their rage to believe a fiction that seemed to threaten their very existence. He heard a high babble of voices outside the house; men shouting, women screaming and children calling from house to house. A moment later, White Coffee was back in the room. He hauled Jarrah out of his chair by the hair of his head and slammed him against the wall.

"The Jews are coming, Jarrah! Tanks and trucks and planes. They're coming for you, aren't they? That's how important you are! All the rest was a trick. This is the big killing, isn't it?"

Then Idris Jarrah saw the joke and he laughed and laughed in the face of his tormentors.

From the observation post, the spectacle unfolded itself in a weird slow motion, like a maneuver of fire ants, seen through a giant's eye.

The tanks came first, two columns of them, trundling over the plain, churning up dust and pebbles, shaking the air with the rumble of their engines and the rasp of their tracks. From opposite ends of the plain, they converged upon the toy village, a parade of long-snouted planetary monsters, driven by goggle-eyed creatures in helmets and chinstraps. They were relentless and invulnerable. When the villagers saw them they fled in panic, snatching up chattels and children, streaming out of the township in a pathetic exodus towards the hillside caves. To the men in the observation post the flight was a Lilliputian flurry dwarfed by the immensity of the sunlit plain and the menacing processional in the foreground.

After the tanks, driving parallel to the lines of the convergence, came the infantry in trucks and carriers, puppets with mushroom heads and fungus-colored clothes, and little guns whose muzzles pointed to the sky. Seen thus, at a distance, packed in their metal boxes, they were like toy troops, ready for the senseless happy slaughter in a child's game.

They were near the village now. The leaders of the columns were almost abreast. They swung away to cast a ring of armor and armed men around the township. Before the ring closed, they halted. The tankmen trained their guns on the buildings. The infantry scrambled out of their trucks and ran forward, crouching, to shelter under the iron flanks of the monsters. There was a silence now. The dust began to settle. Then came a crackle of rifleshots, which echoed faint and futile across the hills. After the shots, a huge distorted voice

began calling on the villagers—if any remained—to leave
their homes and follow their neighbors into the caves. They
would not be harmed, the voice promised them, but if any
man fired a shot or was found with a weapon on his person,
he would be killed without mercy. The call was repeated,
once, twice, and again. Then, under the watchful eyes of the
gunners, the last frightened folk crept out of their homes and
hurried away. The ring of tanks closed around the huddle
of empty habitations. The troops moved in to prepare its
destruction.

High up in the dazzling sky two Mystères were engaging
three Jordanian Hunters in unequal combat. To the men in
the observation post, the battle was a flashing of sunlight, a
scrawl of vapor trails and the distant sound of cannon fire.
It ended when a broken shape tumbled out of the sky, trail-
ing smoke and fire. They saw the two Hunters dive low over
the Jordan hills while the Mystères broke off the battle and
screamed homeward.

The Chief of Staff caught at Baratz's arm and pointed
across the valley. "Look at that, Jakov!"

Baratz focused his glasses and saw, on the shoulder of the
Hebron road, a convoy of open trucks each filled with Arab
Legion troops. He swore, savagely. "God Almighty! They're
mad! Open trucks and infantry! I hope to hell Zakkai re-
members his orders. If he hits them now, it's a slaughter."

The words were hardly out of his mouth when the tanks
opened fire, laying a barrage of shells across the road. The
trucks halted and the men piled out, dispersing along the
rocky hillside.

Baratz heaved a sigh of relief. "Full marks for Zakkai."

The tanks fired again, blasting the stationary trucks and
then laying down a creeping barrage along the mountain
road. They were still firing as the first demolition charges
went off and fountains of smoke and rubble began to rise
out of the village. For twenty minutes there was a confusion

of gunfire and scurrying men and buildings that spouted fire or collapsed like card houses in a puff of dusty air. Then there was only a small white mosque towering over a ruin, and the tanks pounding desultorily at the scattered legionaries, while the infantry piled back into the carriers and drove back towards the border. The tanks fired a last salvo and turned to shepherd them home, unscarred, unhurried, in a barren triumph.

"And that," said the Chief of Staff sourly, "is that. Very neat, very efficient. Let's go back and balance the books."

"We can't," said Jakov Baratz. "The final bill hasn't been presented yet."

JERUSALEM, ISRAEL

By five in the afternoon the accounts had begun to take shape. The Prime Minister had already cast up his own ledger and was less than happy with the balance.

"I must say, Chaim, I'm rather surprised at the casualty figures. Discount the Jordanian figure of forty-three dead and write it down to the more probable twenty or thirty. That's still very high. You promised us . . ."

"We promised nothing." The Chief of Staff was tired too and was not disposed to courtesies. "We told you the risks. You accepted them. We won't be made scapegoats."

The Prime Minister drew in his horns like a snail. He tut-tutted a little and then pressed the question obstinately. "I'm not looking for scapegoats, Chaim. I'm asking for an explanation."

The Chief of Staff delivered it, curtly. "We do not and we cannot have a complete knowledge of what happens on the other side of the border. We guess that, when the attack was launched, the police post called for help from the Arab Legion. They're bright and they're well trained. None of their commanders would dream of sending light-armed infantry in

open trucks against heavy armor; so we conclude that the
police call did not specify that we were in action with tanks.
It's the bane of all field commanders. Poor reporting. . . .
Now when the Jordanians arrived we could have hit every
damned truck square in the middle with a homing shell.
That would have given you a real massacre. We didn't. We
laid a barrage across the road and gave them time to disperse.
But we still had to keep them out of the village. That ex-
plains casualties."

"There's one casualty that requires some more explanation." This from the Defense Minister, coiled serpentlike in
his chair. "Amman radio reported the discovery of a man
who had been beaten, tortured and then shot in the chest.
His body was found in one of the houses which was not
demolished. They've promised to publish photographs in
tomorrow morning's press and to send full documentation
to United Nations."

Jakov Baratz gave him a flat and hostile answer. "If that's
true—and I'd have to see the body before I'd believe it—we
had nothing to do with it. It takes quite a time to conduct
a real torture session. Our boys were too damned busy with
the demolitions to worry about that sort of nonsense. A shooting, maybe. I can't guarantee every man in the Army. Torture? Plainly impossible in the time."

"Another question for you, Jakov." The Foreign Minister
was more polite. "We've had two garbled news reports from
Damascus about the breaking of an Israeli spy ring in Syria.
Do you know anything about it?"

"I wish I did. Our man sent us a message after midnight
last night. He gave us some important information and then
asked to be pulled out because he thought he was blown.
We've had nothing since. I read the reports. They could be
true. My guess is they haven't caught our man yet. I could
be wrong. We're tapping our other sources now."

"It makes a beautiful propaganda piece, Aron." The

Foreign Minister grinned ruefully at his gray senior. "A reprisal attack with twenty to forty dead. A spy scandal in Damascus. An Arab found tortured and shot in the village after we leave. I'm going to need double salary for my next visit to United Nations."

The Prime Minister chose to ignore the joke and ask another unhappy question. "What do we know about press reactions?"

The Foreign Minister answered that one in the same vein of black humor. "All that we've seen are bad. Jewish Goliath beats Arab David. Brutal and futile displays of strength. Bullying tactics. Incitement to hostilities. Aggravation of the difficulties of an honest but harassed government—to wit Jordan. They tone it down a little towards the end. But the headlines are all against us."

"And the diplomats?"

"All puzzled. Most of them unhappy."

"So how will we come out at United Nations?"

"No promises, Aron. And let's put that on the record now. At best we'll get a vote of censure, fairly unanimous. At worst we'll get an outright condemnation by a small majority."

"Small comfort either way."

"We have a corpse on our hands, Aron. Let's bury it quickly and not wait to put portholes in the coffin."

For a fleeting instant a faint smile brightened in the melancholy eyes. "But let's dress him up a little for the funeral, eh? Our enemies say we've got the best propaganda machine in the world. So could we please get it to say some nice things about Israel?"

THIRTEEN

TEL AVIV

Jakov Baratz drove back to Tel Aviv through the early darkness, railing silently at the devious ways of politicians. They demanded impossibilities—bricks without straw, battles without blood, diplomacy without deceit. That they would never get them, made no matter, so long as there was a printed record of their noble intentions and patient helots to carry the burden of their defaults. They played upon man's most obstinate illusions. They offered a guarantee of felicity for a temporary delegation of power. They were always afraid because the guarantee hung around their necks like a stinking sea bird and they could never get rid of it unless they named themselves fools or liars.

For them, the soldier was always the serviceable scapegoat. They loaded all their historic sins on his back and shoved him out into the desert to purge them in a primitive trial by combat. If he won, they brought him back with garlands round his neck. If he lost, they buried him in a footnote to more glorious chronicles. They were concerned about the numbers in a casualty list, but the bloodied men and the broken lives were always anonymous to them. A spy scandal in Damascus meant gibes in the assembly of the nations, the derision of fellow professionals. But who spoke a prayer or a word of care for the unknown soldiers in the international underworld?

Yet as his anger cooled, he saw that the contradictions of the political life were only one aspect of the larger paradox that plagued him more and more as he grew older: the desperate folly of violence, and the driving need of men to resort to it; the cry for communication in the human solitude and the futile dialogues in which men spoke a lie and a truth with the same words; the high reach for human dignity and the shabby despotisms that despoiled it. Perhaps old Franz Lieberman was right when he affirmed the positive working of evil in the world and the eternal battle to hold the good in balance against it.

But how could you hold the balance in the world when it was so hard to hold it in yourself? Jahweh Elohim had shouted for centuries against the iniquities of his Chosen, but even He had never rooted them out—by captivity or exile or dispersion or Roman massacre. Tonight he, Jakov Baratz, had forced himself to quit Jerusalem, knowing that, if he stayed, he would sleep with the wife of a man at bay or under torture in a cellar in Damascus. A small treachery perhaps—in all the circumstances, hardly a treachery at all— but another addition to the tally of wrongs which he had not yet been able to forgive himself. He had not even called Yehudith, so that she was still in ignorance of the Damascus reports. He would call her from Tel Aviv, when and if he had firmer news.

He had other matters to preoccupy him, less urgent but far more grave than the fate of an agent or a network. The tone of the Prime Minister's meeting had been ominous. The Hebron affair had turned into a disaster of the first magnitude. It had given the Arabs a company of quite genuine martyrs, one unexplained torture victim and a heap of rubble inside their frontiers—clear testimony to the aggressive brutality of an upstart nation. They would have their day in court and they would get at least a qualified verdict in their favor. Then, flushed and righteous, they would exploit their advantage. The Syrians, untouched and unscarred, would shout the loudest for revenge, for defensive action against unspecified threats, for blood in return for blood. They would launch new actions in Galilee; when their fire was returned they would cry aggression. . . . And because they already had one verdict they would feel confident of getting another. So the cycle would begin again, the sawtooth wheel would spin faster and faster until it exploded into lethal fragments of steel. . . . And Jakov Baratz was paid to be ready against the day of the explosion.

When he arrived at his office, he called for a cup of coffee to still the hunger pangs, and settled down to scan the papers that had accumulated during his absence. The news from Damascus was still garbled. Two agents—one a woman, one a man, both specified as "Syrian traitors in the pay of Israel" —had been arrested. Investigations were continuing. More arrests were expected soon. Secret transmitters had been found, together with incriminating documents which would be published at a later time. After that there were the usual battle cries, and calls for eternal vigilance. There was a note from the duty officer saying that all Fathalla's codes were presumed compromised and had been canceled as a matter of course.

Friendly embassies had supplied a few scraps of extra information. Both the Syrian agents were thought to be dead. All government departments were under investigation and there were indications of a large-scale manhunt for an Iraqi named Selim Fathalla. So far so good—or so bad. An agent on the run was better than a broken man talking his head off under the lights. But the network was gone and, at a time when it was most needed, there would be no earthly chance to rebuild it quickly. He debated a moment whether to call Yehudith and then decided against it. No point in giving her a sleepless night. Tomorrow would be soon enough.

Then he began to speculate about Fathalla's escape route. He carried his coffee over to the map and tried to plot how a man might break out of the secret suspicious enclave which Syria had become since the Baathists took over. It was a fruitless exercise and he gave it up quickly. There were too many *if*'s: if Fathalla had money and documents, if he were wounded or whole, if he were armed, if he had transport or friends or private contacts along the frontiers. And the final *if* was the one Fathalla had accepted at the date of the contract: "If you win, there is no reward; if you lose, there is no redress. Patriot or adventurer we buy you as you are, and you live or die at a private risk."

In fair conscience Jakov Baratz could walk away from Fathalla; but he could not walk away from the map. It held him in a strange hypnosis. There, if you had eyes to read, the story was written—past, present and at least some of the future. The texture of the land imposed the texture of the history enacted upon its surface. The texture of the land imprinted itself upon the men who inhabited it for a space and were buried under its soil. Change the contour and you changed the men and the history, all at once. You changed their cults and their fables and their visions and even their gods.

When Abraham the Wanderer marched out from Ur of the Chaldees he came, as the Bedouin came now, with a private god and a private promise and a private tribal life of flocks and herds and familial alliances. The promise was simple and final: "For all the land that thou seest I will give to thee and thy children forever." The promise made no sense to the petty kings of Canaan because they did not acknowlege the God who made it. And twentieth-century Israel, who claimed the same inheritance under the same covenant, was challenged on exactly the same grounds.

The Semitic empires of Assyria and Babylonia and Phoenicia and Syria had risen and fallen, but in new shapes they threatened again and Egypt restored, though not yet in the

seven years of plenty, was restless again in an imperial dream.
If they marched, they would come by the same roads as their
forefathers had used, gathering to their banners the folk
whom Israel had extirpated from the Land of Promise.

They shouted the same cries at the rallying points: that the
God of Israel was a jealous god who would not live in peace
with Baal and Dagon and Astaroth and a very tolerant and
civilized Allah; that the Jew, who bent like a reed in an
alien land, was rigid as a cedar in his own and spread his
shade only on the circumcised; in subjection they would
welcome him as a dweller in the Fertile Crescent, as an equal
they dare not risk him.

And this was the terrible irony of history, that you saw it
repeating itself and yet were powerless to change it, because
it took its course inexorably from the texture of the land.
The river flats were fertile still, as they were when Joshua
tumbled the walls of Jericho. Water was still precious as
rubies in a parched land. There was salt in the Dead Sea.
There were fish in Kinnereth. There was black gold under
the desert sands. Seaport cities were still a prize. And men
were jealous of them always.

Strangely too, almost sardonically, the land fomented the
jealousies and nurtured the hates, because the history of ancient vendettas was scored into the living rock. This was the
threshing floor that David bought from the Jebusite, where
Solomon built his temple and where now the Moslem kneels
but never the Jew. Here the Romans crucified Christ at the
plea of the Sanhedrin, and Christians have squabbled for
centuries under the shadow of the everlasting mercy. Here
at Yad Vashem we commemorate, with haunting austerity,
the memory of six million dead. There, beyond the barbed
wire are the hovels of the expatriates who pay the debt on
which Europe defaulted. There is the museum which we
have built to show how man, in this chosen corner, groped
upwards from the Stone Age to the rocket ship. Down there,
in the desert, is the atomic reactor which may one day make

the warheads to annihilate him. . . . All there. All written on the map, so harsh and palpable that Baratz was tempted to brush his hand across the surface to feel the sand and the flint and the living pulp that grew out of it and crawled upon it.

Tomorrow was written there too—but not all of it. Only the battle lines were clear. How, if the enemy came, the hosts of modern Midian, the tanks would strike southward twining around Gaza and El Arish, and driving onward to the Bitter Lakes; how they would break through the pass Abu Agheila and sweep the southern deserts and roll eastward to the Gulf of Aqaba. How the pincers would close around Jerusalem and the assault troops would storm the Galilee heights and the planes would sweep the skies clean and come back like homing eagles riding the winds of morning. All there. All written in advance against an expected day of reckoning.

But the afterwards was not written. There were no prophets to foretell it, no psalmists to sing it. Jahweh Elohim sat silent in a silent heaven. He had spoken so long and so eloquently, was he weary at last? Or was he there at all? Had he ever been? What if the Covenant was a vast but beautiful lie foisted by a wandering genius upon his pullulating tribe to hold them together for ten thousand years of illusory hope and interminable suffering? Why then the long nightwatch and the battles to come and the long mourning of Rachel bewailing lost children?

Go home, Baratz. It's late. Tomorrow is another day. Clean shave, fresh linen, early on parade. The British taught you that and look what happened to them!

LEBANON

Selim Fathalla awoke to a sound of bells. It was a long and pleasant wakening without anxiety and without regrets. His limbs were heavy, his movements languid and painless. When he opened his eyes he saw white walls, a bar of sunlight from an arched window, a bedside table covered with a woven cloth. On the table were a handbell and a plastic tumbler full of water. A note in Arabic was propped against the glass. He wanted to read it, but he felt too relaxed and euphoric to make the effort. He closed his eyes and counted the strokes of the bells. He had no anxiety about his future and strangely clear convictions about his past. The strange thing was that the conviction gave him no anxiety. He could review it now calmly as if he were a spectator at a film, too confused and kaleidoscopic to touch the emotions.

In the film, Selim Fathalla was mad. Adom Ronen was mad too. They had hilarious dialogues about their joint and several afflictions. Adom Ronen would talk in Hebrew and Fathalla would tell his tangled story in Arabic. When one laughed, the other cried. When one shouted triumph, the other was cringing in fright. They made an elaborate art of the mirror-experience, so that there was no longer one mirror and two men, but a thousand mirrors and ten thousand men, bloated, elongated, split lengthwise and crosswise, cracked in prisms and put together in a laughable patchwork.

Time itself was a dimension of their insanity. Daylight was dark; night was horrifying day; past and present were jumbled now; single moments were frozen in eternities. The earth too lapsed into a fluid folly. Mountains dissolved into valleys, grapes grew on thorn bushes, fig trees sprouted out of naked rocks; flat plains heaved themselves into lunar mountains or opened into dark pits under their feet.

There were monsters, too, in the crazy landscape; but, disfigured themselves, they seemed to have pity for harmless babblers. There was an old woman with a hump on her back, who offered them grapes and the blessing of Allah. There was a one-eyed giant in the hills, armed with a staff and surrounded by shaggy sheep who gave them water and cheese and told them prodigious tales of his youthful lecheries. There were the tousled girls who found them lapping muddy water and brought them to shelter under a tent of hides. There was the dwarfish fellow, drunk and bawling, who perched them on a load of cabbages and drove them over the hills to a city and a sea. . . . And behind all these pantomime personages stood Emilie, pale as death, staring at them in eternal accusation.

In the city they kept losing each other, in the frightening press of strange people. They wandered about, in a series of frantic searches, Selim mumbling for Adom, Adom groping about for the twin without whom he would die; both looking for Emilie who had suddenly rejected them forever.

They came together at last, in an olive grove on the hillside. They ate green olives and were sick and then they lay down under the trees to sleep. The dream ended there . . . and it was so divorced from the white-walled present that he felt no curiosity about how it might have continued. He noticed that the bells had stopped. He dozed again.

When he woke the languor was diminished, but the heaviness in his limbs was gone. He reached out to the table, drank a mouthful of water and read the note. It said simply: "If you need anything, ring the bell." He rang it. He was curious now, and a vague wariness woke under the languor. A few moments and a short bearded man in a long black robe entered the rom. He was smiling. He seemed to approve what he saw. He said in Arabic:

"Good morning. How do you feel?"

"Still sleepy. But well. Thank you. Where am I?"

"In a monastery."

"Oh." He was still heavily cushioned against surprise.

"Our Lady of Ephesus. It gets its name from a picture we have."

"I see." He didn't see at all. But it was simple to accept the exotic information.

"It's a Maronite foundation."

"Where?"

"In Lebanon. Not far from Beirut."

"How did I get here?"

"We brought you. The brothers found you in our field under the olive trees."

"How long have I been here?"

"Two days, two nights. The doctor kept you asleep. He said that was best."

"What doctor?"

"He'll be coming to see you very soon. A pleasant man. Would you like some breakfast? Coffee. Fresh bread and honey. We make the honey ourselves."

"Thank you."

"It won't be long."

He went out. Fathalla lay back, digesting the information. It seemed satisfactory, there was no menace in it. He threw back the covers and sat on the edge of the bed. Then he saw that his feet were bandaged. He set them on the floor and stood up gingerly. There was pain, but not too much. He hobbled to the window and looked out into a small cloister, planted with orange trees and oleanders. An old monk was pacing between the pillars, reading a book. Fathalla moved gingerly to the door and tried the handle. It was not locked. He opened it and looked out into a long, whitewashed corridor. There was an ikon at one end and under it a small table with flowers and a blue lamp. All the doors in the corridor were similar to his own. He went back to bed.

A few minutes later the monk came back with a tray of coffee, sweet rolls, butter and honey. He made a blessing over the food, wished Fathalla a good appetite and went out. Fathalla ate slowly, savoring every sweet mouthful. The languor began to recede and a grateful strength infused itself into his body. The door opened again and a tall, spare fellow in a blue silk suit stepped into the room. He introduced himself.

"Good morning, Mr. Ronen. I'm Dr. Silver. Enjoying your breakfast?"

"Very much. Thank you. I'm waking up now."

"Good. But take it easy. You've been heavily sedated." He sat on the foot of the bed and surveyed his patient with a quizzical, professional eye. He said: "In case you're wondering. I'm an American citizen. I teach at the American University in Beirut. I have a house just below the monastery. The monks use me as medical adviser."

Abruptly, Fathalla realized that they had been speaking in Hebrew. Suspicion broke through the euphoria and showed itself in his eyes. He demanded:

"Why do you speak Hebrew? Why do you call me Ronen?"

Dr. Silver laughed easily. "I'm a Jew. Though I don't advertise the fact in Lebanon. I went to school in Los Angeles. Your name? You gave me that under the first sedation. You talked to me in Hebrew too. Do you have another name?"

"Yes."

"And another language?"

"Yes."

"You had a rough journey. You walked a long way. And obviously you didn't eat very well."

"I don't remember."

"You will. It's important that you do remember. I'm speaking medically, of course. You must not attempt to thrust unpleasant memories behind you. Especially now. The sedative is wearing off. The anxieties will come again. If you are prepared, you'll weather them." He opened his bag and brought out a folded newspaper printed in Arabic. He did not offer it to Fathalla but held it still folded in his lap. He talked on quietly. "I am a Jew. The monks are discreet and have no wish to embroil themselves with the police because of an act of charity. There are reports in the Syrian and Lebanese press of a certain—incident in Damascus. From your talk when you came here and from what I read in the papers, I would guess that you were involved in it."

"And if I were?"

"Naturally," said Dr. Silver gently, "you will want to get back to Israel as soon as possible."

"That would be a natural conclusion—if the first proposition were true."

"But you have no money and no documents."

"I have money in the Phoenician Bank in Beirut."

"It might be dangerous to draw on it, just now."

"I hadn't thought of that."

"How are your feet?"

"A little painful. Not too bad."

"You'll need new shoes. You walked the others into ribbons. I'll bring you a pair of soft ones this afternoon."

"You're very kind."

"Finish your coffee and let me take a look at you."

The examination over, Dr. Silver pronounced himself satisfied. But he added a caution:

"Don't push yourself, Mr. Ronen. Get yourself a long leave. Psychic traumas take a long time to heal. And you've collected quite a few."

"Yes."

"Medically you're ready to travel now. I think we should ship you home this evening."

"How?"

"Do you like fishing?"

"I've never tried it."

"I keep a motor cruiser down at Sour. We might drive down there this afternoon, cruise out a few miles and throw over some lines. It's just possible we might drift too far south and be picked up by an Israeli patrol boat. How does that sound?"

"Too simple to be true."

"I'll come back about three. I'll bring some new clothes. You wouldn't be seen dead in the others."

"I damn near was," said Selim Fathalla. And then for no reason at all he began to cry, softly and desolately, like a lost child.

JERUSALEM, ISRAEL

"He will mend," said Franz Lieberman judicially. "He will be scarred, like all of us, after the battle with the dark messenger; but he will mend in time."

"Not without her," said Jakov Baratz moodily.

"No. Not without her."

They were sitting under the fig trees in Yehudith's garden, sipping iced tea and waiting for Yehudith to come to them. She was in the house now, at Adom Ronen's bedside, soothing him into sleep after a passionate outpouring of nightmares that had left him ravaged, shrunken and fearful of a moment's solitude. The experience had shaken Baratz. He had never seen a man so humiliated, so enmeshed in guilts, so hideously haunted by cruelty and death. Ronen had wept and shouted and lapsed into long, disjointed monologues of lament for Emilie and Bitar and the nameless victims of his failure. He had clung to Yehudith like a baby, burying his head between her breasts, pleading for her not to hate him, not to let his child despise him.

Franz Lieberman had watched it all, wise in the therapy of purgation, waiting for the inevitable moment of exhaustion; the sad prelude to despair or restoration. It had come at last: a spent man lying back on the pillows, waiting for the mercy of sleep, Yehudith, pale, wet-eyed, and half ashamed of her unwary pity, waving them out of the room.

"So what do you want me to say, Jakov?" The old man quizzed him with brusque affection. "That she can't love him? That she'll do a noble duty till he's well again and then come back to you?"

"True or false, Franz?"

"False," said Franz Lieberman promptly. "She doesn't know it herself yet. But we do. The hero's come back, carried on his shield. He has wounds to weep over, sins to be forgiven, a need for loving that makes her feel a whole woman again and wipes out her first failure with him. Can you match that?"

"I loved her, Franz. I still do. I thought she loved me."

"She did. She does. A month from now, if you like to work at it, she'll give you any proof you ask. And Ronen wouldn't fight her or you. He'd wear it like a hair shirt, in penance for the little dead girl in Damascus. But Yehudith would always come back to him and to Golda."

"Why, Franz? Why?"

"Because when you grow up, Jakov—and let's face it, half the people in the world never do—you learn that there's always a bill to pay for being born. Nobody can pay it all at once, so you do it on the installment plan—with interest. We all slip up on a month or two, or a year or two, but we're not very happy until the account is straight again. You've got debts to Hannah. Yehudith has debts to Adom. Come to that we all have debts to him. So, you have yourself a big love affair, and after every night you crawl out of bed and hate yourself a little bit more. Some people can take that for a long time. I don't think you could. I don't thing Yehudith could either."

"And who pays us, Franz? For God's sake who pays us for what we spend and don't get back?"

"Nobody, Jakov. We're paid in advance."

"With what?"

"With life!" There was a sudden fire in the old, wise eyes. "Just with life—short or long, happy or unhappy. One breath of air, one look at the sun, one smile on a child's face, one taste of the apple of knowledge, even if it turns to dust and ashes in your mouth. Add it up, man, and tell me honestly if you can claim you've been cheated!"

For a long moment Baratz was silent, then he looked up and grinned wearily. "You're an old fox, Franz. I should know better than to talk to you."

"For this advice," said Franz Lieberman cheerfully, "I get one hundred Israeli pounds in private session. You're military. You get it for free. At least appreciate it. . . . Now say good-bye to the girl and take me back to the hospital."

He said his good-bye in the kitchen, with Golda clinging to her mother's skirts. There was no passion in it, only regret and a hint of relief and long, sweet tenderness. Their words were banal, because there were none to match the might-have-been and none to blot out the torment they had witnessed in the bedroom. They kissed lightly like friends and walked hand in hand to the door.

"You'll come to see us, Jakov?"

"Later, yes. If there's anything you want. . . ."

"I'll always ask."

"Shalom, Uncle Jakov."

"Shalom, little one."

"Shalom, Jakov, my very dear."

Now there was nothing left to do but make the ritual visit to Hannah and drive back to Tel Aviv to the long, full days and the restless empty nights.

When they reached the hospital, Franz Lieberman led him in silence down the corridor to the community room where he had seen Hannah on the day of his first visit. There were the same little groups playing the same childish games, fiddling with the same, endless little tasks. There were the same nurses, watchful and solicitous. Hannah was there too; but they had managed to coax her out of her corner and she was sitting at a table watching a nurse arrange flowers in a bowl.

She still had the same slack, adipose look, the same listless
and lackluster eyes. She took no part in the work; but she
was watching at least, and when the nurse offered her a flower
to hold, she took it and held it firmly as if the tiny task were
important. When the flower was taken from her, she made
no resistance, but when she was offered another she took
that too. Franz Lieberman watched the scene in silence.
Baratz asked:

"When did this happen?"

"This morning for the first time."

"What happens now?"

"She will repeat it over and over again. She will come to
expect it. If, for any reason the ceremony is denied to her,
she will withdraw again, cheated and unhappy. She has
stretched one little finger and touched the surface of reality.
She may stop there; she may stretch a little further, to fondle
the flower, to smell it, to hold its color to the light or even
to put it in the vase. We don't know yet."

"May I talk to her?"

"Not this time." Lieberman frowned a warning. "If when
she makes this first brushing contact with a reality she has
rediscovered, it raises the faintest echoes of the reality from
which she has fled, she will retreat like a snail at a finger
touch. It takes a great patience to restore the most elementary
confidence. Only very special people can do this work."

"But the time it takes, Franz!"

Franz Lieberman shrugged and smiled a little sadly. "Only
we are conscious of time. There is none for her. Just the
single moment in which she feels the faint, unidentified
pleasure of holding the flower. She would hold it all day, if
we let her. . . . It is when she begins to feel regret and to
reach out by herself that the cure begins. It's the great paradox, Jakov. Pain is a healer too. You know that."

"I'm learning it."

"Good girl!" Lieberman whispered the words of approval

as the nurse laid down the flower and asked Hannah to pick it up for her. He gave a little sigh of regret when she sat, unresponsive, staring down at the bloom. "Well . . . we'll try again tomorrow."

"Can you give me one hope, Franz?"

"A very little one. But yes . . . a hope. Which of us can ask more?"

"None of us," said Jakov Baratz softly.

MASADA . . . JANUARY, 1967

The helicopter lifted off the desert floor, crabwise, in a cloud of sand, and clawed itself up the steel wall of the sky. It climbed westward, swiftly over the Wilderness of Zin, and then turned southward in a wide sweep towards the painted hills of Makhtesh Ramon. Below, the desert baked in the afternoon sun, a pitiless place to the stranger, but to the knowing, and the patient, and the strong, a place of visions haunted by the memory of past glory.

Here, in the folds of arid hills, were caves and holes where men had lived, millennia before the Patriarchs. Here Abraham wandered for a space, driving his herds along the route which was now a tarmac road from Beersheba to Eilat. Here came the caravans of Solomon hauling copper from his smelters in Etzion Geber and trade goods from the Gulf of Eilat. Here the Nabateans had lived, taxing the caravans, building their towns and farming the wilderness with water stored from the winter rains. Here the Byzantines had built Abde and Subaita and then abandoned them to the lizards and the scorpions. Here, now, lived the hardiest of the cactus breed of Israel, growing oranges in the sand and the shale, probing the wind-blown waste for minerals, planting their outpost farms farther and farther eastward towards the cleft of wadi Arabah.

Tomorrow it was to be a battleground. The fire ants were

on the move again, down the road from Sde Boker, fanning out through the foothills to assault the pass of Mitzpe Ramon. Hung high in the dazzling air, Baratz and the Chief of Staff watched them come, matching their moves against the battle plan, playing an aerial chess game with tanks and guns and carriers and masses of anonymous men. This was Operation Maccabee, repeated every year for ten years, with the same units; commented upon, revised, tested again and again, against the day when it would be mounted in a bloody reality against another pass in another place.

The real objective was the pass of Abu Agheila, key to the Sinai Desert, where in the campaign of 1956, Israel had suffered grievous losses in an assault against blockhouses and heavily defended gun emplacements. If the Sinai campaign had to be fought all over again—and every threatening pointer said that it would—Abu Agheila would have to be retaken. But this time, the cost must be kept to a minimum. In Israel every life was precious because, without men, the desert would creep back and eat up the pastures and wither the pine trees and fill the cisterns with sand.

So Operation Maccabee was no routine war play. It was a rehearsal for survival and the Chief of Staff directed it with tyrannical thoroughness while Baratz probed for the weak places in the script, a cold, meticulous analyst and a brutal critic. At this time, more than at any other, the nature of their trust became clear to them: two and a half million lives, ingathered from the whole world, camped in a narrow perimeter, beset, outnumbered by tens of millions, a child country, matched against giants terrible in their armor.

They cruised for nearly an hour, and then, because the movement of troops had slowed and the deployment was halted to feed and water the men, the Chief of Staff shouted over the clatter of the machine, "Let's give ourselves a break, Jakov."

"Just as you like, Chaim. Where do you want to put down?"

The Chief of Staff thought about it for a moment and then made a slightly shamefaced suggestion. "Would you like to make a sentimental journey?"

Baratz grinned and shouted back, "Anywhere you say."

The Chief of Staff tapped the pilot on the shoulder and gave him the course. They turned northward until they picked up the township of Oren and followed the tarred road between the twin ranges of Bagadol and Hakatan, until they came to the junction of the highway that ran from Beersheba to the Dead Sea. Here they turned east towards the cleft and saw the great salt lake, locked between the rocky escarpments, shining like a silver shield in the sun. Sodom lay under them now, a potash town, crouched on the water's edge, with raw cliffs, white and ocher and yellow, towering at its back. They changed course again and followed the water northward until they saw the great flatheaded bulk of Masada towering out of a tumbled desolation.

"Circle it." The Chief of Staff tapped the pilot again. "Circle it and put us down."

As they banked and began their spiral around the great plateau, they fell silent, awed by the monstrous majesty of the place, familiar yet terrible, sacred, glorious and full of bloody memories.

Twenty-two hundred years ago, Jonathan Maccabeus had fortified it. A hundred years later, Herod the Great had built himself a palace on the escarpment, a fantastic, paranoid place, with bathhouses and granaries and storehouses for arms, and huge wells that held water enough for an army, and stuccoed chambers and pleasure rooms for the monarch and his minions. When the Parthians took Jerusalem, he had retreated into the wilderness, shutting himself in with a wall and thirty-seven watchtowers that commanded every approach to the plateau. There was no glory yet, only a mime of mad actors, sybarites strutting in a dead landscape in sight of a festering sea.

Then the day came, when Titus cast a trench about Jerusalem and laid siege to her and crucified her fugitives on the lip of the ditch and starved her defenders into submission and flattened the city into a ruin and enslaved her survivors. It was then that Masada was remembered. Eliezer ben Yair gathered his Zealots about him with their wives and children —a thousand souls—and led them into the Wilderness of Zin and west to the deserted fortress. They camped on the table of barren rock, swept by the desert wind. They rebuilt Herod's walls with their bare hands. They opened the storehouses and the armory and found the wherewithal to live and fight. And they waited. . . .

As the helicopter circled low around the rim of the rock, Baratz could see the façade of the pleasure palace, and the serried lines of the granaries and the casemate walls and the cisterns of Herod. He saw the precipitous snake paths up which the Zealots had dragged their protesting tribe and the ragged cliffs they had scaled to reach their refuge.

. . . And then, the Romans had come, outraged that so small a band should still defy the eagles and the legions. Flavius Silva led them, ten thousand men. He camped them at the foot of the rock and built a wall all about it and camped his legionnaires in permanent quarters to besiege the citadel. They brought in Jewish slaves for laborers and servants and they too waited, while the great Silva surveyed the problem. They could afford to wait, because Rome was great and eternal and her empire stretched from Parthia to the Pillars of Hercules. . . .

The Chief of Staff pointed downwards to the valley floor where the eight camps of Flavius Silva were still visible, rows and rows of tent floors and sleeping platforms enclosed within the classic ramparts. Baratz nodded, but against the noise of the rotors he could not speak the thought that was in his mind: that this was a symbol of Israel itself—walled in by boycott and blockade and belligerent rivals. They would never starve her into submission but they could and they did reduce her, bleeding her capital into arms, cutting the life-lines of her trade, blackmailing those who wished to do bus-iness with her. But she still held out—as the thousand on Masada had held out for three years against the ten thousand Romans.

. . . Finally Flavius Silva made his plan. Using the labor of Jewish slaves, he built a great ramp of earth and rock from the valley floor to the walls of the citadel. He hauled his rams and catapults to the top of the ramp and began to bombard the defenders with stones "of the weight of half an hundred-weight" blackened so that the defenders could not see them. When the stone walls were breached the Zealots repaired them with wooden beams, so laced and backed with earth that they rocked with the rams but would not break. Then Flavius Silva set fire to the wooden wall, but the desert wind blew the fire back in their faces and they retired, knowing that by morning they could enter and take the fortress without trouble. . . .

The desert wind was not blowing today, so the pilot set down the helicopter without difficulty on the northern end of the rock. They stepped out, stretching themselves grate-fully, and then walked together to the place where, nineteen hundred years ago, the Roman fires had blazed through a night of terror and magnificence. Neither man spoke. There was no need of words. They were twins drawn back into the womb of the same folk-memory. The same voices spoke to them both out of the past: the voice of Eliezer ben Yair, exhorting his doomed army to a final heroism, the voice of the renegade chronicler recording the outcome.

". . . Let us die then, before we become slaves under our enemies, and let us go out of the world, together with our children and our wives, in a state of freedom. This is what our laws command us to do; this is what our wives and chil-dren crave at our hands; God himself has brought this necessity upon us; while the Romans desire the contrary and are afraid lest any man should die before we are taken. . . . Let us leave them an example which shall at once cause their astonishment at our death and their admiration of our hardiness therein. . . .

"So they presently laid down all they had in a heap and set fire to it. Then they chose ten men by lot out of them, to slay all the rest; every one of whom laid himself down by his wife and children on the ground, and threw his arms about them, and they offered their necks to the stroke of those who by lot executed that melancholy office; and when these ten had, without fear, slain them all, they made the same rule for casting lots for themselves, that he whose lot it was should first kill the other nine, and after all, should kill himself.

"Accordingly, all those had courage sufficient to be no way behind one another, in doing or suffering; so, for a conclusion, the nine offered their necks to the executioner, and he who was the last of all, took a view of all the other bodies, lest perchance some or other among so many that were slain should want his assistance to be quite dispatched; and when he perceived that they were all slain, he set fire to the palace, and with the great force of his hand ran his sword entirely through himself, and fell down dead near to his own relations. So these people died with this intention, that they would not have so much as one soul among them all alive to be subject to the Romans. . . .

"Now for the Romans, they expected that they should be fought in the morning, when accordingly they put on their armor, and laid bridges of planks upon their ladders from their banks, to make an assault upon the fortress, which they did; but saw nobody as an enemy, but a terrible solitude on every side, with a fire within the place, as well as a perfect silence. . . ."

The Chief of Staff thrust his hand into the pocket of his tunic and brought up a small shard of pottery, inscribed with

a Hebrew character. He smiled and held it out to Jakov
Baratz. Baratz nodded and brought out another one to match
it. The archeologists had a name for them: "ostraca." They
were the personal tokens of the Zealots of Masada, used for
the drawing of rations, and perhaps for the last fratricidal lot-
tery on the mountaintop. They were the last answer to the
last question. The symbols inscribed on them were the only
words that made sense in the Babel-tower of politics and
legalities and family quarrels, and split loyalties. Sooner or
later, believing or unbelieving, every man had to find one
inch of soil on which he would stand and defy the world.
Sooner or later, he had to say: "This is all I know. It is not
enough; but so be it." Sooner or later, prophet or mounte-
bank, he had to take his own small shard of truth in his hands,
write his name on it and toss it into the bowl, prepared to
live or die by the draw.

"Full circle," said Jakov Baratz. "Twenty years and we're
here again."

"Do you remember the words, Jakov?"

"I remember them."

They clasped hands, pressing the potsherds into their
palms, and recited the old oath of the Haganah and their own
covenant with the new Israel.

"Masada shall not fall again."

About the Author

MORRIS L. WEST, a native Australian, was born in Melbourne in 1916. When he was fourteen he began studying as a postulant with the Christian Brothers order but left twelve years later without having taken final vows. After serving with Australian Army Intelligence during World War II, he became a partner in a flourishing recording and transcription business but left it when he discovered that he preferred to write for himself rather than for sponsors.

A stay in Italy resulted in his book *Children of the Sun,* a study of the street urchins of impoverished Naples, which became an English best seller in 1957. There followed two novels published in the United States under the titles *The Crooked Road* and *Backlash,* in 1957 and 1958 respectively.

In 1958, also, Mr. West returned to Italy as Vatican correspondent for *The Daily Mail,* and he then absorbed much of the technical background for a new novel. *The Devil's Advocate,* published in 1959, promptly became that rare phenomenon in publishing—a book universally hailed by critics as a major creative work while selling, in various editions, more than two million copies. Mr. West followed it with more major successes: *Daughter of Silence* (1962), *The Shoes of the Fisherman* (1963), *The Ambassador* (1965), and now, *The Tower of Babel* (1967).

Mr. West, with his wife and four children, presently lives in Rome, Italy.

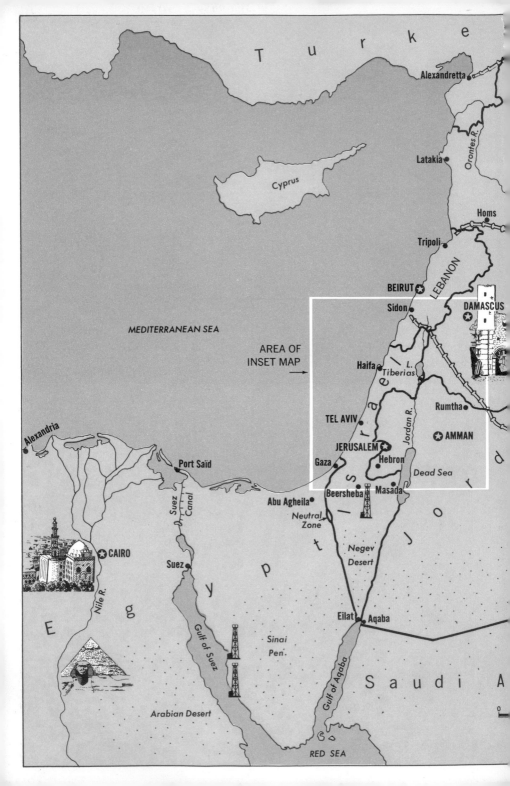